# LOST LOVE, LAST LOVE

# ROSEMARY ROGERS

# LOST LOVE, LAST LOVE

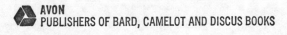
AVON
PUBLISHERS OF BARD, CAMELOT AND DISCUS BOOKS

# LOST LOVE, LAST LOVE

# Part One

# "A SUBJECT FOR GOSSIP . . ."

## Chapter One

೦∾೦

Even among the glitteringly dressed crowd at the grand opera ball they stood out from the rest—the tall blue-eyed millionaire-adventurer from California and his lovely copper-haired wife. They were an exceptionally good-looking couple, of course, but that wasn't all. It was the suddenness of their appearance in New Orleans that had the gossips' tongues wagging—that, and the *rumors*.

After all, everyone knew that Virginia Brandon Morgan was the stepdaughter of Sonya Beaudine, formerly of New Orleans herself. And almost everyone had heard the talk—much more than sly whispers—about Steven Morgan's liaison with a certain Italian opera singer as well as his wife's defiant flouting of convention while she visited Europe not so very long ago.

"Isn't it true that they were married a bare few months after she'd been widowed? A Russian Prince, didn't the newspapers say?"

"I heard that she had a child while she was in Europe—I wonder what she did with the poor little mite! Does *he* know, do you think?"

"My dear, I vow I wouldn't want to be in her shoes if that was

true and he did find out! He doesn't exactly look either tame or—
or *safe*, does he?"

The lady who had spoken gave an exaggerated shudder, even
while her eyes continued to watch Steve Morgan. In spite of herself she couldn't help wondering secretly what it might feel like to
be married to him. Even if one couldn't trust him an inch, it
would certainly be *exciting*. . . .

"I think we are the subject of a great deal of conjecture, darling!"

Slightly slanted green eyes, the exact color of the emeralds she
wore, sparkled to match the young woman's smile. The steps of
the dance swung Ginny and Steve away from each other and then
back again.

"Has it begun to matter to you?"

"No . . . I suppose they'll always gossip about us. Why should
I care?"

"Bravo." His voice was slightly derisive, as if he meant to let her
know he saw through her put-on insouciance.

"I *don't* care!" Ginny said defensively, and then, meeting his
raised eyebrow she surrendered with a small laugh. "Oh—very
well! I just don't like to feel as if I am on exhibition, that's all. I
vow, some of those old biddies had their glasses turned more often
on us than on the stage this evening. Steve—why did we have to
come?"

"We had to make a public appearance sometime, my sweet.
And I must say you're looking uncommonly fetching tonight.
Considering how quickly Madame Elise whipped that gown up
for you. . . ." He pretended to study her critically, even while his
fingers tightened over hers.

"You like me better this way?"

"You're a provocative little bitch—dressed or undressed; and
you know it too!"

Through his narrowed blue eyes he was seeing her, for an instant, as he had seen her during the last month they had spent together, journeying through the swamps. Tangle-haired, half-naked
—a green-eyed Amazon with a holstered gun on one hip and a
knife at the other. His mistress-wife.

How they had hated each other, fought each other, loved each
other! And even now—could they ever be sure of one another?

They had been married for over four years and had been together continuously for less than half that time.

"Do we really know each other?" Ginny wondered, her eyes staring back at his, knowing by instinct that he was thinking the same thing. "How will it be with us four years from now?" There were some questions she didn't want the answers to—not now, not yet. The opera singer . . . had he loved her? Did he mean to keep mistresses . . . would she be able to keep him? And having children . . . that was bound to affect their relationship in ways she could not guess.

"They certainly seem to be wrapped up in each other. It's almost embarrassing to see a married couple *look* at each other that way! Do you think . . . I mean, all those stories, the gossip . . . it can't be true, can it?"

"Of *course* it's true!" The speaker, an elderly lady whose bosom was almost smothered with diamonds, sniffed. Inwardly, Mrs. Pruett enjoyed her younger companion's indrawn breath—the widening of her eyes as she leaned closer so as not to miss a single tidbit.

"I used to know Sonya Beaudine," Mrs. Pruett continued. "In fact, I remember when—" She cut herself off, almost as if she had been talking to herself, as she suddenly remembered she was in company. "Well—let's just say I remember a great deal! But as for the *gossip*—well, my dear, it's all true of course. Why, less than a year ago he was here to hear his paramour sing—and she brought the house down too. Such a voice!"

"But . . . but his wife? They appear to be so much in love. . . ."

"I'm sure they are," Mrs. Pruett said forbiddingly. "And why not? I've heard that he married her a scant few months after she'd been widowed—and her first husband was a Russian Prince, no less. I'm sure they're a very *modern* young couple—or so I've heard."

The ladies of New Orleans were not alone in their whispered comments. Some gentlemen professed themselves to be quite enchanted by the beautiful, half-French Madame Morgan.

"A pity she's married. What magnificent eyes!"

"A lovely figure too. Hmm . . . I would imagine that in a chemise she would be quite adorable."

"Better keep your voice down, Andre my old one. I've heard her husband is a dangerous man. There are rumors. . . ."

"Ah yes—one hears these rumors. And about her as well. I was in Paris last year and had the opportunity to see the lovely Ginette on a few occasions. Each time with a different escort—she was quite the rage, and it was said the Comte D'Arlingen, a former fiancé, was on the verge of leaving his young bride for her—until she went off to London with an English Duke. I wonder if her husband is aware?"

Lucian Valette, to whom the last, rather sneering question had been addressed, shrugged his shoulders. He was used to his friend and his friend's penchant for pretty women—especially those who belonged to someone else. And Andre was also an excellent shot, having had his training under the famous Pepe Llulla. Of course dueling was officially outlawed now, but here in New Orleans the tradition of the Code Duello died hard, and the authorities were more than likely to look the other way when engagements of honor took place.

"My friend—who cares? You observe—they are together, and seem content enough. And, by the way, Bernard Pruett looks to be a happy man tonight. Do you think it's because the fair Althea Pennington has chosen to smile on him?"

The other man's shoulders moved under his close-fitting jacket. They were broad and well muscled, and several pairs of female eyes languished as they looked in his direction—a fact of which he pretended to be unaware.

"She's looking for a husband—and young Bernard has more money than sense. She'd best persuade him to elope with her before his dragon of a mother gets an inkling of what's afoot, though!" A rather cruel smile curved the speaker's chiseled lips. He touched his mustache. "*La mère* Pruett would never countenance an eight-month infant as the heir to the Pruett millions, and if Althea is clever enough to follow my advice she'll be well off."

Valette shot his friend a sharp look, although he forebore making a comment. Inwardly he whistled to himself. So *that* was how the land lay? It had been less than two months ago that he'd taken a drunken wager with Andre that the one woman he'd never bring to bed was the lovely Althea Pennington—spoiled, adored and well-chaperoned daughter of an irascible Yankee banker. So he'd actually pulled it off—and had Miss Pennington looking for a husband in a hurry? Andre never lied about his conquests—he didn't have to. Women flocked to him and only his reputation as a deadly marksman kept angry fathers and husbands from challenging him.

"So I owe you one of my matched bays, eh?" He shrugged resignedly. "I should have known, I suppose! Damn, but you have the most infernal luck with the ladies! I wonder if there is one of them you couldn't get?"

"If that is another wager, Lucian, I'll take it—for the other half of your matched pair. Let's see—whom shall it be this time? A married woman, perhaps—they are always harder to get to, especially if their husbands aren't too old. Name her, my friend—but please, I must insist that she be attractive. You know how fastidious I am!"

The tempo of the dance changed, and Steve Morgan led his wife back to her seat. From across the room, a phalanx of bejewelled dowagers watched them critically.

"Well—he's certainly attentive to her! One must grant him that, I suppose."

"In *public*, my dear! Aren't they all? But he *is* a handsome man, for all that. His dark complexion gives him a saturnine look. Do you think he means to dance with his wife all evening?"

"Marie-Clair Valmont! You're surely not hoping he'll ask your daughter to dance? He's a married man."

Madame Valmont smiled insincerely at the speaker, her "dearest" friend.

"Quite so, Agathe. Much safer to dance with a married man, under the eyes of his wife, than with a known philanderer like Andre Delery."

Her barb was rewarded with an unbecoming flush that stained Agathe's already rather mottled complexion.

"Andre Delery paid formal court to my Therese, and well you know it! My husband turned him away. . . ."

"Oh? He certainly did not appear inconsolable the next day when he escorted Rose Thierry to a private supper at Antoine's, did he? And by the way, when *is* dear Therese returning from

France? The poor child must be quite bored in Provence—she's with her grandmother, you said?"

A blonde, still-attractive woman in her middle thirties danced by with her husband, a distinguished-looking older man. She acknowledged the ladies, who all smiled back, with varying degrees of surprise and cattiness concealed behind their expressions.

"Dear Sonya! She doesn't look very much older than when she left here, does she? I wonder if her hair is naturally blonde still. . . ."

"I wonder how she really feels, being presented with a stepdaughter who promptly makes her a grandmother! Poor Sonya! Remember when we all used to wonder about that handsome young Union officer who was always escorting her carriage to and fro during the war?"

"Oh yes—the one who fought a duel with his commanding officer over a quadroon woman—didn't they execute him? She used to vow she hated him for his insolence and the way he would *look* at her, but I—"

"Yes, yes. We all used to whisper that she protested a trifle too vehemently! Come to think of it, don't you think that son-in-law of hers looks a trifle like her Yankee Captain? That pitch-black hair and those eyes—"

"It seems to me, Amelia, that you must have spent a considerable amount of time studying that particular Yankee yourself!" Mrs. Pruett interrupted acerbically. "Being *friends* of Sonya, don't you think we should concentrate more on our plans for entertaining her and becoming reacquainted rather than in dragging up old gossip?"

"Well—*she's* a fine one to criticize!" one lady sniffed to a companion behind her fan. But she spoke in an undertone, for Mrs. Pruett managed to overawe them all with her husband's money and her arrogant bearing.

"Some of those women have knives for tongues!" Sonya Brandon whispered heatedly to her husband once they had run the gauntlet of curious stares. "Oh, William, I do wish you had not made us come! Ginny and Steven are accustomed to being talked about—I used to think sometimes that they deliberately *invited* gossip of the most unpleasant kind. But New Orleans used to be my home, and I know most of the people here. I cannot say that I relish—"

"My love, you know very well that that is exactly the reason we are here. Because you know everyone, and they accept you as one of their own."

William Brandon smiled down at his wife, giving her small hand a reassuring squeeze. Inwardly, he was concerned. It was unlike Sonya to be so difficult, and it had taken a new diamond bracelet to persuade her to accompany him here. He had thought she would enjoy meeting all her old friends again, but instead she had protested quite vehemently, forcing him to be unwontedly stern with her. Why were women so unpredictable, even after several years of marriage? After all, *he* had not too much reason to want to visit New Orleans, a city that would always remind him of Genevieve, his first wife. Lovely, fragile Genevieve whom he had adored with all the ardent passion of first love—his first love who had not loved him back, for all her show of docility at first. She had cried each and every time he made love to her, no matter how kind, how tender he had tried to be; until at last he could not bear to touch her at all.

William Brandon—*Senator* Brandon—deliberately shook his mind free of the past. Let it be! He was a pragmatic man, a man of considerable ambition and shrewdness and political savoir faire. When he had received his son-in-law's telegram, dispatched from Shreveport, he had perceived immediately that it would be good policy to come to New Orleans and lend some respectability to his daughter's first venture back into polite society since her somewhat hasty trip to Europe which had produced so much gossip.

The Senator's lips firmed, thinning slightly. A man less used to schooling his features might have frowned. He must make an opportunity, very soon, to talk with Virginia. He had been appalled by certain disclosures Sonya had made after *she'd* returned from Paris. And the fact that Ginny had turned up in Texas, without having had the courtesy to let him know she was back in the country at all. . . . He was surprised that Steve had taken her back; but that, of course, was Steve's affair.

"William, I'm becoming a trifle fatigued. Please let us sit down."

"You're beginning to sound quite petulant my dear. You are not *sulking* are you?"

Her husband's voice had hardened slightly, and Sonya forced a smile.

"Of course I'm not! It's true I didn't want to come, and I'm still not completely *easy* about being here, but here we are, after all! And look—even Ginny has decided to sit for a while. I'm sure she's as thirsty as I am."

"A charming man, the Senator. So handsome! He's a Virginian, is he not?"

The ladies' whispers favored the Senator, even Mrs. Pruett unbending so far as to bestow a smile and a nod in his direction.

"She's lucky to find a second husband even better looking than her first. You'll recall Raoul Beaudine? He was as handsome as he was wild."

Sonya Brandon sat down beside her stepdaughter; neither of them had very much to say to the other once they had exchanged mutual, polite compliments on each other's gowns. Sonya had chosen to wear rose-pink satin—a shade so dark it was almost red, while Ginny's form-fitting dress—with its daring décolletage—was a turquoise watered silk, a cunning blend of blue and green.

Sonya thought resentfully that one of the things that angered her most about Ginny was the young woman's almost unconscious air of arrogance—of not caring a whit for anyone's opinions or feelings. "She's always been selfish, and still is," Sonya thought. "It doesn't matter to *her* what other people may say. And as for him . . ."

Ginny had half-turned away to laugh up into the face of a young man who had sauntered over to speak to her. Sonya recognized him as Lucian Valette, the son of an old friend—an *older* friend—for Madame Valette had been of a generation removed from Sonya's.

Had they been formally introduced? It was really too bad of Ginny to be so familiar to a virtual stranger, and to allow him to be familiar enough with her to engage her in a low-voiced conversation, obviously laced with effusive flattery. "It's really Steven's fault. If he hadn't let her run wild in Europe so that *he* could flaunt his mistresses in public—"

Sonya's agitated thoughts were interrupted by Steve himself, and to her annoyance he merely raised an amused eyebrow at the spectacle of his wife flirting far too openly with another man. "*Belle Mère.*" He bowed formally over Sonya's hand while she flushed angrily. How *dare* he? He knew how it infuriated her to be addressed in public as his mother-in-law. And he knew how much she hated him, how much she . . .

Afterward, Sonya could only think that it must have been sheer rage that paralyzed her throat, not allowing the words of haughty refusal her brain formed to escape. He had asked her to dance, drawing her unwillingly to her feet, and William, misinterpreting her almost frantic glance in his direction had merely smiled and nodded.

Damn him! Sonya almost never swore, but the words swirled around in her mind. The last time they had danced together had been in New Orleans, on an occasion she could not forget, no matter how hard she had tried. The Governor's Mansion, and he had been in uniform. How she had hated him that night, how she had tried to keep on hating him, even when he was in her bed, his hands on her body, his teasing voice calling her "Sonya-sweet." Damn him! Why must he force her to remember?

Sonya found herself hoping fervently that no one else would. Adeline Pruett had sharp eyes and a long memory. Far too well she could recall Adeline whispering to her that after all, there was nothing in keeping oneself amused if one was *discreet*—why shouldn't women have as much enjoyment as men did?

Oh God, it seemed so impossible that she could actually have had a wildly passionate affair of the senses with this same man who had become, by an ironic twist of fate, her stepson-in-law. No —not ironic, it was monstrous!

Struggling to keep her composure, Sonya said coldly, "I wish that you had not forced this dance on me. I'm not as much a hypocrite as you are, Steve Morgan. Don't you have a conscience?"

She remembered, too, his rather sarcastic smile.

"You ought to know better than to ask, Sonya-sweet. Or do you prefer *Belle Mère?*"

Her indrawn breath was like a hiss, and she would have pulled herself free of his arms if they had not tightened to trap her.

"I would much prefer to sit the rest of this dance out. If you please!"

"Well, I don't please!" He frowned down at her for an instant, black brows drawing together. And then he surprised her by apologizing. "Sonya, I'm sorry. I didn't ask you to dance to provoke you. But as long as we are all planning to be in each other's company for some time, don't you think a truce is in order?"

"Is that all you wanted to say to me?"

Lines crinkled at the corners of his eyes when he smiled at her.

"No, not exactly. There were a few questions I wanted to ask you." Somehow, Sonya had the feeling that his smile was put on like a mask, to cover something else. There was a knife-edge tension in him that she could feel with her senses, frightening her. She stayed silent as he continued: "You know most of these people here, don't you?"

It was a question she didn't understand then, and would not for some time to come; not even when he continued his light, almost bantering queries as to who was who exactly among the crowd of people surrounding them. Why did he want to know so much?

# Chapter Two

❧

"My dear, I wish that you would not make your dislike for Steven so obvious," William Brandon commented mildly later when they were in their room.

His wife continued to brush her hair until it crackled, and her voice sounded stiff and sharp as she retorted: "Then I am sorry, William, but I am no hypocrite! He should not have asked me to dance. He should know very well that *I* have never forgiven him for the way he tricked and humiliated us, even if you have chosen to forget."

There were times, Sonya thought viciously, when she would have loved to blurt out everything, to . . . to purge herself. Steve Morgan's arrogance, the way he had taken it for granted that she would fall in with his request to furnish him information on all her friends, was insupportable! Why did he have to be married to Ginny? And why, after his mysterious "disappearance" for the past few months, did he have to turn up again?

Even after her husband had fallen asleep beside her, his breathing heavy and even, Sonya had to will herself to lie still instead of tossing and turning restlessly. Intolerable! Intolerable that she was here, back in her old home again, and in the same large four-poster bed that had so many memories for her. "I should have insisted on selling the plantation," she thought feverishly. "And I should never, never have come back here!" She had a premonition that something bad, something ugly, was going to happen, disrupting all their lives. Steve Morgan had always brought trouble and now she wished that, scandal or no, Ginny had stayed in Europe.

Two doors down the hall, Ginny too could not fall asleep at once. Damn Steve—where was he?

He had made love to her, and then, with a light kiss and no word of explanation, he had left the room. Where had he gone? Worse thought—to whom? "He's been away for over an hour now," she thought unwillingly. "But I won't demean myself by getting up to go looking for him. He'll think I don't trust him, and then we'll have a quarrel." Had he been angry with her for flirting with that nice young Lucian Valette? He hadn't said anything afterward, although she had reproved him laughingly for annoying poor Sonya so.

He'd raised one devilish black eyebrow. "How? By asking her to dance? What a stubborn woman—she hasn't forgiven me yet, you know."

"Well—I don't know if I have either. When I remember . . ."

"There's a lot I remember too, my love."

And what had he meant by that? The trouble was that they had not yet had enough time together—that they were too intent on not quarreling to be able to be perfectly frank with each other about everything in the past. They loved each other, but was loving enough to prepare them for a lifetime of being *married*? And after a while, would love leave? Would they grow bored with each other, hate each other perhaps?

Ginny had left a window open, and she saw the thin draperies flutter violently in a gust of wind. She got up, crossed the room and stood looking out the wide windows. Even the breeze was warm tonight! She heard the rushing sound of the wind through the trees that surrounded the house; like the ceaseless crashing of ocean breakers beneath the gallery of the house in Monterey. The house where Steve had taken her after he had killed Ivan on the deck of the Russian ship.

Even now that particular memory of blood and violence had the power to make Ginny shudder, reminding her of the dark side of Steve's nature—the side that Paco Davis had warned her about so long ago. How she had hated Steve that day! How she had stormed and cried and threatened . . . all the while fearing him too.

She could still hear Steve's voice, sounding harsh and uncompromising.

"You're an addict—do you know what that means?"

"No more powders, no more tonics to make you sleep. You're not going to need them, from now on. You'll find that out."

It had been the beginning of a nightmare she'd thought might never end. Why did she have to remember, especially *now*, when that painful time was so far behind them both? Ginny closed her eyes, trying not to think at all, but the night seemed to be made for memories, and the warm wind breathed across her body like the touch of fingers fluttering lightly over her skin—sounding again and again like the ocean, taking her back and back. . . .

Back to a time when she was shaken by chills at one moment, burning hot the next, her body bathed in sweat. Every inch of skin seemed to itch, as if fine needles were being driven into her flesh. She writhed against the sheets that seemed to entrap her in their minutest folds, screamed defiance of hands that held her down. Her head seemed to swell, and then contract as an iron band was tightened around it; slowly, slowly. She was being tortured, deliberately, and *he* was doing it.

"You want to kill me! You're destroying me just as you did . . . no! God, don't touch me! Don't . . . don't."

Her hair had lost its sheen and hung dull and damply matted about her face and shoulders. When she tried to tear it out of her scalp by handfuls, they tied her wrists to the bedposts.

Fluids were pouring down her throat. Soft food, that she promptly vomited up. She screamed until her throat was sore and only animal whimpers escaped from it.

"Don't touch me . . ." she whispered hoarsely, even in her sleep. "Don't—oh don't! I hate you—you're going to kill me too. . . ."

She heard voices talking in undertones, coming from a tremendous distance away, without being able to understand what they were saying. Felt hands on her body that were alternately cruel and kind. They tried to make her listen, but no one listened to *her*, no one cared. She wanted to die, but they wouldn't allow her that privilege either. And part of the time she dreamed, when she was too exhausted to struggle any longer and lay limply against the crumpled sheets, hearing the voices that never stopped.

"Oh Christ! Are you sure this is the only way? She's in agony, and to tell you the truth, I don't know how much more I can stand either! If I'd known . . ."

"She's strong enough to stand it, and so are you, if you'll get some sleep and some food inside you. She's not going to die, I can guarantee that much."

"That much! What the hell do you mean? I'm warning you, Doctor, if anything happens to her . . ."

"And, by God, I'm ordering you out of this room! If you expect me to do the job you paid me to do, you'd better start following my instructions yourself, sir! I've treated similar cases before, and during the period of withdrawal, it is essential that the patient be kept as calm as possible. She starts to scream whenever you come near her! Now it's obvious to me . . ."

For two days they had heard nothing from him and he had left the room and left the house. He returned on the evening of the third day with the beard-stubble thick on his face and not a word of explanation. And this time, Dr. Matthews greeted him with a thin smile.

"She's better. The convulsions have stopped, and she's able to take some nourishment again. It's only a suggestion, mind, but I think you should wait at least until tomorrow before you attempt to see her."

"Your tactful way of telling me she's still liable to fly into hysterics if she sets eyes on me?" Steve Morgan's fingers rasped irritably across his stubbled jaw, and the doctor, observing the lines of tiredness and strain on his face, the bloodshot eyes that told of too much liquor and too little sleep, gave a professional noncommittal shrug.

"She's your wife, and—this problem between you isn't any of my business, of course. But speaking as a doctor, you look as if you could use some rest yourself. An emotional, angry scene at this point . . ."

"You're right. At this point I would find it very difficult to keep my temper! Good-night, Doctor. If you'll excuse me now, I promise to present myself in a more respectable condition in the morning."

Ginny heard the low murmur of voices. Unconsciously she had kept alert for sounds ever since she'd heard the sound of horses' hooves passing her window and the voices of the *vaqueros* had warned her of *his* arrival.

She felt so weak! So drained of everything—strength, emotion —and yet she found her heart beating far too fast with a kind of sick, frightened anticipation. The voices murmured on and on or was it only her imagination? She listened for a certain footfall, and heard the distant slamming of a door, echoes bouncing off the numb edges of her brain. Would he come bursting in here, blue eyes hard as sapphires, live with hate or disgust? Or would they be as empty of feeling as hers?

Her room—had it been *his* room once?—was set slightly apart from the rest of the house; built on a slightly lower level into what seemed to be a niche in one of the enormous coastal mountains that fell steep-sided to the ocean. To reach it from the living room one had to walk down a covered passageway, wood-floored, open to the gardens except when the enormous shutters on either side were closed.

She knew all this because the nurse had told her, even drawing a small sketch for her. And she had looked down on the narrow, crescent-shaped beach that seemed to be directly under the windows that formed one whole side of her room. She had seen the ocean breakers foam in, to break with deceptive gentleness over black rocks, slide insinuatingly up the strand.

"There's a lovely terrace just outside—when you're better you'll be able to sit out there and enjoy the sunlight and the clean sea air."

When she was better? Why had she been so ill? What had he done to her? There were still bruises encircling her wrists to remind her that she had been tied to her bed like a captive animal. Tortured. And *he* had ordered it, had sat by her and watched her suffering for days on end, listened unmoved when she begged for release.

"If you will only *give* me something! For the pain—I can't stand it, I'm going to die from it! If you're going to kill me, why can't you do it quickly? Why?"

She thought he had stroked her hair back from her face and had murmured something gentle, pretending to reassure her, but that was all it had been—pretense, for the benefit of the others, the doctor and the nurse. Why couldn't she remember everything? Why were some things so blurred and indistinct?

Ginny moved uneasily under the light covers, longing to throw them off. But then the nurse would come in and cluck-cluck disapprovingly as she pulled them up again.

Was she really on a ranch in Monterey, or in a private sanitarium—the kind that Ivan had once threatened her with?

Ivan. . . . No! Oh God, no—one memory she wasn't ready to cope with yet. Steve had killed him. Horribly. But why, why?

She thought she heard footsteps, and closed her eyes quickly, trying to force her breathing back to normal. Footsteps pausing outside her door, and then moving on. Long, angry strides. Walk of a stalking predator. She remembered Paco Davis' voice, from long ago—how long? "Those *guerrilleros* don't give any quarter, and Steve's one of the worst of them. I could tell you things. . . ." But he hadn't told her. And she had had to find out for herself.

Ginny waited, knowing he would come, not knowing how she would feel. Only the nurse came, in the end, bearing a bowl of hot broth, her professionally cheerful smile pasted onto her fat white face.

"You still awake? My, my! And we all thought you were asleep. You need rest, you know. And your husband's back. He'll be glad to see how much better you are, won't he? I'll help you sit up and you must finish every drop of your broth. It'll put some color in your cheeks when he comes in to see you tomorrow."

Nurse Adams kept up a flow of determinedly cheerful chatter while Ginny forced herself to finish her "supper."

Why did the woman have to talk so much? And treat her as if she were a child? She was tempted to make a scene—to throw the soup back in the woman's face and demand that she should be allowed to get up. But it was all too much trouble, and in spite of herself she had begun to feel drowsy again. Ever since she had started to become aware of what was going on around her, all she wanted to do was sleep. Even sitting up was almost too much effort.

He wouldn't be coming to see her tonight. He didn't want to. He'd been indifferent enough to stay away—how many days had it been? And now he preferred to put off the time of their meeting for as long as possible. Perhaps he was wondering what to do with her, now that he had her. An unpleasant, unwanted responsibility. After all, a mistress was one thing—an instrument of pleasure, easily and conveniently discarded when one tired of her. But a wife . . .

That was what they talked about the next day, when Steve finally came to visit her, carrying her out onto the terrace she'd been promised but had never seen until then.

Clean shaven, the livid red of the saber cut on his face already fading into a thin line that would only prove more intriguing to the women who always watched him, Steve looked more of a pirate than ever. But his manner was that of a polite stranger.

He had deposited her in a chair, and asked if she was comfortable. But he would not sit down himself, preferring to lean recklessly against the wrought iron railing that looked down the rocky cliffside to the ocean below.

His eyes, slightly squinted against the morning sunlight, were the color of the ocean where it joined the sky, beyond the breakers. Just as unfathomable, their expression impossible to read. Suddenly, she didn't know what to say to him; how to act. What did he want of her now?

Nurse Adams had brushed out her hair until it shone again with something of its old fire, and had tied it back with a green ribbon that matched the ribbons threaded through the tiny eyelets that embroidered the edges of her lacy wrapper. Ginny had looked at her reflection in the hand mirror the nurse had held up for her—slanted green eyes like pools in the whiteness of her face—cheekbones far too prominent. She was too pale, and she was ugly. She'd had a fleeting vision of Concepción's gold-tinted, glowing face, red lips curved in a triumphant smile. "Esteban and I—we are the same kind of person. We understand each other. . . ."

She didn't understand Steve any longer, if she ever had. When he looked at her so impersonally, neither anger nor passion was in his voice when he spoke. Unconsciously, her chin came up, giving her a rebellious look.

"I'm glad you're so much better. Perhaps we can talk now."

"About what?" She sounded sullen. "I'm sure you have everything decided already. Have I been punished enough yet?"

"Punished!" For just an instant his eyes blazed into hers, and then, with deliberate control he said, "I had hoped that by now you were capable of understanding why I brought you here."

"To . . . to torture me! I know what you're capable of when you're angry—or had you forgotten? What escapes me is why you couldn't let me go away. You—"

"You weren't being tortured." Still the same carefully controlled tone. "You were on your way to being an opium addict. And this was the only way to—Ginny, I've seen what happens to

people who acquire the habit. I've been in opium dens, peopled
by human skeletons who escape from one hell into another, not
even realizing after a while that they're alive. The cure is painful,
and I'm sorry you had to suffer through it. But at least you *are*
recovered now, or so the doctor tells me."

"You should have let me die! It would have been more convenient, wouldn't it?"

"You're still being unreasonable, Ginny."

"Does that mean I have to be 'cured' all over again? Are you
going to keep me a prisoner forever, or just until the scandal dies
down? Oh, for God's sake! I'd rather you were honest with me for
a change! What happens now, Steve? A divorce, after a discreet
interval? Or am I to be sent away to some quiet place, where you
can forget. . . ."

"I haven't forgotten a damn thing! And nor have you, it seems.
But there's going to be no divorce, Ginny. Not yet, anyhow. A
month from now, we're going to be married again for the benefit
of the public. In church, with your father giving you away. And
half of San Francisco at the reception afterward. They might
whisper, for a while, of how soon you became a bride after you
were widowed. And they'll say you were my mistress before. But
it's better than being called a bigamist, isn't it, sweetheart? And in
time they'll stop whispering and accept."

He called it a "civilized arrangement"; Steve, who was hardly
civilized himself! Purely to prevent a scandal, they were to be formally remarried; her only obligation being to play the contented
wife for some months afterward.

"I gave your friend Count Chernikoff my word I'd let you
travel to Europe within a year. You can make up your mind about
a divorce then."

"And until then?" Ginny's voice was almost a whisper, she only
hoped he did not see how white her knuckles were from grasping
the arms of her chair.

"Until then I propose that we attempt to keep up appearances.
I'll make it a point to be gone as much as possible; I'm sure you'd
feel more comfortable if I am. A year, Ginny. And I'll settle
enough money on you so you'll be independent, no matter what
you decide to do afterward."

He made it sound so reasonable and practical and completely
cold-blooded! After all, what real choice did she have?

"What about your mistresses?" Ginny demanded later, and he lifted a black, quizzical eyebrow.

"And your lovers?" Leaning back in his chair, Steve regarded her inscrutably. "I hope, my sweet, that we are both sensible enough to practice a reasonable amount of discretion. Between us, we've already given the gossips a field day. Why not give their wagging tongues a chance to talk of something else for a change?"

They were facing each other across the dinner table by candlelight, talking as if they were uneasy partners in some impossible scheme. Less than a year ago, they would not have bothered with the dinner. No—only a month before, he would have carried her off to bed, over her halfhearted protests. But now, when they were about to present themselves in public as husband and wife, a barrier lay between them, with neither of them able—or willing—to surmount it.

Both the *Alta California* and the *Chronicle* described the wedding in detail. Headlines in the latter newspaper announced: *First Marriage for Senator Brandon's Daughter, According to Catholic Church.*

The more conservative *Alta California* referred to the young bride as "the recently widowed Princess Sahrkanov," reminding its readers of the tragic accident at sea that had claimed the Prince's life. But both newspapers agreed that the bride and her new bridegroom made an exceptionally handsome couple, and that the reception given afterward by the bride's father surpassed even the magnificent wedding party thrown by a certain New York millionaire to celebrate his daughter's marriage to an English peer.

The house on Rincon Hill blazed with lights, and the dancing went on until dawn, followed by a "surprise" breakfast party at the Palace Hotel. It was only after this that the bride and groom made their traditional escape, driving off in a magnificent new carriage, specially ordered from England and drawn by matched thoroughbreds.

Tired out to the point of exhaustion, her head aching from the effect of too much champagne and too much tension, Ginny fell asleep; barely stirring to murmur something unintelligible when the carriage stopped and Steve carried her out in his arms and up a winding staircase.

Her first thought, on waking, was that she was still dreaming. Where was she? What had happened to her? She lay alone in an enormous bed with a carved mahogany headboard, wearing a nightgown of thin, pale green silk that seemed to cling to the length of her body. And it must be late evening. She could see a faint, violet-colored glimmer of light outside, through full-length windows. Someone had lit a fire in the room, and its orange glow quarreled with the fading daylight.

And then recollection came, faint and half-blurred at first; bringing with it an uneasy sense of apprehension.

She had actually been married—again—to Steve. This wedding even more unreal than their first: the brilliance of candlelight at the high altar, the high voices of the choir, her own stumbling voice making the required responses. Steve's voice sounded stronger—and unemotional. Like the brush of his lips over hers afterward.

During the reception, smiling, he had whispered to her: "I know what a good actress you can be, Ginny. Remember that we are supposed to be too much in love to have wanted to wait longer to be married. You can do better than *this!*"

"And you . . . I notice you found it hard to tear yourself away from Concepción. It reminds me too much of our *first* wedding!"

His eyes narrowed at her lazily.

"What a good memory you have, my love! You must tell me sometime how *this* wedding compares with *your* last!"

Before she could retort he had forced her to dance with him, holding her so closely that she became breathless before the music ended. And after that . . . after that he had hardly left her side, setting himself out to play the devoted, attentive bridegroom. How dare he talk to her of acting!

And yet . . . Ginny sat up in bed, frowning with the effort of remembering. She had fallen off to sleep almost as soon as they were alone together in the carriage; her head resting on his shoulder. He had put his arm around her . . . and after that? She thought she remembered being carried in his arms . . . the low murmur of voices . . . a door being kicked open. Who had undressed her and put her in bed? Suddenly, and quite unexpectedly, the young woman felt a flush warming her cheeks. How ridiculous! She must guard against the sudden feeling of weakness that seemed to overwhelm her for a moment. Now she remembered this room and this bed. Steve had brought her here before,

and on that occasion, had practically raped her, his body a punishing, driving instrument of anger. Just because he had been kind—
even gentle—last night was no reason for her to trust him blindly
as she had done before. He knew what he was doing; it suited
him, for the moment, to keep her tame and content.

Ginny gave an angry, imperious tug at the velvet bell rope,
stretching languorously after she had done so. Whatever Steve's
motives were, he had taken her as his, in the eyes of half the
world. They had made a bargain, and this time she would not
allow herself to be hurt. No . . . nor would he find her a placid,
complaisant wife! He had forced this situation upon her for convenience' sake—perhaps her father had something to do with it.
Well, she would play her role to the hilt—see how he liked it!

Ginny shivered uneasily—wanting to return to the present and
trapped, in her dream, by the past. Trapped . . . by the wedding,
by the emptiness between them. It had barely been nine months
ago that they had traveled back to San Francisco from the Penin-
sula after their honeymoon, and for once they were not surrounded by other people. While her maid packed for her, Mrs.
Morgan shared an intimate dinner with her husband on the glass-
enclosed terrace that looked out over the city and all the way to
the distant curve of blue water where ships rode at anchor, their
lights shining against the encroaching darkness.

Every now and then—and especially at moments like this, when
they were alone—Ginny would find herself smitten by a feeling of
unreality. Was it really possible that she was married to Steve,
and that they could remain strangers to each other? He could talk
to her about business affairs, laugh at her, even tease her. But the
constraint between them still remained.

"He's bored with me already," Ginny thought, and lowered her
eyes as she pensively reached for the glass of white wine that stood
beside her plate. "It was foolish of me to expect . . ." But what
had she expected? That Steve would demand she stay with him,
when it had been he who had made all the arrangements for her
trip to Europe? He had done so after that horrible weekend house
party at the house of an actress. Almost every other man there
had brought his mistress, but *she* had insisted upon going.

"Why not? I know everyone. It sounds like fun. And you don't
need to think I'll be jealous if you decide to wander upstairs with

that little blonde you paid so much attention to the other night."

He had raised his eyebrows at that.

"Does that mean that I must not display any jealousy either? I noticed you had several admirers among Madame's friends."

"Oh!" she had shrugged carelessly. "But at least they are all real people! I am so tired of hypocrites, and pretending to be respectable when I am not."

He had burst out laughing at that—but he had not been laughing when he came up the staircase of the actress' house, looking angry and impatient, and had caught her being kissed on the landing by a young man named Peter. He was an English actor, quite well known, but she had only allowed him to kiss her in order to soften the blow to his pride when she informed him firmly that she did not intend to spend the night with him.

Wondering why she felt so guilty and so awkward, Ginny had struggled to extricate herself from the young man's too-tight embrace. After all, she thought defensively, she had left Steve alone with Madame herself. They had gone out on the terrace, and had already spent an unconscionable time there when Peter, who had been whispering in her ear all along, had offered to show her to her room.

Steve himself seemed to be the only one of them who was not in the least taken aback. The look that had been on his face only seconds before had been wiped away, leaving only a bleak sarcasm, and he had made her a formal bow.

"Excuse me for interrupting, my love. I only wanted to wish you a pleasant night."

She had spent an extremely unpleasant and sleepless night, all alone; for she had quickly got rid of Peter after that. And had seen Steve again at their very late breakfast, when neither of them had made any reference to the previous night, or how it had been spent.

"He's made love to me, but has never once told me he loves me," Ginny thought. The short, happy time they had spent together in Mexico, both penniless, sleeping wherever they could in the wake of an army, seemed dreamlike now. He had loved her then, but it hadn't lasted. She tried not to think of the way he had killed Ivan. *That* too, fortunately, seemed impossible; as if it had happened in a nightmare. Not jealousy—Steve was no longer jealous of her. He had merely been reclaiming a possession. And now, less than a year after they had been formally married, he was already tired of her and had not shared her bed since that weekend.

With a flash of her old fire Ginny said to herself, "but I'll be damned if I'll let him see that it matters to me! If I don't have anything else left of the green girl I used to be, at least I have some pride."

She had spent some time in the sun, and her face had regained something of its peachy-gold tint, making it glow in the candlelight. Her green, slanted eyes looked enigmatic and mysterious, as she toyed with the stem of her wineglass and then raised it suddenly, draining it.

"Were you drinking some secret toast of your own? To Russia? Or to France, and old memories?"

The glass Ginny had been holding smashed against the fireplace, and she looked at him challengingly.

"Why should I drink to old memories? The past is dead. I prefer to look ahead."

"You should have told me," Steve said dryly. "I would have joined you."

For a dangerous moment the impulse swept over him to kick aside the table that separated them; to sweep her into his arms and push her down on the carpeted floor, taking her among the litter of broken crockery and glasses. Forcing her to admit . . . to admit what, for God's sake? That she had become the kind of woman who would respond to any man's caresses, providing they were delivered forcefully enough? He wasn't able to forget that it was all his fault. Too selfish to think of *her* future, he had delivered her to the wolves, in more ways than one. If he hadn't let his infernal pride and jealousy blind him, she would never have been subjected to Carl Hoskins—or Ivan Sahrkanov. Or the powders that helped her forget. Now she blamed him for everything, and the rational part of his mind could understand why.

When she had been half out of her mind with the longing for opium, screaming her hate and distrust of him, he had promised himself to be patient with her. This time, there would be no more force. He would let her get everything out of her system and win her back to him of her own accord, without coercion. But it hadn't worked out that way.

She was an accomplished mistress and lover, but she wasn't the same woman who had once offered her throat to his strangling hands while she swore that she loved him. Or the same half-tamed creature who had used a knife to fight for him.

It was just as well they would be separated soon. They both needed time apart from each other to readjust.

Time . . . suddenly it seemed to rush by far too quickly; like the passing scenery seen through the windows of the expensively constructed private cars on the new railroad that linked two coasts of a vast continent.

They were shareholders in both the Central and Union Pacific railroads, and as such, their passage across America was as smooth and as luxurious as if they had merely been holidaying at some weekend resort.

Steve had recently made her a present of some of his shares, and Ginny began to feel as if she were part owner herself as they sped through days and nights, with a constantly changing country-side unfolding through the windows.

Unless she joined the Senator and Sonya, though, she would have spent most of her time alone in the luxuriously appointed car that was hers and Steve's. Steve himself spent most of his time playing poker with some acquaintances he had discovered, and once, the night before they were supposed to arrive in New York, she could have sworn she smelled some woman's cheap perfume on him when he formally—and a trifle drunkenly—kissed her good-night.

Ginny had been wide awake and angry when she heard him draw aside the heavy velvet curtains. She stiffened, closing her eyes resolutely when he bent over her.

"Are you playing the traditional wronged wife, Ginny-love? It doesn't suit you. And I'm far too tired to think of raping you. So . . . good-night."

Steve's lips, warm and somehow teasing, brushed against her temple, trailing down to her earlobe. The power he had to excite her body was diabolical! She would almost have welcomed his presence beside her in her wide, comfortable berth, if only so that she could quarrel with him for the rest of the night. But he left her. And that, too, was something she had grown used to during the past months.

They had separate rooms, and when they did come together in bed it always seemed as if Steve was taking her merely because there was no other woman available, to sate his own uncontrollable desires. And it happened, usually, when they had both been out somewhere and were tired or had had too much to drink. They joined each other like animals, each trying to seek a kind of forgetfulness in passion without feeling. He never looked at her, as he had done before, and muttered under his breath: "I want you, Ginny! And if you don't take off your clothes quickly . . ."

No—now her maid undressed her, and helped her on with her expensive, sheer nightgowns and negligees. And when Steve came to her—*if* he came to her, it was only when she had just started to fall asleep, or was too worn out to protest. And then, soon afterward, he would leave her again, preferring to sleep alone, she'd no doubt. Yes, Ginny was aware of the gossip around town—of the women who envied her secretly because she had a husband who would take her everywhere with him and treated her as if she was his mistress instead of his wife. Even Sonya, her soft mouth hardening, had commented on how *odd* it seemed.

But it was really her fault. *She* had faced Steve in the beginning, insisting that she was not going to be treated as a poor fool of a wife.

"Since we have come to an agreement, our arrangement ought to be fair. I don't see why you should have all the advantages. I would like to enjoy myself too."

Surprisingly, she had not enjoyed herself at all, but she would have died rather than admit it to *him*. He took her everywhere, and treated her in public as if she were his mistress—but she was not even *that*.

In a very short time, she would be sailing for Europe. Not even the thought that she would be meeting the Tsar of Russia, and was in all probability his daughter, could stir her out of her strangely depressed mood.

And as usual, depression made Ginny sparkle on the outside. They were to spend a week in New York. She took the staid society there by storm. Not only was she rich, married to a young and handsome husband who was himself the object of much feminine curiosity; but she was half-French, well-educated and intelligent.

Rumors had filtered this far from San Francisco about the young couple; New York wondered how many of the rumors were true. No one could tell, not even the writers for the gossip "rags," who were not above bribing servants to get their information.

Steve Morgan, tall, dangerous-looking, with the saber cut on his face adding to the whispers ("he's fought several duels, both here and in Europe . . . *one* story has it that he and his wife were openly lovers even before her first husband died."), was in New York on business, with his father-in-law. His lovely young wife, with her intriguing green eyes, would be leaving very shortly for Europe with her stepmother. In public, they seemed happy and perfectly suited. In private—but who was to know what happened in the privacy of their hotel suite? Since they had arrived in New York, Ginny hardly saw her husband unless it was at some public function. Her days were spent either shopping with Sonya or visiting. Her evenings did not end until dawn lightened the sky and she had barely enough energy left to fall across her bed.

When they were not both acting for the benefit of other people, Steve behaved as if she had already left. Even his occasional desire for her body seemed to have waned. Not once had he entered *her* room in their suite. When she had breakfast, it was alone. A sense of sheer humiliation kept Ginny from asking where he was after the first day.

"Mr. Morgan said you should sleep as late as you liked, ma'am. He was gone real early."

She had insisted on keeping Delia as her maid, and the girl had learned to be wooden-faced of late. Moreover, she seemed to be slightly afraid of Steve, having heard all the old stories from Tillie, no doubt. And Ginny wouldn't demean herself by asking questions.

She felt time rushing by, buffeting her with the wind of its passage. Not even to Sonya could she admit her real feelings, but especially not to Steve, even if he had spared her some of the precious hours he spent away for her. Ginny was positive now that he was anxious to see her go. She must have been mad to imagine, to hope foolishly that he might suddenly change his mind and tell her he wanted her to stay.

There was a grand bon voyage party—the kind of affair the newspapers snobbishly referred to as a "soiree"—given for them the night before they were supposed to sail for Paris. Held in the grand ballroom of the hotel they were staying at, there must have been over five hundred guests. And yet the next morning the newspapers would refer to it as a very exclusive gathering of close friends. Ginny hardly knew any of them.

Her nerves were all on edge, and she tried to hide her exhaustion by laughing a lot and flirting with all her partners when she danced. Last night they had gone to a private ball, and had returned to the hotel after breakfast. She had not seen Steve after that until he had come, quite unexpectedly, into her room to find her rummaging through her jewel box, trying to decide what she should wear with her new bronze watered-silk gown.

"You're keeping everyone waiting, love." And then, quite casually, he had presented her with the Aztec necklace. She called it that because she had seen its facsimile in a museum once and had admired it. Heavy gold, encrusted with jewels, she need not wear another piece of jewelry with it. It fitted closely around her neck and reached to the curve of her breasts, exposed by her low-cut gown. It was beautiful and barbarically splendid, and would make her the envy of every other woman present.

"Oh, Steve!" she murmured, wide-eyed, and he laughed.

"You can thank me for it later. We had better go down now."

Once they mingled with their guests, she lost him again. And Ginny's air of gaiety was almost feverish. How many hours left? She and Sonya were to sail with the early morning tide. He had paid her off with a fabulous piece of jewelry, and no doubt the thanks he expected would be a discreet divorce later, with no fuss.

By the time dinner was announced, Ginny had almost stopped caring. She had had far too much wine to drink already, to dull the strange ache in her heart. And she was holding her arm out to the man who was to be her dinner partner, laughing at something he had said, when Steve appeared from nowhere, his face unexpectedly angry.

"Have you said your good-byes to everyone?" And without giving her a chance to reply: "Good. I've already made our excuses to your father. You're having dinner with me."

His fingers closed over her wrist, and in spite of her resentful tugging they were as inexorable as steel manacles.

Ginny's face began to burn. Everyone was staring at them! He practically dragged her down the length of the room, past all the couples who were going in to dinner, past the dowagers with their raised eyebrows, and her tight-lipped stepmother, and the waiters with their discreetly shuttered faces. Up the carpeted staircase; turning to look at her only once, when he inquired with dangerous politeness if she'd rather he carried her all the way upstairs?

At the door to their suite she tried to hang back again.

"Steve! Have you gone completely mad? What will Delia—"

"If you were going to ask me what Delia would think, or any of those people downstairs, quite frankly, I don't give a goddam! And I told Delia to get some sleep, so it's useless your calling out to her, if that's what you had in mind."

She almost fell across the threshold of the room, and she heard the door slam behind her, the ominous click of metal as he locked it.

The drapes had all been drawn, and the gaslights turned low, so that she seemed to be enclosed in the heart of a velvet box.

"If you hope to wear that dress again, take it off. Get rid of all those ridiculous layers of garments you're wearing—everything but that necklace."

He was already ripping carelessly and angrily at his own clothes, without taking his eyes off her.

Ginny took a deep breath and faced him defiantly, her eyes narrowing.

"If you want me naked you can take my clothes off yourself, Steve Morgan! I'll be damned before I'll undress for you like . . . like some trollop!"

"What the hell else do you think you are? You little green-eyed slut, I've been patient with you long enough. It seems you're the kind of woman who only understands and deserves one kind of treatment."

Speaking through gritted teeth he advanced on her, and in spite of the sudden pounding of her heart, Ginny refused to give ground. She gave a smothered gasp when he put both hands in the deep vee of her gown, ripping it down to the hem. And she cried out softly when he finally lifted her naked body and dropped her across the bed, his fingers catching in the rippling mass of her tumbled hair as he lowered himself over her.

She felt . . . she felt like a captive slave girl being taken by her conqueror. Quite by instinct she struggled angrily against his domination of her, clawing at his back with her nails until he tugged cruelly at her hair, pulling her head back to press his lips against the hollow at the base of her throat. For a moment she stayed rigid, and then, with a sudden sigh of surrender her arms clasped his body closer to hers; her fingers caressed his back, and instead of struggling to escape she arched her hips against his, legs twining about his hard-muscled thighs.

The Aztec necklace bit into her flesh and his, as he leaned closer into her. The gaslights seemed to flicker, making the room expand and then contract around them. Lips and hands reexplored and rediscovered each other as their bodies moved apart and then joined again, making new patterns against the crumpled bed linens.

The Senator's guests downstairs had finished dinner, and the dancing started once more; along with the inevitable whispered speculations.

With Steve's arms still holding her closely Ginny drowsed off and then was wide awake again, her voice murmuring husky love words against his bare shoulder as she exulted in the resurgence of his desire for her.

After this—after they had suddenly found each other again, surely he would not let her go away from him! If only he would say so—if only he would announce that he had no intention of letting her escape him!

"Steve . . . ?" she began, but he wouldn't let her finish. He was kissing her, fiercely, possessively, stopping all thoughts, everything but feeling. It was as if both of them refused to consider the morning that lay crouched outside the windows just beyond this night—waiting to tear them apart.

As it did. Shouldn't she have guessed it? But how was she to know that a faint grey light filtering in through carelessly drawn drapes and a frightened, insistent knocking on the door could wipe away a night of passion as if it had never happened?

She was on a ship again; warmly dressed, bonneted and pelissed against the chilliness of a misty morning. There was a pearly light that seemed to come from everywhere, and the fog leaned sleepily against the gently swelling bosom of the sea.

What a sadly depressing hour for leavetakings! Even the tattered sheets of fog seemed shabbily dispirited. And she was on board a ship again—a schooner. Its white sails were just beginning to be unfurled, its polished rails that would shine brightly in the sunlight were now misted with minute droplets of water. Everything seemed damp. Even Ginny's skirts felt limp as they clung to her limbs, and when she brushed away straying tendrils of coppery hair from her face, they seemed moist.

The lamps burned brightly in the luxurious stateroom she was to share with Sonya, and it seemed far too crowded; the heavy scent of hothouse flowers almost stifling. It seemed that all their guests of the previous evening had insisted on coming aboard to say their noisy farewells. A table had been set up in one corner of the large cabin; snowy white tablecloth bearing an assortment of covered silver dishes that still steamed, and bottles of champagne.

"A toast!" Over and over again she heard the words, as glasses were lifted and drained. An elderly man that Ginny vaguely remembered meeting told her reassuringly that they were bound to have a calm voyage. .

"Traveling's best at this time of the year. You'll have the sunshine with you all the way, as soon as you leave the harbor."

As if she cared! As if she cared about anything but the fact that Steve had said nothing, done nothing except to hurry her, in case they missed the tide.

Last night . . . but perhaps last night had only been a kind of farewell. *His* way of getting her out of his system for good.

Ginny's eyes went back across the room to where he stood, as they had done too many times already. Clean-shaven, as elegantly dressed as any other man here, he bore no resemblance to the naked savage who had taken her so fiercely only hours before. Her lips still felt swollen and aching with the force of his kisses. Did everyone here suspect what had happened when he had dragged her upstairs with hardly a word of explanation? Was it really important? Seeing them today, in the cold grey light of a spring morning, they must seem just another married couple, already too used to each other to be upset by a separation.

A shaft of sheer anger cut into the bleak cloak of lethargy that Ginny felt envelop her. That woman—smiling flirtatiously up at

Steve, holding her glass up to touch his lightly. Who was she? And how dared they flirt so openly, before she, his wife, had even left?

Quite suddenly, almost as if he had sensed her look, Steve glanced toward her, his eyes a dark, inscrutable blue, their expression half-hidden by those ridiculously long lashes she had once teased him about. Her head back, Ginny looked back at him.

Steve had already forgotten the woman who stood so close to him. Half-mockingly, catching Ginny's sparking eyes, he lifted his glass to her. How cold and angry she looked just now, her hair discreetly tucked under that concealing bonnet, her gown high at the neck and long in the sleeve and of dove-grey silk that made her look like a Quaker until you saw those eyes, and that mouth. His little green-eyed witch! He remembered, only too well, the frantic beating of her heart against his chest, like that of a captured forest creature. Small, incoherent moans through parted lips. Ginny—siren-nemesis; the kind of woman who could lead any man on to his destruction. How she could fight and scream rude invectives at one moment, only to yield with complete abandon the next. How she continued to elude him, even when he managed to force the surrender of her body! If only, in the stormy months that had passed, she had given him some sign that she had changed her mind about this ridiculous trip to Europe; but now Steve reflected grimly that his own pride, if nothing else, would have made him insist that she must go. He wanted her to have every opportunity to find her own destiny; to be completely free to make her own choice, so that when she did it would be hers alone. It was better this way, not only for her sake but for his own peace of mind. There had been far too many occasions recently when his own infernal jealousy had almost broken the bounds of the tight controls he had set on himself.

Steve's eyes had taken on a brooding, almost measuring look as he studied her. Suddenly, as if she could not bear to meet his gaze any longer, Ginny turned, and slipped out of the cabin, letting in a draft of cool, damp air before she closed the door behind her.

"Excuse me," he murmured mechanically to the pretty brunette who stared up at him pouting slightly, a disappointed look spreading over her face.

He drained his own glass, and poured out two more, tipping the obsequious steward who acted as bartender. And then, against every practical, rational warning in his mind, he followed her.

She was standing alone by the rail and he handed her the glass without a word. Her eyes, a sullen, opaque green, met his for a moment, and then, tilting her head, she swallowed the champagne as if it had been water, without pausing; throwing the glass over the side in almost the same motion.

"Bon voyage, baby," he murmured over the rim of his glass, before he followed suit.

Abruptly, she turned away from him, gloved hands gripping the polished rail so tightly she thought her fingers might snap. A sharp breeze, ruffling the face of the water, tearing the transparent strips of fog into shreds, outlined the curves of her slim body, and Steve felt her skirts whipping against his legs. He was on the point of speaking, of saying something light and casual, when she said his name aloud, her face still turned resolutely away from him.

"Steve . . ."

And now, quite suddenly, as if the veil of doubt and misunderstandings that had existed between them all these months had lifted for an instant, he could sense the fierce struggle that went on inside her. The tug-of-war between pride and emotion, as she kept her face turned toward the ocean as if she didn't dare face the answers she might find in his eyes. The same damned emotional seesaw he tried to deny in himself; only, Ginny had more courage. Not helping her, not answering her appeal, he saw how her shoulders squared at the same instant she tipped her chin up defiantly.

"There's something I have to ask you, you know. Steve, do you . . . do you want me back?"

He hesitated for a fraction too long while he searched for the right thing to say; saying carefully at last:

"I want you to do whatever *you* want to do, Ginny."

And soon after the words were out he was cursing himself again for being a coward. How damned pious and cautious he had sounded! But at least she was braver than he. Steve damned her persistence and her utter desirability as she swung her head around to look him fully in the face, unashamed of the sheen of unshed tears in her eyes.

"Then . . ."—she kept her voice carefully steady, her eyes never leaving his—"then perhaps I should have phrased my question differently. And perhaps this time you will give me an unequivocal answer! Do you . . ." She bit her lip suddenly before going on in a controlled voice: "What do you feel about me, Steve? If you care—how much do you care? I must know—don't you see that?"

Feeling himself trapped and taken by surprise, Steve said lightly and almost too quickly:

"Why, I'm crazy about you, baby. Haven't you always known that?"

For a moment, seeing the green lights sharpen in her eyes, he thought she was going to slap him, and knew he deserved it.

And then a tinny, magnified voice put a distance between them.

"All visitors ashore! All visitors ashore, please. This is the last call."

Whatever angry words she had been about to say were drowned out in the inevitability of that warning.

Her eyes turned solemn and wide, searching his face for the answer he grudged her.

So many things not said! Words of love, and trust, or even jealousy. Under her childlike, questioning look the twisted half-smile of self-mockery vanished from Steve's lips. He looked angry and impatient and frustrated and—yes, he actually looked unhappy!

He put his hands on her shoulders, his voice harsh.

"Ginny . . ."

She shook her head at him.

"No—don't! Don't say anything more, Steve. I don't want . . . if you can't say the words, then show me. Damn you, Steve, tell me the truth *this* way . . . !"

Suddenly, violently, completely uncaring that the deck was suddenly crowded with people, Ginny flung her body against his, arms going up to clasp themselves around his neck as she stood on tiptoe; lips already parting as they reached hungrily for his.

And he wasn't able to resist her. His arms took her and crushed her body against his as if he longed to break her, at the same instant that his mouth took hers with a hard, hurtful savagery that made her moan softly, even while she triumphed in her victory. He might *say* what he wanted, he might kiss her almost as if he hated her for having trapped him, but he loved her—he loved her! Every instinct, so long dormant, seemed to tell her that now.

He kissed her as he had that evening in Vera Cruz, when he

had first admitted he loved her. When he had said he was besotted by her, and had possessed her hungrily while he murmured soft Spanish love words against her burning skin.

Anger and passion turning into tenderness when he felt the sweetly giving, damnably familiar molding of her body against his —salt taste of her tears. Transformed into a raging frustration when there was an embarrassed cough behind them, and her father's voice, gruffly reminding Steve that the boats were leaving. "They're holding the last launch for us. I think . . ."

Ginny's face was white and tearstained, her eyes a deep, almost murky green as they stared into his face.

He seemed to slide his hands up her back with an effort— fingers clamping down on her shoulders as he moved her away from him.

In an undertone, black brows drawn together in a frustrated scowl, he swore at her in Spanish. "Perdition take you, you green-eyed witch! Did you find your answers? What more do you want from me—my scalp to wear at your belt?"

Before she could answer him, or indeed, perfectly comprehend what he had muttered at her through his clenched jaws, his hands fell away from her and his face became darkly unreadable again.

This time, his kiss was politely formal, a mere brushing of his lips over hers.

"Take care of yourself, *querida mia.*"

Ginny stood there, clinging to the railing for support; feeling as if she had taken root there and might never be able to move from that spot again. And watched him leave her without once turning his head.

Would it always be that way? Ginny felt as if she were coming back very slowly to reality after the ebbing away of a nightmare. There was a picture in her mind, etched there. Steve—walking away from her. How many times had he done so—how many more times would he do so?

"You're being morbid!" Ginny chided herself. "Don't dwell on the past . . . not on *that* part of it, anyhow."

She stretched, breathed deeply, and turned from the window trying to compose herself for sleep. She didn't want to be lying awake like any typical jealous wife when Steve returned. And it was going to be different for them, this time. Very different.

# Chapter Three

ॐ

In spite of all her good resolutions, however, Ginny found herself transformed into a virago by the next morning. It was Steve, of course, who brought it on himself—daring to join her in bed with the sun shining brightly outside; strolling in nonchalantly from the dressing room with his hair still wet and his eyes bloodshot.

He'd just come home! How dared he? She had meant to feign sleep, but her quickened breathing gave her away, and Ginny saw a smile that mixed taunting with teasing lift a corner of his mouth. She sat bolt upright, eyes sparking green fire.

"You're a trifle *early*, aren't you, Steve?"

"To tell the truth I'm surprised to find *you* up at this unconscionable hour, my sweet. And you always look your most adorable when you're angry. Do you mind moving over? I haven't had too much sleep myself."

"Oh! You are a . . ." Sheer rage made Ginny breathless—she wanted to tear at him with her nails until he lost that damned sarcastic grin.

He dropped to the bed beside her, fending her off with a lazy, almost insolent ease—his grip on her wrists increased until she cried out again, this time with pain.

"Stop it! Damn you, Steve, you let me go, you're hurting me, and it's you who deserve . . . oh, I'd like to show you exactly what you deserve. Do you think I'm some foolish milksop wife who'd believe you spent all of last night in your dressing room? Or that you were playing *cards* or some other such ridiculous masculine excuse? I won't put up with—"

"If you don't stop shrieking at me like a shrew, sweetheart, you're going to force me to show you what *I* won't put up with—

and that includes temper tantrums when I come to bed needing
some sleep! Ginny, I mean it. You'd best stop struggling, unless
you mean to incite me to something else besides violence!"

She caught the sudden narrowing of his eyes as they studied her
angrily squirming body, and gasped with righteous outrage.

"Oh no you don't! If you think I'd let you use *my* body after
you've been with God knows *what*—why, I'd rather . . . I'd rather
we went back to sleeping in separate rooms as we used to."

His mouth hardened, and an ugly note Ginny remembered all
too well crept into his voice.

"There are a few things, madam, that you ought to get through
that pretty little head of yours. One of them being that it's my
right to *use* your body, as you so aptly put it, any time and any
way I damn well please. Yes, even if I've already been with—how
did you phrase it?—God knows what!"

Why did she bother to struggle? He moved his body over hers
in the same lithely vicious movement as he yanked her pinioned
wrists up over her head.

And her "Steve, no!" came too late as he said with almost murderous softness, holding his face close to hers:

"And the next time, love, you might have the courtesy to ask
me where I've been, before jumping to conclusions! Wasn't it you
who talked about trust some weeks ago?"

They were both panting now—he with anger and she with her
efforts to get away. Dark blue eyes and flaming green locked in another kind of contest, and like a cornered vixen Ginny bared her
teeth, daring him to try to kiss her.

"You brute! Must you always use force on me?"

"Must you always provoke me to it?"

"Damn you! I won't let you rape me!"

"If you'll stop struggling like a wildcat it won't turn out that
way." And then, as if gauging her temper, he went on tauntingly,
"Unless, of course, this is really the way you prefer me to take you
. . . in which case, my sweet, you really ought to have told me before and I'd have been happy to oblige."

Glaring at him, Ginny compressed her lips. He was baiting her,
and she wouldn't let him! She'd match him in any game he
thought he could play!

Suddenly, her body became completely inert. With a small

sigh, she let her eyelids close resignedly as she said in a bored voice:

"Oh, very well! I should know well enough by now that you're much stronger physically than I, so what is the point? Do what you want with me, Steve, but pray *do* try to come to an end of it quickly, would you? I am famished for breakfast—and you did say you needed to sleep."

She heard his indrawn breath, and it was only with a tremendous effort of will that Ginny kept her eyes closed. She didn't quite dare to meet his eyes, in any case, for she was beginning to develop a sinking feeling that this time she had gone too far.

"Is that how you managed to keep your lovers tame?" Underlying the deceptive softness of Steve's voice was a vibration that she had not heard recently—a note of throttled fury, mixed with disgust that almost made Ginny tremble. In the same voice, he went on almost conversationally, "You sound just like a whore, you know—but then, I should have remembered that that is what you are . . . have you done well at your profession recently?"

Her lips had gone stiff, but now, having gone this far, she forced herself to reply tonelessly:

"Not as well, I'm sure, as you have at *yours*, whatever that may be at this particular time. You know whores so *well*, Steve dear! And you trained me after all, didn't you?"

Somewhere in the back of her mind she could almost *hear* a small, despairing voice that was hers, asking "why are we saying all these horrible things? How did this all begin?"

Looking down at her averted face, Steve had the almost insane impulse to strangle her. Vicious-tongued little bitch! How dared she needle him, provoke him, and then lie there like a martyr waiting to be torn into pieces? And he'd thought he actually had her almost tame!

"It seems I didn't train you well enough, perdition take you! But I intend to remedy *that!*"

The sudden short laugh he gave as he released her had the effect of making Ginny's eyes fly open. She had expected—no, she was not sure exactly what she had expected. Certainly not his next action, as his long, angry strides took him to the large armoire that held her gowns.

What was he up to this time? And would she ever really come

to understand the wild, unpredictable stranger-lover she found herself married to? Steve could play the role of gentleman—urbane and sophisticated—to the hilt, when he chose; but perhaps she should have remembered the savage that always lurked under the surface. Unaccountably, Ginny felt a ripple of fear go through her. What was he doing, rummaging among her clothes?

She tried to make her voice as icy as possible.

"If you don't mind I'd really rather have my maid do that for me!"

She winced as he practically ripped one of her favorite gowns—a brocaded silk—from its quilted hanger, and swung around, narrowing his eyes at her in a particularly nasty way.

"But I do mind. Get dressed, Ginny. And be quick about it."

She almost gave vent to a hysterical burst of laughter. Was it possible that he was actually asking her to get *dressed* rather than to undress for him? Had he gone crazy? And then he flung the gown at her, and her incipient hysteria gave way to renewed fury.

"I will not, Steve Morgan! I'll not be ordered around by you or any man!"

Instead of reacting, he merely awarded her a sarcastic inclination of his dark head.

"Madam, you have five minutes—while *I* get dressed again. After which time . . . well, you reminded me a few minutes ago how much stronger than you I am, did you not?" And then, his voice hardening, "Don't test my temper, Ginny. Because dressed or undressed you're going to take a ride with me. I've decided to satisfy your curiosity as to where I was all night."

She remembered riding with him once, a long time ago, unwilling and half naked—his rifle pressed warningly beneath her breasts. She remembered the feeling of having her clothes ripped from her body, the stickiness of his blood against her naked flesh, and buzzards circling overhead against a hot blue sky. And half-walking, half-dragged along with him through the oozing swamp mud with the trees closing out all light, like a green, miasmic cage. So many things, all part of the eternal battle that was constantly being waged between them. A contest of wills, of stubbornness.

And before he swung abruptly on his heel and left her, Ginny could have sworn she saw the same recognition in his eyes as well.

She was dressed and waiting for him when he came back into the room, freshly shaved and dressed. Steve's black brows drew together in a frown as he let his eyes assess her insolently. Damn the contrary, unpredictable little witch that she was! He had expected resistance at the very least—at worst, to have something thrown at his head while she stood with her feet planted apart and dared him to force his will on her. But instead, here she stood facing him; fully dressed, perfectly calm, and looking annoyingly fetching into the bargain.

A part of his mind applauded her, even while he scowled. Ginny's smile was artificially bright.

"Do you like it? You've never seen me wear this gown before— it was really shockingly expensive of course, but I couldn't resist it —is that why you chose it for me to wear?"

The brocaded polonaise was draped cunningly over an underskirt of green slightly darker than the tiny sprigs that decorated the oyster satin brocade—drawn into a bustle that ended in a tiny train. The bodice of the gown was extremely low-cut, fitting her to perfection. It was a ball gown—hardly suitable for morning wear, and that was one of the reasons why he'd chosen *this* particular gown; out of sheer perversity.

"You'd best wear a shawl to cover your shoulders," he said shortly, choosing to ignore her subtle challenge.

Tempted to stick her tongue out at him as he held the bedroom door open for her, Ginny forced herself to smile sweetly again, hoping her insincerity showed.

"Why, *thank* you, Steve. How considerate of you! And are we going for a long ride? Because I really should leave a message for Sonya. . . ."

"I've already taken care of that!" His voice warned her to be careful how far she carried her play-acting, and Ginny thought with vicious pleasure that she really hadn't seen him so angry in ages!

An hour later, when it had grown much hotter and Ginny could feel herself positively *steaming*, her face flushed and pearled with sweat under the big veiled hat he'd forced her to wear, it was her turn to become angry. Even the discovery that they were entering the city of New Orleans did nothing to lessen her mounting rage and—yes, she had to confess to herself that she was beginning to feel slightly apprehensive as well. One never knew, with Steve! And when he was in one of his black rages . . .

Ginny glanced sideways at him from beneath her lashes, but his profile was gravenly impassive. He had hardly spoken one word to her, even when she had attempted to get her sweetened barbs under his skin; and sullen silence was her final recourse. But when they arrived at their destination, he would soon find out that her false docility was exactly that—a pretense. "I will not allow myself to be bullied," Ginny told herself rebelliously. "And Steve is going to find that out!"

Strangely enough, even without looking at her, Steve could almost sense her thoughts. She was an extraordinarily stubborn woman, as he had good reason to know! She might bend when she had to, but she would never let him break her—did he want to? Most of his anger had evaporated by now, and he had even begun to feel slightly foolish for having let her goad him into this crazy expedition. He should have gone ahead and taken her as he'd meant to—willing or not. No matter what hateful and cutting words they used on each other, their bodies spoke a different language. Yes, he should have remembered that, and instead of being back in New Orleans feeling infernally tired and irritable, he might have been soundly asleep by now.

The light carriage that Steve had insisted on driving himself turned abruptly into a wide, tree-shaded avenue lined with imposing brick and brownstone houses, most of them at least three stories high. *Basin Street*—Ginny read the sign and her nose wrinkled. Such strange names the people of New Orleans chose for streets. Was Steve taking her to visit some old friend of his whose existence he'd chosen to keep dark? No—that would be too pat a solution. Without her knowing it, Ginny's chin had tilted defiantly. She wouldn't satisfy him by asking, or even by seeming interested in his alibi. She would make him see that she didn't really care what he had been up to all night. What she really objected to was this long and tedious drive from the comparative coolness of the plantation house by the river to the hot and humid atmosphere of the city. She was already sticky with perspiration—and thirsty into the bargain. It was typical of Steve that he hadn't been considerate enough to allow her the time to have breakfast before he'd dragged her off in his usual high-handed fashion!

The carriage jerked to a stop just then, interrupting Ginny's thoughts, and a small Negro boy dressed in a uniform with gold buttons shining proudly against his red jacket came scurrying up to take the reins that Steve tossed at him carelessly. His face broke, split in a white-toothed grin as he caught the coin also spun his way with his free hand.

"Thank you, *sir!* I'll be sure an' take real good care of the horses, sir."

Under lashes almost as long as Steve's the boy's liquid brown eyes studied Ginny curiously as the tall gentleman handed her down from the carriage.

This lady looked a lot different from most of the other ladies who came in the daytime. For one thing, he'd never seen a dress quite as pretty on any of *them,* and from the glimpse of her face he caught through the thick veil, she had a mighty pretty face as well.

Steve too was slanting a look at her as he gave the knotted gold bell cord a sharp tug that brought an elderly man, also in uniform, to the wrought iron gates that barred entrance to the narrow passageway fronting the street. Beyond it, Ginny could see the top stories of a house that was set some way back from the street itself, its white-painted shutters closed against the hot sunlight. The brick-and-stone passageway was arched, and deliciously cool in contrast with the heat outside. Small torches set into elaborately patterned wrought iron sconces reminded Ginny in some way of Mexico; an impression that sharpened when she heard the soft splash and tinkle of water up ahead. A fountain! Twin marble cherubs holding tilted pitchers poured an unending stream of water into the circular pool below them. And there were more trees here for shade with benches set under them.

The manservant who had unlocked the gates for them now bowed them through the imposing mahogany and brass front door to the house itself, his smile somehow knowing as well as obsequious. He had seemed to recognize Steve, from the way in which he'd greeted him. Ginny could have stamped her foot with vexation. Why had he left her bed last night? And why was he so ... so overbearing that he'd made her lose her temper so that now pride wouldn't let her ask him the questions she was dying to ask?

A pretty mulatto maid took Ginny's lace shawl and, thankfully, her hat—and now, without the encumbrance of that tiresome veil, she was able to see around her much more clearly.

"Will you want to have refreshments first, sir? There's a parlor free, if you'd rather. And I'll tell madam you're here, I don't think she was expecting you back this early."

Everything in the entrance hallway was subdued and in good taste. A hatstand, a few mirrors in gilt frames that made the room seem larger, and a really exquisite crystal chandelier. And who was "madam" Ginny wondered wrathfully. Was it possible that Steve intended to introduce her to his latest mistress? She tugged her elbow away from his overly polite grip and had opened her mouth to tell him she was not going to stand for any more mystery when she heard a door open, and a woman's voice, rich and rather languorous murmured:

"Oh—that is all right, Belle. As you can see, I am awake already. You can go back to whatever you were doing. . . . Steven? Well, she was right, I did not expect you to be back so soon! You did not sleep at all?"

Tall, slim and blonde, the woman drifted forward with both hands outstretched. Her perfume was expensive, Ginny noticed unwillingly, and so was her gown. And she was undeniably attractive—how dared Steve? What did he have in mind?

She was to find out. With mounting disbelief Ginny watched Steve take the woman's hands as he kissed her casually before he had the effrontery to say:

"Hello, Hortense. You're one of the few women I've known who contrives to look quite ravishing no matter what time of day it is! And no, I wasn't able to fall asleep after all"—Ginny caught his sideways look and felt her hands clench into fists—"so I decided that I'd bring a companion back with me. Do you have a room?"

Hortense, her glance sizing Ginny up and then dismissing her, laughed gently as if he'd said something very funny.

"Whatever you want, *cher ami!* It's all yours, eh? You like the gold and white room—the one with all the mirrors?"

# Chapter Four

❧

At first, Ginny found herself ridiculously torn between the desire to give vent to hysterical laughter or scream with pure fury. Even for Steve, this was surely going too far! After all, she was his *wife* now, how dare he bring her to a place like this? She was no longer the frightened, half-cowed girl he had once kept as his captive whore in a room at Madame Lilas' house in El Paso. And yet, as that particular memory flashed into her mind, Ginny could not help the shiver of fear that shot up her spine. Could he get away with it? *Would* he?

They faced each other in a room that was incongruously light and airy, with its grilled windows overlooking a garden. A room furnished in the French Provincial style—charming and elegant until one noticed the mirrors that were everywhere; cunningly placed to reflect the enormous bed from every angle. Like experienced duelists, they were both on guard without seeming to be.

So far—after a single abortive attempt at protest—Ginny had, with lips compressed, forced herself to remain silent. Downstairs, her vehement "Steve! . . ." had been silenced by his none-too-gentle grip on her wrist and the almost *waiting* look he had given her. She had the feeling he had anticipated her making a fuss, and was prepared for that too. No doubt he'd overpower her or have her overpowered and carried upstairs, willy-nilly—no, she wouldn't allow herself *that* degradation!

Hortense had looked at her, smiling a vaguely polite smile. "Oh, you mustn't feel shy! We're very discreet here, as Steve will tell you. You won't run into anyone else while you're here, I assure you!" And then, to Steve, with more vivacity, "And will you care for breakfast? Along with some champagne perhaps? I can have it sent up in just a few minutes, so that you will not have to wait."

True to her word, a servant had knocked on the door almost on their heels, bringing the champagne in a silver bucket—two bottles of an excellent vintage.

Now, after an inscrutable look, Steve said politely, "You'll have some champagne, won't you?" And turned away to pour it without waiting for her assent.

Ginny sucked in a deep breath as she strove to keep her composure. When it came to games, even the cat-and-mouse kind, she'd show him she was as good a player as he. She took the glass he handed her, meeting his unreadable eyes with what she hoped was careless insouciance, touching the rim of her glass to his.

"How very obliging of you to go to all this trouble—just to make sure I believed your explanations for your absence last night! Or did you bring me here for breakfast? If so, what a nice surprise!"

His eyes seemed to darken slightly as they narrowed on her, but he awarded her a slightly caustic smile of appreciation.

"Touché, my sweet," he said softly. "I see you've learned how to fight back with honied barbs rather than your sharp claws. You should show me *this* side of yourself more often, it might make for a better relationship between us."

She gave him a tiger-smile—a mere flattening of her lips as they curved upward. "How convenient that I please you in *some* way! Should I add 'my lord and master' as women do in the Eastern countries? And as for the . . . this relationship between us—what is it, Steve? Rehearse me again in my role—is it subdued, submissive wife? Mother? Slave? Understanding, undemanding mistress perhaps?"

Only from the tautening of the muscles in his face and the sudden hardness of his mouth did she know he was angry. He raised his glass to her before tossing off its contents and immediately pouring himself more champagne.

He didn't answer her yet because he didn't trust himself to. It infuriated him that she refused to give ground; and worse— refused to lose her temper, thereby giving him an excuse to tear her clothes from her body and take her, as he had done so often in the past. The hell with the patience he had exercised in all the months after their formal marriage in San Francisco! She'd left him and gone to Europe, where she'd looked up all of her old swains and collected more new ones. *And* she'd had the impudence to produce twin infants, without having the courtesy to inform him he was a father—if he *was* their father after all! Damn her. She had no right to be such an unpredictable, unexpected female—and she deserved to be taught her place, or—what had she called it, voice dripping with sarcasm? Her "role."

Steve eyed her dangerously, of half a mind to do exactly what his loins prompted him to do, without bothering to look for excuses. Her anger-sparked green eyes looked challengingly into his, as if she was actually daring him . . . and perhaps she was, the little vixen!

She was saved by the arrival of their breakfast—oysters on the half shell, baguettes still steaming hot, butter that looked as if it had been freshly churned that very morning, and a pot of honey. The smell of coffee was heavenly.

"How very homey," Ginny purred as she sat down to eat, helping herself without a glance at him. She had the feeling, all the same, that he was of half a mind to have her for breakfast. "Do you get such royal treatment every time you visit this . . . place, Steve? Oh, do sit down and join me—you make me nervous, pacing about like a caged beast! And you did order this feast, after all."

She was relieved to see him take the chair opposite her, long brown fingers toying with the stem of the wineglass as he studied her through lazy-lidded eyes. He hadn't said a word to her in minutes. What was he thinking of? What was he planning to do with her next? Ginny felt rather like the intended victim of some sleek-muscled beast of prey. He was *stalking* her, that was it! Waiting to catch her off guard. . . . Well, she would attack first.

"Do you make a habit of frequenting places like this, Steve? I have often wondered why men who are . . . reasonably attractive to the female sex should need to purchase the favors of . . . whores. Mmm—these oysters *are* good! Is it true that they are considered—"

"Ginny." His voice cut flatly across her speech. "Yes, to both your questions. As for what you *wonder*—since you are not a man, it is not something that you would understand in any case. And this particular . . . um . . . house happens to belong to me. I won it in a poker game last night, when our mutual friend Mr. Bishop, who usually wins, threw in four aces in order to allow me to win that particular pot."

Ginny sat bolt upright, almost choking on an oyster. "Mr. Bishop? You mean he is here in New Orleans? Did he have any excuses to offer for not turning up before? Why, if Renaldo and Missie had not misled the soldiers *and* the Sheriff we might both have been killed!"

"If that had happened, I'm sure Mr. Bishop would have been regretful but resigned. Jim is an eminently practical man." Long legs crossed before him, Steve lounged back in his chair, noting with wry amusement her sudden stiffening as the first part of his speech registered belatedly.

"You won this house, you said? You won a . . . a whorehouse in a game of cards? And what were you doing playing cards at all? What was Mr. Bishop doing? You know very well that if he's here it's to persuade you to do something for him—what is it this time? Steve—you *did* refuse him?"

She had the impression, as she watched him, of a shutter falling into place, closing her out. He sounded too studiedly casual as he shrugged. "Even Jim Bishop takes a vacation occasionally. And you've a bad habit of jumping to conclusions, Ginny-love. As you did earlier this morning, if you'll recall."

"Don't try to fob me off, Steve!" She leaned forward urgently, trying to force his attention from his sudden appetite for breakfast to *her*. "Mr. Bishop never travels anywhere without a reason, and I know that as well as you do."

He raised an eyebrow at her, drawling: "You must tell me, sweet, how you came to know Jim so well. You told me he traveled all the way to Mexico to see you?"

"Ohhh . . . ! But you're impossible!"

"I'm sorry you find me so, madam." How she hated it when he called her "madam" in that drawling, sarcastic tone! But his next words made her rigid with anger and apprehension. "Perhaps you would prefer to travel back to Mexico without the burden of my company. In any case, I'm sure you're anxious to get back to your children, and I find I have some business here that might take me some time."

"Running a whorehouse? Why—since you've called me one

often enough—perhaps I can be of help. Is that why you brought me here?"

"I brought you here because you're a spitfire who needs taming." He came out of his chair in one easy motion, catching her under the arms and lifting her up and against him. "And because it's an unwritten law that the owner gets a sample of the merchandise before he decides if it's good enough to put up for sale. In fact, I might just decide to keep you here. It might be a good way to make sure you stay out of mischief—and on your back, whenever I want you."

His calculated, deliberately brutal words had the effect he meant them to have, rendering her almost mindless with rage.

"You . . . you bastard! No . . . I'll never be . . . you won't ever make me . . ."

"No? Don't challenge me, Ginny." Ruthlessly, as he used to in the old days, he cut off her attempts to scream invectives at him with the brutal force of his kiss that bent her head back so far she thought her neck might snap. She felt her head spinning, her thoughts becoming jumbled and incoherent. It simply wasn't fair! She must be possessed. Desire was an insatiable demon inside her and Steve was the devil, making her unable to think, only to feel, to want. Need mounted with the feel of his body molded against the length of hers, throbbing hardness like a promise against her thighs . . . oh God! Would she ever really belong to herself again? Why Steve, who had hurt her before and continued to . . .

Without knowing why, she was clinging to him fiercely as she returned his kiss, standing on tiptoe. He was hers after all—he wanted her. Hadn't he told her she was an obsession with him? He wanted her as much as she wanted him, and no matter how they tore at each other and fought each other the desire that kept bringing them together was inescapable.

They fell together on the bed, coming together savagely without preliminaries, without wasting the time it would take to undress completely. And whether it was hate or whether it was love, it was feeling and it was passion and that was enough.

The same moment, for Sonya Brandon, brought only annoyance. It wasn't like William to leave the house alone without being considerate enough to tell her where he was going, and as for Ginny and that . . . that husband of hers, they still had not returned.

Ginny, Sonya thought angrily, should really have more self-respect than to go out riding with Steve after he'd had the effrontery to stay out all night! Even the servants were whispering, and Ginny's maid had told Tillie that they'd been quarreling furiously when the girl had come upstairs to wake her mistress.

The man doesn't have any scruples! Sonya's face flushed pink when she remembered how few scruples he'd had in his dealings with *her*. And he'd dared remind her. . . . Sonya met her own china-blue gaze in the mirror, hand going up automatically to pat at a straying wisp of hair. The new hat was really very becoming. Tilted slightly forward to shade her eyes it made her look—well—younger. Not that she was *old* yet, of course. All her friends had complimented her on the fact that she'd hardly changed at all. And that really charming young man had actually flirted with her, paying her extravagant compliments even after she'd had to remind him primly that she was a married woman. What was his name? Ah yes—Andre Delery.

And then, Sonya being essentially pragmatic, gave a mental shrug. He had probably been attentive to her in order to wangle an introduction to Ginny. In fact, he'd almost reminded her of Steve Morgan; in a certain way they resembled each other—if not in build exactly, in bearing. She'd sensed an element of danger beneath M. Delery's charm, having noticed how respectfully other men treated him in spite of his youth.

"You'll be needin' the top buggy, ma'am? And would you want me to come with you?" That was Tillie, walking softly as usual. Sometimes Sonya wondered how much the girl overheard and what she really thought, but she soon brushed such absurd questions out of her mind. What did it matter? Tillie was loyal at least, and that was what counted.

"Oh . . . well I did think I would take the buggy as it's such a short ride to La Terre Promise." Still wondering at her husband's absence, Sonya sounded a trifle distracted. "Charles can drive me there and bring the buggy back. I'm sure Mrs. Pruett will make sure I am returned home—and perhaps you could press my blue taffeta for tonight? We are to have dinner at Antoine's with some friends."

Sonya reflected that it was really much better not to take Tillie along, especially since Adeline Pruett had insisted that they simply *must* have a long and intimate chat.

"Just the two of us, my dear. What a lot of catching up we have! And I'm dying to hear all the latest gossip, of course. This is such a backwater compared to the circles *you* must move in now! Although"—voice lowering conspiratorially—"we didn't exactly lack for *some* excitement in those years during the war, did we?"

All of which had reminded Sonya uncomfortably that Adeline Pruett, then an older, sophisticated woman whose husband was off to the war, had been her closest confidante in those days she tried so hard to forget. Well, Sonya thought resolutely as she went downstairs trailed by Tillie carrying her parasol, today she would no doubt learn exactly how much dear Adeline remembered.

"Sonya dearest! How nice of you to come. I had almost feared this intolerable heat might keep you away. Bernard, *do* ring, won't you? Let's see—you've met Bernard's friends I'm sure . . . Lucian Valette . . . Andre Delery . . ." Mrs. Pruett sounded a trifle distrait, quite unlike her usual formidable self, but Sonya, still feeling slightly sick from the oppressive heat outdoors, did not have time to wonder at her friend's manner. Bernard Pruett, a rather vacuous-featured young man who took very much after his late father, had already rung for refreshments and was showing her punctiliously to a chair. Sonya smiled at him warmly, even while she wondered a trifle guiltily at her feeling of *reprieve*. She really was not in the mood today for Adeline's prying, as she no doubt would have done—especially if, as Sonya feared, Adeline had recognized Steve in spite of the mustache he'd grown.

Sipping her glass of chilled white wine Sonya found herself growing quite vivacious after a while. It was so seldom one ever saw the redoubtable Adeline Pruett the least bit discomfited! But Bernard, it appeared, had brought his two closest cronies along to help him beard his mother with the announcement that he had become engaged last night to Miss Althea Pennington. Personally, Sonya could not see why there should be any objections to the match—Miss Pennington was an acclaimed beauty, and her father's millions matched those of the Pruetts. Of course, she wasn't from one of the old Creole families, but what did *that* signify in this day and age? Besides, Bernard was of age and in control of his own money—it was high time he cut loose from the strings his mother kept on him!

Sonya's manner sparkled as becoming spots of color touched her usually porcelain complexion. After all, she thought with a mental toss of her head, Adeline—for all that she was a dear soul —must learn that she couldn't have everything exactly her way forever. And wasn't it *nice* that she, Sonya, still contrived to look quite young and attractive while Adeline herself had grown somewhat matronly and old during the past ten years?

"Do you know that I was quite desolated when I found out you were married? I said to Lucian, 'it can't be, she's far too young! . . .' Will you accept it not as presumption on my part but sincere admiration if I make bold to tell you that last night you were by far the most beautiful woman at the Opera Ball?"

Andre Delery was an accomplished flirt of course—how did men learn so young these days?—but his flattery was rather amusing, Sonya thought. It was nice to feel, for a change, the center of attention instead of constantly being forced to play second fiddle to Ginny. And there was nothing exactly *wrong* with flirting back just a little, was there? It was a game that they all understood, here in the South, and not to be taken seriously, of course. Even Adeline herself would realize that.

Mrs. Pruett, no fool, could almost read Sonya's every thought; but she was far too annoyed at her son and his cowardice in breaking the news of his engagement to that upstart Yankee banker's spoiled daughter to pay very much attention at the time. How dared Bernard bring his friends along with him as if for *protection* from her, his own mother? He knew very well that her usual logical way of presenting things would serve to deter him from such an impulsive step, and so he'd decided to be positively *underhanded* instead! Why, in heaven's name, did Bernard have to take so much after his late father?

Much to Mrs. Pruett's further annoyance, her son, with a wiliness she could hardly credit, decided to take his leave of her at the same time his friends excused themselves, using as a pretext a polite offer to see Mrs. Brandon home before it became too late.

"Oh, Adeline!" Sonya cried with mock dismay, "and I had *so*

looked forward to a long and comfortable gossip with you. We
must make up for it soon; perhaps you'll visit me?"

The journey back to the plantation was so much more pleasant
this time, in the comparative coolness of early evening. And it was
pleasant too, to have the escort of three young and eligible males.
Sonya felt quite like a young girl again, especially during those
moments when the other two dropped slightly back and Andre—
he had begged her to call him that—rode abreast with her, the
deep and somehow searching look in his eyes belying his lightly
frivolous conversation. She felt flattered that he chose to entrust
her with his confidence—the story of his past life, the fact that he
was, surprisingly, older than he looked. He told her it was a pleasure to be able to talk to a woman who was mature enough to understand.

"You're so easy to talk to! In fact, you are the first woman
I've—" He cut himself off quickly as if he'd said too much, and
Sonya blushed with pleasure at the implied compliment. Why, he
was really such an *earnest* young man, under the debonair and
worldly wise exterior he presented to everyone!

If it had been Ginny, now. . . . It was with a stab of annoyance that Sonya remembered her stepdaughter, who had almost from the first proved such an embarrassment to her. Ginny,
no doubt, would have had all three men dancing upon her attention while she flirted shamelessly with them. And of course, they
in turn could hardly retain any respect for her. Certainly, one
could not imagine a young man like Andre Delery admitting to
*that* brash young woman that he enjoyed her conversation. He
would probably—and Sonya found herself blushing at the thought
—do more than *flirt* with Ginny. For all the respect that he
showed to *her*, Sonya had the feeling that M. Delery was something of a lady-killer.

And, in fact, this was something that Mrs. Pruett went to great
pains to confirm to her "dearest Sonya" sometime later that same
evening, when the women once more found themselves thrown together in the same box at the opera. It was, Sonya was to think
later, an evening of disasters. She should have developed a convenient migraine and kept to her bed, and she would have done so if
William hadn't been so unreasonable. First her husband, usually

the most understanding and *civilized* of men, and now Adeline Pruett—who could hardly afford to talk, Sonya thought angrily—had seen fit to warn her against being seen in the company of M. Delery, who was, Sonya was beginning to think, a much-maligned and misunderstood gentleman.

"Adeline's jealous, of course, because she's aged so—why she's let herself become fat and positively *dowagerish!* But there's no excuse for William acting as if he didn't trust me after all the years we've been married when I haven't given him the slightest excuse. . . ." It was really too much to expect her to put up with, Sonya found herself thinking, with an unusual spurt of rebellion. No—it just wasn't fair, considering how lightly they all glossed over Ginny's antics.

# Chapter Five

❧

Had Sonya Brandon but known it, Ginny herself was far from happy that same evening, although she would never admit it or show it. Sheer rage filled her, and being angry always gave her manner and looks a new fire, as Steve had pointed out on too many occasions—choosing to ignore the fact that it was usually *he* who was the cause for her fury. And this time he had gone too far. No matter what the cost to their tenuous relationship, Ginny's spitfire pride made her vow silently that she would show him once and for all she would never submit to his cavalier treatment.

Ginny paced the confines of the gold and white room like an angry young lioness, her cloud of copper hair swinging to her waist. Her lamplit reflection first scowled and then smiled back at her as she rehearsed the role she would play that evening. Her eyes narrowed; she planned exactly what she would do. Oh yes, Steve would be surprised. He had badly misjudged her if he thought she'd be as easily intimidated as she had been on that *other* occasion when he'd kept her captive in Madame Lilas' pleasure house in El Paso. Since then she'd learned a great deal, and Steve ought to remember that!

Soft sounds began to filter up through the carpeted floor as the house began to come awake. Faint tinkle of a piano, a woman's laughter, a man's rumbling bass voice. There was even the faintest odor of incense to add an exotic flavor to an already exotic setting. A setting meant for seduction and acted-out rituals of "love" that was bought. There would be other rooms such as this, of course— each with a slightly different motif, but all serving the same purpose. And on this particular floor the rooms were rented out during the day to lovers wishing to be discreet and private—married women and their paramours—men with their more "respectable" mistresses. The house of assignation by day became an elegant brothel by night, catering only to the elite and the very rich; serving only wine and champagne. Meals were cooked by Parisian chefs and the ladies held "conferences" with their clients by appointment only!

Ginny was aware of all this as she seated herself before the mirrored dresser and pulled out the top drawer. Steve, being a man, hadn't thought to inspect the drawers and the twin armoires the room boasted, but *she* had—since she'd awakened to find both her husband and the gown she'd worn had disappeared. Obviously, the regular occupants of the gold and white room delighted in dressing up. There were not only men's and women's costumes of various periods and fashions, but a treasure trove of cosmetics and perfume as well. Green eyes beginning to sparkle with a mixture of excitement and malice, Ginny studied herself carefully before she picked up a small pot of lip rouge and began to apply it, her mind already racing ahead. The trick she had played before, in El Paso, would serve her again—only *this* time she would not allow herself to get trapped. . . .

"Gentlemen—" The man's voice was very slightly slurred, but carried all the same a tone of authority that made all heads in the smoky card room turn in the direction of the door. Henry Warmoth, Governor of the State of Louisiana, stepped in, bowing with a flourish to the young woman whose hand he held. "I give you—Helen of Troy!"

She posed for them with a graceful assurance that bordered on arrogance—well aware of the vision she presented, enjoying the various degrees of shock and stupefaction painted on the faces turned to her.

The white gown she wore was artfully draped to bare one peach-tanned shoulder and one shapely leg up to the thigh. Crisscrossed, thin gold cord bound it under her breasts, emphasizing their delectable curves. If one looked closely enough, it could be seen through the filmy material that she had lightly rouged her nipples; and if a man's eyes traveled higher they were trapped by the red, kiss-inviting mouth and the slightly slanted emerald eyes that both mocked and challenged. Her hair, gleaming like freshly minted copper under the chandelier, put the gold ribbons she had

threaded through it to shame. Masses of it, bound up with ribbon
—how far would it fall, unbound, and how much would it cover?

Pleased with the effect he had created, Henry Warmoth
laughed.

"Am I not lucky? There was a slight contretemps—my lovely
goddess had locked herself into her room by mistake, and a candle
overturned . . . a slight mishap that might have been worse had *I*
not been passing at that moment. And, since she is a veritable
Aphrodite, how could I resist her command that I escort her
downstairs to the lucky man who is her partner for the evening?"
He looked around inquiringly, adding with obvious sincerity in a
slightly lower voice, "Needless to say I would give almost anything to exchange places with whichever of you gentlemen has the
privilege. . . ."

Smiling into their stunned silence, Ginny let her eyes travel
from one reddening face to another, her voice like honey.

"Senator Brandon! How lovely . . ." and, ignoring his choked
exclamation: "And Paco Davis—I vow, you've been neglecting me
lately, I'm not sure if I'll forgive you. How is our baby?"

From the pleasure of seeing Paco choke on his drink she turned
her limpid gaze to another familiar face, meeting cool grey eyes
that had had time to shutter themselves.

"Jim *darling* . . . how could you keep me waiting so long? I did
exactly as you told me . . . and you said you couldn't wait to see
how the gown suited me. . . . Oh, I haven't made you too *angry*,
have I? I mean, I'm sure all these nice gentlemen understand . . ."

The Governor cleared his throat and threw his shoulders back
to state rather belligerently that should the *gentleman* wish to
continue with his card game why *he* would be more than glad to
volunteer to keep the lovely Aphrodite happy. . . . At which
point she brushed a definitely provocative kiss on his flushed
cheek and whispered that she'd be glad to entertain him tomorrow night if he'd speak to Hortense.

It was at this point that Mr. Bishop, with a resigned sigh, rose
to his feet to take charge of matters that had already gone too far.

"Gentlemen, please excuse me. And er . . . Aphrodite? Yes, let
us by all means repair upstairs, shall we? I hadn't realized I'd kept
you waiting."

Their smiles met and clashed—his thin and warning, hers

curved and triumphant. He had taken the hand that the Governor reluctantly relinquished when Steve Morgan returned to the card game, to freeze in disbelief at the spectacle of his wife, whom he considered safely locked in the room upstairs, now dressed in a diaphanous Grecian costume that revealed almost everything she had to offer. She had the added effrontery to smile sweetly at him as she leaned languishingly against Jim Bishop's shoulder.

"Hello, Steve. Are you having a pleasant evening? I know *I* am!"

There was a moment when he almost lost his head. Ginny could not help flinching slightly at the leap of murderous rage in the dark blue eyes that narrowed dangerously at her. It was only Mr. Bishop's warning cough that brought sanity back. Steve's face grew wooden, and only the slight twitch of an angry muscle along his jaw warned of his barely held-back fury. He wanted to strangle her, and she knew it. Ah yes, it would be a long time before Steve ever took *her* for granted again!

Ignoring his ugly look and the ominously polite inclination of his head that he accorded her at last, Ginny held tightly to Jim Bishop's arm as that gentleman escorted her punctiliously upstairs.

"Madam, I don't quite know what to do with you! Your behavior this evening . . ." Mr. Bishop was justifiably annoyed; in fact he had forgotten his usual self-control far enough to bring out a cigar as he paced about the room to which Governor Warmoth's "goddess" had led him.

But as he might have expected, he thought to himself with a resigned sigh, this particular young female had always been willful as well as hot-tempered. Now, she displayed absolutely no remorse whatsoever.

"*My* behavior, Mr. Bishop? Hah? And what do you have to say to my husband's locking me up in this room, having brought me here under threat of force? You men are all such hypocrites! Frequenting whorehouses and mouthing sanctimonious moral lectures. . . . Well, you might save your breath on *me!* And"—her green eyes reminding Mr. Bishop too vividly of a crouching puma —"you might use it to better advantage by telling me exactly what you are all up to. You, Paco—even my father, of all people—playing *cards* . . . can't you think of a different excuse?" She all but stamped one slim, sandaled foot. "And as for Steve . . . well he deserved this little trick for what he did to me. And don't give me that . . . that fishy-eyed look either, or talk about *secrets*. I recall very well the time you came to me in Mexico, wanting me to help you. If you trusted me then you can trust me now. Mr. Bishop, I insist on knowing!"

But by this time Mr. Bishop had recovered some of his usual aplomb. With that particularly uninflected intonation that was so much a part of his character he said coolly: "But, my dear young lady, I am merely here on a vacation! Even busy men like myself are allowed some rest and recreation, you know! Steve and I ran into each other purely by chance, I assure you—and since the meeting did take place I thought it might be an opportune time to . . . ah . . . recapitulate events of the recent past, shall we say? Really, madam, I don't quite know why I am explaining any of this to you, except that you created quite an embarrassing situation downstairs! Did you have to pick the Governor of Louisiana to be your . . . er . . . rescuer? If he should happen to recognize you at some social function. . . ."

"Then of course he will believe that his eyes are playing tricks on him—or that I have a double! No, no, Mr. Bishop, it just won't wash, and I'll not allow myself to be fobbed off. What's Paco doing here? Or is he on vacation too?" She flashed Mr. Bishop a scornful look. "My goodness, I wonder how the country is being run with her most valuable men off playing cards—or were you waiting your turn to go upstairs?"

"Now really, madam, you go too far!" Mr. Bishop said cuttingly, giving her a look that was meant to quell her.

Ginny shrugged one bare shoulder as she sat gracefully on the edge of the bed, slightly alarming the gentleman with an unconscionable show of leg.

"Perhaps I do!" she offered with a charming smile. "But if you'll try telling me the truth you might find that I could be more useful on your side than against you, you know! And I can fight almost as well as a man—ask Paco! Or ask Steve—that is, when he is through throwing a temper tantrum."

Mr. Bishop found himself nonplussed—one of the few occasions in his career when he felt that he had almost been bested.

What an unpredictable little termagant! What could one do with a woman like her? And why had Steve Morgan, who had been one of his coolest-headed operatives, allowed himself to become so entrapped by her that he forgot caution?

To tell the truth, as Ginny gave a sigh and lay back against the cushions, Mr. Bishop found himself becoming quite nervous. What on earth was she up to now—surely she didn't plan to play Potiphar's wife?

Downstairs the once-lively card game had disintegrated, much to the young Governor's disappointment. He wandered off to look for Lucille, the lovely octoroon he'd had an "appointment" with, and left to their cups the dull, glum-faced fellows his Aphrodite had greeted. Perhaps he'd take Lucille to the opera with him, just to shock the sour-faced old biddies who thought they were still arbiters of New Orleans society. In fact, he'd have even more fun dragging along Oscar Dunn, his straitlaced Negro Lieutenant Governor—especially if he arranged for plump and blue-eyed Sigrid, another of Hortense's "ladies" to come with them as well.

Once Mr. Warmoth had left, it was the almost apoplectic Senator who spoke first. "If she dares tell Sonya . . . ! By God, Steve, I had thought you—"

"She's not the most biddable female in the world, is she, sir?" Steve Morgan's almost indifferent comment was belied by the blazing blue eyes that he unshuttered briefly before he gave his attention to pouring the contents of half a bottle of bourbon into the glass he had just drained.

"If you blame *me* for that—" the ruffled Senator began heatedly before Paco Davis interposed.

"Don't you two think we ought to rescue the poor Mr. Bishop?" His voice shook slightly and when he happened to meet Steve's furious look Paco gave way to a guffaw of laughter. "*Dios!* Amigo, I'm sorry. My apologies to you too, Senator. Of course you couldn't know, but when she said . . . when she asked me that, about our *baby* . . ."

"You forgot to tell me about the baby, I guess!" Steve said in a cold, flat voice. "What the hell was that all about? Goddammit, Paco, if you can't give me an answer that makes sense you can call yourself lucky if you end up in a hospital again!"

While Paco was making his hurried explanations, Senator Brandon, unamused, decided he'd best return to his wife. He hoped fervently that his daughter would see fit to hold her tongue—*and* come to her senses. And if Steve saw fit to give her the beating she deserved, he for one would certainly not interfere!

The Senator, in his present mood, had quite forgotten his curiosity about the business that his son-in-law had invited him here to discuss. Whatever it was, it would keep. And he had another appointment much later on that night—a meeting he had no present intentions of discussing with Steve; not until he'd managed to find out where Steve's sympathies lay in Cuban affairs.

It had turned out to be an altogether frustrating evening, in fact, for everyone concerned, including Ginny, who had found Mr. Bishop immune to both her threats and her blandishments. He had lit up a cigar that smelled abominable and made her feel quite sick, and he had insisted blandly that he was merely on "vacation," an occasion warranted—or so he said—by his need to have Steve tie up some loose ends for him.

"As a matter of fact, I intend to return to my . . . er . . . duties tomorrow. Tonight was in the nature of a celebration." Mr. Bishop sounded impatient to be gone, and Ginny, much to her frustration, could read nothing in his face, nor in the hooded grey eyes.

"And Paco? . . ."

"I believe Mr. Davis intends visiting relatives in Mexico—he is still officially on leave. I daresay"—and a cloud of blue-grey cigar smoke gave Mr. Bishop a slightly demonic look for a moment— "he would be glad to accompany you back to the Alvarado hacienda. You must miss your children, I'm sure."

"Mr. Bishop, you're a . . . a man without any scruples at all, aren't you?"

He inclined his head slightly.

"You have discovered me, Mrs. Morgan. Precisely. May I wish you a very pleasant journey home, and my . . . er . . . thanks for your assistance?"

He was dismissing her. Just like that. And how effortlessly he had turned the tables on her! The thought made Ginny grit her teeth and want to scream out with rage and frustration. Her seductive posing forgotten, she swung bare legs to the floor, only to stare in disbelief at the closing door. Damn him too—with his threats to have her sent back home, now he'd no more use for her help! And Steve—was that what he intended too?

A tap at the door made Ginny start, realizing uneasily that she didn't really want to face Steve yet. But it was only the woman he'd called Hortense, gliding in before Ginny could respond.

"Oh—hello, dear, you look really magnificent, you know!" Hortense sounded as vague and whispery as she had earlier. Her knowing eyes studied Ginny and looked away into the mirror while she patted a curl into place. "I should have knocked, I suppose, but I didn't realize . . . that is, when Henry Warmoth began to positively *rave* about you—only I didn't know it was *you*, so I came to find out . . ." She turned to look at Ginny again. "Would you like to stay on, *cherie*? Is that why he left you behind? Really, men are so thoughtless sometimes! He might have mentioned . . . why, I could have had several appointments lined up for you, you're different from my other girls, and I like to offer variety, you know. Have you had much experience, love?"

Ginny had a wild feeling that she was on a speeding train that was rushing her backward through a tunnel of time. She was back in El Paso, with Lilas sizing her up and Lorena, the French-Canadian who had befriended her, giving her advice she didn't want to hear. Steve's captive. . . . "Is that why he left you behind?" the woman had said. The thought had filled the girl she then had been with terror. But that had been before she had learned what terror really was—before Tom Beal had made her a *thing*.

With an effort, Ginny wrenched her mind back into the present. She wasn't a captive and this was *now*. She was Steve's wife, and he couldn't discard her as he pleased. She smiled artlessly at the woman. "Oh, of course I've had experience. Steve is *such* a particular man! But as for staying on . . . I really do need a little time to make up my mind, and I'd promised a friend I'd meet him at the opera tonight. I wonder . . . if there's a gown I might borrow? Or a cloak, perhaps? This is hardly . . ." Ginny looked down at herself deprecatingly as Hortense blinked a few times, obviously adjusting her thoughts.

She said doubtfully: "Well, I suppose . . . of course I could lend . . . but I wish now that I'd come up before. He took Lucille and Sigrid with him because he thought you'd be busy for the evening . . . and he can be *so* generous! You wouldn't lack for anything if you pleased him. . . ."

It turned out that Hortense could lay her hands on Ginny's own ball gown, given to her maid for pressing. And the same vaguely amiable and obliging woman lent Ginny her own smart carriage to take her to the opera.

"If any of the others see you they won't try to steal you away to their establishments . . . we have our own code here, as you'll find out. And do come back tomorrow, I can promise you won't regret it. I never ask for too large a cut and I'm generous, ask any of the other girls. . . ."

"I should take her up on her offer, see what he says then . . . oh, God, how did we start squabbling again? Why do we do these things to spite each other? I won't let him send me off to Mexico without him. . . ." Ginny's thoughts went round and round like the carriage wheels striking sparks from the cobbles over which they jounced. Her temper warred with her fear that this time, *this* time Steve might stay angry at her. He was so unreasonable!

"But I'll take one thing at a time, and I won't let him browbeat me either. . . ." Repeating it over and over again stiffened her spine.

# Chapter Six

❧

There were always lookers-on outside the grand French Opera House on the corner of Bourbon and Toulouse streets. They came to watch the singers themselves, and to discuss their latest admirers; they would watch, with avid interest, the ladies and gentlemen who were fortunate enough to enter there—compare the ladies' finery and whisper about scandals. . . . Oh, it was a fine pastime for the poorer folk, and especially on a balmy evening such as this!

On this particular night, however, there seemed to be quite a number of late arrivals—an unusual occurrence, unless the singing promised to be indifferent. But no, surely that could not be the case with the truly magnificent Adelina Patti introducing a new opera, *Mignon*, for the first time in the United States. Why then should there be so many comings and goings? "Something's in the air!" the whisper went around. And here was the Governor himself with two opulently dressed women, one on either arm ("Aha, we know where *they're* from!"), followed by a decidedly uncomfortable-looking Oscar Dunn who looked as sleepy as if he'd just been dragged out of bed. With his usual aplomb, Mr. Warmoth acknowledged the slight cheer that went up.

And then, just before the end of the first act, a young woman of exceptional beauty that set everyone to puzzling as to who she was arrived in a closed carriage and went hurrying up the steps. Was she late for an assignation? Was she the handsome tenor's latest flirt? So unusual for a lady to arrive at the opera unescorted—that is, if she *was* a lady, and not the pampered mistress of some rich carpetbagger. It was hard to tell the difference, these days!

Ginny's late arrival had not been missed by anyone, it seemed. It was all she could do to hide her vexation. The polite argument with the gentleman who had to make sure she was an invited guest took exactly enough time for the first intermission to bring everyone thronging downstairs for refreshments, and she thought she had never been studied so curiously and so critically before! It was with a feeling of relief that she recognized one of the young men she had been introduced to the previous night—at just about the same time *he* recognized her and came up to inquire if perhaps he could be of some assistance to her.

"How kind of you! In fact, you would be rescuing me . . . I was delayed by some silly mishap to the carriage . . . no, nothing serious, but late or not I couldn't *bear* to miss tonight's performance! Is my . . . that is, is Mrs. Brandon here? I was to join her, but I have no idea with whom she is sharing a box. . . ."

Andre Delery kissed her hand, holding it against his lips just a little longer than necessary.

"It would be my pleasure to escort you to Madame Pruett's box. In fact, I was on my way there to ask the ladies if I might bring them some refreshment, but I must confess that you have helped bolster up my courage! I have the decided impression that *la mère* Pruett imagines I have been leading her precious Bernard into mischief. Her looks have been quite frigid of late! But tell me . . ."—he smiled into her eyes with an easy, charming assurance that reminded Ginny strangely of Miguel Lopez, who had been her lover once—"would you permit me to offer you something —some champagne perhaps?—before I have to tear myself away from your company? I hope you will not think me impertinent. . . ."

"Well . . ." Ginny was on the verge of making some polite excuse, imagining poor Sonya's disapproval should she accept M. Delery's offer; and then, out of the corner of her eye, she saw Steve.

He was far too busy to notice her, his attention concentrated upon a dark-haired Spanish-looking beauty with a voluptuous figure. It didn't matter that the girl in question was with an older man who might conceivably be her father. It was enough that Ginny, feeling a wave of fury wash through her, recognized the same Ana Valdez who had once been Steve's betrothed.

And was *that* the real reason why he had been at such pains to keep Ginny away from the opera tonight? Oh, no doubt he believed that at the very least he'd taught her a lesson—that she'd either stay where he'd left her or go straight home. But instead, she intended to bring herself to his attention—and to everyone else's, for that matter!

Ginny's eyes dropped with mock demureness as she played with her lace and ivory fan.

"You are a true gallant, M. Delery! But I mustn't keep you away from your friends—I'm sure you're here with a party of friends. . . ."

"Madame, I assure you that, *au contraire*, I'm here entirely on my own! I'm sharing the box of my old friend Lucian Valette, but I'm positive he won't miss me! Please . . . it would give me the greatest pleasure to perform some small service—let me be honest —to prolong the pleasure of your charming company."

It was a little game that they played out before she finally accepted the offer of his arm and the champagne he promised her. Andre Delery, through his lazy-lidded eyes, had already made note of the fact that that charming Madame Morgan's husband had arrived earlier—and without his wife—joining certain people that Delery recognized quite well. The thoughts that flashed through his mind were carefully screened by his smile.

An interesting situation, this. And quite convenient for *his* purposes as well. The woman was quite lovely, with a mouth that promised all kinds of pleasures to a man who could please her. And what was more, she had had a quite unusual past, to judge from the gossip he'd heard yesterday. Perhaps his fortuitous encounter with her might just turn out to be the proverbial killing of two birds with one stone? Whatever the outcome, it did not seem that he could lose. . . .

The lithe, sleek-muscled Andre Delery reminded Ginny of a Spanish dancer. With his dark Creole good looks and flashing smile he was obviously a lady-killer who was used to having his own way with women. And his suggestion that she, a married woman, might jeopardize her reputation by being seen openly in his company had been impudent, of course. But under the circumstances. . . . Ginny's chin lifted stubbornly. She could look after herself! And so, she was sure, could M. Delery. She put her hand on his arm and saw his rather cynical smile flash down at her as he said softly, "You have made me the most enviable man here tonight, I assure you! I can hardly believe my luck."

To Sonya Brandon, her rebellious stepdaughter's sudden and unexpected appearance on the arm of Andre Delery was the last straw—turning an unpleasant evening into a catastrophe. Sonya was, in fact, almost beyond words. First William, deserting her inexplicably with the lame excuse that some urgent "business" had come up—leaving her to endure Adeline Pruett's scarcely veiled curiosity and hints about a past Sonya would much rather pretend hadn't happened. And then Steve had turned up *without* Ginny— sitting in a box right across from theirs with some people Sonya had never met before. "Rich Cubans," Adeline had whispered to her. "What a coincidence your son-in-law seems to know them. Especially the young woman . . . rather pretty—in a full-blown sort of way—isn't she?"

By this time, Sonya was gritting her teeth as she vowed to herself that she could not—no, she *would* not—stand another moment of Adeline's company. . . . And how could she ever have looked upon the woman as her *friend?* She had all but come right out with her sly insinuations—stopping just short of telling Sonya bluntly that she recognized Steve Morgan as the same Yankee Captain who'd once been her lover. And of course Adeline would conveniently not choose to remember that she had *encouraged* that unfortunate, insane affair—having practically *wormed* a confession from her first.

To have Ginny suddenly materialize . . . and, even worse, to hear her announce that she had accepted M. Delery's invitation to join his party for supper after the opera—would Sonya mind telling Steve?—no, *that* was absolutely the last straw, and Sonya developed a migraine that was quite unfeigned.

How could Ginny be so devoid of sensibility as to throw herself in such a blatant fashion at M. Delery? Didn't she realize that her rash and unconventional behavior could lead to a duel? Steve Morgan was such a violent man . . . a cold-blooded killer—didn't Andre realize what might happen? Sonya felt her hands become clammy as a wave of nausea almost choked her. William—where was William? She wanted to go home!

"Now listen here my dears—and I hope you'll pardon an older

woman's bluntness?" Adeline Pruett's pragmatic sharpness cut across the tension, focusing their attention upon her. "Andre Delery, I've known you for too many years not to speak my mind, and well you know it! It just will not do, you know—these may be modern times, but there are some things that society *here* will not tolerate. To take a young married woman off with you to supper under her husband's nose is asking for trouble, and I'll not permit it, d'you hear? And don't *you* start frowning at me either, young woman! *You* ought to know better yourself, as a matter of fact. And if you were thinking that what's good for the gander is good for the goose, well take my advice, it isn't! Men can get away with anything, and it's something we women have all got to learn to put up with—at least, till things change. It's *your* reputation that's going to be lost, not his. And you've got more than just yourself to think of, haven't you? Is it one child or two now?"

"Whew—what a Tatar! Madame Pruett has always terrified me."

Sonya thought, of course M. Delery did not look as if anything or anybody could frighten him—and a tremor of laughter underlay his whispered words, but at least he was a gentleman, and making an effort to make them all at ease in spite of her sullen stepdaughter, who of course could not bear to be thwarted! As for herself, Sonya could feel nothing but relief and, yes, gratitude toward Adeline for coming to the rescue. So relieved was she that she pretended not to notice when Andre Delery's fingers brushed hers. It was an accident of course . . . he was just being extra nice to her to make up for Ginny's unfeeling behavior.

Warm fingers touched hers again under cover of the darkness in the box, and Sonya caught her breath, ashamed of the warmth that rushed into her face. He whispered, his head bending down to hers: "I'm sorry if I helped cause . . . you are an exceptionally sensitive lady, aren't you? I could tell from the beginning. Is the headache any better?" And then, so softly that she could hardly hear: "How cold your hands are! I wish I had the right to warm them."

Ridiculous, of course! She was an older, *married* woman, and he was being far too bold, she should put him in his place—kindly but firmly. And yet Sonya could not stop the silly pounding of her heart, and another—less practical—part of her mind was whispering that after all she wasn't too old to *flirt*. What was wrong in that?

Ginny was far too busy with her own thoughts and frustrations to be aware of any of her stepmother's turmoil. Steve—with that unpleasant young creature Ana of all people . . . and more than likely it was with *her* that he'd been last night. Was there no end to his perfidy, his string of women? And why must she be expected to endure it? Had the daggers her narrowed green eyes were throwing been real, her husband would have died of a thousand wounds already. The opera could not interest her any longer —Ginny's mind was far too fully occupied with plans for getting even with Steve. And if the stone-faced Mrs. Pruett had not intervened, *she* and not that bitch Ana would have had all his attention by now. The best way to defend herself from being hurt by Steve's cavalier attitude was to pay him back in his own coin—to fight him every inch of the way. And that was why she had continued to hold him—so far.

Unconsciously, Ginny's small white teeth had begun to worry her lower lip. A small sigh escaped her. Why did it always have to be this way? And just when they had almost begun to know each other, to be almost-friends. "We're two ill-tempered, stubborn people," her mind warned her. And didn't she know Steve almost as well as she knew herself?

"Damn your deep-forested eyes my love! I'm not sure that I enjoy being snared this way. . . ." Had he only been joking when he'd told her that some days ago? Or had it been a subtle warning?

Perhaps I'll never understand Steve, or what it is that keeps me loving him. And does he really love *me*, or are the words he says merely words to keep me content and malleable? From anger and frustration that made her want to scream out loud, Ginny's mood had turned introspective, subdued. Oh, God! How much longer must they keep on squabbling, not really trusting one another, always on guard? She should have stayed on in Europe and saved herself all this pain and anguish. Suddenly, a fit of depression caught her as if in a vise, and tears of self-pity stung behind her eyelids. How futile it had been, after all! All the anger, all the misery, the constant seesawing between hate and love. For what?

To hold on to a man who would not be and could not be held unless it was on his own terms? To spend her life wondering what security was like? "I don't know what it is I really want," Ginny thought dolefully. Not even the thought of doing battle with Steve could cheer her up.

It was as if Mrs. Pruett had read her mind. The older woman inclined her head rather stiffly to whisper behind her fan that for all the attention the singers were getting tonight they might as well leave as soon as the next intermission began. Perhaps at that time, if Mrs. Morgan wished to join her husband . . . ? Back stiffening, Ginny responded with cold civility that no, she would not dream of interfering with her husband's *business* engagements. But perhaps, if Mrs. Pruett had no objections, arrangements could be made for her to go home?

Mrs. Pruett's short laugh sounded rather like a snort.

"You're a spunky young woman, aren't you? I like that, believe me, although I was forced to be blunt a short while ago—for your own good. You remind me a little of myself at your age, although *then* I'm sorry to say I lacked your air of self-assurance. Wish I'd had half the freedom you seem to have! But that came much later, when the war made me a widow and I had two daughters safely married off. Hmph! *Now* I pretty much have things my own way but what good does it do me when I'm too old to enjoy my freedom? What I *did* learn, though, was discretion. A clever woman can get away with practically anything she chooses too if she's discreet and if she's careful in her choice of lovers. Do you get my meaning?" While Ginny still sat stunned by these completely unexpected and almost shocking disclosures, her hostess, still fanning herself vigorously, leaned even closer, to whisper significantly: "Andre Delery now—*not* the right choice at all! I know he's a fine-looking young man and an accomplished flirt, but he's dangerous. Hot-tempered to a fault and far too fond of dueling. I've heard he isn't discreet—not when he's among his cronies, anyhow. And if I hadn't guessed you as too clever to feel fascinated merely because I've warned you about him I wouldn't say a word. Andre's . . . ambitious. Likes to use women—in more than one way! Well . . . I've said enough, I suppose! And at least you're a good listener!"

"What did she expect me to say? She hardly gave me a

chance." And yet, Ginny found herself rather intrigued by Mrs. Pruett's unexpected and flattering revelations, although she found it difficult to imagine that the stern-faced matron had ever taken lovers. And as for her warnings about Andre Delery, that young man seemed to hang politely on Sonya's every word, making Ginny wonder if perhaps she had mistaken the glint in his eye earlier. He didn't seem at all dangerous now, and in any case Ginny had too much on her mind to concern herself with M. Delery. Like Sonya, she too was wondering where Senator Brandon was spending the evening. And Steve—where did *he* plan to spend the night?

When the lights came on to mark the end of the second act, neither Steve nor his companions were anywhere to be seen, and Ginny gladly acceded to Sonya's suggestion that they leave early as her head was simply splitting.

Mrs. Pruett offered them her carriage—*she* would ride home with Bernard, she announced firmly, causing her son to exchange unhappy looks with his fiancée. And Andre Delery gallantly insisted upon escorting the ladies as far as the plantation—his way home lay in the same direction, he assured them.

Afterward, Ginny was to think of a stage being set—but how could they have known it then? She herself had been far too occupied with her own thoughts to wonder about anything else. She had made a decision to face Steve, to force him into a serious talk. Couldn't he see for himself that they couldn't go on in this fashion? She was barely aware of Andre Delery's presence, for he had joined them in the carriage, leaving his horse to trot alongside.

He was aware of her, though, for all that he had fastened his open attention upon the blonde-haired woman. *Her*, Virginia Morgan, with her arrogant, flame-haired beauty and barely cleft chin she could raise stubbornly while she stared a man straight in the eye. He had already promised himself that he would have her, and his instincts told him she was ripe for the taking—bored and made angry by a husband who flaunted his mistresses far too openly. Oh yes, he would have her for certain, but not yet—not quite yet. And the waiting only sharpened the intensity of his desire for her. Let her wait—and in the end she too would come to heel like all the others.

# Chapter Seven

❧

"Wonder if the bastard's ears are burning?" Paco Davis' white-toothed grin flashed under his thin black mustache as he looked across the table at Bishop, who returned the grin with one of his thin, mirthless smiles.

"I would very much doubt it. I'm sure M. Delery is quite used to being a subject of discussion around these parts. The point is —we know he's being paid. He's even paid his tailor! The question is—who's paying him, and for what, exactly?"

The question was rhetorical, for Mr. Bishop had more than a good idea of the kind of services M. Andre Delery was being remunerated for. He was a noted duelist in a city where "meetings of honor," although illegal, were still quite commonplace. But whereas in the past the man had usually fought the husbands or male relatives of the women he'd made targets of, in more recent months he'd taken to challenging men with certain political beliefs. The troubles in nearby Cuba had sent Cuban émigrés scurrying to New Orleans to drum up support, either for the Spaniards who wished to hold on to what was almost the last of their rich acquisitions, or the rebels who sought self-government. There was also a third class of person to further complicate matters—the American would-be filibusters, out to turn internal conflicts in nearby countries to their advantage.

If Jim Bishop had been less self-contained he would have sighed. As it was, his face showed no expression at all as he glanced across the room to meet Steve Morgan's shadowed blue eyes. He hoped that Morgan was keeping his mind on business tonight, instead of his sharp-tempered wife. A pity, what marriage could do to an otherwise good man.

Wisps of cigar smoke trailed languidly toward the window

Steve had just opened. Outside, the stars were beginning to look jaded and dim, already preparing to be eclipsed by the rising of the sun.

Steve rubbed one hand impatiently across his beard-stubbled jaw, wishing that Bishop would come to the point. Not for the first time, he wondered how in the hell he'd gotten himself talked into this particular bit of intrigue. Steve's black brows drew together in the beginnings of a frown. In fact, now that he'd had time to think about it, he had the definite feeling that he'd been maneuvered into the position he found himself in right now. A few weeks ago, Bishop could have had his friend Colonel Belmont call his soldiers off from their overenthusiastic search of the swamps for the outlaw "Manolo." Instead, he'd been forced to run, taking Ginny with him—dodging not only bullets but the natural predators of the swamps as well. And then, arriving in Shreveport at last, he'd "run into" Paco Davis. Created coincidences always presaged Jim's reappearances in his life, it seemed!

Steve said sarcastically: "Why don't I just *ask* the hot-tempered M. Delery that question? Maybe he'll get mad enough to tell me —or make me made enough to make him."

Bishop surprised him by giving him a thoughtful look before he shook his head slightly, and with some regret. "I don't think you should provoke a duel with the man. Not yet. No—we know he's pro-Spanish, and no longer as short of cash as he used to be. And of course, we know what he's doing. But . . ."—the grey eyes hooded themselves for an instant as Bishop took the time to light another cigar—"it is your father-in-law's activities that I am mainly concerned about. A pity that our carefully arranged meeting with him was interrupted. If he's already met . . . the other gentleman we've had our eyes on and has committed himself, do you think he might still be persuaded to . . . ah . . . change his mind?"

"I don't know." Steve walked back to the table and dropped his long length into a chair, reaching for a glass. "Damn it, Jim, I'm not the Senator's keeper, and we're still getting reacquainted, in a way." He gave an unwilling grin. "He was understandably rather upset about the way I dropped out of sight, you know. And I don't think he's quite forgiven me yet."

"Me, I find it hard to believe you two can talk politely. Remember the first time we got together to talk about that gold he was shippin' across to Mexico? And now . . ." Paco leaned back in his chair, shrugging pacifically at Steve. "Now, maybe it is the same kind of thing, eh, amigo? He's an ambitious man, the good Senator Brandon. I do not think he has changed too much. What do *you* think?"

Bishop watched them both, his mind still moving methodically over his collection of facts, sorting them out and piecing them together to form a patchwork whole. Paco was right—Brandon was still an ambitious, even a greedy man. And Brandon was suddenly interested in Cuba and Cuban affairs, even to the extent of dickering over the purchase of a plantation there. A rundown plantation with a price he couldn't afford. Why? And somehow, there was a connection with Andre Delery as well. And the pretty young widow of a Cuban landowner, Ana Dos Santos, who had once been Steve's betrothed. . . . Lots of varied pieces to this puzzle, but he would fit them all together eventually. The President had been most emphatic in his instructions that the status quo with Cuba *and* the neutral position of the United States must be maintained. At least for the time being, Bishop's mind amended cynically.

He leaned across the table. "Gentlemen, it's almost morning and we're all rather tired. I suggest we all give some thought to what we've been discussing and arrange to meet again tomorrow. In the evening perhaps? Let's see what the day brings."

The day started far too early for a number of people, and to some others it brought surprises as well. Lucian Valette had fully expected to sleep until late in the afternoon when he had flung himself upon his bed, fully dressed and feeling abominably queasy from all the liquor he had consumed. His valet would undress him and, when he finally awoke, bring him a tall glass filled with a decoction that was Pierre's own and guaranteed to cure even the worst hangover. The last thing Lucian expected or needed was to be shaken rudely awake in spite of his anguished groans—barely managing to open bloodshot, aching eyes to confront the grinning face of his friend Andre Delery.

"No—no! Whatever it is I am not in the mood to hear it. The noise inside my head is too loud. . . . *Bon Dieu!* How is it that

Pierre let you in? I will assuredly get rid of the rascal—and challenge *you*, my friend, as soon as I feel better!"

"Nonsense! For you know you couldn't get rid of Pierre—and that *I* would kill you if you challenged me . . . my reputation, you know! Wake up, Lucian, and pay attention. See, I've had your good man mix you one of his special drinks to clear your head, for it's important that we talk."

Still clutching his aching head, Valette sat up sullenly, wondering as he did how on earth his friend contrived to look so fresh and so alert after what must have been a sleepless night. But by the time Andre had finished talking, Lucian himself had lost all traces of sleepiness, only a slight throbbing in his temples reminding him of his excesses of the night before.

"You are surely not serious? When we took that foolish wager I did not mean that in order to accomplish your object you should challenge the husband! Just think, *mon ami*, of the consequences! He's not, after all, one of *us*, and his position . . . what I am trying to say is that it could be a deuce of a scandal! Worse, the consequences for *you* . . ."

Delery's hazel eyes narrowed as they came to rest on his friend's flushed, concerned face.

"Would you imply that I might be afraid of consequences? But no, I'll not seek a quarrel with you *mon vieux*, considering your *mal de tête*. Besides . . ." And here Delery smiled limpidly, "I happen to need your assistance. Not in the *accomplishing* of the matter, you understand, for that will be easy—the groundwork is already done and the bird is eager to fly into the trap! Have I ever failed with a woman? Or failed to kill an adversary? This particular adversary will challenge *me*, in front of witnesses I'm sure, leaving me with no choice but to . . ." Spreading his hands, Delery shrugged. "You comprehend? However, I need information. The man's friends. Particularly those with whom he met last night. I understand that after the opera you spent the rest of the night at a certain house on Bourbon Street?"

While the two young men talked, most of the occupants of the rambling plantation house that was still referred to as "the Beaudine House" were already awake. Ginny, coming downstairs to seek refuge and an early breakfast in the tree-shaded garden, found to her surprise that her step-mother was already up, and obviously of the same mind.

The two women looked at one another and it was Sonya, pale except for two spots of heightened color in her cheeks, who spoke first.

"There's no need to stand on ceremony. Sit down." And in the same conversational tone of voice: "The servants are all agog with gossip, of course. No matter what our differences are or have been, we might as well pretend that nothing's amiss, don't you think?" In the face of Ginny's silence, Sonya's knuckles whitened on the arm of her chair. "*Your* husband has not returned, has he? And mine came to bed two hours ago, with some story of having played cards all night. He is asleep and snoring now."

Under her composed exterior, Sonya was seething with rage. How could William shame her in front of all her old friends? Staying out without the courtesy of a *real* excuse for two days in a row—and to think that yesterday William had actually dared reprimand *her*, merely because she'd accepted the escort of three much younger men. Not that M. Delery was really *too* much younger than she, come to think of it—he had told her laughingly that in spite of his youthful appearance he was several years past thirty.

She watched Ginny subside into a chair across from her, still unusually silent except for a murmured "Oh? . . ."

Perhaps Ginny was better prepared to deal with male perfidy after all. No doubt *she* was already planning who she would take as a lover to be revenged on Steve. And Ginny, judging from her past, took lovers and amorous escapades extraordinarily lightly. Worse, she'd always managed to get away with it too! "It's not fair," Sonya thought rebelliously. "She's always contrived to have everything turn out *her* way in the end."

She watched almost maliciously as Ginny pulled off her hat and began to fan herself languidly with it. The younger woman looked as if she hadn't slept a wink all night—which was probably the case. There were dark circles under her eyes and an unusual pallor to her face. Had she really imagined that she could change a man like Steve Morgan?

Ginny was thinking the same thing as she continued to fan herself more to keep her hands busy than to cool herself. She was aware of Sonya's scrutiny and anger, but after all, what did they really have in common? Of late they had seemed to deal more directly and honestly as adversaries than as friends. No, she didn't feel in the mood to confide in Sonya, or join with her in recriminations. She didn't, as a matter of fact, want to *think* any more at this moment, having done too much of that as she lay awake in bed.

The servants were bustling about, bringing steaming platters to the table that had already been laid for four persons. Ginny reached hungrily for a hot, flaky croissant, watching the butter melt on it. She said casually, and more for the benefit of the servants than anything else: "Are breakfasts in Louisiana always this elaborate? Five and six courses . . . how does one manage it every day?"

Sonya shrugged. "It's a matter of custom and habit. One gets used to it." Her china-blue eyes met Ginny's and she continued in the same conversational tone, "But does one ever get used to being . . . *neglected* and openly humiliated? How do you put up with it?"

"I don't."

The servants had gone, and the need for discretion with them. Ginny's too-abrupt retort made Sonya's lips tighten.

"Oh?" she said pointedly. "But you are still his wife. Didn't you travel all the way here to find him and persuade him to take you back? Forgive me if I've drawn the wrong conclusions, but . . ."

The stubborn, angry tilt of Ginny's chin was all too familiar.

"Well, you have. But it really doesn't matter to me. Steve and I . . . you never could quite understand how matters were between us, could you? And I doubt that you ever will. But he goes his way and I go mine. Please don't expect me to be as upset as *you* obviously are!" Seeing the light of battle leap into Sonya's eyes Ginny added impatiently, "Oh come! What would be the point of more quarreling between us? I think we know very well where we stand with each other. Why not let it be?"

"It's all so easy for *you*, isn't it? You have always felt free to follow your whims without a thought for anyone else or . . . or the pain and the scandal you might be causing. Whereas *I* . . . ohh! As you just said, what does it matter? Enjoy your breakfast, do. I think I will go riding."

It had only been an impulse, of course. Sonya was to tell herself that later. She had not been able to stand sitting there with that . . . that little trollop outfacing her arrogantly. And it had been so long since she had gone riding by herself, feeling the easy gait of her mare under her and relishing the feel of a slight breeze against her flushed cheeks. No—it had been years since she had taken this particular path leading to the river bluff. And this time she would take care to avoid the old stone warehouse.

After Sonya had taken her abrupt leave Ginny found her appetite had waned. She didn't need a large breakfast. The croissant and café noir liberally laced with cognac was quite sufficient if she didn't want to become plump; hateful thought! Almost, Ginny wished that she *hadn't* allowed herself to wrangle with Sonya—an exhilarating ride was just what she needed to blow away the cobwebs from her mind and start it functioning properly again. For all the tossing and turning and the endless thinking she had done last night she had still not reached a decision or formulated any kind of plan. She only recognized, with a kind of fatalism that was new to her impulsive nature, that matters could not go on this way. Once and for all, she and Steve must have it out.

"I do love him . . ." she thought, and they had come so far apart in so short a space of time that the thought startled her. "But if we continue this way we will only destroy each other and whatever it is we feel about each other now." Steve—was it anger or indifference that kept him away from her? She had to find out, and brave the consequences. Thank God for the pride that stiffened her spine! No, she would not run away again, as Sonya had just done. And whatever she forced from Steve this time would be the truth.

"And the truth shall set you free. . . ." Why did that phrase, repeating itself over and over in Ginny's fevered brain, sound like a . . . a *knell?* A half dozen times she was tempted to turn back; to tell the disapproving old man who drove the light buggy that she had changed her mind. He would be even more disapproving when he found out the nature of the house to which she directed him. There would be more below-stairs gossip and Sonya would be horrified. But she didn't care, Ginny told herself stubbornly. She had to find out.

"Here," Ginny said, arousing herself purposefully from the reverie into which she had fallen, "please let me off here. And you don't need to wait, for my husband will bring me back."

Ginny had, in spite of herself, allowed herself to imagine all kinds of situations in which she might find her husband—more to arm herself against him than to whip up righteous anger. The one image that Ginny had *not* conjured up for herself was that of Steve sleeping alone.

Steve Morgan had, as a matter of fact, not intended spending what remained of the night by himself. He had almost decided to tell both Jim Bishop and his friend Paco to go to hell, he was buying out. And damn it, he was going to find Ginny and make her see, once and for all. . . .

And then, a yawning and sleepy-eyed Hortense had given him the note. A thick vellum envelope with a seal he recognized all too well—its contents brief and laconic. Bishop's trump card? It was almost too much of a coincidence that a letter from his grandfather, forwarded by Renaldo, should reach him here—and at this particular time. Looking down at Don Francisco's sprawling hand, Steve had found himself trying to read between the lines, even while a sense of fatalism overtook him. It seemed as if everything pointed him toward Cuba. But what possible business could his grandfather, of all people, have to transact in Cuba that was so important he had gone there himself in the middle of what promised to be a bloody revolution? Damn the old man's stiff-necked pride! He could at least have sent for Renaldo. And he had not regained his former strength and vigor after his stroke—he should not be traveling anywhere by himself.

Steve swore feelingly before he carefully burned the letter in the marble ashtray. Coping with his grandfather was something he never had relished. And now it looked as if he would have to cope with Ginny's inevitable tantrums as well—just as soon as she realized he would be sending her on to Mexico by herself.

The first paling of the sky outside the open window made Steve close his eyes purposefully. He had a feeling he was going to need all the rest he could get today. . . . And why in hell was it that as soon as he sought sleep his mind became jumbled with a myriad picture-images? Other times—the keyed-up feeling that always preceded the beginning of a new assignment. Ginny had accused him once of deliberately flirting with danger. "I guess I've just got a restless devil soul, sweetheart," he'd teased her back.

Ginny—temptress, tigress, siren-nemesis. No matter how hard they battled each other she was the kind of woman who could keep a man eternally curious as well as cautious. A green-eyed vixen with sharp teeth and claws. . . .

It took him a few seconds to adjust from the dream to the reality, and his first reaction to seeing her there staring down at him was to take her in his arms. But reason banished instinct, and the little sleep he'd had was enough to sharpen his mind. Meeting her questioning eyes Steve let the hardness show in his, knowing he had to make it easier for her to go away from him—and easier for him to send her back.

# Chapter Eight

◈

"Good-morning. I thought we might have breakfast together, as we did yesterday. We need to talk, don't you think?"

Steve's eyes narrowed at her before he gave her a smile that was a mere twist of his mouth.

"Do you really think so, madam? And by the way—where did you spend the night?"

So he was determined to be unpleasant. An unconscious sigh escaped Ginny's parted lips before she firmed her resolve.

"Steve—please don't. I'm tired of being at war. What happened to the honesty we promised each other?" Almost desperately she searched his face for some sign of softening, but found only coldness there as he shrugged, swinging long legs off the bed and beginning to pull on his pants as if she were not present. She couldn't even see his face as he said indifferently, "I had no idea we weren't being honest with each other . . . according to our respective lights, that is. Did you want to discuss something in particular?"

She was persistent—he had to grant her that! Her mouth tightened mutinously as if to tell him she recognized his tactics very well.

"As a matter of fact—yes I did. I wanted to discuss our . . . the relationship between us. I am not . . . not happy with the way it is, Steve. Are *you?*"

He looked up at her impatiently. "Jesus Christ! You came here for breakfast and pointless questions? We're married—and you've told me we have twin children who should be *your* main responsibility. If you're not happy living my way, there is no reason that you should not live in a fashion less upsetting to you. I've been a more than understanding husband so far, haven't I? As long as you'll try to remember to be more discreet than you were last night I'll try to curb my damned temper—is that fair enough to suit you?"

She stood her ground, her eyes bright with what may either have been tears or fury.

"Am I supposed to . . . to be punished? Is that the reason for your studied cruelty, Steve? Or do you really prefer to go back to living the way we were before I went to Europe? I'm afraid you'll have to answer me if you want to be rid of me."

"I had the idea that *you* were more than content with our style of life, my love. And with your own when I'm handily not around. No doubt when you're back in Mexico you'll find excuses to travel again, although I'd really prefer it if you waited until the children were older before you leave them again." He gave a short laugh. "God, but you're becoming a persistent nag! You might remember that I don't care to have my movements questioned."

He was being cruel on purpose—there was a reason for it. But telling herself that did nothing to soften the blow to her pride. All that was left was to make her exit dignified.

"Very well, Steve. I'll remember that—if you'll remember how I too despise jealous scenes." She shrugged lightly. "Do you suppose Hortense will provide me with breakfast? Or perhaps Governor Warmoth is still here. . . ."

It was perhaps unfortunate for them both that there was a knock on the door just then. They had been looking at each other —Steve with his hastily donned shirt still unbuttoned while he tried to fathom what lay behind his wife's sudden shift of mood.

"May I come in? They told me you would be expecting me . . . oh!"

"Do come in—I'm sure he *was* expecting you! And you mustn't look worried, I'm sure Steve will explain that we are a very *modern* couple and each have our own set of friends—although sometimes it's amusing to compare notes!" Ana Dos Santos, her brown-velvet eyes wide, did not look as if she had grown too much more mature since Ginny had last seen her. She stood pressed against the doorpost as if for protection, her gaze fixed on Ginny. "You *must* try the oysters," Ginny continued, "they are excellent—and so is the champagne. And since I can see I'm now *de trop* . . . darling—excuse me, Ana—I won't be home for dinner tonight.

Henry has invited me to a reception he is giving at the Governor's Mansion. *Au 'voir*—and do enjoy yourselves!"

Ginny's feet carried her past the startled young woman and away from Steve's suddenly wooden face. And as long as she kept that tableau fixed firmly in her mind, she wouldn't break down. Halfway downstairs Ginny heard the door close on the landing above.

William Brandon watched Ginny walk across the entrance hall toward him and only his own anxiety prevented him from noticing her unusual paleness. He remembered belatedly that he was still annoyed at her, and his voice was curt.

"My God—where has everyone hidden themselves? Where is Sonya?"

"I have no idea, except that much earlier this morning she said she was going riding. Why don't you look for her?"

"Now listen here, Virginia! Just because you're a married woman now does not mean you may talk to me in that impertinent fashion! And as for your behavior last night—"

"I have not told Sonya where you were, if that is what you are worried about. Do you mind letting me by? I've been out myself and have rather a headache."

"Her" room was only a temporary refuge. Lying in bed fortified by an icepack fetched by her solicitous maid, Ginny tried to think clearly, but only one thought made any sense: She must leave. And since Steve himself had set her carelessly free to follow her own inclinations if she chose, she would do exactly that. Ginny closed her eyes, willing herself not to feel pain—to find numbness. "So it's over. It's really over at last, and how strange it feels!"

Through her open window she heard Senator Brandon's voice, shouting for one of the grooms to bring a horse around from the stables. Was he going to search for Sonya? *He* was a man too—it was perfectably acceptable for them to take their pleasure any way they chose, but their women must be above reproach—untouched and untouchable. Suddenly, Ginny found herself wondering about Sonya who, after all, was much younger than her husband. Had Sonya loved her *first* husband, who had left her this house and its attendant lands? Had she ever had lovers? Sonya, although rather plump of late, was by no means an unattractive woman; and certainly Andre Delery had seemed to think so.

While Ginny was trying to keep her vagrant thoughts on anything but her own choices for the future, Sonya, on the other hand, was beginning to wish desperately that she was safely back home, blaming Ginny for her own impulsive behavior.

If William had not behaved so badly and if Ginny hadn't provoked her, she would have quite brushed out of her mind the memory of Andre Delery's whispered pleas that she allow him to join her on one of her rides—when she was alone—so that he might again talk with her and share with her a book of French poems he had brought back with him from his last trip to Paris. She had thought him such a charming and unusually sensitive man, but of course a clandestine meeting with him—or any man for that matter—would have been unthinkable under *normal* circumstances. M. Delery had made it clear he respected her, of course, and that he valued her opinion and her conversation—she had no reason to mistrust him for he was accepted by all of her old friends. And yet . . . oh, God, how could she have been so unbelievably stupid and thoughtless? She had not really expected to see him—she had only wanted to be alone, to be riding again as she used to do in the old days. Oh, she had already told herself all of these things, none of which excused the fact that Andre Delery had been waiting for her and she had permitted him to engage her in conversation.

The grove of trees on the river bluff was very old, having been planted by one of the earliest settlers in the area. Sonya had always enjoyed the picnics they used to have here in the leaf-screened shade. She and Raoul, her handsome, laughing young husband who had courted her and captured her girlish imagination and married her. And had loved his quadroon mistress most of all. . . .

It had been a long time since she had walked among the trees, listening to the sounds of the river below the bluff. A long time since she had sat laughing with her back against an ancient, gnarled tree trunk; she was a little drunk from the chilled wine Andre Delery had brought.

"Bread and wine—a book of poems translated from the Persian, we are told. It was you I thought of when I first read it; I had to share these things with you."

"You sound like a poet yourself, M. Delery! But you know, of course, that I can't stay. I . . . I really shouldn't have come at all, only I suddenly felt as if I—"

"Please . . . a few minutes, now that you are here? Did you know that I was wishing you here, calling you with my mind?" At her confused, rather startled look he laughed, and caught her hand. "Don't look so nervous, I swear I don't mean to compromise you. What harm can it do to share a few moments of all this beauty and peace with each other?"

She had allowed him to persuade her; and afterward she could not have told why. At the time it had seemed merely natural to stay and talk a while, after he'd gone to all the trouble. She had to tell him gently that he'd do much better picnicking with a young woman closer to his own age—an unmarried woman. But in the meantime he read her poetry, and sat close to her; offering her still-warm chunks of freshly baked bread with white goat's cheese, to be washed down with wine. She wasn't doing anything *wrong* after all. But how long had it been since she had done something impulsive? How long since she had enjoyed herself so much?

Andre Delery saw to it that she enjoyed herself as he set himself out to charm her out of her awareness of time. He also made sure that the crystal-and-silver wine goblet he had thoughtfully brought along was kept refilled. He read poems to her and told her droll anecdotes that made her laugh; all the while carefully gauging how long it would take. And then, when he heard the first faint sounds he had been waiting for he interrupted the story he had been telling her, leaning so close that he could see the startled look in her eyes.

"Wait—don't move! There is a small spider . . . no need to alarm yourself, I shall brush it off, so. . . ." All in one movement his fingers brushed against her hair at the back of her neck while she made a small outcry of fear. What more natural than with the same movement he should turn her head toward him and kiss her parted lips?

It was a scene that implied more than really existed, of course. A kiss—and it seemed as if they both lost balance so that Sonya

was now leaning backward with Delery's body half covering hers
when they both heard the embarrassed coughs.

"Oh—a thousand apologies old friend, but I did not know . . .
how could anyone know you would pick this particular place for
*your* trysting too?"

Sonya thought she would die a thousand deaths. Indeed, she
would much rather have dropped dead at that moment than be
forced to face them all. The carefully blank faces of Lucian
Valette and Bernard Pruett and the openly inquisitive stares of
the two young women accompanying them.

Valette's stammered attempts at an explanation only made
matters worse, of course. While he explained that they had come
by river—it was so pleasant a day, it had been an impulsive idea—
Sonya straightened her clothing and wished she dared burst into
tears. There were servants carrying hampers and blankets and
cushions. Bernard's fiancée was accompanied by a middle-aged
aunt who frowned at Sonya with obvious, purse-lipped disapproval, while the girl herself went red and white in turn—and
Andre stumbled over *his* explanations.

"Lucian! Well I must say—I met Mrs. Brandon out riding and
persuaded her to rest in the shade for a while . . ." Andre Delery
did not seem to be the kind of man to sound so embarrassed and
at a loss for words. He looked at Sonya and mouthed the words
"I'm so sorry!" But after all, what good did *that* do her reputation? Sonya knew New Orleans society and she knew that the gossips would have a greatly exaggerated account of this by evening—
a story to be whispered in drawing rooms and over card tables.
Soon everyone would be buzzing with it!

Everyone started talking at once, as if to try to gloss it over—
everyone except Sonya, who could not have spoken if her life
depended on it.

It was this strained, stiff picture that caught William Brandon's
choleric regard as he rode his horse up. And his presence was, as
M. Delery was to tell his friend Valette much later, purely coincidental and a bonus thrown in their direction by the gods themselves! The Senator was to have found out that his wife had been
surprised with her lover through the inevitable gossip; instead he
had walked in on the carefully staged scene and had drawn, quite
swiftly, the inevitable conclusions.

* * *

"For heaven's sake! You *must* try to keep calm—hysterics are not going to help you, you know!" Ginny's voice sounded sterner and more impatient than she meant it to, but Sonya in hysterics was something she was not used to coping with. "Go on—it will help you to speak to me about it. What happened then? Couldn't you have explained? Surely he gave you the benefit of—"

"I tell you, I tell you—oh, my God, how would you understand? You weren't brought up here as I was! They are to fight a duel—there's no way to . . . to . . . I want to die, I want to die!!"

"But you won't. Sonya, *listen* to me! Don't you see that the only way to get over this is to face—and to *out*face them all? You must—for your sake and . . . and for my . . . father's as well. Let me talk to him, and I'll get Steve—"

"No! No, no, no!" Sonya's voice rose in a wail. "I can't face him—not either of them, I'm guilty, I'm guilty—it's my punishment after all these years. . . ."

"Now you are talking quite nonsensically! And here's the Doctor come to give you something for your nerves—I'll see what I can do to stop this nonsense and you must promise me you'll try to make yourself calm. You're not helping anything by remaining in such a state, you know!"

In spite of all her rallying words, Ginny found herself shaking when she left Sonya's room. It was not *this* way that she would have wanted her mind taken off her own problems. Poor Sonya! Ruled by convention for all of her life, only to be trapped and condemned by it. And as for her father the Senator fighting a duel —*that* was even more ridiculous! It would make the scandal much worse, and the consequences were unthinkable. He should have trusted in his wife; why were men so touchy and so doubting? Like Steve—always believing the worst of her. . . .

Ginny finally realized how cold her hands were when she felt their numbness as she clasped them together. Angry at herself the next moment for acting like a ninny, she left her stance by Sonya's door and went downstairs, hoping to find the Senator still there. He must be made to see that fighting a duel with Andre Delery would ruin him politically while ruining his wife socially. Yes, that would be the best way to go about it. And if that didn't work then Steve would know what to do. Ginny's mouth twisted for an instant. Steve would never back off from a duel. The first time she had seen him, looking down from her hotel room window in San Antonio, he had killed a man in the dusty street. And she had been forced to watch him kill with his bare hands on the deck of a ship the Russian Prince who had been her "husband." Steve's way of preventing an encounter between the Senator and Andre Delery would probably be to challenge Delery himself. And why should she care? She had known—or should have—from the beginning what kind of man Steve was. And he had not once pretended to be anything else. So, therefore, the fault was all hers and the illusions were all hers as well as the dreams—the fairy-tale endings of "and so they lived happily ever after" that made all the sad parts and the bad parts right for the Princess and her Prince or the Knight and his Lady, in the fairy tales she had read as a child.

The whole household seemed hushed—the somehow *whispering* silence seeming to be intensified by the lengthening shadows, the subtle fading of slanted sun through open windows. Walking down a strangely empty hallway that was still permeated by the lingering smell of lemon wax, her mouth determined, Ginny was suddenly reminded that they had guests coming to dinner that night. Or had someone sent messages? Was *she* supposed to take charge?

Hoping to confront the Senator in his study, where he had locked himself in, Ginny found the door standing open—a frightened-looking butler informed her that the Senator had gone out again—and no, ma'am, he surely hadn't mentioned where-all he was going. And then her hoped-for confrontation was replaced by another she wasn't quite ready for yet.

"What in hell is going on around here?"

Steve, of course. Black brows scowling as she turned to face him with her chin elevated.

"Well?" His eyes squinted down at her as if he was taking her measure and had decided to attack first. Ginny glared at him, fighting back.

"Are you going to give me a chance to tell you?" And then, very succinctly, she did tell him—a detached part of her mind almost enjoying the look she surprised on his face before he closed it against her.

At the same time, amazingly, he took her arm, leading her with him into the study with an impatient jerk of his head at the servant. He had no right, after his blatant rejection of her, to try to be *kind!*

"How did she become so friendly with Delery? Damn, I'd almost thought *you* were his target. Didn't you notice anything between them?"

"Dear God! After all that has happened, *that's* all you have to say?" Suddenly so furious that she was shaking, Ginny snatched her arm from his grasp, stepping backward. "You thought I was his target. . . . How casually you can say that! And . . . and . . . oh! . . . sometimes I wonder if I know you at all, or if you have any *real* feelings for anyone that are not dictated by expediency or what *you* want. Don't you care about what might happen? About the consequences of what took place this afternoon? Sonya's prostrated with shock and self-blame, poor creature, and she's really not the kind of woman to engage in that kind of thing, she's always been so straitlaced! I'm sure she met him by accident and that my father, like a typical male, made far too much of it. . . . I was going to talk to him, but he's gone somewhere and I'm afraid. . . ."

He was watching her steadily now, with that new, closed expression on his face that she particularly resented—only the sardonic curl of his lip betraying any emotion at all. He was watching her instead of listening and the discovery only infuriated Ginny to the point that had she dared she would have struck out at him to force some reaction from him that was at least *real*.

The careless shrug of his shoulders under the formfitting jacket of dark blue broadcloth only added fuel to her fury, as he said sarcastically: "I'm sure your er . . . father would have made sure to inform you where he was going and why, had he known of your concern, my love. But now that I'm back and you've been kind enough to explain everything to me . . . you *have* told me all, I presume? Or did Sonya happen to meet Delery under the mistaken assumption that she was protecting *you?* Because you're right on that score at least, I really can't see Sonya running off to a clandestine meeting with any man as obvious as Andre Delery. . . ."

If he had been egging her on to just such a reaction he succeeded. Speechless with rage, Ginny slapped him, feeling her arm jolted all the way to the shoulder when he caught her wrist.

"You bastard!"

"I should act like one and slap you back, Ginny. Don't push your luck, or you might have some ugly bruises to explain."

"It wouldn't be the first time, would it? Damn you, Steve! I won't be treated this way, I won't live this way! I want a *normal* life, do you hear me? Not . . . not an armed truce or a forced surrender and never being quite certain . . . oh damn, damn! I want —let me go! I want a divorce, you said I could have one, remember? And I'd rather not let this . . . our marriage drag on until we both end up hating each other. . . ."

She had forgotten about her father and about Sonya, and about whatever it was that had started all this. Without realizing it she had begun sobbing with rage and with hurt and most of all with frustration because he was making her act this way and *she* was the only one to show any feeling at all, as usual. He just stood there looking at her with that infernally caustic twist to his lips and one eyebrow cocked. He didn't care, or he would have gathered her into his arms. And only a month or so ago he'd told her again that he loved her and would never let her go—did he only feel that way because his pride didn't want the world to know she'd left him? Was pride all that held them together?

Now he dropped her wrist, leaving her to massage it sullenly while she fought to control her telltale temper. And his voice sounded disgusted—slightly impatient.

"Ah shit, Ginny! So you're still harping on that theme? My answer's still the same—no. No divorce, my sweet. Think I want to be the target for some other sweet young thing looking for a husband? Uh-uh—once is enough. And in any case, right now is a mighty poor time for another juicy scandal, don't you think? I'm afraid you'll just have to put up with being a married woman until I decide it's time our ways parted—*formally*, that is. And in the meantime, if you're sensible, you'll be discreet—just as I intend to be. That way we can both have our cake and eat it, and when you've stopped throwing tantrums I'm sure you'll agree with me."

He might just as well have slapped her back and have done with it—she would have infinitely preferred that honest, *human* reaction to the coldly cutting and almost inhuman logic he was

foisting on her. It all had to be his way, of course! Her feelings
didn't matter to him at all—as if they ever had! And yet Ginny
felt as if her next words were being forced out of her by some
compulsion she couldn't control; by something she *had* to know.

"You don't love me any longer? Is that what you're trying to
say?"

"Goddamn it—*love!* Is that all a woman thinks about? You slap
my face one instant and tell me you hate me and the next you're
demanding that I love you. . . ."

She hated the way he shrugged, the way he was looking at her as
if she made him long to be gone from her. She hated the offhandedly impatient way he added, as if to a recalcitrant child: "Of
course I love you, Ginny. You're my wife, and the mother, so you
inform me, of my children. But we've both played enough games
to know we need some outside excitement as well, don't we? Oh,
I'll admit you have the capacity to make me infernally jealous at
times, but I'll try to curb that tendency if you'll do the same.
Does that satisfy you?"

What would have satisfied her was to have made him furious at
her—to have him kiss her angrily and savagely and make love to
her while he told her he loved her and wanted her and she was his
and no one else's and he'd beat her if she strayed—but instead he
was politely stepping aside to give her "freedom"—the same kind
of freedom *he* obviously wanted. And did his changed attitude
have something to do with Ana? Ginny wanted to scream that
question at him—to scream and rage and stamp her foot and
throw a real tantrum, however he had put her in an untenable position from which there was only one way to escape with her pride
intact. Wiping tattle-tale tears away with the back of her hand
Ginny said shakily:

"Oh damn! Why do I always cry when I am in a rage? And
why do I let you bait me?" She faced him with her chin up, daring him to try to disarm her now. "I suppose I shouldn't let you—
and I won't in future. And I . . . I'm afraid I'm not very good at
playing the hypocrite, but with you to instruct me I'm sure I shall
*try* and do well in the end. Please do think about a divorce, won't
you? I'll try to be discreet about my affairs of course, and I agree it
would create a difficult situation just now, but if I should happen

to fall in love with some man I shall go away with him, you know, divorce or no. I refuse to live with *that* kind of a lie."

He watched her leave the room with her dignity intact and her back straight. He didn't make a move to stop her, even when all his instincts pushed him to do just that. Go after her and spin her around, forcing her to admit she hadn't meant a single bitter word she'd said—any more than he had.

# Chapter Nine

❧

Mr. Bishop was both annoyed and perturbed, but he hid his feelings quite well, having had much practice in doing so. Nevertheless, there was a slight edge to his usually uninflected voice that made Paco Davis rather uneasy.

"It seems that they are cleverer than we gave them credit for being—and especially to strike so quickly and in such an unlooked-for direction! So the Senator is seeing a lawyer—redrawing his will, one assumes? And the meeting with Delery is . . . ?"

He knew the answer to that one as well as Paco did, but the pause was deliberate, as he relit his cigar and sent a mild question across the table with his look.

Resignedly, Paco supplied the answer. "They are *supposed* to meet tonight, I've been told. The unusual hurry is because they don't want the authorities to hear about it and take steps to prevent such a thing. Shall *we?*"

Bishop appeared to be considering the blunt question as he leaned back in his chair studying the bluish-grey whorls of the smoke ring he'd just blown. He had decided he *was* annoyed—it always irked him to feel himself outmaneuvered.

Paco leaned forward, his black eyes suddenly bright.

"Hey, maybe *Steve* should push this Delery into a fight, huh? What could be more natural, after all? The Senator is his father-in-law, and it's well known that Delery likes to *kill* his opponents, that's why most of the men around here are so damn scared of him. . . ."

"And you ought to know better than to imagine it would work," Bishop said coldly enough to make Paco give an exaggerated wince.

"Well—it was an idea."

"Not a very smart one. We want Morgan in Cuba, and we want

him to remain an unknown quantity—at least for as long as possible. And in any case, if he fights Brandon's battles it would humiliate the Senator himself. No, I think there are other ways to circumvent this ridiculous duel without being too obvious about it. . . ."

Thoughtfully, Bishop leaned forward to steeple his fingers under his chin while he detailed the "other ways."

"Gotta hand it to him!" Paco thought grudgingly. "He's a cold-blooded son of a bitch, but a smart one for sure!"

It was a conclusion that Steve Morgan, when he came stalking in to join them with the scowl on his face mirroring his black mood, was forced to agree with. All the way back into town he'd been toying quite pleasurably with the idea of forcing some sort of immediate meeting with Andre Delery that would have relieved some of the temper and tension within him. But of course it was Bishop, with his cool head, who had come up with the obvious and most practical solution of all. The easiest way to prevent the duel was, of course, to invoke the law and have all the parties involved arrested. Oh, of course it would mean some attendant unpleasantness, but in the long run . . .

Steve Morgan, his jacket removed and his ruffled linen shirt open at the neck, deigned to lift an interested eyebrow. "And once we have them in jail . . . ?"

"Well, at least it buys us time, huh?" Paco offered helpfully.

Bishop looked sour as he said with unusual shortness: "That will be *my* problem." He looked from one to the other and added softly, "And in the meantime perhaps you gentlemen will prepare for an imminent departure for Cuba?"

"I cannot believe it! Just like in the old days—and *then* you used to argue with him, but today you didn't. Hey Steve, you're not listening to your old amigo—"

"Shut up, Paco."

Steve was still in the same black mood he'd been in all day, and the large quantities of warm liquor that he and Paco had managed to consume since Bishop's stiff-backed departure hadn't helped; nor had his attempted concentration on the map that Bishop had obligingly left for them to memorize. Steve frowned over it, wishing that Paco would stop needling him.

Cuba. Strange that he'd never visited that island, even though he had an uncle there. Or was it a cousin? Shit—some distant relative he'd hardly been aware of. Stranger still that his grandfather, who detested traveling, had suddenly decided to take off on some mysterious errand to Cuba on his own. His letter, full of sarcastic admonitions and outright orders (". . . when I advised you to take some time away from the hacienda in order to see to outside business I had no idea you intended to stay away for over a year . . . and now that I find that very urgent personal matters force me to leave at once for my estates in Cuba, I trust you will not find it too inconvenient to return to Mexico . . ."), had not once mentioned the nature of the urgent personal business that had sent Don Francisco on this journey. Or the acquisition of any estates in Cuba. None of this was at all like his grandfather! Was the old man on the verge of senility to set off to Cuba in the middle of a revolution? And then Steve remembered unwillingly that when Mexico itself had been caught up in bloody revolution, Don Francisco had been one of the few large landowners who had refused to budge from his hacienda. No—his grandfather was afraid of nothing, and once determined on a course he would let nothing stop him . . . perhaps they were more alike than either of them cared to admit! Both stubborn—although there were some that would call it being pigheaded or overly prideful.

Deliberately, Steve smothered the sudden image that flashed unwanted into his mind. Ginny, his vixen-eyed termagant. Her back straight, chin tilted defiantly as she countered his temper and his calculatedly hurtful thrusts. Damn her pride and her resilience. And the unwavering truth in the face of his own dishonesty.

"You must know that map like the back of your hand by now, the way you've been scowling at it. Or do you have something else on your mind?"

Steve looked up at Paco and pushed the map across the table with a shrug. "Yeah. And she's waiting upstairs for me."

"I don't know how you do it! Wish I had your luck—that kind of luck, that is. Quite a coincidence your running into your ex-fiancée here, huh? And her being a recent widow and all. I guess she's forgiven you for jilting her?"

Steve grinned. "She blames it all on Ginny."

Whether Ana was waiting for him or not, Steve Morgan proceeded to take his time about joining her, Paco noticed. Paco also wondered, as he had many times before, why women put up with the kind of cavalier treatment his partner meted out to them. The only one who hadn't—and had won him—had been Ginny. And there had been a time when Paco had thought it was going to work. But he wasn't so sure any longer. He found himself wondering how Ginny had taken the news that her husband was going to Cuba, leaving her to return to Mexico on her own. If she hadn't changed too much since the last time he'd seen her, she'd probably be angry. Especially if she knew about Ana. Paco, who'd seen Ginny angry, couldn't repress a grin when he remembered the knife fight she'd had with Concepción. Jesus! What a day *that* had been.

"Thinking about something funny?" Steve said disagreeably. Paco noticed that Steve was still scowling, this time at the food a waiter had just brought in.

"Nope. Just smiling because I'm real hungry and that gumbo or whatever they call it sure smells good!"

What in hell was bothering Steve? He'd ordered supper, and now suddenly he was pushing his chair back from the table, leaving his portion untouched.

"Then you won't mind if I leave you to the serious business of eating, my friend? I guess I'll go upstairs and take a bath before I take care of . . . my appetite. I'll see you later."

Unoffended, Paco shrugged equably. "Sure. Me, I can't wait to find out exactly how Jim is going to stop that duel—without *us*. It's enough to hurt a man's feelings, don't you think?" His teeth flashed in a grin. "And I'd sure like to see the Senator's face when he's hauled off to jail!"

Tactfully, Paco hadn't brought up the subject of Sonya Brandon who had started all this, and who, he happened to know, had once been Steve's mistress. Steve hadn't mentioned her—or her part in the whole affair—either. But then, Steve had always tended to be close-mouthed. It didn't stop Paco from wondering though, even after Steve had left the room. What had made Sonya Brandon, after all the years of conventionality that had elapsed since the war, decide to rendezvous with an obvious rake with a reputation—and right under the nose of her husband? Either the woman was stupid or she had been deliberately used in order to get her husband out of the way. No doubt Bishop had already thought of that angle.

Ginny, feverishly concentrating upon keeping her mind on *any* subject but the sudden unbridgeable chasm that had opened up between her and Steve, had begun to wonder about the same thing. There was something strange and almost too coincidental about the whole sordid affair. Why would a man like Andre Delery—quite young, undeniably handsome and attractive to women, suddenly decide to pay court to a woman much older—and very much married into the bargain? Delery had made no bones about showing he desired *her*, and it wasn't conceit that made Ginny think that—she'd met far too many accomplished flirts like Delery *not* to know it. And yet he'd suddenly turned his attention to Sonya. Why? And why, instead of being careful and taking his time, had he rushed matters so? For that matter, why had Sonya?

Her father hadn't yet returned to the house, and in spite of a suddenly raging headache Ginny decided to seek Sonya out again. Never mind that her stepmother was still in a state of prostration. She had to face reality and be made to realize that remaining in a state of hysterics wouldn't help her. Maybe, ironically enough, they could even help each other.

"Of *course* I never agreed to meet him! How could you think it of me?" Sonya, sitting up in bed with her face all blotched and puffy, her eyes swollen into slits, was a pitiable sight, but Ginny went on with her questioning remorselessly.

"I didn't mean to imply that. But don't you see that you must talk about it and come up with a story that will . . . that will hold water? All you've done is cry—"

"Oh!" Beginning to sniffle again, Sonya cried out reproachfully, "How unfeeling you are! But then you've never cared a jot for . . . for convention or the feelings of others, or . . . or—"

"It doesn't signify what *I've* done in this case," Ginny said, trying to keep her voice even. "And I *am* trying to help you. Do stop going *on*, Sonya, and tell me exactly what happened. Then perhaps I might be able to help you in some way, if only by talking reason to my father when he returns."

It took her, all the same, a considerable amount of time to get the whole story from an alternately sullen and sobbing woman who seemed ready, at the drop of a hat, to pin the blame for everything on Ginny herself. And yet, at the end of Sonya's recital, the younger woman believed her. It would be so like Sonya to do exactly as she had done! Enjoy a surreptitious flirtation without admitting to herself that that was what she was doing—and to be unprepared for the consequences. But it wasn't Sonya's part in the whole train of events that was a matter of concern. Andre Delery continued to be the part of the puzzle that wouldn't fit.

And damn it, Ginny thought violently, why had Steve forced her into the quarrel they'd had before she could tell him of her already half-formed suspicions? Why had they suddenly started quarreling again when they were around other people? She closed her eyes against the treacherous pain that flooded through her without warning. Yes—like Sonya she would have loved to have given way to the luxury of tears; she wanted to throw things, to beat at the walls that enclosed her, to scream out loud. But she would, of course, do none of these things. As she had promised Steve, she would put him out of her mind and make herself a polite stranger. She had survived without him before and she would again. And no one—*no one* would ever see the pain, and after a while it would go away, leaving her really free.

"Think about it!" she commanded herself, and unconsciously her back stiffened. "Yes, think about how wonderful it will be to belong only to myself again, to be in control. I'm going to live my own life from now on." And with that die finally cast she wouldn't let herself remember those miserable months she'd spent traveling around Europe with a string of attentive escorts who hadn't really mattered at all—no, not even Michel, her former fiancé. After a while, when the twins were older, she'd take them with her and go back to Europe. Back even to Russia, where the man who was the Tsar was in all probability her *real* father. No yearning this time. She'd forget Steve and help him forget her.

With her resolutions made, Ginny turned her mind again to the problem at hand. The duel, of course. Her "father" the Senator, fighting a duel? Somehow, it still seemed unbelievable. William Brandon wasn't the type, although in this case she supposed he'd been left with no alternative—something that Andre Delery had planned? And if so, for God's sake, *why?*

"I should really ask him that myself," Ginny mused, taking pins from her hair and letting it fall loose across her shoulders. "I could tell, just by watching his face, if what I suspect is true or not . . . like most men, he wouldn't expect a woman to have a mind."

Her face in the mirror looked pale and hard, her eyes like green stones. Ginny grimaced at herself, picking up her silver-backed hairbrush to tug it through unruly strands of hair. And then belatedly the implications of her own thoughts froze her arm in midstroke. Why not? Yes—why not? She could look after herself very well—her experiences as a *soldadera* had taught her that much and more. And it would be something to do, a challenge. Above all, it would make Steve furious. Yes, and the ubiquitous Mr. Bishop—whom she hadn't quite forgiven—too.

# Chapter Ten

❧

Such was Andre Delery's confidence in himself that soon after his morning's encounter with Madame Brandon *and* her husband he had proceeded to visit all his usual haunts in town, pass the time with his old friend and mentor Pepe Llulla and order a new suit of clothes from his tailor. Then he enjoyed a pleasurable hour or so in a discreet house of assignation with a new mistress— none other than the sister of one of his close friends, conveniently married to another friend. He had always had a fondness for Berthe, but she, knowing more about his escapades through her mother than most other women, had always managed to stay aloof until she'd heard of her husband's octoroon paramour.

She wanted, Berthe told Andre, to be taught how to excite a man—drive him to the verge of madness. Andre had pleasure in teaching her, and in the process had enjoyed Berthe's lush body himself. They would meet again.

In the meantime . . . sighing, Delery took out his gold fob watch and looked at it, noting the hour. He supposed he had better go home to his apartments, take a leisurely bath and change clothes. He would be meeting the foolish Senator Brandon exactly at five minutes to midnight—it always pleased Andre to set this hour for the duels in which *he* was the challenged party. By midnight it would all be over, and he would be richer by a considerable amount of money which would be placed discreetly in his bank account. His chiseled mouth stretched in a hard smile. An easy way to make a fortune for a man like himself who infinitely preferred a life of leisure to a life of toil at some profession!

Climbing the stairs, Andre Delery planned his evening. Dinner with friends, among them Lucian Valette. The theater, where he would make an appearance and establish an alibi. And after the duel he would probably visit his favorite gaming establishment,

run by another old acquaintance. Tonight he felt lucky, the cards
would run in his favor!

"Monsieur . . ." his valet, Jean-Baptiste, was a Frenchman and
spoke only French. Master and man understood each other very
well after six years. Was it possible that the wiry, dark-haired
Frenchman was somewhat concerned? Surely not about the duel,
that would be too much! Pausing in the act of shrugging out of
his closely fitting jacket, Delery raised an interrogatory eyebrow.
"Yes?"

The valet cleared his throat awkwardly. "There is . . . that is
. . . the truth is I did not know what to do. You did not tell me
you were expecting a visitor, but the young lady is . . . ahem . . .
she is extremely attractive, monsieur. And speaks French also. She
said—"

"It's not important. She shall tell me whatever she said to you
herself. She's extremely attractive, eh? Coming from you, Baptiste,
that's quite a compliment. Is she waiting in the little salon?"

"*Oui*, monsieur. And I took the liberty of offering the young
lady a glass of sherry. I also told her that you might not be back
until much later, but she insisted that she would wait."

"Did she?" Delery's mouth curled slightly as he wondered if he
was going to be annoyed, bored or pleasantly surprised. Women!
They were always full of little tricks. But he knew very few of
them who would be bold enough to visit a man's apartments in
broad daylight, unless the "lady" was not really a lady. His jacket
removed, he unbuttoned his vest, handing that too to his wooden-
faced servant, deliberately giving her and himself time. This was
his apartment after all, he would be comfortable in this heat and
perhaps if she interested him would encourage her to do likewise.
To be considered also was the matter of killing a man within a
few hours.

A fastidious man, Andre Delery hesitated a second before he instructed Jean-Baptiste to prepare his bath in the *larger* tub. "And
be sure there are extra towels and perfumed soap—if she stays the
lady will join me."

Jean-Baptiste inclined his head, handing his master a glass of
chilled white wine to fortify him. Not that he needed it—
M. Delery was a rare one for the ladies indeed. He, Jean-Baptiste,
had known him to take three of them, one after the other, in one

hot afternoon. He watched Andre Delery walk across the small foyer with his graceful swordsman's gait to open the door leading to the petit salon and step inside.

The waiting had been almost intolerable, but the sound of voices from outside had at least prepared her for his entrance. Ginny had not been able to sit; the chairs in the small room she found herself in were too small to accommodate the bustle of her stylish afternoon gown, and in any case she was nervous, now that she was here.

However she might have felt inside, there was no show of agitation in Virginia Morgan's manner as she turned away from her study of a small oil portrait when the door opened.

"M. Delery—how good of you to receive me unannounced." Her voice was cool and composed as she held out her gloved hand.

It was Delery who could not hide his surprise at seeing her there. For an instant—and then, like a true gambler, his eyes became hooded. "And I, madam, can scarce believe my luck!" Like her, he too spoke in French. He took her hand and kissed it, holding it as he went on teasingly: "Shall I guess why you have come or . . . merely hope?" As he spoke he wondered if at this point she would play coy and pretend annoyance. She was really a most intriguing woman—a flame-haired gypsy with a passionate, wanton mouth.

Ginny, guessing his game, made no move to free her hand although she resisted slightly when he made an equally tentative attempt to draw her closer.

"M. Delery, I came to speak to you about . . . well, about my stepmother. We haven't been getting along too well recently, as I'm sure you'd guessed, but I hate to see her in such a state. Tell me"—and she deliberately let her voice quiver slightly—"is it really true? That you *didn't* have an assignation with her, that is, and met quite by chance? Poor Sonya swears to it, and I promised myself that I would do all I could to convince my father of that fact before you two naughty men fight your silly duel! And of course, who else would I come to for the truth but *you?* And you will tell it to me, won't you? From the first I had a feeling that I could rely on you to be completely honest, even to the point of bluntness, because . . . because you don't really *care* enough to pretend, do you? I mean . . ."

His voice sounded playful although his eyes had narrowed speculatively at her. "And you, *belle* madam. Can I in turn expect complete honesty from you? Is that *all* you came here to find?"

"Well . . ." Deliberately Ginny let the word trail out, and then she gave a little, nervous laugh. "Well of course I'd be honest—I usually am, unless I discover other people aren't. And I came here to find *you*, I suppose I've made that fairly obvious, haven't I? I do want to know about Sonya. She's always been so . . . so staid and stuffy, always criticizing *me* for flouting convention, and what happened this afternoon just doesn't seem possible, you know. Nor the duel either. My father is so pigheaded!"

Now he caught and imprisoned both of her hands, saying softly: "Come, madam, don't disappoint me! You came here, you said to find honesty, and I have the feeling it is not in your nature to talk as much and so fast as you are doing now. Will it encourage you if I answer your first question? Well then . . ." Taking her silence for assent he squeezed her hands slightly. "Being a gentleman I can tell you only that I did not have the opportunity to make love to your charming stepmother. We were, unfortunately, interrupted by some of my friends who had decided to picnic at that very spot. And as for our meeting itself, well . . . who can tell? I had asked her to meet me at the river bluff—she neither agreed nor disagreed. I waited, being a patient man when I want to be, and *voilà*, by *chance* she said, the charming Sonya appeared. What could be more natural than . . . conversation? A pity indeed that your father should have arrived so inopportunely. . . ."

"But I suppose that even if he hadn't your friends would have gossiped and he would have found out in the end and had to challenge you anyway—isn't that so?" Ginny widened her eyes at him with pretended innocence and then, because he had begun to gaze at her thoughtfully, she awarded him one of her more charming smiles. "Now don't *you* go and disappoint me, M. Delery. I'm really not stupid, even if I do talk too much and too fast on occasion. And on this occasion what I'm wondering is—why Sonya? She's older than you are and very much married—to my father. And . . ."

"Do continue." Delery's strong fingers still held her fast, and now his smile matched her own. "You intrigue me. And more so now, if I may say so, than you did at the beginning—or when you arrived at the opera without your husband and permitted me to escort you to your box. Did it pique you that I paid all my attention to your stepmother instead of to you?"

"Oh, no—I thought you were being polite. And had I wanted your attention on me then, I think I would have managed to engage it. Now, to get back to my father—and to Sonya of course—I was merely asking myself if it was indeed a coincidence that your friends turned up when they did? Or whether there was some reason why you would *want* to challenge my father to a duel?"

This time he laughed, throwing his head back, but Ginny noticed that his laughter did not reach his eyes, which again were fixed on her.

"You have a charming imagination, madam temptress, to match your other charms. And you continue to intrigue me. Did you come here with the intention of . . . er . . . offering me some consideration *not* to fight your father?"

"Money," Ginny said shortly and succinctly, dropping her smile. "More, of course than you're being paid to kill him. And of course you really should think very carefully of the consequences to yourself if you should succeed, although I doubt that you will. My father has *friends*, shall we say, who watch over him. Something—an unfortunate accident perhaps—could befall *you*. Had you thought of it?"

"I am thinking that it's *you* who have come here to duel with me—and your words are as sharp as your wits. I pay you homage, madam! However . . ."—his lazy voice, dropping, becoming sharper—"you must surely understand that this is a matter of honor, and your father challenged *me*, not the other way around. Alas, I have no choice!"

"You could do the honorable thing and elope—"

"Ah, but then he might kill *me!*"

"If I told him he was wrong to assume that Sonya and you—"

"I'm afraid he surprised us in a most compromising position."

Now Ginny had the feeling that he was toying with her, and she disliked it immensely.

"M. Delery, I offered you . . ."

"Yes. But you know it won't do now, don't you? You see, I am being honest in my way. What if I had pretended to accede to your request if you would give me . . . yourself?"

"Well, since you were gentleman enough not to, the question doesn't arise, does it?" Green, slightly slanted eyes met his levelly. She was the kind of woman *not* to look away—and who would retreat with grace when she had to. Delery was tempted to keep her. After all, she'd arrived on her own; she'd hardly have dared tell anyone where she was—or would she?

"I'd better go now. I've intruded on your privacy for long enough." Now her hands tugged against his, and it was with extreme reluctance that Delery released them.

"I hope I haven't made you unhappy. And who knows? No one is perfect, I might miss."

"Or you might not be there."

He had to admire her cool impudence. She was, in reality, quite a woman, and now more than ever he wanted her—willing or unwilling, although he'd soon change the latter into the former!

"If that is a warning I thank you for your concern. And I look forward to our next meeting."

"So do I," Ginny said without inflection.

"Nothing ventured . . . nothing gained." Wasn't that how it went? For all that Andre Delery had denied none of her accusations, Ginny had the annoying feeling that he had bested her. Especially by remaining a gentleman to the end. But all the same, she'd had to *try* to do something—perhaps as much for her own sake as for Sonya's or the Senator's. To stay in her room, pacing its confines in frustration, had seemed unthinkable. And on the other hand, there had been the thought of Steve's reactions if *she'd* succeeded in preventing the duel.

"I shouldn't waste my time thinking of his reactions," Ginny thought dully. "It's really over between us. Finally."

A sudden pang shot through her, bringing unwanted tears to her eyes, even while she told herself fiercely that she was only weeping for the wasted time. Why hadn't she realized that two people as different and as stubborn as she and Steve could never live together the kind of life that other, normal married people led? The only real bond between them was of the flesh—there was no understanding, no real closeness borne of trust and a feeling of companionship. "Ah!" she thought now, "why do I bother to go over and over it? This time I am really going to make a new and different life for myself, on my own accord. I don't care—I *won't* care what he does any longer, as long as he doesn't interfere."

Had she really been surprised when none other than the ubiquitous Mr. Bishop himself "just happened" to be riding past in a rather shabby hired buggy as she emerged into the sunshine of the street after her wasted visit to Andre Delery?

"It's really not very safe for a young woman—an attractive married woman—to be walking by herself on the streets of New Orleans," he'd said severely. "No, really, madam, I do insist on offering you a ride to wherever you are going. And I must also insist that you do not interfere . . . please rest assured that the duel between your father and M. Delery will not be fought—I still have some small influence in certain quarters. And now, about arranging for your return to Mexico . . ."

Hardly giving her an opportunity to protest, his dry, coldly unemotional voice had gone on and on, demolishing all her arguments with reason and logic. Didn't she want to rejoin her children before they forgot her? Was she aware of the fact that Don Francisco had had to make an urgent journey to Cuba and that Renaldo had been just as hurriedly recalled to oversee the running of the hacienda? His new bride was very young and would be lonely without the companionship of another woman closer to her own age.

In the end, Ginny had subsided into stubborn silence, thinking her own thoughts behind a mask of cool indifference. No, she wouldn't give him the satisfaction of asking him how Steve fit into his schemes, whatever they were this time. Steve was of no concern to her any longer—hadn't he made that much very clear?

# Chapter Eleven

❧

In spite of gossip, in spite of scandal, one must hold one's head high and outface it as if nothing at all had happened. That was the only way to act; so that even if there were the inevitable whispers no one could be really *sure*. One must smile and chatter inconsequentially to one's friends and not cancel a single engagement. . . . Everything, in fact, must seem quite *normal*, even if it was not.

Ginny found herself astounded by Sonya as the long evening wore on. She hadn't expected to find Sonya up and about when she had returned from town in a mood for nothing more than the comfort of her bed and a cold compress for her head. And yet, here she was seated with Sonya and the Senator at the opera again —feeling the focus of all eyes on their box. How could Sonya bear it? For all that she wasn't overly fond of her stepmother of late, Ginny could not help admiring the other woman's fortitude and courage tonight as she nodded, smiling at friends; and in between talked animatedly with her husband as if nothing was wrong or ever had been between them.

"Why must we all act the hypocrites when everybody must know by now exactly what happened?" Ginny had stormed when she had been told that their plans for the evening would *not* be canceled—they would go to the opera and attend a ball afterwards, just as usual. "What good will putting on a . . . a facade do when underneath it everything is crumbling?" And she had been talking of herself and Steve as well; she really didn't feel up to facing him again, not until she had had time in which to rearm herself.

Surprising her, however, Senator Brandon had cut across her vehement protests, his voice unusually hard and stern: "For once, Virginia, you will please do exactly as I say, even if you do not understand why. There is a certain unwritten code of conduct among us Southerners—call it a form of etiquette if you will. But we do not air our dirty linen in public. No matter how we may really feel toward one another." And here his eyes had flicked over Sonya's taut, white face like a blade of steel, bringing bright color in its wake before he continued: "There is no need for anyone else to know it. We will present a united front to the rest of the world—is that clear?"

"Does Steve know this?" Ginny had cried out rebelliously. "He's not the type of man to conform to any code of conduct—he always does exactly as *he* pleases anyway! I'm sure he will have conveniently forgotten that we were to go out tonight."

"Your husband will be there," the Senator said shortly. "And no matter what quarrels you two are engaged in I trust that you will behave with decorum and dignity."

Dignity indeed, Ginny thought furiously now, feeling her back stiffen. And where was Steve while she sat here alone—the very picture of a neglected wife? No, she wouldn't put up with it another moment longer—even if her father *was* to fight a duel tonight, she wasn't going to sit here pretending to a crowd of people she hardly knew that anything was amiss. She would leave at intermission.

As soon as the house lights came up, Ginny, in fact, rose to go when suddenly the door to their box opened, freezing her in place. Recognizing Steve, her eyes began to glitter dangerously. Decorum and dignity indeed! If he did not have the decency to display any, why should she? And since *he* had been the one to insist that there would be no divorce she would damn well persuade him otherwise, by being as nasty and as obnoxious as she could—let him swallow *that* for a change!

Her father and Sonya had turned around. Steve, standing back to hold the door open, was making his casual, polite apologies.

"I'm sorry that I was delayed, but a carriage had overturned a few blocks away and we had to take a more circuitous route to get here. May I introduce the Señora Dos Santos and her father-in-law, Don Ignacio Dos Santos? They're from Cuba, although the señora and I have known each other almost from childhood. . . ."

For a few moments, as Steve made the formal introductions,

Ginny could feel a whirling sensation in her mind as jumbled, incoherent thoughts fought one another to escape, leaving her literally speechless. Somehow, quite by instinct, she must have acknowledged the pair—a rather smug, sweetly smiling Dona Ana and the tall, spare man who was her father-in-law. She must have smiled through lips that had suddenly gone cold and stiff, while Steve was politely rearranging chairs—somehow managing to make sure that he sat between Ginny and Ana, while Don Ignacio moved to the front of the box to sit on the other side of Sonya. And now he had with his usual devilish cunning ensured that she couldn't make a scene without being made to appear stupid and rather pitiful—the wronged wife! No, Ginny found herself thinking vengefully, she wouldn't give him *that* satisfaction; she'd show him instead that she could play a role and act the hypocrite just as well as he could. And somehow, she would contrive to get even with him—then let them see which one of them looked more of a fool!

To that end, Ginny leaned across Steve with a falsely brilliant smile while she engaged a somewhat surprised and wary Ana in conversation, very much aware of the tautness of Steve's arm under hers.

"I am really sorry that we have not had enough time to converse about old times. It's really remiss of Steve not to have brought you along before to some of the very boring affairs we've had to attend since we've been here. But do tell me how you've fared since we last met? Your husband . . ."

Dona Ana pursed her full lips, looking down at her lap as she said in a soft voice, "I . . . unfortunately, señora, my husband passed away very tragically, less than a year after we had been married. I am a widow." She sighed tragically, looking at Steve as she went on softly: "I had to come away—so many memories! The plantation is very large, you know, and takes very many men to run it, but my father-in-law, such a kind man—insisted that his overseer could manage it, with the help of a cousin. And so, we came here. New Orleans has always been one of my favorite cities. I remember visiting here once as a very young girl, and my husband brought me here on our honeymoon. . . ."

What a good little actress she'd turned out to be, Ginny

thought viciously as the younger woman let her words trickle out into silence. And as if on cue Steve said shortly:

"Why don't we change the subject? Ana came here to get away from unhappiness."

Traitor—traitor! Ginny wanted to rake her nails across the side of his face; instead she leaned back in her chair with a shrug that she hoped showed bored indifference.

"Oh, of course. Let's see—why don't *you* pick the topic this time, dearest? That is, if we must converse to show all those curious people who have their opera glasses turned on us how enchanted we are with one another's company."

There was a little indrawn breath from Ana that sounded like a hiss, and the girl seemed to lean closer to Steve, who turned his head with a smile that was belied by the hard, warning look in his narrowed blue eyes.

"You always were a consummate little actress, my love—you can do better, can't you?" And then, through his teeth he added in a much lower voice with a cutting edge to it, "Better, I hope, than being foolish enough to visit your latest lover's apartment by daylight, for all the world to see! I thought I'd warned you to be discreet?"

It was fortunate, Ginny thought through the red mist of rage that filled her mind, blinding her eyes, that the lights were dimmed at that moment to signal that the second act was about to commence. For her smiling mask dropped as she swung her head around to confront him with blazing, contemptuous eyes.

"*Warned* did you say? Warnings are for those who fear them, *Mr.* Morgan!" Flinging the formal "Mr." at him as if it was a weapon she added in the same low, breathless voice, "And as for *discretion,* let me inform you that I intend to see my lovers as openly and as often as you do—shall we have this clear between us?"

She could almost *feel* the blue fury of his eyes; as physically as she sensed the flare of his nostrils, the hard, angry slant of his lips and the tension in him that was like that of a big cat about to spring. Oh, God, how well she knew him! Too well, it seemed sometimes.

"What is most clear, madam, is that, as usual, you overstep your bounds! I will not have my wife behaving like a slut, do you understand me? This evening we'll play out our roles for the benefit of New Orleans society—and tomorrow you pack for Mexico. If you continue to neglect your children, my dear, I shall have to take them from you, as an unfit mother!"

She heard his carefully measured, icily cold words drop into the sudden blank space in her mind—and could not believe what she was hearing. This could not be Steve, whom she had loved harder than she hated, for whose sake she had suffered so much. No matter how they had fought, no matter what they had done to each other, *this* was something she didn't deserve, as monstrously unfair as his cold threat had been.

She felt herself breathe faster—so hard that her chest was almost bursting, and she felt as if she were drowning in frigid water. To have him say what he had—and worse, to have it said in Ana's presence, making it scornfully clear that he was packing his recalcitrant wife out of the way so that *he* could be free. Intolerable!

She must have made some choked sound, for suddenly his fingers clamped over her wrist so painfully that she almost moaned with pain—would have, if that pain hadn't been dulled by the agony swirling inside her.

"No scenes, if you please! Or has your survival instinct failed you? Damn it, Ginny, it's high time you grew up! After all, you yearned for motherhood; why don't you be one for a change?"

"Let me go, Steve. Do you enjoy using force on me? And no—I won't make any scenes. It . . . it seems as if we have already said all there is to be said between us, doesn't it?"

Even she could hardly believe it was her own voice she heard, coming to her over a vast, empty space. A sound as small and without feeling as the rustle of dry straw, followed by silence that went on and on inside her in spite of the music and the singing that filled the theater. And after a while he released her and she leaned back in her chair, feeling him lean back in his—with his attention turned once again on Ana, who was whispering to him while her hand rested possessively on his arm.

"No—I won't make a scene. He isn't worth it and I won't give him the satisfaction of vanquishing me again. It's finished between us, and it's much better to say nothing. What does it matter anyway? What does anything matter?" Once, long ago, those same words had scarred her consciousness from being repeated over and over again—a litany of hopelessness as she trudged bare-legged and bare-footed behind a wagon. Long ago . . . and how she had changed, how everything had changed. Except . . . that it really didn't matter, this time it would pass and go away. Every-thing—feeling, and even pain.

"You are very stern with your wife," Ana murmured with a sidewise look at the man beside her. "Is that the sort of treatment that I escaped? I think you frighten me—a little!"

She caught the white flash of his reckless smile as he looked down at her, and her talk of being afraid was only half a lie.

"What you escaped, *pequeña*, would have depended on how you behaved. What do *you* think?"

She caught her breath at that, wondering why this man excited her so, making her long to be even closer to him than she was now—oh, much closer! Feeling the heat that spread throughout her body, centering and melting in her loins when he touched her.

"I think . . . I think that neither of us was ready then. I was very spoiled, wasn't I? And I had no idea what marriage really meant. There was much I did not know."

"And now you think you do?" he teased her, and caught the sheen of her lips as she wet them nervously with her tongue.

She said demurely, "Oh—now I am still learning! I find it . . . very interesting, with the right teacher."

Dona Ana had had more than her share of "teachers" since her short-lived marriage—one of them being her own father-in-law, who fortunately was not a jealous man, although a generous one. But naturally she had no intention of letting Esteban know that. Nor had she let him know that she had schemed to run into him after learning quite by chance that her former *novio* was actually here in New Orleans. In fact, she had persuaded Don Ignacio to postpone their return to Cuba indefinitely, planning to ac-complish exactly what she had managed to do—the catching of Esteban's interest. The fact that Esteban had a wife did not sig-nify in the least, although Ana could not help a feeling of spiteful triumph at scoring over the same woman who had once treated her so contemptuously and had, in fact, married him under Ana's very nose. No—she'd never forgiven the woman for that, and she was enjoying her revenge and would continue to enjoy it after his wife was out of the way. Because she had made him interested enough in her to talk of coming to Cuba with her. Ana thought she would like that very much!

If only it could all be over quickly! Over the storm of music roaring in her ears, Ginny was too much aware of *them*—Steve and that bitch Ana with their heads close together, shoulders touching as they whispered, leaving her alone in icy isolation. Not that it mattered, except that all she wanted was to be somewhere else. All her earlier passion and fury had evaporated, leaving her empty of all feeling.

Let Steve have Ana—let Ana have him for as long as she could keep him! And oh, God, let this evening end soon!

She did very well during the final intermission, leaning forward to engage the hawk-faced Don Ignacio in conversation and presenting him with just enough view of her breasts in the deep décolletage of her gown to hold his attention. He left the box with the Senator to fetch the ladies some refreshment—iced champagne of all things, in crystal, thin-stemmed glasses that seemed too fragile to hold; and somehow he contrived to shift his position so that now he was seated on the other side of Ginny.

Oh, but she was so good at flirting! It gave her the perfect opportunity, besides, to turn her back on Steve, pretending he did not exist. And Ginny, fortified by champagne and in a hell-bent mood, was all sparkle and glitter on the surface, as Don Ignacio was discovering happily.

"Champagne in crystal—how did you contrive it, señor? I love champagne, even if it does make me a little silly!"

"You are far from being a silly woman, señora. In fact, you are easily the most intelligent young woman I have encountered. Quite a dangerous combination, taken with your beauty, if you'll allow an old man the liberty of saying so."

"And you are by no means an old man, Don Ignacio—but then I'm sure many women have told you so! I have always been more at ease in the company of gentlemen who are *mature*."

Don Ignacio, who had imagined Steve Morgan's wife to be a typical American female, self-assertive and lacking in conversation, was more than pleasantly surprised, even while he could not help wondering why this woman's husband should choose to ignore her for little Ana, who while being pretty was not remarkable. Even if they had once been affianced, why should the man who was known as Esteban Alvarado in Mexico pay such open court to Ana—right under his wife's nose? Unless he was punishing her for some misdemeanor—paying her back in her own coin perhaps?

None of these thoughts showed in Don Ignacio's hooded dark eyes or his lean, rather craggy face. He was a shrewd man, a builder of a sugar empire he meant to keep intact at all costs, and he was used to getting his own way. If he made up his mind to have the obviously unhappy Mrs. Morgan, he was sure that he would. As for Ana . . .

Here he could not help an impatient inward sigh. Ana he had picked himself as the right wife for his younger son Alonso, a reckless young daredevil of a boy. She had been a virgin, eminently suitable, and an excellent rider to boot—Alonso had insisted on that accomplishment in a wife. But alas, Alonso's recklessness had not been tempered by his becoming a husband, and he had been killed in a riding accident, leaving the pretty Ana a widow, in need of comfort.

Don Ignacio had mourned his son's death—he had been fond of the boy who had been his mother's favorite. But he had two older sons who were fortunately still alive to carry on the family name and heritage, and Alonso had always proven himself wild and undisciplined. God gave, and God took away. Life was harsh sometimes, but one had to go on living.

To that end, Don Ignacio had comforted the weeping girl-bride who had proved unexpectedly passionate and responsive in bed. He had no feelings of guilt about this—she had met him halfway, after all, and he was responsible for her now. When he became bored, he allowed her to take other lovers, all of whom he picked for her, without her suspecting that he did. And he had brought her to New Orleans on this business trip to find her a husband. Now he wondered if perhaps he had, after all? Divorce was not entirely unheard of; and after all Ana had been Don Francisco Alvarado's choice of a bride for his grandson and heir. It just might be possible . . .

After she had drained her second glass of champagne and Don Ignacio had assiduously poured her a third, Ginny decided that after all she might as well enjoy the evening since she was supposed to pretend to do so. She had also decided that she detested and despised Steve and rather liked Don Ignacio, who obviously appreciated *her*.

The fact that Ana's father-in-law appeared to be quite taken with his wife had not escaped Steve Morgan's notice either, and he wondered angrily why the sight of Ginny, flirting openly with another man, could still tempt him to violence. Was there nothing, no threat he could make short of keeping her locked up, that could subdue her reckless defiance? Ginny continued to frustrate him and irritate him, just as she had from the very first time she had entered his life—did he continually have to swallow that bitter pill?

There was an instant, when they all rose to leave the theater and his fingers brushed Ginny's cold shoulders as he politely helped her on with her wrap, where Steve wanted to hold her, feeling the silky softness of her flesh under his hands for just once more. But that was weakness—damn it, Ginny *was* his weakness, blinding him to logic and the old, cold pragmatism that was all that had ruled him before. He felt her flinch away from him and turned to Ana, offering her his arm. The hell with Ginny, she needed to be taught a lesson! This time, he wasn't going to soften.

They were, all six of them, part of a glittering crowd that poured from the Opera House, pausing outside to look for familiar carriages among those that thronged the street.

Senator Brandon glanced at his gold watch before tucking it back into his vest pocket—a habitual gesture that would have passed unnoticed except for its significance on this particular occasion. Sonya's face whitened, and Ginny shivered slightly in spite of her heavy silk shawl, causing Don Ignacio to murmur solicitously in her ear, "Are you cold? There is a fur robe in my carriage. . . ." She replied mechanically—words she could not afterward recall. How to explain to the nice, concerned man that the coldness that made her shiver came not from the light breeze outside but from deep inside herself? It must be close to midnight—the Senator was looking impatient, his face set and stern; the lamplight bringing out the deeply scored lines that betrayed his age. Was he afraid? What had Mr. Bishop meant by saying that the duel would not be fought?

"Look, there's our carriage!" Ana said suddenly, and then, with an arch upward look at Steve, "Will we all be dining together?"

As they started down the steps, Ginny's shawl slipped from her shoulders, and Don Ignacio bent gallantly to retrieve it. She supposed numbly afterward that that must have been what saved his life, but during that instant all she was aware of was a sudden flash of light and a cracking explosion; a riffle of wind past her cheek.

Someone screamed, breaking the split-second hush that froze them all—and it seemed as if the sound released total pandemonium and more sounds that re-echoed and reverberated. Horses neighed and whinnied, panicking as swearing, perspiring men fought to hold them back from trampling the equally panic-stricken crowd that began to scatter wildly in all directions, milling down the steps from the Opera House into the street, those on the street rushing for alleys and doorways. There were more screams and yells.

"It's a riot!"

"They're shooting at us!"

"Goddamn those reconstructionists anyhow!"

Standing frozen, still not quite comprehending what had happened, Ginny felt a violent push send her to her knees as Steve's angry voice grated from above her: "Christ, don't you have any sense? Want to get yourself shot too?"

Shot? What had he meant? Who had been shot? She felt a protective arm go about her shoulders and pressed her hands against her ears to keep out the sounds of screaming that wouldn't stop, going on and on until she wanted to scream too.

"No! No, no no, no-o-o-o!" Why was Sonya hysterical again?

Ginny attempted to struggle back onto her feet in spite of the crowd that seemed to press even more closely about them, but Don Ignacio, still kneeling at her side, held her firmly, although she could feel his arm tremble.

"No, señora, please don't look!" In his agitation, he spoke Spanish. "*Dios*—it was meant for me, I think! Had I not stooped just then . . ."

"Who . . . ?" She almost screamed it at him, fighting against his restraining arm, but it was some stranger in the crowd who answered her.

"Dear God, it's Senator Brandon, he's been assassinated!"

# Chapter Twelve

❧

Afterwards, although she continued to function like an automaton, Ginny continued to feel thankfully numb, like a walking statue. It was almost like those blurred, unhappy days when she had been married to Ivan and was the Princess Sahrkanov, shielded from life's unpleasantness by a cocoon of opium. Indeed, with a feeling of defiance she had obediently taken the sleeping draught the Doctor had given her, knowing it contained laudanum to give her pleasant dreams. Just once wouldn't hurt her— there was too much she didn't want to think about.

She had heard Dr. Maddox say that her father was not dead but critically wounded and in need of full-time nursing; that even if he recovered there was the grim possibility to be faced that he might never walk again. She had seen to it that her stepmother, driven almost mindless by shock and remorse, was sent to bed with a stiff dose of the good Doctor's elixir to put her to sleep. And she had listened to Don Ignacio's shaken explanations—he was a man with many enemies in Cuba because of his pro-revolutionary sympathies . . . how strange to think of the distinguished-looking older man as a revolutionary!

"You must understand—I own several very large sugar plantations, and they are widely scattered. Two of them are managed by my sons and are in provinces held by the rebels. So, naturally . . ." His expressive gesture, palms upward, had made further explanation unnecessary. Don Ignacio was obviously a practical man who would adopt whatever politics were expedient. Just as obviously there were those who would prefer him out of the way as a warning to others like him. Señor Dos Santos was sure the assassin's bullet had been meant for him. "It wouldn't be the first time; they tried once or twice in Cuba, and that was partly the reason that I am here in New Orleans instead of in Florida where there is actual fighting going on between the two factions. If not for your shawl . . . ah, but I am sorry your father stood just behind, for the world I would not have endangered anyone else—"

"You could not have known, of course. My father will recover, I'm sure of it. He's a strong, healthy man, didn't you hear the Doctor say so?"

Oh, she made all the right moves, gave all the right answers—except to Steve, who had mercifully deposited his precious little Ana somewhere and came striding to find her; almost snatching her from Sonya's bedside.

"I want to talk to you, Ginny." His voice sounded uncompromisingly harsh, and she couldn't see his eyes nor quite make out the expression on his face in the dimness of the hall. She didn't really think she wanted to look him in the face again.

"I have nothing more to say to you. You made it clear how things stand between us." Making an attempt to wrest her arm from his grasp she felt his fingers tighten, holding her there before him as if she were a criminal caught in the act of escaping.

She could tell what an effort it cost him to keep his voice controlled and pitched lower—noticing, as he must have done also, the streak of light spilling like a sword's point from Sonya's partly opened door. The sword was between them now she thought, lifting her head mutinously.

"Ginny . . ." And then, between his teeth, "Goddamn it! You might have been the one!"

"Do you wish I had been? That would have been convenient, wouldn't it?"

He dropped her arm then, and she saw his black, angry frown.

"No. It would most decidedly have been damned inconvenient if you'd been shot, because I'd have had to postpone my visit to Cuba. And for the same reason I don't want to have you exposed to any more danger—the Señor Dos Santos, whose attention you seemed to enjoy so much, is a dangerous man to be close to, my dear."

She was glad she'd forced him to drop his mask of false concern! End it, her tired mind jeered at her. End it quickly before his mood changes again and he snatches you into his arms.

"So were you, Steve, for as long as I've known you—which isn't really very long, is it? And if that's all you had to say to me, consider your point taken. I shall certainly be packed and ready to leave New Orleans as soon as I possibly can—even *you* must admit I can hardly do so at once, as much as I'd like to? As soon as I learn of my father's condition—"

"Stay with your father then—and out of mischief, if you can manage that much! I'll make arrangements for your departure to Mexico, and for an escort. *A demain. . . .*"

Turning on his heel with that blunt "till tomorrow," he had actually started to leave her—no doubt eager to join the waiting Ana. And later, Ginny was to tell herself that it was only incipient hysteria that made her clutch at his arm, her voice as sharp as her digging nails.

"What do you mean? Arrangements. I won't be arranged for, do you understand? I can make my own arrangements, thank you! You bastard—for all I know *you* might have . . ."

And now she was sorry, but it was too late. Even in the dim yellow light she could see the furious sheen of his night-blue eyes as he swiveled round to face her, the sudden grip of his fingers on her arms almost paralyzing her.

"I might have *what?* What the hell are you implying? Once and for all, Ginny, you need teaching a lesson. Several, in fact! But before that you're going to explain yourself. . . ."

From behind the half opened door Sonya moaned—her moan rising into a high-pitched scream of guilt and self-pity.

"I didn't mean for it to happen! How was I to know that he would want to kill him? Oh, God—Oh, God!!"

The soft murmur of comforting voices smothered that pitiful cry, and the door slammed shut, leaving them in darkness. Blindly, angrily, Ginny snatched her arm away and made for her own room. Hopefully, *he* would have the decency to leave her alone tonight. No doubt he was anxious to return to his waiting Ana!

But when she fumbled humiliatingly with the doorknob in the dark, it was *he* who reached over her shoulder, trapping her between his body and the door, to open it. And as she almost fell inside the room it was he who caught her up to prevent her from falling; kicking the door shut behind them both.

"For God's sake—*leave* me now! There's no need to overplay your part—the Doctor and the nurses are impressed, I'm sure, by your concern and your devotion—as they were before in Monterey. Don't you remember, Steve? . . . You were out to be revenged upon me then as you are now. . . ."

She lost her breath as he spun her around to face him with her wrists imprisoned behind her back.

"And you, you hypocritical little bitch! What is *your* revenge? *This?*" She felt the bodice of her gown tear, freeing her breasts, and in spite of her struggles felt his lips tug at her peaking nipples.

"Stop it, Steve! If anybody's the hypocrite, *you* are! No—*don't!*"

"You *are* a hypocrite!" And then he growled in Spanish, *"Perdición*—perhaps I am too! But it's dark in here and I can't see the hate in your face. It's just like too many other times which *I* remember even if you don't since you've become a wife—and not just the willing, passionate mistress I remember too well."

Each one of his words was like a dart thrown at her most sensitive places, making her gasp with a mixture of pain and rage. But he was right, she was a hypocrite, for even while her mind and her words railed at him her body was already surrendering; not just giving in but actively aggressive as her hips began to move against his—softness inviting hardness—and her mouth opened eagerly under the fierce kisses he attacked her with.

There was no light in her room with the shutters and the drapes drawn. What happened there between them was an act meant for darkness and a shrouding, later, from remembrance. But like the door to a cage springing open to let a tiger escape, everything that had been held back or hidden between them erupted into an explosion of violence and of passion.

They were like animals as they tore at each other's clothes—and at each other's flesh. He pulled her down onto the carpeted floor. The thin wire of physicality that drew them to each other strummed and grew taut and held as they passed hours without knowing minutes.

She moved her body to lie opposite his, her thighs open to him. Ginny forgot her arguments as she let herself reciprocate; his hardness and strength filling her and stifling all words, all protests, all thoughts.

Their bodies, at least, had declared a truce, even if there were words between them that could never be unsaid and questions that would never be asked or answered.

From the thick rug that carpeted the floor he carried her to the bed; and presently they slipped from the bed and back onto the floor. It was a battle in which neither was the victor, neither the loser, but a battle nonetheless. He made her do everything—anything—and want to do it; and so she triumphed over him and with him, finally lying inert and almost insensible in the hard embrace of his arms and his legs holding her captive.

And all the love words and all the obscenities he had whispered to her had been in Spanish—as hers had been to him. It had been like falling backward or escaping into wish-fulfillment dreams. Wasn't wanting the same as loving? Was it? It didn't matter, as long as there was something there—but those were only half-asleep, half-aware thoughts that came from feeling and not from rationality.

When she woke, with her bed all damp and rumpled, covers trailing onto the floor, he was gone. To Ana, no doubt, as she should have expected, should have *known*. He had used her and abused her and she had let him, but for both of them it had been a kind of farewell.

"It meant nothing . . . nothing. . . ." The words sounded hollow in her mind and by concentrating Ginny found that she was able to push everything out of her mind by pretending it hadn't happened. It helped that Steve seemed to make a point of staying out of her way in the days that followed while she, for her part, make a point of locking her door. If he had *really* wanted her, he would have broken it down; but as it was he did nothing—nothing at all; and neither did she.

Her mood of detached isolation carried Ginny through the next few days as if she had been walking in her sleep. Sometimes she felt as if she was, indeed. The Senator lay in a state of drug-induced unconsciousness, Dr. Maddox having stated solemnly that any sharp movements of his body or attempts to rise out of bed might fatally move the position of a bullet that was lodged against his spine. It was Ginny who spent most of her time in his room, still hardly able to believe that the waxy-faced, *old* man who lay so still under the white linen covers was the same vital, handsome man who'd had the ladies simpering when he smiled in their direction. There were also two nursing sisters that the Doctor had recommended be brought in, and Ginny was thankful for his suggestion, which allowed her to sleep at night. As for Sonya, she too needed nursing, for a mixture of shock and guilt had almost deranged her. If she wasn't weeping hysterically and screaming out loud that she wanted to be allowed to die, she seemed to slip backward in time, acting during such periods as if her husband was still alive.

"My dear—we are sorry. So sorry! If there is anything we can do . . ." Ginny became used to dealing with the stream of sympathetic callers—mostly old friends of Sonya's. As for Sonya's condition, she would parry their sometimes curious inquiries with the answer that Sonya was being kept sedated; she was extremely upset and the Doctor had forbidden her any visitors. The only one of Sonya's friends who did see her was Adeline Pruett, who marched in and up to Sonya's room without bothering to have herself announced. But even that formidable grande dame was taken aback to discover the true state of her friend's mind.

She had begun, bracingly, with: "And what's this nonsense? Why are you hiding away? Sonya Beaudine, you ought to know better than to think that *this* kind of behavior is going to stop the tongues from wagging! Where's your backbone, my girl?"

The good sister who was on watch in her chair by the window obviously did not know what to do—whether to stay and guard her charge or leave the room to summon a member of the family. While the nun fumbled nervously with her beads, her mouth open, Sonya sat bolt upright in bed, looking very much a girl again with her hair hanging loose over her shoulders and her blue eyes wide with apprehension.

"Oh, Adeline, is it you? Oh, I'm undone—do you think they all know? How *could* he have . . . even if he *is* a Yankee, he should know better than to flaunt his affair with a quadroon bitch! And to think that I . . . that I let myself—"

Madame Pruett, who prided herself on being unshockable, actually gasped.

"Sonya—"

"Do you think they'll shoot him after all? He deserves it! Doesn't he, Adeline? Oh, God, I must have been mad, quite mad to jeopardize everything for a man like that, knowing what he is

like! An animal—nothing but a crude savage of a man like the Indian savages he lived with . . . oh, *please* tell me no one else
knows, I couldn't *bear* it if they suspected."

Gathering her wits about her, Adeline Pruett walked quickly up
to the bed to grasp her friend's hands, while at the same time trying to signal to that silly-looking nun to go and fetch someone—
the Doctor or Sonya's own maid.

"Now, now love, there's nothing to worry about on *that* score,
you know I'm the only one who knows and you can be certain I'll
be the last person to open my mouth on the subject!" In an aside
over her shoulder she said to Sister Therese, "Go and fetch Tillie
—the girl will know what to do! And hurry!"

Accustomed to blind obedience to a voice that reminded her of
her own Mother Superior, the black-robed nun scurried from the
room. She supposed it was all right—the two ladies seemed to
know each other very well, and from the look of her dress and
jewels, the older woman was obviously well-to-do.

Leaving the door half open in her confusion the poor sister almost ran down the corridor, only to cannon blindly into the tall
man who emerged from the Senator's room, obviously in a hurry
himself.

Steve Morgan swore unthinkingly before he realized who he
had bumped into, and then offered only a perfunctory apology;
he was in a devil of a temper anyhow—his rage directed, as usual,
toward Ginny, who had been successfully avoiding any conversation with him for the past three days. *This* time, he had decided, they were going to have it out. Damn her, what kind of
game did she think she was playing this time? And where was she?

That was the question he snapped at the scared-rabbit of a
sister who was looking at him in a terrified fashion, with her coif
all askew and her mouth hanging open.

"Where the . . . I beg your pardon sister, but where's my
wife?"

The sister, forgetting all her carefully learned English, began to
stutter in French: "Madame Brandon . . . her friend asked me
to—"

"Will you please inform my wife that I wish to see her at
once? And if she's in hiding you may also tell her that it is my intention to find her!"

His face as black as thunder he strode past the confused woman and into Sonya's room, only to be greeted by a shriek from Sonya herself.

"*You!* Oh, you monster—how dare you show yourself here in *my* bedroom after you've been with . . . with that trash? What are you doing here? How could you escape?"

It was all Mrs. Pruett could do not to throw her hands up in despair. Of all the people who could have showed up at this particular moment, while her poor friend was obviously reliving the past! For almost the first time in her life she was at a complete loss as to what to do next.

"What in hell are you talking about?" Steve kicked the door shut behind him unceremoniously and stood glaring coldly down at the distraught Sonya, whose eyes seemed to become wider and wider as they searched his face. Tears began to spill from them as she whimpered:

"How can you talk to me like that? I thought you loved me, and yet you went from my bed to *hers*. Did you have to seduce her too?"

He stood as if frozen, hardly hearing Mrs. Pruett interject testily: "It might be best if you left quickly. As you can see she's suffered a lapse in her memory and imagines it is still—that time during the war when you . . ."

"Good God!" But this time he said it more quietly, still staring down at Sonya—a Sonya he hadn't really remembered nor thought about since a faraway time. He'd become used to thinking of her as Brandon's wife—Ginny's stepmother . . . now suddenly she was looking at him with the same china-blue eyes that held a mixture of terror and longing—and the Pruett woman was taking it all in!

But Sonya seemed to have forgotten that there was anyone else present. Sonya was still weeping, her eyes red; she could hardly believe he was here, coming boldly into her room in broad daylight when he was still under arrest—did he expect her to shelter him? What *did* he want of her? An unwanted shiver shook her body as she looked at him—the tall, hard length of his body that she now knew so intimately, the deep blue of his eyes that were narrowed at her now, the slight, familiar flare of his nostrils. Oh, God, she thought despairingly, why does he have this power over me? Why do I want him so?

Her half-screamed tirade suddenly died away in her throat when he muttered harshly: "Now look, Sonya—*listen* to me, will you? There's something I have to—"

But she didn't want to listen to any more of his lies. No, they didn't matter, all that mattered was that he was here and he wanted her—hadn't he always told her that? "I want you, Sonya-sweet. Isn't that enough for you?" It had to be enough, if that was all she could expect of him. William had gone away and *he* was here, her half-savage lover; and hadn't Adeline advised her wisely to take her fun and her pleasure while she could?

Sonya had, as a matter of fact, forgotten Adeline Pruett's presence entirely, as all her attention, her frustration, her rage and her need became focused upon *him*—Captain Steven Morgan, out of uniform and looking devastatingly and unfairly handsome in well-cut civilian clothes.

He was saying something to her, but she interrupted him, her voice husky with tears. "No—I don't want to hear any more! It doesn't matter, do you hear? Why do you keep standing there? You're not usually so hesitant. You were not so slow that day of the storm when you took me by force! What's stopping you now? Aren't I more beautiful than she is? My skin's whiter, look—"

"Christ, Sonya, stop it! And I'm not here to rape you. Will you listen to me for God's sake?"

Steve made the mistake of grabbing for her wrist as she made as if to tear her nightgown away from her breasts, and with a swiftness that surprised him she put both hands out to cling to him, swinging bare legs off her bed as if she meant to rise.

"Now, Sonya . . ." Adeline Pruett began firmly, ashamed of herself for having been too entertained to break in earlier. But another voice, younger, clearer, made all of them freeze in their places to form an odd tableau.

"Why should she believe you when it is one of your habits to rape helpless women? You cannot deny that, can you, Steve?"

Afterward, Steve was to reflect bitterly that Ginny could not have chosen a better—or a worse—moment to make her presence known. And he supposed that she had derived no small satisfaction from seeing the expressions on all their faces as they had turned their heads to face her slim, unrelenting figure, standing just inside the door.

Dark smudges against the paper-white of her face seemed to emphasize the frosted emerald brilliance of her eyes, their cat-slant even more apparent than usual. She didn't look at Steve but at Sonya, who stood clinging to him now, shaking her head and asking over and over as petulant as a child, "Who is *she*? Is she another one of your women?" And Ginny could even feel sorry for Sonya—poor, pitiful Sonya who'd had to carry *this* secret with her all these years.

No, Ginny decided, she didn't want to look at Steve, who hadn't said one word—who still never said a word to stop her when she went on conversationally, "He's really no damn good—and not at all worth yearning for, you know. And if you do—I'm not one of his women. I'm just . . . a visitor here. On my way back home."

And when she turned and left the room Steve said nothing and did nothing to hold her back, even then. Of them all, only he understood the manner of his wife's leavetaking and the message she meant him to have. And because there was nothing he could do or say at that moment without making both her and him look ridiculous, he let her go—knowing it could be forever and knowing too in that moment that she was still the one woman he wanted wholly for his own and perhaps would always yearn for.

# Part Two

# "THE SEARCH FOR LOVE . . ."

## Chapter Thirteen

❦

Without knowing why, or even really willing it, here she was—on a ship that sailed over a calm sea with only the slightest whisper of a breeze to cool her flushed face. Dancing rays of sunlight reflected off the translucent green-blue water that rushed by, breaking into tiny miniature suns within each foamy droplet that flew into the air. She leaned as far as she dared over the warm mahogany rail, enjoying the dampness of the salt spray on her face and hair; eyes closed as if in ecstasy. And what would it feel like indeed—to give herself to the sea, like some sacrificial virgin of old? She had read somewhere that drowning was an easy death—not as painful as drowning in one's tears. "But tears are not for me!" she thought fiercely, opening her eyes again and narrowing them against the brilliance of sea and sky. Not a pirate sail on the horizon this time; she was really free!

"I belong to myself—I shall always belong to myself!" she had said with pride, lifting her chin in the old way that Steve would have recognized and been wary of. But she hadn't been addressing Steve two days ago when she had gone down to the wharf to buy her passage to Vera Cruz.

"What a fortunate coincidence—running into you here," Andre Delery had drawled in his lazy, slightly sarcastic voice. In spite of the fact that she had hoped not to encounter anyone she knew, Ginny had not flinched.

"Yes, what a coincidence indeed. And are *you* traveling somewhere, M. Delery?"

He had given a slight shrug, looking down at her with his polished-mahogany eyes. "If fortune is with me we may be traveling together—or, do you think that would be stretching coincidence too far?" And then, without giving her a chance to reply he had smiled, taking her hand. "Come, can I persuade you to sit down to a cup of coffee with me? I can promise you that you'll be as safe in that café over there as you were in my apartment. Or are you afraid of gossip?"

She had retrieved her hand, but she had accepted his offer, thinking "why not, what difference will it make now?" Delery had been having dinner with friends when Senator Brandon had been shot, and in any case he didn't appear to be the type of man who would resort to shooting at an enemy from some dark alley.

The coffeehouse he had pointed out to her was clean, and they were shown to a table apart from the rest, somewhat to the rear of the room.

"Havana is full of coffeehouses," Delery said, apropos of *what?* Ginny wondered cautiously, although she put on a look of interest that did not fool him.

"Oh. Is that where you're going, to Cuba?"

"You are breaking my heart. You don't really care. And I was hoping to persuade you that you might enjoy visiting Havana. It can be quite an exciting city, especially if you haven't been there before, and after all, from here Cuba is on the way to everywhere. Don't you have Cuban friends?"

Ginny said, stirring her coffee carefully: "If you mean—oh, of course you do, you have a certain . . . waiting look in your eye! They're really friends of my husband. We don't always share the same friends."

"How very perceptive you are, and how wise as well. I have always wondered what it might be like to be married." Here he gave a slight shudder. "But not enough to try it. I do not enjoy bonds of any kind."

"You go from one subject to another very easily. What shall we talk of next?"

At that he actually laughed, throwing his head back in a fashion that made him seem almost boyish. "Do you know, I am quite enjoying this little tête-à-tête with you! I suppose you've been told this before, but you're really quite an unusual woman!"

"Thank you." She waited, and after a short pause he said casually:

"I had heard—one picks up all kinds of rumors around town, you know—that you were leaving soon for Mexico to rejoin your husband. That *is* where he has gone, is it not?"

Ginny sipped her café noir and considered her answer. "Did you really want to know where I am going or where my husband has gone? Perhaps, to save time, you might be more direct? It might amuse me to answer some of your questions if you will answer mine."

"Ah, but you drive a hard bargain! But very well—I had merely wondered why your husband would choose to escort a pretty young Cuban widow to Mexico leaving his beautiful wife behind to play nurse . . . is that direct enough?"

Having half expected he'd try to take her off guard, Ginny didn't change expression.

"Quite. But I'm sure you already know the answers. My husband had urgent family matters to attend to in Mexico, and Ana Dos Santos is going back to her parents whose hacienda adjoins that of my grandfather-in-law. And as for myself—both my father and my stepmother, thanks in part to you, need *someone* capable of managing matters until he is well enough to go back home. So . . ." She let her eyes meet his levelly. "And you—the duel with my father was all very carefully planned, was it not? Why did you want him out of the way? Or were you merely obliging someone else?"

"You're a clever woman—clever enough to be an adventuress!" He leaned back in his chair and smiled at her, his teeth white and even against his olive complexion. "Did you guess that it was really *you* I wanted all along? I had made up my mind to have you too—even if it meant abducting you."

"As a hostage?" Ginny said curiously and then she shrugged. "After you'd killed my father no doubt. . . . It's been done before—my being taken as a hostage I mean. The person who did it afterward regretted it very much."

She was proud of herself—there was not a tremor in her voice to give herself away, nor had she lowered her gaze from his.

Like a good swordsman, Delery continued to attack.

"Perhaps this person did not realize what a rare prize he had taken. You'd not find *me* so lacking in perception. No, I do not believe I would regret taking you. I find you . . . quite fascinating! And what do you think of me?"

"That you are far too sure of yourself for one thing. But, does it matter?"

"It might. I think we'd deal together far better as friends than as adversaries, don't you agree?" And then, quite urgently as he leaned forward, lowering his voice, "Your passage was booked on the *Anna B.* to Matamoros. I believe you are supposed to sail, accompanied by several other persons, on Friday? So then why are you looking for a ship that will take you to Vera Cruz? Please—don't break my heart by telling me you're running away to a lover!"

"You followed me. Or you were listening." She didn't make it an accusation—just a bald statement of fact.

"I made it my business to find out as much as I could about you. I'm a very methodical man in some ways. And I have many friends here in New Orleans. There is always bribery, besides. Even Henry Warmoth is open about the corruption that is rife here!"

A feeling of unreality had been creeping over her as he kept talking. Now, when he captured her hand that lay listlessly on the table, Ginny noticed how strong his fingers were.

"What are you leading up to?" She hoped her voice sounded steadier than her nerves. His eyes seemed to darken as they studied her.

"Don't disappoint me by implying you haven't guessed! Couldn't you look upon it as an adventure? You look as if you've lost some of your fire and sparkle of late—wouldn't you like to have an adventure?"

She could hardly believe any of it, but her instincts told her he was quite serious, and her eyes widened.

"Don't be a coward! Haven't you ever wondered what it might be like to start a new life—or wanted to? To be a person you'd much rather be than yourself? Look there, through the doorway at that beauty with the tall masts. They're getting ready to unfurl her sails, do you see? She'll take you anywhere you want to go—they say her owner is an eccentric who hides in his cabin and never comes out except at night, to study the stars, but who cares for that? The *Amaryllis* will put in at Nassau and at Havana and Jamaica and she might even stop for a day or two in Vera Cruz before she sails across the Atlantic. I have reserved a passage for two persons aboard her. Come—haven't you ever had the urge to gamble? I wouldn't treat you badly. Let's try it for a week or two, and if you still want to get off at Vera Cruz, well—*c'est la vie!*"

He was quite mad! But all the same . . . Ginny moistened her lips.

"Had you really planned to—and if I tell you I am not at all in the mood to gamble or have an adventure? . . ."

Still holding her hand he lifted his shoulders expressively. "Ah—then what choice would I have? I'd rather have you willing than unwilling, but I'd intended to have you anyway, you see. I've made . . . er . . . certain arrangements—"

"I'd really rather not know about them!" Suddenly, she began to laugh, wondering whether it was from hysteria or a sense of suddenly breaking free. Free of everything—bonds and boundaries and responsibilities and memories. To be a new person, starting out fresh. Could it be possible, or was *she* quite mad too?

She had intended all along *not* to go escorted—like a prisoner being returned to her jail, she had thought rebelliously—to Mexico, although it had suited her to pretend meekly to go along with all the plans that had been made for her. What she *had* planned was to go to Vera Cruz by herself, and from there to the little hacienda, which was the only place she could think of as her home. And after that—she hadn't thought. Perhaps she would send for her children—surely Don Francisco at least would not deny her that right? One step at a time, she'd told herself—and now here she was, actually intending to take not a step but a leap into space!

"I have no clothes!"

"Oh, but I've already thought of that," he'd said agreeably. "I'm told I've very good taste, so please trust me."

That was when Ginny had reminded him that he must not think at any point that he had bought her, or that she belonged to him. And still agreeable, he'd made her a formal bow of acquiescence.

And that was how she had come to be here—feeling the warmth of the sunlight on her neck and shoulders and the cool salt spray against her face. A woman who was listed on the ship's manifest as Genevieve Remy ("You may call me Jenny," she'd told Andre solemnly) whose memories were all new and would start from two days ago. A very lovely woman, to judge from the admiring looks cast in her direction by the male passengers on board, all of whom envied the man they thought to be her husband.

For a pretended "husband" who was to be her companion for at least the next few weeks, Ginny had to admit grudgingly that she found Andre Delery's company not too unpleasant or constrictive. It was as if they had taken each other's measure at the beginning, so that neither of them now needed to waste time on the usual little games and coy subterfuges; and in this respect at least their relationship reminded Ginny of her liaison with a certain Colonel Miguel Lopez in Mexico. "The difference is," Ginny thought now, frowning into the sun as she turned away from the ship's rail, "that I was still too full of dreams and romantic notions then. And of course I couldn't know that I would have been much better off putting *all* of my past behind me. Perhaps I should have married Michel. . . ."

"How beautiful you look this morning, my love. But then, you're always lovely." His arm slipping around her waist, Andre Delery bent to kiss salt-damp lips, murmuring against them, "And you always taste delicious too—which reminds me, we have been invited to sit at the Captain's table tonight. Shall we do so and brave all the inevitable questions from curious ladies? Or do you think you'd rather have a headache instead?"

There was unmistakable arrogance in the way her head jerked back, soft lips hardening.

"I don't intend to run from anyone! And as for the questions . . ." Suddenly, her eyes began to glimmer with mischief. "I know—I shall pretend to speak only French or Russian. *You* can answer their questions."

She had intended to return to the cabin they shared in order to change—the sea spray had ruined her gown and damp strands of copper-gold hair clung to the nape of her neck and her temples. But Delery seemed perversely determined to keep her there with her back to the rail, while he seemed to study every detail of her appearance with close attention; bringing a slight flush to Ginny's cheeks. She said nothing, having learned much about self-control during the past two years, but she wouldn't drop her eyes either and after a while he said softly:

"How will I answer their questions? You must admit I don't know much about you—only what little I managed to dig up during a week or so. And I'm not usually curious about a woman once I've had her. You're one of the exceptional few."

"Well, I know hardly anything about you, if we don't count the obvious," Ginny said lightly, wondering why he suddenly made her feel ill at ease. "I was about to go in and change," she added carefully. "Was there anything else you wished to say?"

"Stay here with me for a while longer—the sun will dry you. Surely you're not the kind of woman to be frightened indoors by a little salt water? Besides, I want them all to think that we are two lovebirds on our honeymoon, completely wrapped up in each other. If we don't answer too many questions they might even think we're eloping and be tactful. What do you think?" Without changing his rather teasing tone Delery went on, "And do please continue to look at me—meltingly, if you can manage it. Think about the pleasure I promise to give you when we go back to our cabin together in a little while—and *don't*, I beg you, look toward the bridge, but become aware that you're being watched. Through glasses—I saw them flash in the sunlight a few moments ago."

She shrugged. "So the Captain—"

"The owner's cabin is up there too. It's from there that you're being . . . observed. Not that I blame him, of course, but I'm always curious about mysteries, aren't you?"

# Chapter Fourteen

❦

"Are you Spanish?" they asked her with surprise.

"No, my mother was French and my father American."

"You must have had a Spanish governess then—your Spanish is as perfect as that of any *peninsulare*."

"Well, I spent a great deal of time in Mexico. . . ."

"Ah, that accounts for it!"

Ginny had grown used to the questions, and her answers were always artful enough to disclose very little about herself or her background. At least she had made friends with some of the women on board, who had decided after scrutinizing her dress and her demeanor that Madame Delery was obviously both well-born and rich. And to keep her mind off other things Ginny made it a point to be friendly and to ask many interested questions about Cuba—and about Havana in particular, which pleased them.

"You will enjoy the leisurely life we lead in Havana! And don't think that we don't have our share of excitement either. There is the theater—everyone dresses, of course. And the masked balls and *tertulias* . . . will your husband be buying property there? You must tell him to speak to my husband, he'll give him advice."

"Just remember, my dear, that a lady never, ever walks on the streets in Havana. Always go about in your volante. If you want to go shopping you have only to have your footman—your *calasero*—pull up, and the shop assistants will bring their goods to your carriage for you to inspect."

Ginny found that some of her earlier mood of apathy was slipping away, and she was actually beginning to look forward to visiting Havana. As for the revolution these new friends were talking about, she wasn't in the least interested, why should she be? In any case, she understood that the fighting was mostly confined to the central and eastern sectors of the island, and that in Havana life went on as usual.

Revolution! She wrinkled up her nose at the thought. She had been mixed up in one revolution and that was quite enough for her. No—she wouldn't even think about it any longer; she had no past, and she didn't much care about the future as long as it was different. And as for Andre, he helped pass away the time, and he wasn't *too* demanding. Ginny had learned to parry his questions too, although that didn't stop him from being persistent.

"Your husband—are you sure he's in Mexico? I've heard he's a very rich man—do you think the little Dos Santos could persuade him to help the Cuban rebels?"

They were in Nassau, lying in the rented hotel room Delery had thoughtfully taken when he'd learned they were to be here for two days.

Lying on her side, with the sweat sheening her body, Ginny turned her head languidly, meeting his searching look through the screen of her lashes.

"Why are you so interested in the Cuban rebels? Is that why you're going there? And as for my husband, if I was interested in his plans I would be with him. Do stop trying to wheedle answers I don't have out of me, Andre."

He leaned over her, caressing her breast and shoulder almost absently. "What an enigma you are, to be sure! I have a feeling of . . . tremendous depths beneath those limpid green eyes of yours! What kind of a woman are you, really?"

"Didn't you say you enjoyed mysteries? I'd have bored you by now if you could read me easily."

"Perhaps." He bent his head and kissed her throat, his hand moving lower down, moving the thin cotton sheet with it. "Do you know," he whispered presently, "that I am not usually curious about any of the women I take? But you—you are like a winding mountain road. Always a fresh surprise around each bend. And the more I take you . . ."

As his lips took her and he felt her response, Andre Delery continued to be puzzled, and was annoyed at himself because he hadn't tired of her yet. He had never met a woman who could respond to him with such sensual abandon and yet keep a part of herself inviolate. He needed to teach her nothing about the art of lovemaking, and yet she had never cried out to him that she loved him or pretended any guilt because she was another man's wife nor jealousy and curiosity about his other loves. He was still amazed at the easiness with which she'd come with him—running away from everything and everyone with only the clothes she had on her back and a few jewels. He'd meant to abduct her, of course, but she had almost made it seem the other way around. Damn her for being some kind of witch!

He heard her soft moan and enjoyed the supple writhing of her body—and could not help his own grunt of pleasure as she twisted herself about and began to pleasure him in the same manner in which he possessed her. How had she learned so much? How many men had taught her? God, for all that he'd meant to use her, it seemed as if she in her way was also using him. It was a feeling that Andre Delery neither liked nor was familiar with. He told himself that he must be careful, or he might not find it as easy to leave her when the time came as he'd anticipated in the beginning. And then, forgetting all else, he concentrated only on the fiery contest between them. He would arouse her senses as they had never been aroused before; he would defeat her by making her dependent on him for this . . . and this . . . and *this!*

The afternoon was hot and the room close and rather stifling in spite of an open window that overlooked a grove of banana trees, growing so closely together that they seemed almost to be intertwined. When it was over and they lay spent beside each other they were both panting—the sheets dripping wet from the perspiration that had run off their bodies.

Ginny longed for some cool water to sponge herself with and for air, thinking with longing of cool ocean breezes and mountain streams. But she had not the energy left to stir, and her companion, as if he was able to sense some of her thoughts, had one hand wrapped in a thick coil of her hair. She lay with her eyes closed, and after her breathing had slowed somewhat she found herself listening to Andre's deep, even breathing—a sure sign that he was falling asleep. She herself drifted somewhere in limbo—half in and half out of sleep, on the fringe of dreaming.

Another hot room—a hotel room in San Antonio where a girl called Ginny Brandon was waking up with sunlight spilling onto the floor from open windows, beckoning her to look outside onto

a dusty, rutted street where a man in a dark blue shirt stalked another. And if he looked up at her, a frozen spectator, she would
see that his eyes were the same blue as his shirt. Mocking blue—
unfathomable blue that gave nothing away, especially not love.

"I hate you, Steve Morgan!" Her own voice, crying out in rage
and frustration. And he held her pinned down, half smothered by
the weight of his body; keeping her there while she stabbed him
and stabbed him and he kept making love to her with the buzzards circling far up against the pitiless hot blue of the Mexican
sky. . . .

Why was she crying? Why was she so alone and hopeless and
terrified? This was another room and it wasn't Steve but the
French Colonel, chuckling at her discomfiture while the shadowy,
angular figure of Tom Beal waited outside to take her to horror.

"Steve—Steve where are you? I love you, I love you, please save
me!" But he was turning away from her, his eyes shadowed so she
couldn't read their expression, his mouth hard with scorn.

"Love. What the hell is that? There's only one thing we have
in common, baby, and that's easy to find."

The sound of his voice kept echoing "easy . . . easy . . .
easy . . ." until it faded away with the abrupt snapping open of
her eyes and she thankfully came back to reality, lying there with
Andre Delery's thigh lying heavily over hers and his hand still fast
in her hair. Better Andre than Steve, her own demon from hell.
Steve, whom she must and would exorcise. The devil take him
away! He had no right to haunt her dreams, when she was certain
he seldom spared more than a passing thought for her. No doubt
Ana Dos Santos was doing her best to keep him occupied as they
made up for what might have been if Ginny hadn't stepped into
the picture. She should have admitted to Andre that it was Cuba
and not Mexico that Steve had traveled to—but then, why not
keep to herself the delicious possibility of revenge if they happened
to run into each other in Havana?

Andre murmured and stirred in his sleep, flinging his arm out
widely as if to fight off an unseen assailant. So Andre had his
nightmares too? Waiting until his breathing had quieted Ginny
began to ease herself free. Suddenly the room seemed unbearably
stifling—she felt as if she would drown in the moist, overheated
atmosphere. Yes, she would die if she couldn't breathe clean, cool

air again! And feel the silken kiss of water rippling against her skin. . . . Hadn't she noticed a natural pool, with a small, mossy-rocked waterfall splashing down into it, on one of the walks she had taken earlier this morning? It had been on the other side of an ancient fence that was completely grown over by flowering vines and she had meant to explore further but she'd heard Andre's voice calling to her. "Who lives there?" she had asked the little barefooted urchin who had been her self-appointed guide, and he had shrugged.

"Don't know. House very old—she falling down too like fence. They say boss man he go to Jamaica—much bigger island, that!"

Part of the freedom of belonging to herself was being able to do exactly as she pleased, wasn't it? Naked, Ginny got up from the bed and walked across the room, running her fingers carelessly through the long, tangled masses of her hair. She caught a glimpse of herself in the small mirror as she pulled on the simple cotton dress she had worn that morning—this time without the benefit of stays or bustle to make her look "fashionable." The barefoot Mexican *soldadera* hadn't cared for fashion—only survival. The woman who stood here in her place didn't *look* very different except that she wasn't quite as thin and her face had lost that gaunt, frightened look.

Ginny knotted her hair up atop her head with the aid of a few pins and decided against wearing her smart kid walking boots. On an impulse, she wrapped a brightly colored scarf she had bought from a dockside vendor around her hair so that its coppery beauty was completely covered, tying the ends in a bow above her forehead like tignons the bronze-skinned women of color wore in New Orleans. Now she was ready for her small adventure. Ginny smiled a trifle wryly to herself as she caught herself hoping she would not run into anyone who knew her. It wasn't probable, here in this very small hotel. She had asked Andre to find them a place that none of their shipboard acquaintances would be likely to choose, so that they might relax and be alone. So far they had spent their time probing each other's minds as well as bodies—both adept enough at pretense to savor the game they played.

"But I need some time to myself to think," Ginny said to herself, running barefoot over a patch of thick grass that felt like a mat under her feet. So far she had seen not a soul abroad—

perhaps here too as in Mexico they kept the hours of siesta. The sun beat down on her head, its heat like a golden brand for a moment until she had gained the comparative coolness of a grove of trees. Even the incessant insect noises sounded hushed here—an occasional puff of warm air made the large fronds of the banana trees scrape against one another, sounding like heavy, rasping breathing. Ginny ran faster, hoping she remembered the way, praying she wouldn't encounter any snakes, and at last she came panting and breathless to the dilapidated fence, leaning over obligingly at this point as if its burden of vines had grown too heavy. On the other side of the fence the little pool had deep green lights in it from the sun rays that filtered through leaves.

How delightfully inviting and refreshing the sound of running, dripping, rippling water sounded! Her skin felt chafed from her damp gown, longing for coolness. Unused to trespassers, perhaps thinking her a creature of the tangled green forest like themselves, brightly plumaged birds flew up once or twice, screeching, and then settled down again. Nobody came here—perhaps nobody left here! This had to be an enchanted place, an oasis where time stood motionless.

Without stopping to think any further Ginny removed her scarf and tore impatiently at the gown that confined her, throwing it aside as she let herself slip into the water, instantly submerging all of herself.

Someone, long ago had cunningly widened this place in the stream to form what looked like a completely natural pool, lining it with smoothly rounded stones that now were covered with moss, giving the water its green tone. Birdsong and bee-murmuring, sunlight and shadow. Closing her eyes and abandoning herself to pure *feeling* Ginny thought lazily of a poem by Andrew Marvell that she had always loved. How did it go? Something about ". . . annihilating all that's made into a green thought in a green shade . . ." Oh, but it really didn't matter, she was too lazy to think; sensuously relishing the water's caress, the feeling of her hair floating free about her shoulders.

Her hair was like a swirling rivulet of the purest molten copper, melting into green. Her brows, against the sheened peach face, were dark in contrast and slightly winged as if to match the way her eyes were the barest trifle slanted upward at the corners. They were green—like the emeralds she wore sometimes. And she had a mouth that could make men crazy to kiss it, to find out if its promise of untold delights was real or not.

All these thoughts went through the mind of the man who stood very still some distance off in the shadow of the trees, watching. He had watched her before, when she was unaware of it, but never like this; never quite expecting this complete naturalness. Women of his generation, and especially that class of women who were called "ladies," did not strip off their garments with total unconcern and bathe naked and unashamed in the open. Nor would they run barefoot and half dressed through a forest, quite unafraid, to find this isolated place. It was as if she had heard his silent summons, sensed his yearning. If this had been ancient Greece he would have thought her a dryad—one lovely enough to tempt Zeus himself. His mouth twisted slightly at that conceit. No, he was no king of the gods but a mere man. But even so, more of a match for her than the man she had chosen to travel with, who was *not* her husband. He had studied Andre Delery, had made inquiries about him, and had dismissed him as being of no real importance to *her*. The two of them were, his intuition told him, traveling companions for convenience' sake; they would not remain together. And all the better—for he had felt the pull of his senses from the very first time he set eyes on this woman. He had known even then that he would give everything he had to have her—circle the globe if need be, to fulfill her every wish. But at the same time, knowing all this, his instincts told him that if she was worth having she was worth keeping, and in order to keep her he must teach her to love him—that was the only way in which a man could hold this woman who called herself "Genevieve Remy."

# Chapter Fifteen

❧

Jim Bishop was annoyed. Any other man, Paco Davis thought—wisely keeping his thoughts to himself—would have exhibited all the symptoms of a towering rage. Bishop merely lit one cigar after the other and drummed his fingers on the edge of the table until Paco, in retaliation, began whistling off key.

Jim Bishop gave him a forbidding look, clearing his throat. "You're sure you didn't miss anything?"

Paco looked offended. "Would I do that? I happen to be quite fond of Ginny, apart from the fact that she saved my bacon once. No, I left no stone unturned—that's the right phrase? She's gone —no note, nothing. Her maid was hysterical; she'd been left be-hind to pack, and says her mistress said she had some last minute shopping to do—a hat she had ordered and must pick up. Said she'd be back in time for supper."

Paco heard Bishop's impatient sigh and gave a mental shrug. What the hell, if Jim wanted him to repeat the whole damn thing again he would—maybe between the two of them they'd come up with some answer. And because he was genuinely fond of Ginny, Paco hoped fervently that *his* hunch proved wrong.

He went on patiently, watching Bishop start to trace absent-minded patterns on the table, "Jim, I went over everything—every little detail, every possibility. What do you think? Her milliner never saw her—nobody she knows ran into her. And you told me to be sure and not make it too obvious she'd disappeared, so it took time for this friend of a friend to find out that a woman an-swering her description had asked about buying passage to Vera Cruz. He asked at every single shipping office, and they only remembered her being in one place. . . ."

"Delery. Let's go back to Delery. M. Delery leaves New Orleans

on precisely the same day that Steve's wife disappears. He was going—where?"

"Back to France, on business, he told his friends. They say it's
something he had been planning for some time. Of course the
ship he's on stops at a lot of places, including Cuba. You think
he's going there instead of to France?"

Bishop said thoughtfully, as if Paco hadn't spoken, "We know
this Andre Delery is a not unclever man. We are almost certain
that the money he throws around so freely is Spanish money, and
he earns it by eliminating certain people the Cubans do not like.
Of course he fights a lot of duels too—a sadly hot-tempered man,
isn't he?—and this keeps us from being quite certain. But the 'Af-
faire Brandon' leads me to believe that he had quite definitely
caught on to the fact that our friend Senator William Brandon
was planning to finance a filibustering expedition to Cuba with the
active help and advice of several rich Cubans in the United States.
That would be easy to find out—these Cubans spy upon each
other! But Delery, who's of French extraction . . . with him it has
to be money."

He looked up and caught Paco's watchful, interested gaze as he
paused to light yet another cigar. "Delery has another weakness as
well, hasn't he?" Bishop said softly, and answered his own question. "Women. He has quite a reputation as a Casanova, has he
not? And you started to mention a while back that when he
booked his own passage he also booked a berth in the same cabin
for a lady? A Madame Delery?"

"Yes, sure—but he did that about ten days before—"

"Naturally he didn't get married in the interim?"

Paco shrugged. "Not him! He doesn't seem like the marrying
kind. And anyhow, the female he's traveling with couldn't be
Ginny, if that's what you're driving at. From all accounts they
went on board together, accompanied by mountains of luggage—
mostly the lady's. They were very affectionate . . . hey! If he had
tried to abduct Ginny she'd have been fighting him tooth and nail
—I've seen her fight! She—"

Bishop said drily: "She could have been . . . um . . . willing."

It was clear that Paco hadn't thought of *that* possibility. A dis-
mayed look crept over his face. With a female as unpredictable
and hot-tempered as Ginny, anything was possible!

"Jesus Christ!" Paco swore feelingly. "If that is true and Steve finds out—"

"Steve is occupied at this moment. On business. We can't get word to him until he gets word to us. And I see no reason to . . . er . . . raise an alarm until we have facts to go on." Bishop gave Paco a quelling look and went on austerely: "When *you* get to Cuba, I'm sure I can trust you to say nothing. *I* will take the responsibility of finding the lady."

Although he was used to keeping his thoughts well hidden, Bishop was thinking sourly that the young woman in question certainly seemed to thrive on making trouble—not to mention stirring up a hornets' nest of gossip wherever she went. The trouble with women was that they were never constant, first blowing hot and then cold and never allowing a man to be sure of where he stood! If Ginny had indeed run off with Andre Delery on a crazy whim then she deserved to take the consequences. *He* would try to make sure there was as little talk as possible, and to that end he had arranged for "Mrs. Steve Morgan" to set sail as planned for Matamoros. He would deal with the rest later.

Being the kind of man he was, Bishop didn't crack a smile when he told Paco exactly what his arrangements were. He was brief and succinct, and he listened silently and without any expression at all while Paco blew off steam; leaping up from his chair and pacing about the room dramatically.

"And now I *know* you're crazy and—*por Dios!*—I have to be loco too, to keep right on working for you! *No*, damn it! Me, Paco Davis, I will not dress up as a woman, you hear? Wear a veil, huh! Shit, I'd never learn to walk in skirts, let alone—forget it, Jim! Find yourself some other idiot! I'd rather swim to Cuba than—"

"As to that, you won't have to swim very far. There'll be a fishing boat waiting to pick you up when you conveniently 'fall overboard' the second night out. And until then you will stay in your cabin on the pretext you're seasick."

In the end, Paco would follow orders just as he had been trained to do. Even—if it became necessary—to the extent of telling Steve Morgan that his wife had been lost at sea. While Paco ranted, Jim Bishop's mind had already gone ahead to other matters. He found himself wondering what Steve Morgan was doing, and how much he had accomplished by now. Hopefully, he would have reached his destination by this time, along with the pretty young woman who had volunteered to go back with him. Steve never seemed to have much difficulty in finding women who were helpfully willing to volunteer anything he wanted of them, and Ana Dos Santos was no exception. How very convenient for them all that she should have turned up in New Orleans at exactly the right moment to fit in with their plans!

"I did not want to visit New Orleans," Ana Dos Santos said softly, letting her head rest languidly against the shoulder of the man whose arm encircled her. "But now I am so glad that I did— and that we met again. Do you think it was fate, Esteban?" She felt the slight, shrugging movement of his shoulder and knew she was talking too much again, but she was tired of the silence between them and wanted to bring herself to his notice.

"Don't you believe in fate, *querido?* After all, we were supposed to be married once—and now, so many years later, here we are, traveling together as man and wife . . . it seems *right*, somehow. Don't you agree?"

Why, for God's sake, did she insist on keeping up a flow of pointless, repetitious chatter? Now she had turned her head to gaze expectantly up at him, forcing an answer from him, and Steve had to fight back a surge of irrational anger before he said shortly:

"It'll seem much better when we've reached our journey's end. Making love to you in this rattletrap of a coach has its disadvantages, especially when we are surrounded by such an overzealous escort!"

"But if we didn't have the soldiers with us it would appear suspicious—as if we were not afraid of the rebels because we are allied with them! Please don't let them see you're so angry, Esteban, or they'll think . . ." Her voice, turning coy, she gave a slight, nervous giggle. She wished she could see the expression in his eyes as she murmured, "After all, they think we are still honeymooners, and that all of your attention is upon *me*—and it is, isn't it? Is that why you're angry, because we can't make love properly?"

"Isn't that reason enough for anger?"

He soothed her because he had to, but Steve Morgan had never been the most even tempered of men, and his thoughts were far from pleasant, especially when they dwelt on Mr. Bishop. Damn Bishop and his carefully laid schemes anyhow! It seemed as if more often than not something always came up that blew everything to hell, leaving *him* to improvise the best he could. He had meant to go looking for his grandfather, once his credentials had been established, so to speak, in Havana. He had meant, at that point, to rid himself politely of Ana, who had already begun to bore him. But instead, caution had been forced upon him by certain developments, and the clinging woman, coming cleverly to his "rescue," had declared that they were man and wife, thereby rescuing herself as well. For, as she had inquired with a suitably wide-eyed and innocent stare that had daunted even the irascible Captain-General himself, didn't that make her a citizen of Mexico once more, through her new husband? Truly, she had no sympathy with the rebels—as a woman, she wasn't in the least interested in politics, she left that to *men*.

It was at that point, hiding feelings of anger mixed with grudging admiration for her guile, that Steve had interposed smoothly: "Actually, Your Excellency, it isn't merely to look over my bride's plantation that I'm here. I'd heard that my grandfather, Don Francisco Alvarado, is also visiting Cuba."

The gamble he had taken was a fortunate one after all. General Pieltain's face had cleared somewhat and his eyes sharpened, studying Steve with interest and some curiosity.

"Ah! So *you're* Don Francisco's grandson? You should have said so before, and I would have understood why you wanted a pass. He got *his* from my predecessor, General Ceballos. *I* would never have permitted a gentleman of Don Francisco's age to travel such a distance through rebel country. However . . ."

On the heels of the older man's expressive shrug Steve said quickly, "I understand, sir. And had I not been traveling at the time I would have come in my grandfather's place. But now that I am here . . . have you heard anything of him since he left Havana?"

"No, I'm afraid not. But that may not be a matter for concern, Señor Alvarado—the rancho is in a remote area, and communications aren't too good these days, what with these damned rebels constantly keeping things stirred up!"

He had gone on to make a few rather patronizing observations on the state of affairs in Mexico—self-government indeed! Look how it had ended—with the proud Criollas getting an Indio Presidente in the end! It wouldn't happen in Cuba!

Steve had kept his temper under control. With the condescending Governor, with the ensuing red tape that delayed his obtaining a safe-conduct for over a week, and with Ana who was beginning to act as if they were married in fact. Now he was forced to tolerate an armed escort that made him wonder grimly if he was being protected or watched. Perhaps General Pieltain wasn't quite as easygoing as he had appeared to be? It was a thought. . . .

He felt Ana's hand on his thigh, as she snuggled even closer, her full breasts pushing against his chest with every movement of the volante they were riding in.

"Darling, please don't be cross! I'm sure it couldn't be much further now. And it's really such an honor, you know! Julian Zulueta is the most powerful man in Cuba, and to think that we have been invited to visit. . . ." Ana's voice sounded excited and her fingers began to stroke him. "Esteban, they say he controls even the Governors of Cuba. He . . ."

Underlying her boastful triumph there was a sexual excitement as well that made Ana's breath quicken. Men might control other men but a woman who knew what she was about, who knew how to give and withhold pleasure until a man craved it—why, that was power too! Her father-in-law, who had taken a genuine liking to her, had told her so. He had been warning her, of course, that she mustn't let herself be totally controlled by her former fiancé.

"He remembers me as a *child*, but I've learned so much since then!" Ana thought. "I've learned enough to keep him. I'll make him need me, and then it will be real—I'll be his wife at last, as I should have been and would have been if not for that green-eyed French whore!"

But of course he no longer loved his wife! Hadn't he publicly humiliated the woman by showing her just where his affections lay? Yesterday was yesterday and today was *now*. They were going to be together, she and Esteban, for a long time to come.

Wrapped up in her own plans Ana responded hungrily to a harsh kiss that silenced her chattering. Soon she was making whimpering sounds as his fingers played with her breasts, lifting them one by one out of the low-cut gown that barely restrained their fullness.

Ana's pleasurable excitement would have turned to fury had she known that her companion had only begun to kiss her because he was tired of hearing her voice and bored with her coquettish attempts to tease him into arousal. The trouble was that he could read little Ana's mind almost too easily! There was no longer a sense of anticipation, no more mystery about her. But then, almost the only woman who had managed to keep him intrigued and never quite sure of her was his wife.

Ginny. Quicksilver woman. Would he ever be able to keep her out of his mind?

# Chapter Sixteen

❧

Watching the moonlit ocean made Ginny pensive; and *this* was a night almost too beautiful to bear. How could anyone go to sleep, or sit huddled below over a card table? She leaned with her elbows on the rail, watching the molten-pewter sea, turning her head upward to the ghost-white sails and back again to the ocean itself.

"I could sail this way forever, trapped in time on a phantom ship with no yesterdays and no tomorrow—balanced on the rim of eternity. . . ." Her thoughts were as deep and as moody as the ocean itself, flowing restlessly in as many directions. It would be pleasant *not* to think, to be able to channel and control thought itself. To forget what she wished to forget, like Steve, who had once conveniently developed amnesia. . . . And damn, why did she have to think about Steve, who was the reason for her being here? She should have stayed below with Andre; watching him play cards would have been better than not having anyone to share the moon with. Catching herself sighing, Ginny stiffened her back deliberately. No, she was *not* depressed! And she refused to wallow in retrospection, she was going to look forward to making a new life for herself and her children, and let Steve do the same for himself. Once the wound to his pride had healed he'd soon forget her, if he hadn't done so already with Ana's help! And in any case, she could never forgive him for Sonya—never forget what she'd seen and heard that day. . . .

She looked like a statue sculpted out of white and silver shadowed with black. There were silk roses caught in the heavy coils of her hair, and the faintest scent of attar of roses wafted to the suddenly flaring nostrils of the tall man who stood in the shadow of the mainmast watching her, as he had watched her on so many other occasions before. Once or twice he had wondered if she'd caught the glint of the sun reflected off his telescope—whether she knew or even cared that she might be observed. She was a woman who was used to being stared at, he'd already surmised. And she was quite unself-conscious—unashamed of her naked body and obviously not in the least afraid of wandering off by herself. A different woman. The woman in his stars . . .

A somewhat self-deprecating smile lifted a corner of the watching man's mouth as he wondered if *she* believed in astrology. What was her history, what had brought her here, on board his ship, with an obvious adventurer who was not her husband? Perhaps she was a runaway wife, perhaps a bored and restless woman searching for excitement. Whatever she was, she wasn't ordinary—and he wanted her.

The ship dipped and rose, dipped and rose again as the wind freshened slightly, blowing cool against Ginny's face. Now they were chasing the moon, pure-silver disk against midnight velvet sky. The wind pushed against the full skirts of her gown and blew salt-damp curls against her cheeks and still she did not want to go below and lose the wild, heartbreaking beauty of this night. Nor did she want to be alone with her thoughts. She wanted . . . she yearned . . . but for what? And where and how would this particular "adventure" end? What would be her final destination and her fate? Maybe, on an enchanted night like this, she had only to ask her questions and the answers would be borne to her on a web of moonlight in the wind!

Ginny sighed again and would have turned, willing herself severely to have done with her fanciful moon-thoughts, if a pair of hands had not taken her shoulders from behind and a voice had not said softly in her ear:

"Daughter of destiny, where do you travel to? And for how long have you journeyed, seeking?"

She felt frozen to the spot, not even able to turn her head—perhaps not wanting to. The voice that had addressed her was a pleasant-timbred baritone with a strangely *un*accented accent she found hard to place. The hands touching her shoulders were warm and somehow gentle, almost tempting her to close her eyes and lean her head backward, giving herself up to the crazy spell of the night and the moon.

As if he had sensed the direction of her thoughts he said urgently, "No—please don't turn around yet. Don't you know that this is a magic night? I could feel your thoughts as they tumbled this way and that like waves on a rough sea. And I sensed your yearning, your aloneness, that is why I approached you. I will do no more than this—stand here with my hands touching the flesh of your shoulders and the scent of your perfume in my nostrils—if you wish to talk. And it is far easier to tell secrets to an absolute stranger than to a friend; to confess to a priest hidden behind a grille—isn't that so? But the spell can be broken too, by your turning your head—or by your telling me to leave you in peace."

She did neither. There was only a slight stiffening of her shoulders before she said in a voice as low as his: "*Are* you a priest? Or merely a magician who reads minds? You notice, I am trying not to break the fairy spell by asking outright *who* you are. Is it all right to play guessing games, though?"

She sensed the laughter in his voice and felt more at ease because of it as he answered her with mock solemnity.

"Yes. *That* much, I should think, is allowed. Especially since I have the unfair advantage of knowing the name you travel under, which of course is not your real name. Don't be angry, it doesn't matter. Names are not important, they are, like titles, merely bestowed or borrowed. I have several—all different—myself. What matters is that on a night as lovely as this you are alone and . . . not very happy. I would help if I could, in any way."

"You *sound* sincere. But is anyone, *really?* Why are people so afraid to be completely honest with each other? And say things and make promises that aren't true and were never meant to be true? Ohh—that music! You must be a magician, or else you aren't really *there*. Am I really hearing music?"

The sounds she heard came from a stringed instrument, played very softly. A strange kind of music that reminded Ginny of flamenco but wasn't, although it was equally as haunting in its mournful plaintiveness. A soft, tenuous trickle of sound-song that asked "Why . . . why . . . why . . . ?"

"You are indeed hearing music, and I ordered it especially for you. If you listen closely it will tell you a story and run the gamut of all emotions. But the music, like the night, is merely a stage setting. Or, if you allow it to be, a catharsis."

Ginny caught her breath, feeling the strangeness of it all. It was almost diabolical the way he, whoever or *what*ever he was, seemed to sense her every thought and play upon her emotions. And if she wanted to break the spell all she had to do was . . .

Instead, continuing to watch the moon, she murmured questioningly, "Do you mean that if I—that by bringing all my feelings and emotions to the surface I would . . . somehow feel better? Perhaps you're right. I feel that way sometimes after I've lost my temper."

It was, Ginny was to think afterward, surely the strangest night of her life. Perhaps too much moonlight had driven her slightly insane, or perhaps her wine had been drugged like that of the card players below deck who would be puzzled the next day wondering when and how they had got safely to their beds. But *she* had stayed awake talking to a man she had never met before; watching the moon sink lower and turn golden and drinking dry white wine from a gold-chased goblet that glowed with a myriad different sparks of color as if it had been carved out of quartz. Leaning her head back against him in the most natural way after a while, and noticing that she came only up to his shoulder—and that he smelled very pleasant but *not* of tobacco like most men.

No—she could not have been drugged after all, because she remembered everything so clearly. Even adhering to the "rules" he had suggested in the beginning and not turning around to look into his face. The priest behind the grille . . . a word picture he had drawn. Perhaps that was what he was after all. Or perhaps he was disfigured in some way . . . if he was it didn't matter, because he was kind and caring and made no move to take advantage of her vulnerability. He was, perhaps, the first man who had not done so.

That night, for a change, Ginny slept without dreams to haunt her, waking unwillingly when Andre flung a possessive arm across her body.

"So you're here. . . . Do you know that I cannot remember coming to bed? *Merde!* My head feels as if it is about to explode!"

"Shall I send the steward to you then? I had been thinking in any case of asking him to fetch me some hot water for a bath—I'd like to feel clean when we go ashore."

Ginny avoided the halfhearted move he made to stop her as she swung bare legs off the narrow bed. Andre was an expert and in-

ventive lover but this morning she was not in the mood. Ignoring
his grumbling behind her she flung on a wrapper and began to
brush vigorously at her hair before the small mirror. The smudges
under her eyes were not *too* apparent, fortunately. But they
helped remind her that last night had been real. Unconsciously,
she started to frown into her own reflection. What on earth had
possessed her to tell a strange man, one whose face she hadn't
even seen, so much about herself? "I wonder if I will meet him
again," she mused, "and if I do—will I know him? Why was he so
interested in me?"

"I certainly hope you are going to send for my man when you
have finished scowling at yourself so ferociously? My head . . .
but turn around, let me see . . . yes, you look as delicious as ever,
especially for so early in the morning. I hope you are not sulking
because I neglected you somewhat last night?"

"Oh believe me," Ginny retorted brightly, throwing a dazzling
smile at him over her shoulder as she tugged vigorously at a bell
cord, "I did not in the least feel neglected last night! Such a beautiful moon—it is a great pity you missed it."

She left, as she had meant to do, a thoughtful Andre Delery
pondering over her turn of phrase. "What a little vixen she is! I
wonder . . . but of course she is capable of allowing herself to be
*consoled!* She probably invited seduction, hoping perhaps to make
me jealous. I wonder who the man was?"

As it turned out, Andre Delery soon found his attention concentrated upon other matters of much more importance to him.

When, after a leisurely toilet, he joined some of his card-playing
cronies of the previous night on deck, he found them discussing a
sudden change in course. The owner of the *Amaryllis*, that same
mysterious eccentric they had all wondered about, had suddenly
decided to put in at the small harbor of Gibara, it seemed.

"Rumor has it that it was the first port entered by Columbus,"
Mr. Bartholomew offered. A cigar-smoking Jamaican who boasted
of his unlimited capacity for alcohol, he too appeared to be suffering somewhat from the excesses of the previous night. "Can't say
that I really *care* too much," the gentleman added grudgingly.
"I'm anxious to get home to the plantation myself, and I've been
to Havana before—filthy, unhygienic place!"

"The Captain made an announcement, I guess—one that most

of us seem to have missed!" The speaker, an American from Florida, winced rather exaggeratedly as he massaged his temples.

"Oh yes? And he said . . . ?" Andre Delery's even tones disguised the rage he was beginning to feel at the thought of certain careful planning going astray on a rich man's sudden whim. He composed his features into an attentive expression as the other man continued.

"Said that passage would be arranged for all those having urgent business in Havana. Apparently it's got something to do with our supply of water as well—I really wasn't paying too much attention. But Gibara sounds like a nice enough spot to spend a day or two—and then we'll be putting in at Santiago de Cuba before we make for Jamaica."

"Ah!" Andre Delery said thinly, and then, apropos of nothing: "I wonder, *mes amis,* why we all have such large heads this morning? I could have sworn I drank much, much more two nights ago."

His eyes touched briefly on his mistress—flush faced and fresh looking in a gown of white muslin with an overskirt of apple-green foulard. *He* had picked out that dress for her, the wench! And how had she known so early this morning that they would be going ashore sooner than planned?

# Chapter Seventeen

❧

Seen from the harbor entrance, Gibara was a picture-book town, lying crescent shaped on the steep slope along the bay. Three oddly shaped mountains with scarped summits formed a backdrop against the sky—an obliging Cuban gentleman informed his fellow-passengers that they were named "Silla," which meant saddle; "Pan," or sugar-loaf; and "Tabla," table.

"But of course, what else could they have been named?" Andre Delery was still in a bad humor and he watched sourly as the *Amaryllis* sailed in closer and Ginny, along with the other women passengers, exclaimed at the pretty rainbow-colored villas with red-tiled roofs that dotted the hillside. *She* certainly was in a cheerful mood considering the fact that they were doomed to spend at least two days in this . . . this little fishing village! Delery's mouth twisted as he began to study his traveling companion more closely through lazy-lidded eyes. If she gazed too long in the direction of any particular man now—or avoided one completely—then his suspicions would have something to feed upon. But no, she continued to act just as usual and her gay insouciance made him want to grit his teeth—or shake her by the shoulders. What was she up to? What *had* she been up to? Not used to being uncertain of any woman, Delery was as annoyed with himself as he was with her.

He would have been more than annoyed, he would have been furious had he known that Ginny had no intention of going on to Havana with him. In an introspective mood since her strange moonlit encounter, Ginny hid her thoughts behind her vivid smiles. She was going to Vera Cruz. And from there she would go directly to the little hacienda as she had done before, and would send for her children—learn all over again to become a mother to them. They were *hers*. She had suffered the tortures of the damned to bear them, she had wanted to bear his child and had

borne two children instead. And Steve hadn't cared—if he no
longer cared for her, how could he love the children?

"From now on I'll never leave them—wherever I travel they'll
be with me. I'll make a life of my own for me and for *them*, and
he shan't interfere!"

Armored by her new resolutions, Ginny found it easy to avoid
Andre Delery's subtle questioning. Yes, her first instincts had been
right. Andre was too much like her ex-lover Miguel Lopez, who
had once called himself an "honest cynic." Like Miguel, Andre
was an opportunist, and he had taken up with her only in order to
use her—why should she not use him as well?

She said nothing out of the ordinary to Andre, who continued
to be in a bad mood, even after they had been rowed ashore and
taken to a pretty pastel blue villa that was built, Andre informed
her, like all Cuban houses—the dining room facing the street and
doubling as an entrance hall as well.

"They even take their horses in that way, I believe," he said in
his sarcastic drawl. "And do you notice those iron bars? They do
not believe in glass for windows." He added suddenly, "I wonder
why we have been accorded the honor of a house all to ourselves?
I had expected to be taken to the local *fonda*—if this quaint little
town boasts of one, that is! What do *you* think, petite? You've become unaccountably silent, of a sudden."

"I think that I love this pretty blue house. Look, what a beautiful patio, how cool it is here! And beyond that I have not had
time to think . . . why haggle over a bargain?"

Ignoring the handsome older woman who had shown them to
the tree-shaded patio, Andre caught her by the arm and turned
her around to face him.

"And you, Madame Morgan—bah, such a harsh, ugly name,
that!—are you also a bargain too or have I been cheated?"

She faced him levelly, without attempting to tug herself free of
his somewhat cruel grip.

"Cheated, M. Delery? But I never touted myself as a bargain,
did I?—and I remember telling you I was not for sale. If you
wanted *bargains* you should have looked elsewhere."

Surprising her, Delery laughed. "Touché, madam! And you remind me that you are clever as well as beautiful—and deliciously

experienced. Why would I need to pay for a . . . bargain when you were there for the taking?"

"They came close to quarreling, I think, and then the señor changed his mind and carried the señora into one of the bedrooms. . . ." the housekeeper later related to the owner of the villa. "No—she did not seem to mind . . . too much. He is *muy macho*, that one. Why, just a few hours later he was making big eyes at Conchita, and . . ." The woman hesitated slightly and her employer said sharply:

"Yes? And what else?"

"He . . . it was strange this, you know how bold Conchita is, but it made her feel embarrassed that he should suggest such a thing to her. He . . . desired that she should come to his bed later that night—the bed he shares with the señora."

"I see. And the señora? She did not mind? . . ."

The woman pursed her lips. "Conchita asked this very question. And the señor laughed, she told me, and said that he wished to surprise the señora. He was very persuasive, Conchita said. He told her that . . . he implied that he . . . there would be no trouble, no difficulty, he said. He even offered money. But of course Conchita refused him! She likes men, that one, but she is not a bad girl."

"I am glad to hear that. And since then?"

"Well, this morning, as you know, I said I had to obtain fresh supplies at the marketplace. The señora was sleeping late but the señor accompanied me for some distance. He had to arrange for passage for himself and the señora to Havana, he told me. He asked many questions about who owned the *estancia* and I told him exactly what you told me to say—that I am a widow, trying to make ends meet. . . ."

Ginny had waited, pretending sleep, until she heard the thud of the heavy front door, which meant that Andre had left. Only then did she open her eyes, stretching cautiously at first and then freely and lazily like a cat; letting the covers slide off her body and onto the matting-covered floor. Damn Andre anyhow! She hoped he wouldn't return too soon. Andre with his clever, inventive little sex games that he wanted her to play, just as if she had been a whore he'd picked up in some *maison de tolérance*. She frowned angrily, remembering. Some of his words had flicked at her like whips, leaving their imprint in her mind, although at the time she had merely shrugged his suggestions away as if she didn't care.

"Ah—and I'd thought you a little more honest than most women! And certainly beyond acting shocked! I think you're the kind of woman who has done almost everything—and would like to try what's left to be experienced. Don't disappoint me, petite."

"There are certain things I would not do, though—merely to give *you* a voyeur's titillation! You mistake me, Andre Delery."

"No—I don't think so. At heart, I think you are a cocotte. I think that you would do anything, dare anything . . . and by the way, I am not so selfish as to deny *your* pleasure! I think you would enjoy being made love to by a woman *and* a man. Has your husband never suggested it?"

Why did he have to remind her she had a husband? And why, now, did she have to remember all over again that she had been a whore and worse at one time? All the men in her life, beginning with Steve, whom she had blamed for making her what she was. Some had forced her and some had not. She was here with Andre Delery of her own free will. He had been a stranger, a mere acquaintance, and yet she had run off with him, letting him have the free use of her body. No wonder he felt free to insult her!

Still frowning, Ginny forced herself out of bed, walking naked to the pier glass that had been thoughtfully placed in one corner of the room. She poked out her tongue at her sullen reflection. When she was much younger, she had done the same thing—only *then* she had usually burst out laughing afterward. Now there was no laughter in her, only a strange kind of apathy, a heaviness. What kind of a woman stared back at her—face pale and eyes defiantly brilliant under tangled masses of coppery hair?

"Am I going to let myself turn into exactly the kind of woman Steve has accused me of being? Must I allow *his* behavior to mold mine? After all, I'm no longer a naughty child sticking my tongue out spitefully at a grown-up's back!"

Ginny felt lighter-hearted once she had finished dealing severely with herself. After all, she *had* made up her mind already as to what she planned to do. Andre was not important—she need never set eyes on him again if she chose!

The pretty brown-eyed maid whose name was Conchita seemed

eager to make friends, especially when she realized that the señora spoke Spanish. Perhaps, she suggested shyly, the señora would care to take her bath outdoors in the patio? The house was built around it, of course, and there was no one else here. A marble fountain with two cherubs pouring water from twin urns into one end of a tree-shaded bathing pool made Ginny's mind up for her. Wide steps, azure-tiled like the bottom of the pool, led down into it so that bathers of all heights could sit comfortably. And the water itself was clean and crystal clear—Conchita said proudly that the patron, the owner of this house, had made use of the water from a small stream that ran down the hillside.

"See, señora—there is an opening there for the water to run through, so that the pool stays fresh and clean always. And afterwards, if the señora desires, I will bring fresh fruit—perhaps a *refresco?* Soon it will be very hot."

The bathing pool was tree shaded. There were palms and pomegranates and mignonette and orange trees growing in huge stone urns. Vines grew up the weathered wooden posts that supported the inevitable galería, making this particular house appear more Spanish than Cuban. It was beautiful and peaceful—everything seemed put here for her comfort and enjoyment, and enjoy it she would, closing her mind to all but the present.

Lulled into a state of tranquillity by the cool silken feeling of the water that laved her body, Ginny closed her eyes against the glare of the sun that lurked beyond the trees and thought only of what she should wear and whether she should go exploring. Conchita had mentioned that the cathedral was very pretty, reminding her subtly that it was Sunday—and she hadn't been to mass since she'd left Mexico. Well, in just a little while she would force herself into some semblance of energy. It was too bad, she supposed ruefully, but she really was a hedonist!

From the deeply shaded galería, the owner of the blue-painted villa—who was also the mysterious owner of the *Amaryllis*— watched his guest through field glasses as he had on many other occasions. He watched her to try to find some defect in a body he already thought of as perfect; and he watched her because he had fallen in love with her and could not help it. He was not by nature or inclination a voyeur, and it pained him to have to resort to such devious methods to catch a glimpse of her, but . . . how had

it happened that he, who had always prided himself on his detachment and his intellect, should have allowed himself to come to
such a sorry pass? Spying on the woman he loved—fighting back
the primitive instincts that urged him to go to her, stripping off
his own clothes to join her, naked as a satyr, in the bathing pool.
He wanted her; and that in itself was unusual for him, for he had
women in his life already whom he treated with unfailing politeness and consideration in spite of the fact that desire was not always present. And while he was able to perform as a man, it was
usually his mind that forced him to it, not this tearing urge in his
loins that prompted him even now to throw all caution to the
winds—go to her, take her!

He waited, forcing patience upon himself, because that was not
all that he wanted of this woman. He wanted not only her body,
willing and eager for his embraces, but her mind and her emotions
as well. He wanted her as his wife, and he didn't care anything
about her past.

In the hot stillness of the morning, Ginny stood by the pool,
letting the heat of the sun itself dry her. She was tempted now to
go back in and spend the rest of the day lolling in that deliciously
sensual, cool water, but no—if Andre came back and found her
there naked he would no doubt join her, and *not* for just a bath.

"Which of the señora's gowns shall I bring for the señora to
wear?" Conchita was anxious to be helpful and not at all embarrassed by another woman's nudity. She added hesitantly, "There
is a tear in the bodice of the one the señora wore yesterday—had I
noticed it before I would have mended it."

"You may keep that one—I had grown tired of it."

The tear had been Andre's fault. He had been impatient with
her sudden reluctance and had begun to do what Steve had done
so often—rip her gown from her shoulders, until she'd cried impatiently for him to stop, she'd take the gown off herself. And then,
in spite of herself, her body had responded to his expert caresses;
she had closed her mind to everything but sensation.

Now, brushing aside Conchita's stammered, round-eyed thanks
with her smile, Ginny decided on a pale yellow gown with a
darker gold polonaise that was trimmed with white lace at the
neck and all along the ruffled bustle. A pretty walking gown—in
spite of the heat she was determined to go out. She would find

out if she could go aboard the *Amaryllis* early, so as to avoid a confrontation with Andre. Having come to know M. Delery quite well, Ginny was too sharply aware that he was more than capable of taking her with him to Havana by force if that was what he desired. Far better not to let him know what she planned!

Yet another servant, this time an elderly Negro man Ginny had not seen before, was at hand to open the great, iron-studded front door for her. She noticed the faintest trace of cigar smoke in the large front room, where the inevitable *candela*—a silver dish filled with wood ashes where a live coal burned—had its place on an ebony table by the door so that a gentleman might light his cigar.

Did the widowed Señora Montejo's servant smoke cigars? Or did the handsome Cuban widow entertain many male guests? It was not any business of hers, Ginny chided herself, and then she could not help an involuntary gasp as the intense heat and glare outside seemed to assault her senses. No wonder Conchita had looked at her as if she was crazy—this was obviously the worst time of the day to go wandering abroad.

"There is a volante waiting for the señora," the black man said in a deliberately uninflected voice. "That is, unless the señora wishes to change her mind? It is close to the hour of the siesta now. . . ."

In spite of the lack of inflection in his voice, his eyes seemed to disapprove of her—a young woman, going off on her own without a chaperone! The thought stiffened Ginny's resolve.

"Thank you," she said crisply. "And if the señor should come back before I return you may tell him that I—that I have gone to church."

# Chapter Eighteen

❧

Ginny had meant to throw Andre off in case he returned earlier than expected and decided to look for her; but her first ride in a volante, for all that it was a novel experience, was not very comfortable, and so, when the old, cream-colored cathedral with its red-tiled domes and towers came into sight she called to the *calasero* who rode the silver-saddled shaft horse to stop—breathing a sigh of relief when he did. What a strange vehicle! Two enormous wheels about six feet in diameter dwarfed the low-slung body of the coach itself—one had the uncomfortable feeling of riding next to the ground, and it was hard to see any of the scenery they passed because of the size of the wheels and the dust that flew up behind the horse's hoofs. And then there was the heat as well— what heat! Already Ginny could feel her head begin to throb, her palms become clammy. Even her eyes ached, and all she could think of was the cool sanctuary the old church offered.

"But, señora! There are no masses being said at this hour. Perhaps later on, in the evening . . ."

"I wish to see the inside of the church. It must be very old. You may stay outside, or come back for me—say in an hour? And I don't wish anybody to know where I am."

She hardly realized what she was saying, so great was her desire to escape from the pitiless brand of the sun and into the cool shadows where she could fight off the growing feeling of nausea that suddenly assaulted her senses. She had become extremely pale, with tiny droplets of sweat sheening her face, and the young man sitting on his silver-mounted saddle looked sharply at the pretty señora, seeing beyond her prettiness for the first time as he noticed her pallor. Even her lips looked bloodless, and her hand had been cold when he assisted her out of the volante. He would have liked to have stayed and accompanied her into the church, but the horse was fresh and restive—eager, no doubt, to return to his comfortable stable! It was not safe for any norteamericano, especially a female one, to be out under the sun at this hour—it was *muy estúpido*, but of course it was not his place to say so to the señora herself.

Reluctantly the young ex-slave, whose name was Manuel, turned the volante about and made for the house once more. Sweat poured off his face and soaked his freshly starched collar. He hated this wearing of a uniform that proclaimed him as a house servant. He wanted to be in the mountains with the patriots the Spaniards branded "rebels," following his hero, the brave Antonio Maceo. But instead, because of a certain pair of dark eyes and a pouting, teasing red mouth, here he was, dressed up like a popinjay in livery during the hottest time of the day when any sane person should be taking a siesta.

Suddenly, Manuel's frown gave way to a mischievous grin and he began to whistle. Siesta! Yes—Conchita would be taking her siesta at this time. She would, of course, have taken all her clothes off because of the excessive heat, and half asleep, she might allow him a few more liberties than she normally did. Why couldn't Conchita be like the waterfront girls who knew what a man wanted and weren't averse to giving it to him without playing teasing games, promising everything and then holding out for marriage? Conchita needed a good talking-to. He was a man, not a boy, and he would set her straight once and for all—give her an ultimatum. Either they became lovers or he'd be gone, pouf! And she probably would never see him again—they were saying now that the fighting against the hated Spaniards and the even more detested *peninsulare* "Volunteers," as they called themselves, might go on for years.

Manuel began whistling softly to himself. What a stroke of luck! Due to a whim of the foreign señora he had a whole hour, maybe more, to spend with Conchita. He wondered what she'd say when she opened her eyes and saw him. . . . Manuel's eyes began to sparkle before he crossed himself hastily for luck. Pray God there would be no one else awake in the villa! And he hoped also that the copper-haired señora would find much to interest her in the church. Perhaps she was going there to meet a lover and excitement had been the reason for her pale face and cold hands. All women were beyond understanding!

In the silence of the vaulted cathedral Ginny's ears still seemed to be filled with the deafening rattle of wheels over cobblestones. She had slipped to her knees as soon as she entered, and now she covered her ears with her hands, pressing hard with her palms as she willed the noise to go away. It was some time before she realized that the drumbeat echoes she kept hearing were heartbeats—hers. They kept time with the pounding hammer blows in her temples, each throb a separate pain. What was happening to her? She had been feeling fine this morning, just a little tired, that was all. And now she could hardly keep her thoughts straight. The heat—if she could just get over its effects; if she hadn't finished that sickly sweet *refresco* just to please Conchita she wouldn't be feeling so queasy.

She didn't know how long she stayed there, kneeling all huddled up with her forehead pressed against the back of a polished wooden pew. Had it been an hour or merely a few minutes? Somehow in the end, some of the stillness of the years the old cathedral had stood here in this very place, a refuge and a sanctuary for all the seekers who came here, seemed to melt into the young woman's agitated mind. Lifting her head up with an effort Ginny saw the high altar seeming to glisten with light at what seemed to be a great distance away. Candles—all that light was merely from candles, their flames flickering and wavering until they all seemed to merge into one great glow. Oh—she was really sick, she should never have looked up! For now everything around her seemed to be heaving and moving, even the ground itself. Just as if she had been seasick or trying to walk ashore after having been too long at sea. Ginny gasped and closed her eyes, hoping the strange sensation would go away, but it grew worse instead, and when a low, rumbling noise made her eyes fly open once more she became aware of falling plaster and swaying chandeliers and what were unmistakably screams in the distance. And then at last the primitive terror she'd been trying to push out of her mind crystallized into one screamed thought. *Earthquake!*

Ginny's head still ached, but the pain and the nausea and sensation of vertigo were all subjugated by instinct. Like any trapped and terrified creature she found herself on her feet, her pulse racing and her heart pounding. Escape—run, run! Caught in the grip of blind panic, panting and sobbing out loud, she stumbled toward the door; positive that at any moment the building would collapse on top of her.

"I'm being punished for all my sins . . . I'm going to die. . . ."

Ginny thought she heard a voice calling her name—"Ginny! Ginny!" But of course the voice was only in her head. . . . The sunlight wavered and hurt her eyes just beyond the huge double doors she'd slipped through earlier, and she had almost reached them when with an ominous cracking sound one of the giant chandeliers fell.

If her long skirts had not tripped her at that very moment, Ginny would have been directly in its crashing path. But she was already falling, screaming, and then something hit her a violent blow on the head and blackness swooped in with a rush to swallow her.

Later, people were to say, shaking their heads, that it had been a bad one, that! But earth tremors were common in Gibara, as in many other areas of Cuba, and one got used to them. . . .

"Well, my friend, I'm glad you tell me so! I must say that I had a few deucedly awkward moments, though! Do you ever have any casualties?"

Andre Delery, meeting a few shipboard aquaintances who, like himself, were seeking passage on the next mail boat to Havana, had decided to linger with them in a dockside tavern. It was too damned hot to attempt to go back outdoors in any case, and he was still rather annoyed at his mistress for turning down his proposal of an exciting variation to their lovemaking the previous night. Damn her! He knew she wasn't a prude, she was far too uninhibited for that! But something had been eating her of late, and he meant to find out what it was. In the meantime, having struck up a conversation with the Capitan of the local Volunteers, Andre was wondering idly if she was holding out, the hot-blooded little bitch, for a different kind of orgy from the one *he'd* envisioned—two men, and her in the middle perhaps?—when the first earth tremor jolted him back to awareness of his surroundings.

"It's nothing—we're used to it by now!" The mustachioed Capitan had stolidly gone on drinking and talking, encouraging everyone else in the tavern to do the same. It had not taken him long to find out that this French Creole from Louisiana was sympathetic to the cause of Spain in Cuba—and moreover that he was a friend as well as being a pupil of the famous dueling master, Pepe

Llulla. And everyone knew that Pepe would deliberately call out émigré Cubans who supported the rebels—and kill them, every one!

So now Capitan Carillo offered his new-found friend a cigar, lighting up expansively before he made the judicious pronouncement that *sí*, there were always a few casualties after an earthquake, but they were usually very old people who died of fear or foreigners who panicked.

"Me, I can usually tell when we are going to have one—it gets even hotter than usual, and the air becomes very still . . . one waits—and watches animals. *They* always know!"

It was sometime later when they strolled out of the tavern and started to climb the steeply winding road that led upward to the villa, arguing amicably as to whether they should ride or not.

"You have been kind enough to ask me to have dinner with you and your lovely—ah, I know she must be lovely indeed from the way you describe her—your wife. So I will provide horses, eh?"

Delery shrugged, about to accede, when his eye was caught by a small crowd, clustered around what appeared to be a shattered vehicle of some kind.

"Something wrong?"

The Capitan frowned as he craned his neck, turning back to his companion with a fatalistic shrug. "An accident—unfortunate, but then these things happen. Animals are known to become crazed with terror before the earth begins to shake. The horse must have bolted."

A vehicle, apparently one of those clumsy-looking carriages the Cubans called volantes, had somehow veered off a low stone bridge that spanned a small stream. And judging from the pitying exclamations and fervent signs of the cross being made by the onlookers, the unfortunate occupants of the carriage had not survived.

Capitan Carillo, suddenly all bustling officialdom, shouldered his way through the crowd to peer downward like the rest, beckoning to Andre to join him.

"The clothing belongs to a foreign woman, don't you think? Perhaps a visitor from a ship?"

Mercifully for those with sensitive stomachs, there was not much to be seen of the woman's head, which had been crushed under the weight of one of the wheels and the body of the carriage itself. Only a pool of blood, spreading to soak the livery of a young man who lay close by with upturned, staring eyes, his neck broken.

"Poor young man . . . !" a woman in the crowd murmured, but it was at the woman, or what was left of her, that Andre Delery stared as if hypnotized. Yes—the clothing she had worn was that of a foreign woman, just as Capitan Carillo had surmised. A pale green gown trimmed with a darker green grosgrain piping that had matched her eyes. A pretty, fashionable gown he had bought with a certain woman in mind. *Ginny's* dress . . . dear God! Andre's face paled with shock. Ginny!

Of course, she had been coming to look for him. It would be the kind of wildly impulsive thing she'd do, leaving the coolness of the villa during the hottest time of the day to go sightseeing. And it was that impulsive, reckless quality in her that had made her the almost-perfect mistress. He would miss her, Andre thought ruefully. And not having her with him when he arrived in Havana would change his plans slightly. He had counted on flaunting her openly as his paramour to smoke a certain someone out of hiding, and now he'd have to use different tactics, but . . . after all, it wouldn't be the first time he'd had to change plans at the last minute!

"It's a shame . . . and now I suppose I had better go and inform the proper authorities. Will you come with me or would you prefer that we meet later for dinner?"

Andre had planned to introduce Capitan Carillo to Ginny. He'd planned to set the scene, to conduct the progress of the evening very carefully. She'd refused to share him with Conchita, but perhaps she might feel differently if the third person in their bed was another man? But now he would never know how she might have reacted. *C'est la guerre!*

"I will meet you. I think I had better change my clothes—it has been a very long day."

No use in telling Capitan Carillo anything. While he regretted her death and the manner of it, Andre Delery was more concerned with himself. There was no point in getting himself involved, therefore he would act as if he knew nothing when he returned to the villa for his clothes. He would tell them only that he had obtained passage for himself and the señora on a boat leaving that same night for Havana, and that would be that.

# Chapter Nineteen

❧

It was the hot time of the year, and also growing close to the time of the cane harvest, when the huge sugar mills would be working constantly, the thick, sweet syrup pouring through funnels to drain and dry into the prized white crystals—the *blancos del Tren Derosne*, marketed in large boxes made of imported wood. Beneath the *hormas* or draining funnels there would also be the hogsheads for coarse sugars. The smells would waft on the hot, still air—the odor of the syrup, of the dark, rich molasses, the *aguardiente* that most mills also manufactured.

During this season the pampered wives and daughters of the rich planters did not usually visit the *ingenios*, preferring cooler climates. Many of them, like Julian Zulueta's own family, were scarcely familiar with their plantation houses; preferring to live in town, where there was always shopping, always some form of entertainment or amusement. Only Don Julian's oldest daughter, who had never married, followed her father everywhere, acting as his hostess. A thin, dried out cane-stalk of a woman, she had grown quite comfortable in this man's world, sitting silently on its edges and listening—a square of material for embroidering always lying on her lap as a pretext, although no one ever saw her take one stitch in it. It was whispered that Maria Felipa knew as much about sugar and politics as any man in the country or out of it—a pity, they said, that she hadn't been born a man. Even her taste in cigars and wine was excellent. Visitors to Julian Zulueta's palacio could always be assured of excellent and elegantly served meals; every small detail attended to and just right.

All the same, it was unusual to have visitors descend on them during the harvest season. Zulueta, who had grown used to confiding in his daughter just as if she'd been a son or a trusted associate, felt impelled to explain why he had invited these particular people to spend some time with them.

"It's really to please the Captain-General—and to satisfy my own curiosity. Perhaps *you* might find something out from the woman, my dear. She used to be married to the youngest Dos Santos brother, remember him? A wild young fellow—offered for your sister once, but of course I wouldn't let Innocencia marry a rakehell like that and time proved me right, didn't it?"

Maria Felipa sat patiently with her embroidery on her lap, watching her father pace to the window to stand there looking out for a few moments as if he'd forgotten what he had been saying. But she knew better, of course. Her father was merely collecting his thoughts. Her brown eyes gleamed. Her father was the cleverest man she had ever known—look where he had started, and what he had become! He was the richest and the most powerful man in all of Cuba now, and especially since that fool Miguel Aldama had come out so openly in support of the rebels. Now Aldama was exiled and living in the cold of New York in the United States and his fine palacio in Havana had been burned by an angry mob. Whereas her father . . . ah, *he* had known right from the beginning how it was going to be, and which side to stay on! Her thin fingers tightened over her sewing. He trusted her—yes, he talked to her more freely than he did to her brothers, who spent more time pursuing their mistresses and gambling than they did taking care of the plantations that had been left in their care. If only *she* had been born a male!

Don Julian, relighting his cigar, was frowning thoughtfully now as he resumed his rather pompous speech as if he hadn't paused.

"As for our *other* guest—he's rather a puzzle. Married the widow Dos Santos and made her Señora Alvarado—so we're told. Now they're on their way to inspect her plantation. . . ."

"That rundown place?" Maria Felipa sniffed, her hazel eyes snapping, and when they sparkled like that, her father could not help but feel a twinge of guilt that he'd allowed her to become an old maid. She had pretty eyes, like those of his first wife, her mother. She should have married, only she had been stubborn, hiding her nose in books, insisting on understanding how he conducted his business, always asking questions. . . . At first he'd merely been patient, even a trifle amused, humoring her in the hope that his sons would become ashamed and pay more attention themselves. But after a while he'd begun to talk to Maria

Felipa, and aside from himself, now she was the only one who really *cared*.

"They don't even have their own mill!" Maria Felipa was saying passionately, leaning slightly forward in her chair. "If not for *your* kindness in allowing them to send their cane here . . ."

Don Julian waved his cigar. "Well, well—it was an arrangement made a long time ago. You know I'm a man of my word. But I want you to observe this Alvarado fellow. His grandfather, Don Francisco, is one of the richest men in Mexico—a partner in one of the Queen Mother's estates, I understand, as well as having a half interest in a few thousand acres in the Camagüey province. . . ." Señor Zulueta paused significantly and his daughter nodded, pursing her lips as she continued to watch his face. "It was once a *cafetale*, one of the richest. Recently, they have been importing cattle from Florida—and from Mexico as well, so I've been told. A dangerous area at this particular time, with those damned rebels everywhere. Still, when Don Francisco himself turned up in Havana, demanding a safe-conduct, I persuaded my friend the Governor to provide him with one. Don Francisco also has powerful interests in Spain—his gratitude to me could prove useful, eh?"

The smile of Maria Felipa was a mere thinning of lips that were already thin and bloodless. She resembled her father when she smiled; and already her clever mind had leapt ahead to understanding exactly what her father had had in mind when he invited the grandson and heir of this Don Francisco to visit them on his way to find his grandfather—along with his wife, if wife she really was. No doubt her father was already making inquiries by telegraph—such a useful invention, that! And in the meantime, she would see to it that their visitors were made to feel welcome, their journey delayed for as long as was necessary. Her father was much cleverer than anyone else, a brilliant, far-seeing man. That was why he controlled even the Governors who came and went in Cuba, and why even the unsteady government back in Spain did not dare gainsay him. Hadn't that fool Prim, who'd wanted to hold out an olive branch to the rebels, found that out to his cost?

Now, not wanting to waste any time, Maria Felipa rose to her feet with a rustling of taffeta petticoats under her old-fashioned black bombazine skirts. She had overheard them say that she looked like a governess—a servant. Those empty-headed women who cared only for their hair and their clothes! At least the men appreciated her brain; her father's own contemporaries treated her with respect, even asking her opinion on occasion. She caught a glimpse of her dim reflection in a glass picture frame and looked away from it. Looks didn't last. . . .

"I suppose I had better go and speak to the servants, they should be here at any time now, shouldn't they? I'll take care of everything, Papa."

Her reward was his smile, his look of relief. "I know you will, daughter. I can always count on you."


In spite of the humid, overpowering heat of the blossom-scented night, Ana's hands were cold and trembling, and she kept biting her lips as if to force some color into them. She was sitting bolt upright in bed when Steve came to her—the lamp still lit as if she needed its comfort. A leather-covered volume lay open at her side, as though she had flung it there when reading had begun to bore her. And what was she doing still awake? She had retired some two hours ago, explaining that traveling had overtired her.

Steve frowned, hoping ungraciously that she wasn't taking sick with something. Christ, what was the matter with her? Was she sulking because he'd taken so long to join her in bed? And yet, her first words, spoken in an urgent whisper, brought him quickly to her side, his mouth hardening.

"What . . . what did they ask you? Oh, God, Esteban, you *were* careful, weren't you? I had forgotten—until I saw *her*, that dried-up old witch, watching me with those strange eyes of hers—how dangerous these people are. They could have us both killed, and no one would know. Why do you think there are no other guests? Why are we the only ones? I'm afraid. . . ."

"Be quiet, Ana! If you go into hysterics I'd be forced to slap your face and you'd have to explain the mark I leave, wouldn't you? Now—pull yourself together and tell me what the hell is eating you. Christ, a few hours ago you were all excited at the prospect of being here." His voice was impatient, completely without sympathy or understanding, and Ana gave a small sob, quickly stuffing her knuckles into her mouth like a child when she saw his eyes darken threateningly. Oh, *why* didn't Esteban try to understand? He didn't know these people the way she did. . . . She had forgotten already that, as he'd just pointed out to her, she'd been happy at the honor done to them when the gold-embossed invitation had been delivered to her by the Captain-General himself. She hadn't thought . . . why, right up to the time they'd arrived here she hadn't thought too much about anything but the man beside her, the adventure they had embarked on that would surely tie them together forever.

Ana's glossy, dark brown hair hung down her back unbraided tonight. She'd put a velvet ribbon in it, giving her an almost childlike look. Now, her large eyes were full of tears, and Steve gave an exasperated sigh. Goddamn, it wouldn't do to start quarreling with her at this point—he'd brought her this far and they still had quite some distance to go, to judge from what a surprisingly expansive Señor Zulueta had told him. Perhaps he'd better find out exactly what had gotten Ana so upset.

He said carefully, forcing patience into his voice, "Look—I'm sorry I jumped all over you just now, but I meant what I said about this being no time for you to get hysterical. Why don't you slow down and tell me why you're suddenly so afraid? And do try to keep your voice down. The walls might have ears—or the open windows!" His significant glance toward the barred window that was shaded by an ancient lime tree made Ana so afraid she whispered. But after a while, when Steve extinguished the light and lay beside her, taking her in his arms, she felt better. Safer too. Esteban wouldn't let anything happen to her, he'd promised her that at the beginning, hadn't he?

"I hadn't realized *she'd* be here! But I should have known, shouldn't I? She's her father's shadow, she has a heart like flint, that one! When Alonso died . . . oh, God, I can still remember her *face* at the funeral. She wore a veil, but under it she was smiling. She let me see that she was smiling. When she offered me her sympathies—sympathies!—her voice had joy in it. And she squeezed my hands so hard they were bruised afterward. She wanted Alonso—yes, he told me so himself! But he offered for her younger sister Innocencia instead, and Maria Felipa made their father turn him down. After that she never forgave him, even though they'd known each other since they were children."

Her words tumbled over each other in her impatience to be heard. If he'd only be patient and hear her out. . . .

"Ana—"

"No, please, *please*, Esteban! Let me tell it all in my own way. I must make you understand what they're like. Did you know it's said that Don Julian paid for Prim's assassination in Madrid? His power and influence stretch even there. Even as far as the United States—you saw yourself. That bullet that wounded *your* father-in-law was meant for mine. Did you recall when the conversation at dinner turned to the telegraph and its uses? I caught her looking at me—at both of us. I know what she meant, Esteban! And suppose they find out that . . . that we're not married after all? Suppose . . ."

"Why waste time in supposing? So they find out I have a wife already—hell, I'm just protecting your good name here by saying we're married."

"But then . . . they'll wonder why you're here. . . ."

"I've already told them why." He let impatience creep back into his voice, stilling her repetitious forebodings. "I'm here on business. That's all you know. I'm worried about my grandfather, which is damn close to the truth, as a matter of fact! And I could be looking over your plantation with a view to buying it. So why don't you just keep your pretty eyes open and your mouth shut and let me take care of any questions, huh?"

Beginning to know this man and his moods by now, Ana subsided a trifle sulkily. She was a little bit afraid of him, never quite sure of him. He was what she needed, a strong man—handsome, a magnificent lover, and rich into the bargain. He should have been *her* husband!

With an incoherent murmur, Ana let her flimsy nightrobe fall open as she twisted her body against his, breasts pressing against his bare, warm chest. She knew how to please him in ways she was sure his bitch-wife had never dreamed of. Her breath began to come in gasps as his hands found her roughly. Ah God, she loved it when he treated her like a whore!

During the remainder of the night it had been easy to replace fear with lust. But in the morning Ana Dos Santos found her fear renewed, fed upon a myriad little things. Steve had awakened early and was gone from her side when she at last woke up. She had no idea, at first, where he was, and the slave woman that had been sent to attend her needs only shook her head when she was questioned, pretending (Ana thought) that she knew nothing. Her bovine expression only altered to one of slight surprise when Ana ordered a bath. It was something Steve insisted upon, this constant bathing. Cuban women did not indulge in the custom, and sometimes Ana would much rather have preferred to draw a damp wash rag over her body, but on this occasion it gave her more time. She didn't want to face Maria Felipa, with her mind-searching eyes and clever, venomous tongue. Perhaps if she dallied until lunchtime, Steve would be back. Where was he?

Ana soaked in her borrowed copper tub for as long as she dared. In the end, with the water gone quite cold and her fingers looking unpleasantly wrinkled, she allowed the silent slave woman to pat her body dry, teeth worrying her lip. He'd be back by now. Perhaps he's never left the house. He could be with their host at this moment, waiting for her.

"What will the señora wear?"

"The amber-colored gown—yes, that one."

It was one of her most becoming gowns—more suitable for the town, of course, but she wanted to look her best, it would make her feel better.

There was a tap at the door, and Ana's spirits rose mercurially. Oh, thank God he was back at last!

"Come in," she called, and afterward told herself that she should have remembered that Esteban would not have been so formal, he would have walked in unceremoniously, the blue of his eyes darkening when he saw her naked, her skin turned rosy from the heat. Ana let her lips pout reproachfully as she looked expectantly at the door, but it was not her lover who walked in. It was Maria Felipa.

"Forgive the intrusion, but we had become concerned, my father and I, that you might have taken ill. This is the worst time of the year for traveling." Opaque eyes flickered over Ana's lush body, over the unbecoming flush that rose in the younger woman's face, mottling its marble prettiness.

"I . . . I . . ."

Maria Felipa pretended not to notice that Ana stuttered over her words. What a silly, transparent woman, Maria Felipa thought contemptuously. She had nothing to recommend her but a full-blown kind of prettiness that would soon fade when she began to turn fat. Why were men drawn to her kind? What was this thing called lust that rendered both men and women mindless?

Walking to the window, her body stiff and spare, Maria Felipa gave Ana a few moments in which to snatch her wrapper up and hold it against her. When she turned back to the room her back was to the light.

She made a gesture that caused the slave woman to scuttle away with a frightened bob of her head, and for a few moments the young woman wondered if Maria Felipa had heard her question.

"Please—where is Esteban?"

"That is one of the reasons why I have . . . intruded on your privacy." She made the half-apology sound like none at all, with that slightly sarcastic tinge to her voice, Ana thought resentfully, wondering why the woman seemed to hesitate, deliberately picking her words. Maria Felipa said in her dry, colorless voice: "The Señor Alvarado—or would it be more correct for me to call him Mr. Morgan?—has been with my father for most of the morning. There was, you see, some news of his grandfather. Taking my father's advice, he decided to leave at once, so as to take advantage of the escort provided by the good soldiers who brought you here. I said I would tell you." Pausing shortly, as if to give the dumbstruck Ana a chance to find her breath, Maria Felipa added casually that of course the Señora Dos Santos would be their welcome guest for as long as she desired.

She waited calmly then, for the hysterical tears and ravings that she had expected when she had volunteered to be the one to break the news to "the Dos Santos slut" that her lover had left her without a qualm.

# Chapter Twenty

❦

There were occasions during the next two weeks when Steve Morgan wondered briefly how Ana had fared, and then put her out of his mind. Don Julian Zulueta, as he'd had cause to find out, was an astute man—far too civilized to do anything but send Ana back home to her parents. Steve had other things to think about, and time to wonder wrathfully what in hell's name had gotten into his grandfather.

Don Julian, surprisingly, had not told Steve very much, he'd merely hinted.

"Your grandfather and I are very old friends—business friends. I first met him in Spain. You had no idea? Well, you must forgive me, but before I could speak frankly to you I had to make sure that you were in fact Don Francisco's grandson—you understand my predicament?"

Watchfully, Steve had admitted that he did understand, and Don Julian, a rather plump and balding man whose sharp, cold eyes belied his smile, had waved a deprecating hand. "I used the telegraph—a most useful invention, that!—and I learned . . . many interesting things. You've made quite a name for yourself in the business world, young man! Railroads, silver mines—but apart from a perfectly natural desire to find your grandfather, one wonders what kind of business you are interested in here? Cuba is a country torn apart by civil strife. . . ."

Catching his host's sharply appraising look Steve had shrugged.

"Land, mostly. When there's a civil war there's bound to be land for sale cheap. Sugar land—coffee land. I understand my grandfather's interests here include cattle ranching? In spite of his years my *abuelo* is an extremely astute business man still. But you may rest assured, sir, that while I'm interested in making money I am *not* interested in carving out a little kingdom for myself out here like my unfortunate compatriot Colonel Crittenden some years back."

Don Julian smiled benignly, nodding his head. "Ah yes—very wise! But it's a pity that certain *other* compatriots of yours do not share your good sense, señor. One must only hope that your government will continue to adopt the policies advocated by Mr. Hamilton Fish, your Foreign Secretary."

If he had been wondering what all this was leading up to, Steve hadn't long to wait. Blandly, while pressing more breakfast upon him, Don Julian had asked after the health of his father-in-law.

"A California Senator I understand? A man who also enjoys investing his money in . . . many and varied projects, one hears. A pity—he is recovering well from his wound, I hope?"

"If he knows all that, he's probably been told I was supposed to be headed for Mexico with Ana. . . ." Steve thought grimly although his face stayed impassive.

"Well enough—the last I heard. Naturally, my wife stayed with him."

It wasn't natural that he should be traveling with a mistress masquerading as a wife, Steve thought; but hell, he'd leave Zulueta to draw his own conclusions, he seemed clever enough at doing so!

Surprisingly, the older man had dropped the subject and gone back to Don Francisco instead.

"Ah good! But you must pardon an old man's forgetfulness, I really meant to speak with you about your grandfather—your *abuelo*. Being concerned for his safety in rebel country myself, I contrived to make some inquiries, and although he's safe enough, still it might be wise if you went to him? I can arrange for it if you can be prepared to leave in a hurry. The Teniente who escorted you here and his troop will be departing at noon for Camagüey. It's comparatively safe there now since our good Captain-General Pieltain managed to exterminate Agramonte—he was one of the rebel leaders, you know."

To Steve's further surprise Don Julian had also been thoughtful enough to show him maps—which of course only served to emphasize what pitifully little territory the so-called rebels controlled. The Spanish soldiers were disciplined, well-organized and in control; the sugar harvest last year had been a record one in spite of the hostilities. "I wonder why he's telling me all this?" Steve wondered, the thought striking him that he already had most of the information Bishop had wanted, why stick around? But even with that thought still in his head, his mind was already racing ahead and he could feel the hot leap of excitement that always came with danger and challenge. He knew, even before Don Julian had finished his little discourse—had it also been a lesson? —that he was going to leave for Camagüey province to find his grandfather, and incidentally discover what the hell was really going on in Cuba.

"The fastest—and the safest—way to get to Camagüey is by sea. There is a ship waiting at Cárdenas to take the soldiers there. It will also pick up a large cargo of rum—made right here of course. And so—good luck! Remember me to your grandfather and tell him that if there is anything I may do for him I will consider it an honor."

The obliging and ubiquitous Señor Zulueta had left Steve wondering, and the question in his mind remained to nag at him from time to time. Hadn't his erstwhile host been almost *too* obliging? And what secret had he been hiding behind his smile? The trouble was, Steve thought restlessly, he had too much time on his hands while he was cooped up on the slow, wide-bodied vessel that seemed to lumber through the seas instead of skimming them. The Spanish Lieutenant, a boring young man whose name was De Marco, spent most of the time they spent together talking either about the atrocities committed by the rebels or recent Spanish victories. He boasted of being a man who was married to his career—and a good thing, Steve would think, excusing himself when he'd had a bellyful of the man's long, pointless anecdotes; going topside to stare at the horizon and sometimes catching a glimpse of another, faster ship that would easily and gracefully outstrip them, passing with a perfunctory flutter of flags. Once he saw a clipper ship in the distance, and it could have been one belonging to the Lady Line. It was then that the one memory he had banished sternly to the recesses of his mind slipped out without warning to taunt him. Ginny—green-eyed lady who'd once been his. Virginia Brandon Morgan, his wife. Or had she already made herself his ex-wife? Damn her—and curse his own pigheaded arrogance! Did he really want the kind of wife he'd tried to force her into being? It was Ginny he should have brought here with him instead of Ana—Ginny, who even if she could make him furious enough to want to strangle her, had never bored him, never let him take her for granted. She was the only woman he'd ever allowed under his guard, and the hell of it was that he couldn't push her out of his mind. She'd proved herself a distraction and an irritant from their first meeting, and ever since then . . .

Swearing under his breath, Steve turned away from the rail. *Perdición* take her, the prideful, stubborn little witch! As soon as his business here was finished he was going to head straight for Mexico, and by God, she'd better be there waiting for him! All the same . . . even while he warned himself to get Ginny out of his mind until he was ready to deal with her, the faintest trickle of unease, more instinct than feeling, made Steve grit his teeth and wish they'd let him sail this damned tub himself. He'd make better time than her Captain—an old man who should have been retired a long time ago. Two weeks, and they still hadn't sighted Port Nuevitas, although ordinarily they should have been there by now. But no—every threat of a squall and they'd put into port—without, however, allowing anyone on shore. It all led Steve to wonder ironically whether Julian Zulueta had been trying to teach him the lesson of patience . . . or was deliberately getting him out of the way? No matter what the man's motives had been, Steve hadn't any choice right now but to wait.

Ana Dos Santos too was waiting—she didn't know for what, but she could *feel* it! Like a small animal caught in a trap, waiting for the worse fate of a knife or bullet, she could sense that something had been planned for her. Something bad.

She had been hysterical, just as the cynical Maria Felipa had anticipated. She'd been prostrate, in a mood that swung between dire hatred of Steve for leaving her so callously in the hands of these smiling, over solicitous people, and sheer panic at being alone, forced to fend for herself. And then, when a doctor had been and gone, Maria Felipa came to her room and spoke to her sternly of pride and inner strength.

"I'm sorry to have to be so blunt, but it's women like you who encourage men to trample all over them! He didn't marry you before he brought you over here as his . . . traveling companion, did he? And nor, I'll wager, did he as much as mention marriage to you. Well?" At Ana's choked sob, the older woman gave a sharp, contemptuous sniff. "I thought not! And yet you cheapened yourself enough to accompany him as his paramour. Didn't you expect what happened? I've observed enough to know that men of *his* kind throw away anything too cheaply and easily obtained as soon as they become bored. *Pah!* if you must have a man in your bed why not pick one who is much older and will treat you well?"

"Ohh!" Ana wailed furiously, stung out of her mood of self-pity by righteous anger. "How dare you speak to me so—and especially when I'm forced to remain a guest under your roof? You've always hated me—don't think I haven't known! It's because of Alonso, because he married *me.* . . ."

"You little fool! Do you think Alonso picked you as a bride? It was his father who did that, with an eye to your dowry. And as for your Alonso himself—what a silly, nondescript pipsqueak! Did you actually think *I* could have wanted him? Oh no, my dear—not at all. If I'm single, it's not because of my looks, it's because I choose to remain so, and thus remain in full control of my own destiny. Why, with my father's money I could pick almost any man I chose for a husband—and have him too! Ah, how I despise stupidity, whether it's in a man or a woman!"

With that, Maria Felipa gave her one last disgusted look and marched out of the room; but the next time they spoke it was Ana, swallowing her pride, who initiated the conversation.

"I suppose you're right," she sighed. "About men, that is." Regaining some of her wits, Ana was now determined to cultivate Maria Felipa, no matter what it took. After all, there was no other woman around to talk to, and Don Julian was either out or shut away in his office with his overseers. And Ana was bored, bored, bored! She had to get away from here, but how could she leave, and where would she go?

Now Ana sighed again. "I was hoping that Esteban would help me decide what to do with the plantation. Certainly *I* can't run it by myself! And my father-in-law made me promise not to sell the land out of his family, so where does that leave me?"

"Now you're talking as if you've regained a few of your senses," Maria Felipa said. She was smoking one of her little cigars as usual—they were made especially for her in one of her father's factories. It seemed to amuse her to act as Ana's mentor, at least for the time. Smoke moved in a long, writhing tendril across the room, brushing Ana's nostrils as the other woman continued: "Well I really don't see why you couldn't run the plantation yourself—except that you'd probably run it into the ground! And it's not doing that well in any case. If I were *you*, I'd look around for a man. It's what you're used to, isn't it? A man to lean on, a man to be seen in public with—bah!"

"But—" Ana began protestingly when the other cut her short.

"Never mind. I'm sure you'll find one. My father's expecting a visitor any day now—an extremely good-looking, dashing young gallant—just the type you'd go for, and he's something like your ex-lover. Tell me about his wife."

"What . . . who . . . ?"

"Please. There's no need to stutter. I asked you to tell me about Mrs. Morgan. Her name is Virginia, I understand? What kind of a woman is she?"

Like floodgates opening, Ana was at last able to get rid of some of the accumulated hate and resentment that had been pent up inside her for so long. She talked about Virginia Morgan—who had been Ginny Brandon—her background, the scandal attached to her name and her open, flagrant affairs with other men. And she talked also of Ginny's father, and her stepmother, and the *other* family scandal that had burst upon the shocked citizens of New Orleans just before Ana and Steve had left. And by the time she had finished speaking, Ana had completely forgotten to wonder why Maria Felipa had asked her that particular question. All she knew was that she felt better. Much better!

And later, when Maria Felipa, smiling, relayed to her father the information that Ana had given her, he smiled too.

"I don't know what I'd do without you, daughter. You're much more my child than any of those lazy sons of mine!" He actually chuckled. "Well, well! I expect we'll hear more when our guest arrives. I'm certainly glad he remembered to find out where I'd be at this time of the year—he's quite a clever young man. Resourceful and intelligent as well. Well worth the extravagant wages I pay him. Perhaps, when he's ready to leave for Havana, I should ask him to escort Señora Dos Santos there?"

"She's a stupid, boring woman, and it's been a strain to try to carry on a conversation with her." Maria Felipa shrugged, trying to hide her pleasure at her father's rare compliment. "I'm sure she'll find another protector in Havana, if this Señor Delery who is to be our guest does not find her amusing for a time."

Andre Delery, disembarking at Matanzas, arrived at the Alava plantation by the end of that week, much to Ana Dos Santos' dismay. Of all people . . . ! And then her eyes began to glitter with spite. Why should *she* fear the man, after all? She'd done nothing —she'd been used as a pawn, in fact. No, it was Steve Morgan who had to be careful now, and especially of this man who had a fearsome reputation as a duelist. "It serves him right!" Ana thought. Let him squirm his way out of *this* one. After all, there was much she hadn't dared admit to Maria Felipa without incriminating herself as well. But maybe this M. Delery, who must be fresh from New Orleans, would have more recent information.

Ana looked at her reflection in the mirror, decided she looked her very best, and began to look forward to dinner—and meeting M. Delery who was, she recalled, a very handsome man. And wasn't *he* the one who had been challenged to a duel by that poor Senator Brandon? "A man with a taint of danger. . . ." Someone had once said that of Esteban, in the old days. One of her dueña's croaking old friends. But this was also true of this M. Andre Delery, Ana thought, touching her lips very lightly with rouge; and then smiling at herself, "and I think it makes me intrigued . . . we shall scc how he is, whether he likes me or not." It would be a good way of getting even with the man who had left her here without a word or even a message to tell her good-bye—to take this newcomer as a lover. Why, it was even possible that Andre Delery might offer her his escort back to New Orleans, which she'd much prefer to her parents' hacienda in Mexico. She hoped Esteban came after her—it would give her such pleasure to spit in his dark, arrogant face after she'd told him she never wanted to see him again!

# Chapter Twenty-One

Tired of the feeling of being under benevolent guard, so to speak, Steve had resolved to be rid of the too-helpful Teniente de Marco and his men soon after they had disembarked at the unprepossessing harbor of Nuevitas. Unfortunately, the Teniente was of another mind. It was after dark—there was no decent *fonda* or hotel in the whole of Nuevitas, only whorehouses—and a visitor, a stranger, could not be permitted to travel to Camagüey at night and alone.

"No, no, señor! It is quite out of the question. There are rebel *guerrilleros* everywhere, sometimes even in our towns. Besides, there may be news of your grandfather, the Señor Alvarado, at our headquarters. They have been given instructions, you see, that they should keep in constant touch with the señor—for security reasons, of course. This way, you can find out exactly where Don Francisco might be—and tomorrow I will arrange for an armed escort for you."

It was a wind-chased hellcat of a night with a hint of rain in the air, and it was that, as well as the cooler part of his mind reminding him he needed the information the Lieutenant had just promised him, which kept the polite smile on Steve's face as he thanked the stolid young man.

One more night, he thought. And then, with a slightly caustic smile curling one side of his mouth that was unseen by his diligent "escort" in the darkness, Steve thought back to the time when his temper would not have stood for this delay. He was more cautious now. There would be no point in his haring off on his own way on a night such as this, in a strange country he knew practically nothing about. Ana was to have served as his guide as well as an excuse for his being here, but for some reason he hadn't yet fathomed *they* had seen to it that he and Ana had been separated. He'd find out why in the end—but in the meantime he'd surprised them, perhaps, by falling in so readily with their plans for him—even pretending to accept their thin reasoning for his not saying a formal good-bye to his so-called "wife."

Lights bloomed out of the damp night, and there was the sound of stamping horses and someone plucking desultorily at the strings of a guitar. Walls loomed up before them, and there was a sharp challenge from a sentry.

"Ah!" the Lieutenant said unnecessarily in his stiff voice. "Here we are! The barracks aren't much—you'll understand, I'm sure— but at least the officers' quarters are clean enough, and someone is usually out on patrol; there's always a room or two available. So, señor, let us go in out of this cursed wind, eh? Some hot food and a glass or two of wine would set well with us all, I think!"

Much later that night, when the threatened rain had finally come, falling in angry, gusty torrents that left puddles on the floors and drew fecund odors from the hungry, greedy earth, Steve found himself with time to think and sort out all he'd learned. The young Teniente had been a man of his word—there had been hot food, liberally spiced, and quantities of cheap red wine as well as the inevitable *aguardiente*. Even a young and tolerably healthy-looking woman to warm his bed.

Fortunately, in view of his rather frustrated frame of mind, she had fallen asleep quickly, once satiated, and now Steve lay with his arms crossed beneath his head, listening to her even breathing beside him and the diminishing sounds of the storm outside. To-morrow, if all went well, he would be on his way to Camagüey— with the promised escort, of course. But after that . . .

It seemed Steve wasn't the only person who wondered about Don Francisco Alvarado, and that was perhaps why Julian Zulueta had been so obligingly quick to send him here. From what he could gather from the stiff-necked Major in charge here, no one could be quite certain whether Don Francisco was a prisoner of the rebels, a hostage, or a wholehearted sympathizer and sup-porter of their cause.

The Major had tried to be tactful: "We were told, of course, to give special consideration to the Señor Alvarado—the Marques, should I say? He insisted that he did not use the title. . . . But be that as it may be—it is certainly an extremely ticklish situation, señor! I have not known what I should do, to tell you the truth. We've received messages—written in Don Francisco's own hand, as you've attested. Well—but you've also seen for yourself how short, how ambiguously worded these letters are! He's in rebel country, and I've been unable to send out a detachment of my men to find him, for by doing so I might endanger his life. And they're all up in arms, of course, at what they term the 'murder' of that arch-rebel Agramonte. You see my position?"

Steve did. Just as he had quickly perceived his own situation. He had been sent here, of course, to go to his grandfather. To find him on his own, and to take him away quickly—before he became an embarrassment to the Spanish Government.

Unfortunately, neither the Captain-General nor Don Julian Zulueta had any idea of the mulishly stubborn arrogance of Don Francisco Alvarado, Marques de Santillan, who had always insisted upon doing things in his own way and his own time. Steve frowned blackly into the darkness now, remembering so many other occasions on which they'd clashed, he and his grandfather. Had he brought Jaime Perez, his bodyguard, with him? His terse communication dated some months ago and forwarded to Steve in New Orleans had said very little besides stating the fact that he was going to attend personally to his affairs in Cuba. But it wasn't possible that those affairs included Don Francisco's personal involvement in a rebellion against the Spanish Government —on that much Steve was willing to wager.

Staring into the darkness, he found himself remembering another time and another country, where he had been the rebel—not only in the eyes of the French government of Mexico but in the view of his grandfather as well. Don Francisco had always upheld the authority of an established government, and being Spanish-born himself there was surely no doubt as to where his sympathies would lie. And yet . . . "I wonder why I never knew he had estates in Cuba? He would have mentioned it, surely. . . ." Steve's thoughts brought him to no conclusions, and when the girl beside him sighed and stirred, pushing her rounded bottom up against him, he began almost absentmindedly to caress her moist, willing body. Tomorrow would come soon enough, and with it the answers he sought. Tonight was tonight, and if he couldn't sleep there were still pleasant alternatives to pass the time. As he had learned to do during the years when he had lived one day at a time, Steve deliberately closed his mind to everything but the moment.

At the same moment, but in another place, Ginny was caught in the throes of a nightmare. She had been dreaming that she was dead, buried alive, and then they had dug her out and wrapped her body in a black shroud, winding it round and round until it covered her face and even her eyes. And she was thinking to herself, "How can I be dead and know what is happening to me? But if I'm alive why am I so still and so stiff?" And from a long way off she thought she could hear voices, even though, wrapped in her shroud, she could see no one and recognize nothing.

"I thought I saw her move!"

"She's still unconscious, can't you see? In any case, she mustn't be allowed to move. He said so."

"Be sure there is somebody by her side every minute. And be very careful, especially when you give her nourishment, that you do not let her head move."

"You should sleep . . . sleep . . . sleep . . ."

The last word, in a strangely accented voice, kept echoing in the dark cavern that was her head, growing softer and softer until it faded away completely. And that was when she knew with certainty that she was asleep and all this was a dream from which she'd wake up soon; at least, so she thought at that particular time, but then she was given something to swallow and then her sleep became deeper and deeper until she could hear nothing and think nothing and *was* nothing.

How strange it was! To come swimming close to the surface of consciousness, longing to burst free, but too lethargic to do anything but drift back to the bottom in big, turning spirals in which she was weightless in spite of the now-familiar stiffness and rigidity of her body. "I suppose I've grown used to my shroud. . . ." she thought pensively, and even that thought was not frightening any longer.

Now her long sleep seemed pleasant, a familiar limbo, but the voices she still heard, even beginning to recognize them and separate them, had begun to get louder, disturbing her.

"Why doesn't she wake up? It is not normal. . . ."

"Be quiet—see, she moved again. She'll wake up when he decides the time is right. Don't you understand what has been explained to you?"

They were women's voices—one older, one younger. And sometimes there was also a man's voice that was in some distant way familiar. She thought he talked to her sometimes—*to* her, and not about her, over her head to other people. His voice was low and soothing and painted picturse in her mind that took her away from the darkness and the constant feeling she had of being wound up in her black shroud.

There was no feeling of time passing—she merely floated and sometimes imagined that she was flying and then falling, but her fall was always very slow and cushioned. How very light she felt! It was neither difficult nor unpleasant to stay as she was in a state of non-being; and perhaps it would have been easier, but one day Ginny suddenly realized that she was no longer dead nor half alive nor even asleep and dreaming. She was awake and there was someone singing very softly in a language she didn't understand, although the song sounded something like a Spanish flamenco, sad and sobbing. But that was in another room; the room, or the place that she was in was dark as pitch.

And yet she was aware. It was really the strangest feeling, like being hidden and yet able to see and hear what others were doing. Like being behind a wall with a chink in it that let her hear—the pretended wall in Shakespeare's *A Midsummer Night's Dream.* Or perhaps what she had *thought* she dreamed was partially true and she had been taken for dead and laid in a coffin, a black box. . . . "No!" her mind called sharply. "No, I would much rather I was really dead or dreaming than buried alive."

She must have said something audible, or made some noise, although her heart was beating so loudly with terror that she wasn't aware of it herself. But suddenly she felt a hand touch hers, then take it. Fingers that were warm and firm gently touching her forehead.

"Don't be afraid. There's no need to be; I am here with you as I've always been, as I always shall be. Lie quiet, love, for you have been very ill indeed and must not worry or let fear overcome you in case you have a relapse. Hold on to my hand, hold on tight—I shall not leave you. Dear heart, I shall never leave you!"

Surely, surely, she must be dreaming again? The voice she heard was husky with emotion, but it was a strong voice, belonging, she could sense somehow, to a strong man. One she knew but could not place. Her fingers clutched tightly at his as she struggled to open her eyes but could not. It was still so dark—why, why?

"I'm not . . . not in a cellar, am I? The rats . . ."

"No, hush. Don't even think of such ugly things. You are not in a cellar—by no means! You are in a room, on a comfortable bed—at least, I hope it is comfortable? You have been very ill and you must try to keep calm, to stay that way. Please trust me."

"Am I in a coffin? Is that it? Did they—did someone think I was dead and bury me alive? I think I remember—yes, I do remember that there was an earthquake. I was in a church, and I had begun to run but I fell—something fell . . ."

"Don't think about it, don't worry about anything, do you hear me? You're safe now, and looked after. You must rest, and I will explain everything later, I promise you. Here, my love, drink this."

She felt the cool rim of a cup at her lips—warm, soothing liquid that ran down her throat like honey. She was awake, *awake!* Dear God, why was everything so black, why did she still feel as if she was wrapped in a dark shroud?

"It's not opium, is it? I couldn't go through *that* again, it would kill me! Are you a doctor? You sound like one. . . . Am I really awake or is this part of the dream?"

She could hear her own voice flowing away from her—what an odd experience! It grew softer and fainter until she couldn't hear it at all and felt herself start to float again, down, down and further down until the bright surface she had almost reached was drowned in blackness and she must have fallen asleep again.

The woman's voice sounded cross. "How are you going to tell her? She has had too many shocks, I think, and has been in a coma so long—you said yourself it could be dangerous."

"My dearest sister, I am the doctor! You must not worry. She must get stronger first, and in the meantime, while she sleeps, I shall be talking to her; preparing her for the time when I feel she is ready to be completely aware, and to accept."

"Richard—are you *sure?* I don't want to see you hurt, you know that. How do you know that she will . . ."

"I know it. Please trust me. And when she has her children with her, all will be complete. Have my instincts ever been wrong?"

"No, but . . . but, Richard, is it *right?* You know I'd do anything for you, anything that would make you happy, and *her* as well, the poor unhappy pretty child! But her . . . the man, the father of those children—what of his claim, his feelings? It is not like you to disregard such things, and I suppose that is what worries me most!"

This time he laughed, but sobered quickly. "Ah, Helena! My wise, wonderful, understanding and so-practical sister! Believe me, I disregard nothing. Especially not the fact that *he*, the man about whose feelings you concern yourself, cares nothing for those two poor babes—any more than he cares for the sensibilities of the woman he forcibly married. What kind of a man would neglect his wife, flaunt his mistresses in her face—yes, even her own stepmother was one of them! And he hasn't bothered to take the time to view his children. No, he's traveling in Cuba with a young woman he was once engaged to marry. Can you blame my love for leaving him? She doesn't love him any longer—she will love *me*. And as soon as everything is accomplished we will go away together. We'll be happy, and you, dearest and most understanding of sisters, will visit us often, will you not? You would enjoy being an aunt!"

The woman's rather gaunt features softened slightly although her tone remained acerbic. "Indeed! It's not like you to be such a dreamer of dreams, so impractical. And I've not consented to play a part in such a mad scheme as you suggest. To aid in the abduction of two innocent babes—"

"But it will not be abduction, sister, since you will be helping reunite a mother with her children. They will be *our* children—don't you think it is ironical and yet fitting, since the same blood runs in our veins?"

# Chapter Twenty-Two

❧

"But I can't understand," she said confusedly, "where I have been and where I am now. And what has happened in the meantime. The last thing that I remember it was . . . it was a very hot, still day, and I was feeling ill from the heat so I went to the church, and there was an earthquake. . . . Since then I think I have been dreaming. I dreamed that I was dead or buried alive so that I could hear voices in the distance and see nothing. Am I awake now? Is it very dark? I can't see you, although I hear your voice, and it is familiar to me." She moved her head, and touched it with her fingers. Her forehead felt moist and cool. She felt like a stranger to herself, to her own body. She said fretfully, "Why don't you say something? Who are you? I feel as if I know you and don't know you—it's all very strange. I've been ill, haven't I? What is wrong with me?"

She moved restlessly and knew that she was lying in a bed with clean linens. The top sheet fell away from her shoulders, making her realize suddenly that she was naked under it. The feeling of unreality, of being in a dream within a dream, persisted. A hand touched her hand and held it. That too, she felt, was familiar, like the sudden, cool pressure of lips against hers.

"My dear . . . my very dearest wife. There is so much to explain, and I will do so. But you must promise to lie still while I speak, and to stay calm. You have been very ill for a very long time, and you're still weak. You mustn't exert yourself. . . ."

"But I don't understand! Who *are* you? I do know your voice, and you just said—you just called me your . . . your wife. You're not Steve—your voice sounds a little like his but you're not . . . he's not . . . what is wrong? Why can't I see you?"

The hand she held tightened over hers and the silence seemed to spread and undulate between them; something like the stillness after an explosion. Although it seemed like eons the time that elapsed between Ginny's frantic question and the quiet answer she received was no more than a few seconds.

"But you *will*, my love, and very soon. I am a doctor, you see, and I have learned that there is nothing organically wrong with you. After the blow to your head there was a certain amount of pressure that I was able to relieve—you were in a semiconscious state, a kind of coma, for several months. But no—I can feel your agitation, and there is no need for it. Won't you trust me? As I was saying, there is no *physical* reason why you should not see. But I am a doctor not only of the body, but of the mind as well— I have spent years in the East, sitting at the feet of holy men whom some call 'gurus' or masters—studying cures that they effect that would be called miracles here in the West. So—if you find that you cannot see now you should try to realize that there is some reason why. Inside your mind. When that deeply hidden reason finds its way to the surface of your consciousness and you understand *why*—then you will see again."

Sheer terror made Ginny cling to the hand that held hers. The words that were soothingly uttered hardly made sense to her at that moment.

"I'm . . . I'm *blind!* NO—oh, God, I think I had much rather be dead! I'm afraid . . . I've always been afraid of the dark, and now I feel it pressing down upon me like a . . . like a black velvet pillow, cutting off my breath—I can't breathe—help me! Whoever you are . . ." Sobbing, she lifted herself upward as if to fling herself off the bed, but found herself so weak that she fell back again, still murmuring, "Help me . . . help me!"

The voice she had heard so often in her dreams, talking to her, comforting her, came strongly now to cut off her stumbling, half-whispered pleas.

"I cannot help you unless you want to be helped—you must understand this. You must listen to me, trust me; if nothing else, know and believe that I love you. That we have been together before and will be again. That in past lives and in this one I am your husband and you are my wife. Listen to me and turn all of your mind and your concentration upon my voice now—listen to me, close your eyes. There, you are merely playing a game now of blindman's buff, remember when you played such a game as a child? That is all there is to it. We are playing a game, and I shall lead you into safety and into light. But you must listen çarefully and hear everything I say to you."

And now her cries for help were in her mind only as she clung to strong hands, trying to still her gasping sobs; she began to concentrate on listening to his voice as he had instructed her, because she had to have something to cling to with her thoughts as well as with her trembling fingers. And gradually, as his voice went on softly and unfalteringly—talking to her, soothing her, guiding her out of a morass (or so she felt) and onto firm earth, she became calmer, letting go of the tension within herself and letting his hands and his voice enfold her and hold her closely and safely.

"How do you do it?" the older woman who was called Helena asked some time afterward. "Do you use on her this . . . this process I have heard referred to as mesmerism or animal magnetism? Somehow she does not strike me as being a docile kind of woman—not with that shade of hair, certainly! And yet it is amazing how calm she becomes with you. Has she really begun to accept you as her husband? My brother, I hope that you are not embarked on a dangerous and hurtful deception, or a game that will cause heartbreak and tears. I have heard her call out in her fever for this man she calls 'Steve,' her *husband*. . . ."

"No real husband! She was practically forced into marriage with him, and he has never been faithful to her, never given her anything but unhappiness. She is becoming used to me, she leans on me, needs me, trusts me—don't you see it for yourself? She is beginning to love me. When we leave here together it will be as husband and wife—as a family. You will see, my doubtful one!"

Richard Avery, Lord Tynedale, smiled teasingly at his sister, who did not smile back, but shook her head at him with her mouth pulled down at the corners. Helena Avery was much older than her brother and loved him as fiercely as a mother. She had been proud and happy when he had decided to become a doctor. She had stayed unmarried at home with her mother and father while Richard, who had to have his chance, traveled abroad for years on end, always studying, always seeking. For Richard had a thirst for knowledge, and Helena alone understood when he came home once to explain that Western medicine barely scratched the surface; it was the East that drew him, where it was taken for granted among the enlightened that in order to cure the body the unseen and uncharted powers of the mind must be enlisted as well. Her father, Lord Tynedale, had not approved, and Helena knew why. It was because of her mother, who had been born in the East and had been a Princess and heiress to a mighty kingdom. Only there had been others, guardian of the girl child she had been, who plotted to kill her and supplant her. It had always sounded like such an adventurous and romantic story! The young English Lord who had gone to join the East Indian Company, crossing the border from Afghanistan to Russian-controlled Persia. He had been a spy for the Company, disguised as a merchant. And by some chance he had rescued the young Princess from the men who had taken her away in order to murder her. It was a long story—parts of it Helena did not like to think of. But Richard was truly his mother's child, and always his horizons had seemed much broader than hers, always he had had the urgent, burning desire to travel, to learn, to experience other lands and other cultures. Why, after one of his journeys he had actually come back to announce that he had been to Mecca—what had started out as an adventure had changed him in some way and he was now a Moslem, as their mother once had been.

Yes, Helena thought now, Richard was certainly an extraordinary man—he was the kind who was never still, never content to remain in one place for too long. He had the gift of healing, that much was sure, and had he desired to do so he could have been world famous. How strange that Richard, who had always seemed so . . . so self-sufficient and almost monkish in his ways before, had suddenly fallen in love! Where would this sudden passion of his lead them all, and what of the woman herself? Helena, having been told some of her story, felt sorry for her, but . . . what if this woman that her brother loved so passionately, so madly, did not return his feelings?

As for Ginny herself, it had begun to seem as if she had somehow moved into another world, another dimension where everything was timeless, and there were no boundaries between day and night. Her only contact with life and with reality lay in the different voices she heard, and particularly the hands and the voice of the man who called himself her husband and was con-

stantly with her—attending to her, feeding her and even reading
to her. He spoke to her of her children—"*our* children" he called
them—and promised that soon she would find herself reunited
with them.

"It will not be long now, dear heart. I know how impatient you
must be, and your sorrow grieves me also. But I have promised
you—"

"How can you promise me such a thing? Even if Steve . . . if
Steve is still too busy with other things to take the time, I am sure
that Don Francisco would never allow them to be taken away.
You don't know what he is like. I have learned to love him, and
he is an honorable man, but he is also an autocrat. They are his
great-grandchildren and he would insist . . . no, you don't know
what you are saying!"

She felt the pressure of his lips against the palm of her hand before he answered her cheerfully, if a trifle mysteriously: "Only believe that I do not make empty promises. Don Francisco . . .
well, Don Francisco is known to me. We are related. I think I can
persuade him that the children belong with their mother."

Somehow, even the fact that she was the mother of twin children did not seem very real to Ginny at times. There were even
times when she would feel that she herself no longer remembered
what she looked like. How long had it been since she stood before
a looking glass, smiling or frowning at her reflection? What would
she see the next time she was able to see, if that time ever came?
The blackness she had to live within terrified her at first, especially since she could not help remembering the darkness of a cellar where she had been left helplessly bound—the horrifying feeling of scuttling things crawling over her shrinking flesh, and
blackness, blackness! But after a while, because she had no choice,
she began in part to accept the fact that she could not see, except
with her mind.

"What do you look like?" she asked Richard Avery one day and
he laughed softly, catching her hand and laying it against his face.

"Ah! Curiosity at last, that's a good sign! Feel—and try to picture me, my love. Don't expect a handsome prince, though. I am
just passable looking, and when I was very young the smallpox left
me slightly scarred, can you feel?"

"Yes—but it doesn't matter. What color are your eyes, your hair?"

"Now you delight me! My eyes are blue, a somewhat dark blue. And my hair is black. I am said to much resemble my father, except that I am not as tall, perhaps. But I am taller than you are, my little wife, as you will soon discover when we go walking together. It is high time you went abroad and walked in my gardens. They are very beautifully laid out and it would give me the greatest pleasure to describe them to you."

She made as if to draw back, shaking her head. "No! That is . . . I'm not ready yet, I don't feel . . ."

He sensed her true feelings in the breathlessness of her voice and said gently: "You are afraid, are you not? Of course—it's normal. But you can't remain in bed forever, relying only on massage to keep your muscles from becoming atrophied. There is nothing wrong with your legs, and you must have exercise—now, you see, I am speaking in my capacity as a doctor! I will be with you, at your side, and you will feel much better, you'll see."

"I have become a coward," Ginny said miserably, knowing that it was true. She could *feel* him looking at her and wondered what he saw, wanting to cover her face with her hands, but he was holding them tightly.

"My darling, you are not a coward by any means. You have been through more than most women are called on to experience, and you have survived and become all the stronger for it. You are not going to let a passing infirmity defeat you."

That evening, when it became cooler, she went walking in the garden with him, wearing a silk dress that he told her was fashioned from a shade of green that exactly matched her eyes; and it was not so very bad after all. There were stone-flagged paths under her soft kid walking shoes that were buttoned halfway up her calf, and the perfume of orange blossoms and other more exotic flowers hung in the air. There was a high stone wall all around his estate for privacy, Richard told her. And when she asked, knitting her brows, where his estate was, he answered her that it was in Mexico.

Mexico! And she hadn't guessed, hadn't thought to ask before now. For a moment Ginny felt that everything, even the air around her had gone perfectly still, as her breath caught in her throat. "Mexico . . ." she thought again, and wondered if maybe she was in Orizaba or in Cordoba, where a small group of Southerners had formed a colony after the war. Some of them had grown orange trees. . . . "I have come full circle," Ginny thought, all in the same moment and felt tears she dared not shed sting the back of her eyes when she remembered things she should not think about. She had said so many farewells to Mexico, and yet she kept returning. Was it fate?

Somehow she managed to keep on walking, with Richard's firm hand holding her elbow. She must try not to let Richard see that his casual revelation had been a shock.

"Are you tired, my love? Shall we return to the house now?"

Ginny moved her head in assent—the unaccustomed exercise had made all her muscles ache. And yet once she had walked tirelessly for miles, barefoot and in rags; once she had danced, feeling herself become one with the music, so that she could have gone on for hours—not the decorous waltzes and lancers and schottisches that were so popular in civilized ballrooms but the earthy peasant dances of Mexico that were meant to be danced under the sky.

Ginny felt as if she were looking back on another person—a fiery gypsyish creature who had stopped at nothing to gain her own ends and win back the man she wanted. Yes, she had believed in happy endings then! Unbidden, the thought flashed through her mind, carrying a thread of bitterness with it: "Even if Steve had continued to love me, or at least to want me, he would not, *now*." Steve enjoyed women who were lovely and laughing and unblemished. Once, callously, he had put her through hell to cure her of what he had termed addiction to opium. He would not want a wife who was blind—she never wanted him to know what had happened to her!

She leaned against the comforting firmness of Richard's arm, trying to picture him—to set his picture in her mind so that she might not see those other pictures she'd like to wipe away: Steve with Sonya. Steve with Francesca Di Paoli, with Ana Dos Santos . . . no, no it was enough and she refused to torture herself any longer!

Later, after dinner, Richard came to her room as he usually did, dismissing the soft-fingered maid who had helped her undress. He always came to see her and sometimes to sit by her until she fell asleep. He would read to her or talk to her of his travels all over the world, and sometimes he would massage her feet and her calves with lightly perfumed oils that always imparted a warm glow to her flesh.

Tonight he found her restless, and in some way changed. Her questions were abrupt, instead of being tentative and faltering like a child trying out its first steps.

"Richard Avery—why is it that I did not formerly meet you before? What was all the mystery about? On the ship, I mean, when I was with Andre and you would watch through your field glasses . . ."

Instead of being annoyed and curt with her, he chuckled. "So you noticed, did you? I had the opportunity to watch you on other occasions too. Once in Nassau when you decided to trespass and take a bath in a prettily framed bathing pool that had its own waterfall. Do you remember?"

Ginny gasped. "Yes! But—"

"Don't you want me to answer the rest of your question? I really didn't mean to become a *mystery*, you know, but I tend to be rather shy of crowds and questions—I have been called a recluse, and perhaps I am one! At any rate, I was engaged in some research and the writing of a paper I had promised to present to a colleague in Vienna. So, I was busy you see, and I did not wish to be disturbed. But I found *you* very disturbing indeed, dear heart. In fact, I found you irresistible! That is why I kept following you around like a lovesick calf. And now I'm glad I did or I would not have found you in the cathedral that day."

"And I am glad too, so I suppose I must forgive you for . . . for watching me at times I thought were private. But tell me this, why do you insist that we . . . that I am your wife?"

"Perhaps because I want so much that it should be so!" His voice sounded almost boyish, and Ginny could feel him lean forward to touch her ringless hand lightly. "Besides, I had to tell them something, you know. All the well-meaning authorities who insist upon passports and other formalities! To tell them we were married seemed the easiest way . . . and going deeper than that, I feel it to be true in fact. Someday I will explain, I promise. When you are ready to hear."

"I wish I could see your face!" she whispered. "Then, when you make your explanations, whatever they are, I would be able to tell . . ."

"If I am lying or not?" But he said it gently, and once more brought her hand up to his face to rest against his lips. "Oh, my dearest—listen to my voice. Touch my face so that you will know if my expression changes. You have been hurt by lies and deception in the past, but I swear that I will not knowingly hurt or deceive you. I love you now and have loved you since I first set eyes on you and even before then. You and I have known each other and loved each other many times before in other lives and will do so again. Do you think I am mad?"

"No." Her voice was doubtful, although she tried not to make it so. "But I can see that there is much you are going to have to explain to me."

Then he began to speak to her, and his voice was low and soothing and strong as she remembered it from so many nights before—reaching her even through the veil of unconsciousness. This was the man who had saved her life; a man who loved her selflessly, and who actually believed that their meeting was meant to be.

That night he did not leave her to sleep alone as he usually did. When his explanations were done Richard Avery made love to her with his words and then with his hands, which were gentle and yet knowing, and with his lips, and finally when Ginny felt that she was a bow, stretched almost to snapping point, vibrating with the need for release, he took her with himself and afterward lay beside her, holding her closely and tenderly until they both slept.

# Chapter Twenty-Three

◈

Afterwards, Ginny was to think of that night as the turning point in her restless, seeking life. She had crossed some kind of unseen barrier—gone wildly running, searching for refuge, and had crossed a threshold, hearing the door close safely behind her. Yes, she would think, at last she was safe, and it was Richard who had made her feel that way. She believed him when he told her that her blindness was only temporary. She trusted him and felt secure in his care and his love. Did she really need or miss that wild seesawing swing of emotions that had her either deliriously happy or miserable? Could she want a man she had to fight tooth and nail to keep, never being sure of him in spite of it? Oh, there had been a bittersweet chemistry between them, her and Steve, but it had been built on conflict and intrigue and uncertainty. They had never quite trusted each other, and that was why they had parted so often.

These days it was getting easier not to think of Steve, or anything in the past. There was Richard who listened to her with neither jealousy nor skepticism and was able to explain everything to her—even her own actions. Like a defiant, perverse child she had fallen into one scrape after another, hurting herself more than she'd ever hurt anyone else. How silly she had been! And now she, once so stubborn and willful, bent on having her own way, was quite content to let Richard guide her. He was an exceptionally wise and tolerant man—patient and loving too. She was lucky that he had fallen in love with her!

The passing of time, once painful and seemingly interminable, no longer seemed important as Ginny let the days and the nights dream by—one fading into the other. She had grown out of the habit of asking "what day is it today?" or "what time is it?" Neither mattered, and this time for the best reason in the world—because she was perfectly happy and content.

Helena went away one day—it was to join her mother she said, rather diffidently. Poor Helena, Ginny thought. Not to have a life of her own, a man of her own. She tried to picture Helena as Richard had described her—tall and rather thin, with an ivory complexion and a high-cheekboned face. Dark brown hair—Lord Tynedale had been fair-haired, of course.

"When did he die? And were they happy together, your mother and father?"

For once Richard let a small silence lie between them before he answered her question, and then Ginny could almost imagine his shrug.

"Do children ever really know? I always thought their story was so very romantic, and certainly my mother always devoted herself to her husband. He was crippled after a fall from a horse—it happened a few years before I was born."

"That must have been sad!" Ginny gave a shudder of pity that was mingled with fear. Suppose *she* remained blind always?

"He died a few months ago," Richard said abruptly as if he had intercepted her thought as he had an uncanny way of doing. "But you mustn't feel bad—he'd been ill for almost a year before and he knew he was dying. I did what I could to make him comfortable at the last. He was a good man."

Ginny thought there was a slight constraint in his speech. She wished she could see, then, as she wished many times a day. The utter blackness still frightened her and she was even more afraid of becoming too dependent on others; a kind of cripple.

"Did you love your father?" In covering her own emotions the question slipped out, and embarrassed at her lack of tact Ginny added quickly, "I . . . I suppose I shouldn't have asked that, but . . . I felt heartless at leaving *my* father behind in New Orleans when he was so very ill. I used to think I loved him very much, but I didn't really know him at all, you see. I think he . . . wished to use me. And then when I was told that he was not my real father at all . . ."

The story slipped out then, and Richard was silent until she had finished. She didn't know what he might say until he surprised her by laughing.

"Oh, my dearest love! How parallel our lives have run! Now I am more certain than ever that the threads of our many lives have always been entangled together. You see, the man *I* called father was not my real father either. I wasn't told—and I would not have known had not some papers, a kind of diary, fallen into my hands. When my—the man I had always thought of as my father had his accident he was told that he could not father another child. This was after Helena was born, my poor sister! She should have been a son! For you see, there was the title, the land and the income that went with the title. The last Lord Tynedale was the last of his line, and without an heir everything he possessed in his lifetime would, because of a complicated entail, pass to the Crown. So you see why, in order that my mother and my sister were to be properly provided for, an heir was necessary?"

"Oh, Richard! You don't have to—I can tell how much it pains you to speak of all this. . . ." Ginny felt his fingers tighten over hers briefly, before he said in an even voice:

"No, no—why should it pain me? It was a shock, of course, but I suppose I could understand what went through his mind. He loved his wife and she loved him and was grateful to him for saving her life. And yet . . .

"They talked about it for weeks that dragged into months. And in the end . . . in the end it was agreed upon. My father wrote to an old friend, a very close friend of his boyhood with whom he had lost touch. This man was a widower, also with one daughter who had recently eloped and run off without his consent with a foreigner, to a foreign land. So . . . do you begin to understand at last, my love? How both a plan and *I* were conceived? My father chose my father, and my mother—she is still a beautiful woman, Ginny. She must have been . . . exquisite then. She had been barely twelve when the English 'Milord' rescued her; she was still so young. She . . . did her part as well, and fortunately it did not take long, for my father's friend was virile and strong. I was born nine months after he had left Cuba, the warm friendly land that Lord Tynedale had chosen as a home for himself and his Persian bride."

"And?" Ginny whispered, caught up in her imagination by the story she was hearing. "Did they—this man, your natural father, have you ever seen him? And your mother, did she . . . ?"

"Ah, so you're hoping for a happy ending to this fairy tale? Well, you might call it one, I suppose. Lord Tynedale, knowing that he was close to death, wrote once more to his friend, who had obviously not forgotten, although he'd been gentleman enough to stay away before. He arrived in Cuba a few weeks after my father died, you see? I cannot help but think of Lord Tynedale as my father—and I'm afraid I left soon afterward. An immature reaction on my part, of course, and I would be ashamed of it if I had not met *you*."

It was almost impossible to conceive of, Ginny thought dazedly. But no wonder Richard had blue eyes to clash with his black hair, and no wonder there had been something in the timbre of his voice to stir her with a sense of familiarity—yes, even the long, sensitive fingers that could caress and excite her body so subtly! For of all the unlikely coincidences, it was Don Francisco Alvarado who was Richard's father ("and Steve's grandfather!" Ginny's mind murmured, aghast) and *that* of course was why Richard was so sure that Don Francisco would not refuse to send her children to her.

But what of Steve? What would Steve do when he learned the whole truth of the matter—that he had lost not only his wife but his children as well? And that he was no longer his grandfather's sole heir, either?

"He won't care . . . I'm not sure that he ever believed the children were his in any case. And it doesn't bear thinking of!" Ginny told herself agitatedly. No, she would listen to Richard, who was a doctor of the mind as well as of the body and had told her firmly and positively that from now on she must look forward to the future instead of dwelling in the past. It was exactly what she must do. She had complete faith in Richard—it was amazing how he would calm her and quiet her sometimes fearful moods with the low, soothing sound of his voice. And Richard hid nothing from her, she could count on him to be completely honest. Even to the final, shocking revelation that Don Francisco was now actually married to Richard's mother, and had brought her with him to live in Mexico. It was to them that Helena had gone.

"And now, my darling, I think that you've had enough for one day! I can see you frowning, and any kind of tension is not good for you right now. Only try to remember that you have nothing more to worry about. You are my beloved and my whole passion in life is to make sure that you have everything you want."

Richard's cool fingers touched her forehead lightly and as he continued to speak to her Ginny found herself drifting off into a peaceful kind of half-dream. A few moments ago her head had started to ache, and now she felt no pain at all. She trusted him, and in some strange way she had begun to believe that her life belonged to him since he'd saved it. She had even stopped blaming herself for everything that had happened, for her own weaknesses.

"You are a woman who has survived and overcome all obstacles. What is there to be ashamed of in that? No, my dearest, you mustn't try to tear yourself down, and especially for being a woman with normal urges! You've such a beautiful body that seems to have been fashioned for lovemaking—there's nothing wrong with that! I love you, and yet I'm not jealous of your past or of any of your lovers, whether you thought you loved them or not. You are such a magnificent lover, how can I blame any other man for desiring you? And as for jealousy, *that* has nothing to do with love, only with possession. Stop worrying . . . rest now, and when you wake up everything will seem clear to you."

"Stay with me . . . please." Ginny heard her own voice, sounding breathless.

"I'll always stay with you as long as you want me."

Hands on her body, touching her with tenderness and with knowledge of all her secret places. Not roughly demanding but seeking and giving her pleasure. And forgetfulness, for the moment, of all else.

Sometime later the peace that Ginny had begun, precariously, to enjoy, was ruptured by the arrival of Don Francisco himself, together with his new wife and stepdaughter—and although Ginny was glad to hear that Helena was back, she dreaded the confrontation with Don Francisco that must surely take place. What would *he* think when he learned that she was blind? Perhaps that she was not to be trusted with the care of two young children—he was such a strict, stern old man! How hard it was to think of him as married to a woman much younger than himself who had borne his child—and how strange to think that that child was Richard!

"This is something you must do for yourself, I know that you are brave enough. Smile! He's not going to gobble you up alive, you know. I believe he has a soft spot for you or he wouldn't have come himself."

Richard's words were bracing, but it was hard for Ginny as she sat waiting for the sound of an opening door, not to watch the picture that flashed across the inner screen of her mind. A picture of herself some years ago, facing this same old autocrat and hearing him announce that she must marry his grandson. How many years ago had it been? Time seemed fuzzy, and images ran into each other like spilled paint across an artist's palette. And then, hearing the door open, the sound of a cane slammed against a polished floor and a voice demanding to know what this was all about, Ginny felt as if no time had passed at all. Only this time she wasn't going to give in meekly!

To Don Francisco, as he stood looking at the pretty young woman who sat by an open window with the sunlight burnishing her hair to flame, it was inconceivable that those wide, slanted green eyes could not see him. By God, she *looked* the same, or almost the same—they'd had to cut her hair and it curled about her head most attractively in the style worn by the beauties of the First Empire of France. The stubborn tilt of her chin, as if she challenged his authority before he'd said a word, was the same he remembered. And yet . . .

Recalling why he had come here; still tired from the journey although he would die rather than admit it, Don Francisco sighed as he walked a trifle heavily across the room.

"Genia, my dear—you'll forgive an old man if I sit before we begin our talk? And there is much that we have to discuss—I'd thank you if you'd inform me when you become tired."

As she had dreaded, Ginny could not help the tears that washed down her face before their talk was ended. It was unusual to find Don Francisco so understanding, and most of all to have him ask, haltingly, her pardon for having mistakenly thrust her into a marriage that had obviously made her unhappy.

She tried to say something then: "But I *loved* Steve. Oh please, you don't know me well enough to understand that I seldom do what I really don't *want* to do unless . . . unless I am forced into it." And then, her voice going flatly soft, "I did love Steve. And I thought—dear God, I have been brought up on fairy tales, where everyone lives happily ever after. It's not all his fault, you know! I was never the right kind of wife for him. It ought to have been Ana, who would have been understanding and unreproachful when he . . . went away for long periods. But I—sometimes I wonder if he ever forgave me for what happened to me or for what I *let* happen to me. I think he did love me for a time—or persuaded himself that he did—but . . . what does any of it matter now? I don't know what to say to you, you have been so kind to me, so accepting. But I'm so *tired,* and so . . . maimed! Steve would never tolerate a blind woman for a wife, while Richard—"

"You know everything? The whole story?" She could not see Don Francisco's face, but his voice sounded gratingly husky—not at all the surely arrogant voice she remembered, even after he'd had a stroke.

"Richard has told me some of it. And I *do* understand!"

Uncompromisingly, he told her the rest of it, including the more recent part—his meeting with Steve in Cuba. And it wasn't hard for Ginny to imagine how it had been. She could picture the fury in Steve's eyes, the way his anger must have been tempered by the respect he always, if grudgingly, showed his grandfather.

"He had come a long way to find me. And he stayed in Cuba in order that I might be allowed to leave." Ginny thought, at this point that there was almost a chuckle in Don Francisco's voice; as if he'd been a bad child caught stealing, only that could not possibly be true, could it?

It turned out, though, that the late Lord Tynedale had been a rebel sympathizer, along with his wife, and on arriving at the hacienda Don Francisco, used to unquestioning obedience in all things, had quickly become disillusioned with the Spaniards' way of doing things. He had made friends with some of the rebels and their supporters. He had become annoyed by the fact that the Spanish soldiers thought nothing of appropriating whatever they pleased, whether it be cattle or goats or sheep, in order to feed themselves—and without paying. And in this case it also turned out that Steve seemed to be on the other side. He had wanted his grandfather out of Cuba, but he had been shocked and angry at his grandfather's sudden (at least, *Steve* would have thought it sudden!) marriage.

"We did not agree!" Don Francisco proclaimed with a return of his old arrogance.

"But—"

"It did not matter—a not unusual occurrence! Since Esteban had many friends who were Government supporters I had merely to tell him what *I* wished, and in the end it was done. The last I heard he was on his way back to Havana, in spite of the fact that I reminded him of his obligations here. And of course I did not know at that time . . ."

It was a conversation of broken, unfinished sentences; of significant sighs and pauses. And the end of it very different from the first time they had spoken. Ginny had the feeling that Don Francisco had mellowed—or else still felt guilty for the time when he had not been able to protect her from the French Colonel Devereaux who had arrested her for Steve's crimes and carried her off upon a journey that was to change both their lives forever.

So now it appeared that she actually had Don Francisco's condonation, if not his approval, for the change she proposed to make in her life, and he would even help her to obtain a divorce. It was at this point that Ginny felt the treacherous tears betray her. She felt—oh, God, she didn't quite know *how* she felt! It seemed to her as if for most of her life she had either loved or hated Steve Morgan—his name almost constantly in her mind, and now suddenly that whole part of her life was over and she was starting from the very beginning. Feeling again, starting to trust again—but had she ever been able to completely trust Steve, or her own feelings for him? She could at least be certain of *Richard*, who had saved her life and had never tried to take unfair advantage of her. Yes, she was sure Richard truly loved her, and plainly, even Don Francisco thought the same, otherwise he would not have brought his precious great-grandchildren with him on such a long and tiresome journey.

"I don't know why I am crying!" Ginny scolded herself, even while she felt the warm wetness of tears continuing to gush unchecked down her face. After all, she now had everything she could possibly want . . . didn't she?

Richard stanched her tears in the end. Richard, holding both her hands in his as he kissed her wet cheeks and trembling lips, whispering against them as he did:

"You shall not need to cry for sorrow again my own love. I promise to make you happy. We are going to make a new life for ourselves in a new place—you and I and our children."

As usual, his voice soothed her and made her feel safe. Ginny sobbed retchingly until she was empty of everything—hate and love and frustration and fulfillment and disillusionment. And then she fell asleep in Richard's arms, and in her dreams returned to France and was a young girl of sixteen again, standing tiptoe at the threshold of life with her arms eagerly outstretched to embrace all experiences that lay in wait for her. Now she was free to start again. . . .

# Part Three

# "LOST LOVE"

## Chapter Twenty-Four

☙

Prayers End. The hinged sign at the shabby railroad depot squeaked rustily in the rising wind, and it seemed a logical enough place to get off, considering his present state of mind. "Prayers End"—what the hell! He'd had too much time, sitting in a damned railroad car with no one but himself and his thoughts for company, and the extra miles he'd have to ride through Indian territory would keep his mind on other things. Survival. Maybe even the faint glimmerings of curiosity as to why Sam Murdock had sent for him so urgently. Anything but the same useless, pointless progression of thought-pictures that had haunted him ever since that incongruously sunlit day in Cuba when Maria Felipa Zulueta y Gosalez had put her hand on his arm and told him in her flat, falsely commiserating voice that his wife was dead.

Even now Steve Morgan's mind shied automatically away from that image, going back further to the unpleasant interview with his grandfather that had preceded it.

"You boast of being a free man," Don Francisco had said bitingly, "but *are* you in fact free to follow your own inclinations, or do you merely follow orders? I find it hard to believe that you are here in Cuba on a pleasure jaunt with your latest mistress—or merely because you were anxious to find *me*. Hah!" The snort he had given underlined his words. "You seem to forget too easily and all too often that you are now a married man with a family, which should be your first concern—for let me remind you that I am quite capable still of managing my own affairs. I suppose your friend the ubiquitous Mr. Bishop is behind this?"

Thoughts of his encounter with his grandfather still had the power to make Steve frown blackly. He should have remembered that Don Francisco did not take kindly to interference in his personal affairs, and that he had a tongue as cutting as the riding crop he used to wield so readily. But all the same it *had* come as a shock to Steve to learn that the old man had actually taken a second wife in his eightieth year, the widow of an old friend who had also happened to be a rebel supporter. No wonder Julian Zulueta had been so uncommonly helpful and obliging—so anxious in his veiled fashion that Steve should persuade his grandfather to return forthwith to Mexico.

He'd been able to see to that much at least, thanks to the polite escort of Spanish soldiers who had insisted on accompanying Steve to the late Lord Tynedale's hacienda—the same soldiers who were more than willing to escort the former Lady Tynedale, her new husband and their small entourage of luggage and servants to Port Nuevitas.

At that point, ironically enough, Steve had been of half a mind to leave Cuba himself—send Bishop a cable and a full report by mail and leave Paco, hiding out somewhere with the rebels, to send in his side of the story. But stiff-backed pride had prevented him from more open communication with his irascible and unreasonable *abuelo* and they had parted with cold formality at the docks, Steve bowing over the small but capable-looking hand of his new and still attractive grandmother as he wished her well once more with his voice kept purposefully expressionless.

"I wish you would come with us. . . ." she had said in her soft voice. He had the impression that she would have said more if he had let her, but he had smiled lazily at her as he announced, shrugging, that he had business to attend to in Havana that wouldn't wait.

"*Business* you call it?" Don Francisco had exploded, his blue eyes glittering. "You have two children who will grow up wondering if they have a father! These mysterious disappearances of yours for months on end, with no explanations for those who might worry about you . . . well, I have said all I have to say and will not repeat myself. You have turned yourself into a stranger to all of us."

His grandfather's blunt way of disowning him, perhaps? Steve had not had time to find out, for before he could say anything further there had been a cough at his elbow, a wooden-faced Spanish Corporal sent to inform him that there was an urgent message for him at their headquarters—the señora had traveled many miles . . .

"Go attend to your business, Esteban," Don Francisco had said in a cold, dry voice. "And I shall look after mine."

The señora who had journeyed all the way to Nuevitas to break the news to him herself had been Maria Felipa.

Details. The rest had been details. Andre Delery—Ginny. More irony there or merely fate? He should have remembered her fiery defiance, he should have been warned by her quiet words that day in Sonya's room when he had turned to find her standing rooted in the doorway with comprehension dawning in her eyes. It was then he had lost her, of course. But damn his own ego, he had been sure he'd wheedle her back. Like some typical loutish brute of a husband he had blustered and threatened, ordering her back home when he should have known . . . but what in hell good did it do to go over and over it in his mind? He, and nobody else, was her murderer—as surely as if he'd deliberately thrown her under the wheels of that carriage himself.

"I am sorry to be the one to tell you, but Papa thought it might be best if you heard from a woman. Anything we can do . . ."

Once, he had wanted to kill her himself. Once he'd almost succeeded in doing so and would have strangled her if she had not flung herself against him, pressing her lips against his. . . . Once. A long time ago when they had still been finding each other.

The sound of the wind, skirling around the side of the decrepit building that served as a depot jerked Steve back to the present. Damn memory anyhow. There was no point in going back and back over something he couldn't change. Killing Andre Delery in a much-publicized duel that must have been witnessed by half of Havana had eased none of the ache inside him—Maria Felipa's sudden and surprising offer of her body, her hitherto carefully

guarded virginity (her price for his freedom when he was in imminent danger of arrest and summary execution) had not been able
to erase his urgent and violent need for the one woman he
couldn't have and wouldn't ever have now—Ginny, his flame-
haired vixen, his green-eyed temptress. Prayers End—the name
seemed appropriate enough for his frame of mind.

Not too many strangers got off the train in a godforsaken spot
like this, and the old man who sidled up just as a tall man swung
long legs off the railroad car to stand stretching on the rickety
platform, didn't bother to hide his curiosity.

"You here to see Jack Prendergast, mister?"

He received a frowning look before the man said, with a shrug:
"Well—I guess. He's one of the gents I thought I'd look up while
I was in these parts, anyhow." Hefting heavy saddlebags, he
started to walk toward one of the baggage cars, with the garrulous
oldster scuttling along beside him.

"You planning on stayin' some time then?"

The stranger busied himself persuading his stamping, snorting
horse to leave the comparative security of the baggage car, and
didn't answer.

"Denver House, that's the name of the best durn hotel in
town," the old man volunteered. "That's where all Mr. Prendergast's friends stay when they're passin' through."

"Didn't say I was a friend," the man said in a deceptively mild
voice, but his eyes, catching those of the old man and silencing
him, were a deep, hard blue.

He swung onto the back of the restive horse, headed for the
huddle of buildings that lay some distance to the west, wondering
as he did why they'd picked this particularly remote spot for their
railroad depot. Behind him he heard the old man call:

"You want a cheap place where the food's mighty good try the
Casa Loma. . . ."

Without turning his head the younger man said "Thanks!"
over his shoulder, kneeing his horse into a faster gait as he moved
out toward town.

The old man gazed after him, scratching his head. "Wonder
why he didn't git off at El Paso and ketch the stage instead? Lot
safer way of gettin' to the Prendergast place. . . ."

Two men who had been lounging around talking to the station

master moved out onto the platform, staring after the horse and
rider.

"Another one of Prendergast's hired guns. I tell you, we gotta
put a stop to it or get wiped out!"

"Yeah—we keep sayin' that, but nobody does nothin'. How'd
you know he's one of the Prendergast crowd anyhow? He'd never
be gettin' off *here* if he was."

"Unless he was sent to spy on us. Maybe find out how well
we're organized, maybe—you see all that hardware he was carrying? Packed two guns and a rifle—real new one too. I'm telling
you—"

"You reckon he's the top gun Prendergast was boasting about
hiring? The same one who cleaned all the homesteaders off old
man Brady's range up near Red Mountain?"

"Who the hell else do you think? I'm telling you again, if we
don't *do* something . . ." The speaker, a man in his middle twen-
ties with a shaggy blond beard, looked mad and upset. His face
was red, one hand going up to tug at his whiskers.

His friend spat accurately across the platform, hitting the
tracks.

"Shoot. I'm all for us doin' something myself. Why don't we go
find Milt Kehoe and the rest of the boys? Old Milt—*he'll* have
some ideas, you can bet."

The snaggle-toothed old man, who had edged up close enough
to hear the last said importantly: "I got to see his eyes. Woulda
thought he was a Mex 'cept for them eyes. Real dark blue they
was—an' real cold. Killer eyes." Seeing that he had their attention
he lowered his voice, glancing toward the clerk who stood peering
out at them through the barred window. "And what's more, he
said he aimed to look up Mr. Prendergast. Said they was acquainted. Yep—he sure did!"

The sound of the wind was like women crying—keening for lost
loves, long-lost pasts and never-to-be futures. It blew tumbleweeds
up the street, along with the dust that tasted acrid behind his nostrils. The dust was red and the sky was red, a bloodbath of flame
and crimson streaming down chimney-tall towers of billowing
clouds that presaged a storm in the mountains.

Steve pulled his hat down further over his forehead, scowling.
God, but he was getting fanciful! Maybe it was the strange name

they'd chosen for this town of theirs or maybe just his mood, but where in hell was everyone?

Steve, on the nervous, high-stepping black horse was the only human in sight, although there were other horses tethered to hitching posts along the street. The town was a small collection of ugly wooden buildings huddled together in the middle of nowhere —orange light blooming from windows like coyote eyes caught in the glow of the setting sun. He'd been told that there had been a bigger town here before the war; when the crisscrossing armies of the North and South, playing war games in the deserts of New Mexico Territory had blown it to pieces. Well, some people were just plain stubborn, and gradually they'd started to rebuild, although the why of it was lost on the man who had just reined in his horse and now frowned contemplatively at a faded sign that read Livery Stable.

"Well?" Steve thought, and then, "Ah shit, why not?" One more place to spend one more night before he moved on; and now, as the sun suddenly dropped behind the mountains like a red-hot rock, the bloom of lamplight seemed beckoning, almost welcoming. Not for the first time he wondered grimly why Sam Murdock had chosen this time of all times to take an extended vacation, and why he'd chosen to spend that vacation with "Big Jack" Prendergast, on a ranch in the middle of nowhere. Especially since his partner didn't believe in vacations and had said so on more than one occasion.

"Hell, I'm not going to waste my time wondering," Steve thought grimly. "Let Sam tell me when I catch up with the old bastard."

He'd been doing far too much wondering of late, anyhow. Wasted time . . . not enough time. He swore under his breath. "Why not," he thought again, and coughed the dust out of his throat as he dismounted, long, blue-clad legs making easy work of it so that one moment he was in the saddle and the next, in one lithe movement, standing beside his restive horse, patting his neck while he whispered to a pricked-up ear.

The fat, red-haired man who owned the stable spat. "Damn half-breed Injun!" he thought to himself. The horse was unshod and its rider had dismounted from the wrong side as far as he, Si Barker, was concerned. But then he noticed the tied-down gun snugged low on the stranger's hip and decided what the hell, money was money, and if he had the *dinero* to pay for the care of his horse . . .

This particular stranger looked like a traveler anyhow—the kind who kept moving on, once he had taken care of business. And whatever that business was, Si Barker had no desire to know about it, although he'd already decided that this black-haired hombre was probably a Prendergast gunslinger sent to scout around.

"Milt and the rest of the boys ain't gonna like his bein' here," he thought, his lips splitting to show tobacco-stained teeth in a falsely genial smile as the stranger walked up to him, leading the dust-covered black.

His horse taken care of, Steve headed almost instinctively for the nearest saloon, needing a drink to take the taste of dust from his throat. As small as the town was, there were several to choose from—he decided, whimsically, on the Red Sky. Anyhow, it was closest to the stable.

# Chapter Twenty-Five

❦

The saloon wasn't crowded, as it turned out. Apart from the shirt-sleeved, bored-looking bartender and two men who were intent on a game of chess, an ancient black man sat hunched over the keys of a tinny piano that appeared to be almost as old as he was. He didn't look up when the doors swung open and shut, letting in dust and a puff of hot air, but Steve caught a glimpse of the whites of his eyes before he turned them away.

The chess players glanced up from their game and went back to it, but with less concentration than before. The bartender started wiping hard at the rough wooden counter before him, rattling glasses, and three Mexicans who had been standing together talking among themselves moved to the far end of the room, their dark eyes suddenly wary.

Maybe they weren't used to many strangers passing through— the name of their town probably had something to do with it. Besides, who'd want to stop here? The railroad didn't extend much further and the nearest stagecoach depot was miles away.

"Whisky," Steve said tersely, and felt a disgust at himself for having got off here, just because of a name that had caught his imagination. Morbid. He'd have to watch that. He paid for his drink and tasted it, feeling the fierce rotgut flame all the way down to his belly. It was a far cry from the smooth, carefully blended and aged liquor he'd gotten used to drinking of late—and exactly what he needed right now. From force of old habit, his eyes flicked over the room, noting exits, windows. He felt curiosity in the sly, sidewise glances that were thrown in his direction. Normal for any town that was close to the border and smack in the middle of Indian territory to boot. And the old man at the railroad station had asked if he was a friend of Jack Prendergast. He wondered if that meant that Prendergast ran his cattle this far south. He hadn't in the old days—damn, it hadn't been *that* long ago either! But he'd been in a lot of bars, done a whole lot more traveling since he'd last seen Prendergast, and a lot of things could have changed since then—for Prendergast, as they had for him.

He pushed his glass across the bar for a refill, beginning to wonder if he should follow that old man's advice and try the Casa Loma for a bed and a cheap meal. An early night, and he could be on his way by daybreak or just before. He knew this part of the country. It was funny how many times he'd skirted this town but never been curious or anxious enough to stop.

The swinging doors squeaked open to let in a noisy group of men, bunched together and talking loud. As if he'd been activated by strings, the ancient piano player seemed to sit up straighter as he pounded the keys with more vigor than he'd been showing, and a bored-looking woman of indeterminate age emerged from a back room wearing a fixed, gold-toothed smile.

"Hey, Lottie!" One of the men grabbed her around the waist, giving her a hearty, smacking kiss. She bridled, patting her tightly curled hair.

"Jared Cady—why, what would your wife think? I declare, I find it hard to recollect you're a married man sometimes."

"There ain't any such thing as a married man, Lottie. Only married women!" One of the other men slapped his knee as they all chortled over that one.

Judging from their clothes, they looked to be homesteaders or small ranchers, out for a night on the town. And yet an old sensitivity to danger that had perhaps been too long dormant gave Steve an uneasy feeling. He had seen them glance at him and then studiously look away, pretending to ignore his presence. Reason told him that there weren't too many strangers who passed through this town. A certain amount of curiosity would have been normal, but these men, with their loud voices and jokes, seemed to point up his lonely and negligent stand at one end of the bar as they crowded up against it, keeping a distance between themselves and him.

"Sing us a song, Lottie. Sing 'Dixie.' "

"Sure, anything you say, Milt. But I got to wet my whistle first. It's been a thirsty day."

"Set 'em up for Lottie, Bert. An' for the rest of my friends. Man needs friends around here, right boys? Too many carpet-baggers and land-grabbers trying to steal what's rightfully ours, saying we don't have the rights to our own land, just because we boys fought the war and they didn't. I call 'em cowards and thieves."

"You mean like Prendergast?" One of the men leaned his elbows on the splintery counter top, hunching his shoulders. "Shit, Milt, you know Jack Prendergast for a thief and a man who got his start rustlin' other folks' cattle while they were off fightin' a man's war. You know that fact just as well as I an' the rest of the boys here do."

The man they called Milt lifted his shot glass and tossed down its contents, immediately pushing it back for a refill. Raising his voice, he said:

"Prendergast's a coward as well as being a thief, hiring outside gunnies to do his dirty work for him." Suddenly, his eyes swiveled to the tall man, sun-browned and blue-eyed, who stood silently at the far end of the bar, nursing a drink. "Well! Didn't notice there was anyone else here while we been talking so free. Don't get many strangers around here—land of the carpetbaggers and rene-gades they call this part of the country, not to mention rattlers and scorpions! You ain't any of them, are you, mister?"

Blue eyes met Milt Kehoe's belligerent gaze without flinching, but they were cold and wary too, for Steve had sensed the hostil-ity in the room and was being cautious.

"I'm just riding through . . . mister." He had paused just long enough before adding the "mister" to make it sound insulting, and Kehoe's long face reddened.

"Don't get many folks just riding through this town either. Ain't nothing much to see in this part of the country 'ceptin' cows and dust and dirt—too much dirt. Most of it kicked up by hired guns." He paused and added insinuatingly, "But you wouldn't side with that kind of carpetbagger skulduggery, would you? Bet you was a Johnny Reb, just like us, huh?"

"Didn't get to do any fighting during the war," the stranger said in a deceptively soft, even voice, adding, "It's a long time behind us now, isn't it? And I'm not in the mood for fighting any kind of war right now either."

He finished his drink unhurriedly, flipping a coin on the bar before he straightened up to walk past a taken-aback Milt Kehoe. He noted ironically that, except for the piano player, everyone in the room seemed to have frozen in position, stopping whatever it was they'd been doing to watch. The frightened-looking dance-hall girl they'd called Lottie widened her eyes at Steve and he touched his hat to her on his way to the batwing doors, measuring his steps as he walked. For some reason, there were a bunch of scared and angry people here, and he had the feeling he'd been set up. . . .

"Don't know about you, Milt, but I kin smell a dirty hired-gun carpetbagger a mile off!" The young, tensely excited voice belonged to the blond-bearded young man the woman Lottie had called Jared Cady.

Recognizing the nervous, tensed-up tone in the young man's voice as trouble made Steve pause for an instant, sighing inwardly even as Cady went on tauntingly: "Ain't *nothin'* without them guns—you notice that boys? Ain't even man enough to turn around and face me." A bottle, flung with vicious accuracy, flew past Steve's head to smash at his feet, halting him. He heard Cady's shrilly excited chuckle.

"Hey looky, Milt—he's running, what'd I tell you? Ain't even going to pay for that bottle of whisky he caused me to break."

"Ah shit!" Steve thought, turning slowly to watch the blond man swagger up to him, gun already drawn.

"Pick it up, mister. Bert likes to keep the place clean."

The stranger's eyes were level—cool even as he eyed the gun and then the grinning man who held it. Jared Cady noticed that, and it should have warned him, but he was backed by all his friends and it made him feel brave to face down a professional gunslinger. He said loudly: "Go on—I said pick it up! Every little piece of glass. What you waiting for?" A shot exploded at the stranger's feet and Lottie stifled a scream, but the stranger didn't flinch. "An' when you get that done I aim to take them guns you're packing away before I beat the shit outa you." Cady's laughter was high and keyed-up and his darting eyes invited the crowd's approval now as he snarled, "If you don't hurry I might just shoot a hole in you first! Get to it. Bert was sayin' just the other day he needs a new swampy in here. . . ." He moved the muzzle of the gun threateningly, feeling elation shoot through his veins as the stranger shrugged, acting real meek and resigned. He actually began to stoop over . . . and then his hand chopped up, lightning-swift and vicious.

Cady screamed, clutching at his wrist as the gun flew out of his grasp. "You bastard! You broke my wrist. . . ." Almost sobbing with pain and rage his other arm flailed out, but the stranger moved faster; coldly efficient. An arm to the throat, a chop to the belly. Jared Cady fell back against the bar, retching and moaning, and in the stillness that had fallen the blue-eyed stranger straightened to look around without expression.

"Sure is a nice friendly place you got here," he commented to the stunned-looking barkeep as he lit up a cigar. The second coin he flipped across the bar hit the owner's fat belly and rolled under the counter.

This time, he made it outside, and with the sun gone it was suddenly cold and very dark. Steve drew on the cigar, which was very bad. He let the cigar drop as he suddenly sensed something was wrong. Instinct, maybe; a warning prickling of his nerve ends. Or maybe it was just the *feeling* of movement in the shadows.

A lantern from a window across the street suddenly flared in his face as a shutter was flung wide. He threw himself sideways, cursing under his breath; his gun clearing leather and firing almost at the same instant. But now it seemed as if the shots were pouring at him from too many directions—he felt a leg buckle under him even as he coolly aimed and hit the lantern. No time to reload now, not even to think. Acting on pure reflex, Steve aimed for every burst of fire that bloomed in the darkness; feeling the ugly slam of bullets into his body pushing him backward even while he was trying to struggle upright, using the wall behind him for support.

A shot from behind the water trough hit him in the side, slamming him against the wall again—falling, cursing out loud. And as he forced his body to turn, firing, he sensed movement behind him and tried desperately to swivel and fire again, using the border shift as his left arm became numb and useless. Now he had only one gun—and how many bullets left?

The saloon door opened and Jared Cady, still swaying, held a gun on him.

"You bastard—gonna finish you off for good now."

Steve brought the gun up, discovering he'd fallen again and couldn't get up. He thought he pulled the trigger, but he couldn't be sure because suddenly everything began to fade and his body wasn't obeying the frantic signals of his mind any longer. There was a tremendous booming noise that seemed to explode in his skull, send him spinning through space in a free-fall—very slowly, turning round and round, floating—and a last fleeting thought before all was blanked out: "Christ, I'm dying—" Then nothing.

After the angry crackle and boom of gunfire had ended, the stillness that followed seemed almost painful to ears that were still full of sound. And then suddenly there came a rattle of wheels as a buckboard was driven down the street, and with that noise the release of held-back tension. Now there were voices—shouts, explanations, orders.

"Stop firing, you damn fools, and let's get outa here! We got him. . . ."

"Hey—he got Murphy! And Jared. . . ."

Like a belated footlight, a quarter moon popped its cloud-shawled face over jagged mountaintops, and it could be seen that a woman was driving the buckboard, white-faced and distraught; dark hair flying loose under the white shawl she'd worn against the wind.

"What happened? Somebody, for God's sake, tell me what's happened! Jared? . . ."

"Jared never had a chance, Lizzie. I'm sorry. He was a stranger, one of Prendergast's gun-hung henchmen. He picked a quarrel and just started in shooting. I'm sorry. . . ."

"Hey! Let's get these bodies off the street before the Sheriff wakes up. Sorry, but we'll have to use your wagon, Lizzie. Bert . . ."

"Sure, Milt. I'll see to everything here an' send Doc to ride out to the Cady place right away. Sheriff don't even have to know a damn thing."

"You shouldn't have come out here, Lizzie. I'm real sorry. Here, let me take them reins."

An older man, sturdy bodied, had climbed up beside the distraught young woman, his strong hands controlling the suddenly restive horses who snorted and shied as they scented fresh blood.

"Jared?" she said again in a whimper, and then sobbing, turned her face against his shoulder. Ancient springs sagged and creaked with the weight of the bodies that suddenly eager hands lifted in; blood running over the warped boards.

"What do we do with *him*? I'd like to leave him for the buzzards, he got Jared and Tom and Blackie. . . ."

"We take him along too. We don't want Prendergast to find out just yet. Let him keep waiting—and wondering. Hand his carcass in here, Pete. We kin throw it to the buzzards tomorrow."

It was over an hour's drive to the Cady place, and by then the woman, Elizabeth Cady, was dry-eyed and pinch-faced.

"I knew something was going to go wrong. I begged Jared not to go to town, and after he did I kept having this *feeling*. . . . He shouldn't have taken Fidelito with him, it wasn't a thing for a small boy to see . . . oh, God."

"Hush now, Lizzie, hush. There'll be some of the women to come sit with you tonight. I know it's hard. . . ."

"Jared never had a chance. None of the boys who got it did. He was fast, all right. Wonder what Prendergast was payin' him."

There was more to wonder about after they had reached the house, and some of the men who were unloading the grisly cargo of bodies discovered that one of them at least—the stranger who was Prendergast's hired gun—was still alive.

"The bastard's still breathin', although I sure can't understand how." Milt Kehoe sounded rattled. "I'm gonna finish him off right now. That way—"

"No!" He turned around in amazement as Elizabeth Cady's cold voice stopped him with his gun already drawn and cocked.

"Now, Lizzie—"

"No—" she said again in a dead-sounding voice that became stronger under the gaze they all turned on her; some eyes pitying, some curious. "If he's still alive and Doc can make him well again, he's going to hang. For murder!"

# Chapter Twenty-Six

When consciousness returned, it was like seeing the surface of the ocean from many feet below—mere shadings of light and dark, with shadow images that swam past his barely focusing eyes and then disappeared. He was awake—or alive at least—but where? How? He closed his eyes and when he opened them again (it seemed only seconds later) he was in a small room, bright with sunshine, and there were bandages everywhere on his body, even swathing his head which ached intolerably, like the rest of him. There was also a woman in the room, quite pretty, with dark brown hair and hazel eyes. Her face was cold and sullen as she stood looking down at him, her eyes becoming narrow and hard when they met his. He couldn't understand the look on her face. Why did she hate him? He'd never seen her before.

Steve tried to speak, but even as he thought about it, he realized that he was too tired and too weak to make the effort. He must have made some sound though, because she bent over him, giving him water that almost choked him. He heard her ask in a flat voice that seemed to come from far away if he could talk, and then, in spite of himself he felt the heaviness of his eyelids overpower his will and he slept again.

Now he hovered between sleep and half-waking. Once he was aware that *she*, the sullen-faced woman, was bending over him again, forcing him to swallow some watery soup. And another time it was a man with a silver-sprinkled beard who unwound his bloody bandages and brought so much pain he couldn't help groaning. The woman was there too in the background with her closed, angry face.

"Is he going to live, Doc?"

"Can't imagine why he's still alive, after all the lead he took. He's got a strong constitution, I guess, and you're a damn good nurse, Lizzie. Not that I don't regret fixing him up, in one way. . . ."

The conversation puzzled the man on the bed and he wanted to ask . . . but the thought went away before it was complete and the pain was much worse after the Doctor had left. Although he tried to stay awake long enough to ask the woman . . . to ask her why . . . he must have passed out again.

Next time it was evening. Of what day he had no way of knowing, but the light from outside was reddish and growing dimmer and he was aware that a lamp had been lit in the room. The woman brought him broth in an earthenware bowl and proceeded to feed him, to his continuing humiliation. This time, forcing himself, he was able to mutter "Thanks . . ." after she had finished.

She had begun to get up from her chair, but now she paused, turning to say curtly, "You feeling any better?"

Steve moved his head, closing his eyes against the shooting pains that jagged through it when he did, and without another word she left the room; returning almost immediately with a pair of manacles. Without his being able to prevent her, she secured his right wrist to the iron bedstead.

His frown was puzzled. "Why did you do that? I thought . . . the Doc said something about your nursing saving my life, didn't he? So why—"

"Only so they can hang you," she retorted coldly, turning her back on him. He stared at the door she'd just closed behind her, trying to think, to remember, and found that he couldn't. Even that small effort tired him out and he found himself slipping from reality into sleep again.

The next day she was back, attending to him efficiently and without feeling, just as she would have tended a wounded animal meant eventually for the slaughterhouse. It had to be morning— she had brought him some vile-tasting gruel for breakfast and refused to talk to him at first.

"Why?" He felt strong enough to be persistent. "I'd like to know why they're going to hang me, and why you're so eager for it to happen."

Finally, stung to anger, she turned on him, her voice cutting. "One of the men you killed last week was my *husband*." Her

voice turned bitter. "You came out of nowhere like a prowling
wolf—a hired killer. They told me how fast you were, and that
you deliberately—you never even gave him a chance, did you? So
now you know why you'll hang, and why I'll be there to watch!"

"But I—" He was still frowning, trying to remember, when she
whirled about and left, the slamming of the door intensifying the
pain in his head. He closed his eyes and lay there, feeling pain all
over his body. Reminding him . . . yes, there had been shots. The
sound of gunfire spitting flame at him. The ugly shock of bullets
tearing into his flesh. He had no right to be alive—he remembered
dying!

The window of the room he was in was shuttered now, but the
shutters were old and warped and hints of sunlight filtered in
along with noises from outside: voices; the sound of hoofbeats; a
cow bawling.

The woman—who was she? Had she been there when all the
shooting was going on? And why wasn't he dead? Whenever he
tried to think, his head started aching all over again; whenever he
tried moving, the pain was so bad he became sick with it, retching
helplessly. It was easier to sleep, to die again. . . .

In his half-sleep, half-coma, he moved and thrashed about, not
aware that he had broken open his wounds again. The warm stickiness of blood and the coldness inside made him shiver uncon-
trollably. . . . He was only vaguely aware of all these things, and
he thought he might be awake again because he could hear the
sound of his own voice. What had he been saying? His skin felt as
if it were burning, and he had kicked the covers off. Her hand felt
as cool as ice water on his forehead.

"I think you have a fever again. Drink this."

He was tired of the game she was playing. Why in hell
wouldn't she let him die? But she held a cup firmly to his lips,
forcing him to swallow—he hated the feeling of helplessness and
rage.

His voice, when it finally emerged, sounded husky and almost
disembodied.

"Look, miss—ma'am—" Damn, she looked too young, too girl-
like to have been married.

"You mustn't try to talk." Resolutely she moved away, leaving
him more frustrated than ever. He had begun to wonder whether

she existed apart from his imagination, or if he was in fact alive. He had fantasies—or were they dreams? Maybe he was really dead and this plain, whitewashed room was hell.

He began to study the room, noting that in the daytime the sun streamed through broken slats in the shutters, making patterns on the floor, on the wall. On the opposite wall there was a sampler, and in the corner a small wooden crucifix. Was she a Catholic? Across from the iron bedstead there was an old-fashioned dresser; a crocheted doily on it. Under the window a washstand holding a handle-less pitcher of battered copper and a chipped porcelain washbasin.

This couldn't be a prison, there were no bars. And yet he was a prisoner, the clanking of the rusted iron manacle against the bed reminding him of the fact; and he had been told he was to hang. For God's sake, why? Had he been tried while he was still unconscious, or was this hanging the woman had spoken of to be a lynching in actuality? Why hadn't he seen anyone but *her*? Had there really been a Doctor here the other day, bending over him, changing dressings, or had that been a dream as well?

He fell into a tortured kind of sleep that was full of nightmares in which he could watch himself killing, running, pursuing—riding across deserts and mountains with someone unseen always after him. And sometimes there was someone riding with him. Soft woman-body leaning curved into his, tangle of coppery hair blowing against his face, half blinding him. He was trying to hold on to her, but there were shots and he was falling—gunshots cracking like whips, the feeling of them cutting into his body, bringing agony beyond bearing while he died again—he knew he was dead because he was underground somewhere, locked up, fighting to get free before he suffocated.

He attempted to start up and the manacles clanked against the bed as he fell back weakly, panting as the sweat poured off his body. In his angry mind there was a sense of loss and of pain that was inside as well as outside—mixed with a bitter frustration.

Suddenly the woman was back, her hands touching him—and for once her voice betrayed a trace of feeling. "What on earth have you been doing to yourself? Were you foolish enough to think you could get free?"

He was almost tempted to plead with her, but he forced himself into silence. She had put down the lamp she had been carrying, and he noticed irrelevantly that she was wearing her hair in a fat, demure braid over one shoulder. She had on a light wrapper of some kind, belted at the waist, and when she leaned over him he became conscious of the faint soapy-clean woman smell of her. She put her hand on his forehead and said with concern, her hand now moving impersonally down to his chest, "Why, you're wringing wet! You did have a fever. . . ."

Suddenly their eyes met and held, his desperately searching, questioning—hers puzzled, slowly turning darker as she turned away abruptly as if she couldn't stand to look at him any longer. "You must be thirsty," she said stiffly, and she brought him water. She was always forcing him to swallow something, but this time he was grateful for it.

"Thank you. . . ."

She acted startled, turning aside to straighten his pillow; pull the covers back up over his semi-nudity. He was really noticing her now, as a female. The wrapper she wore was shapeless, but for an instant the curves of her body had been outlined against the lamplight. She turned almost too hastily to leave, hand already poised to pick up the lamp when he said, "No—don't go yet. Please."

She paused with her back to him. "You're going to be all right now, the fever's broken."

"I must talk to you." His voice was impatient. "Surely you can understand?"

"*Understand?*" Her voice grew almost strident, and now she suddenly turned around with her lamp-shadowed face all hollows, hard and implacable.

"Mister, I understand your type all too well! Vicious killers like mad dogs looking for victims to pounce on—the guns you wear are a license to kill anyone in your path, like my husband. You and your kind"—she sounded venomous—"they should have kept you in jail instead of turning you loose—or did you get loose on your own?"

"*Jail?* What do you mean by that?" His black brows had drawn together and his voice had turned as harsh as hers.

She laughed scornfully. "Oh, there's not many secrets you have from *me*, mister. Did you think no one would notice all those scars? You've worn irons and you've been flogged—and they should have finished the job while they were about it! Whatever you did to put you in there, it must have been real bad. You—you're evil, that's what you are. . . ."

He had been listening grimly, waiting for her tirade to run to an end, and now he said in a voice tight with frustration, "My God, you've guessed more about me than I know myself, it seems. So I'm an escaped criminal; and now a mad-dog killer. . . ."

"That's right! And don't you go getting any ideas just because I . . . because I nursed you back to life when you should have been dead, by rights. I'd have done the same for *any* sick animal, even a coyote. And at least you won't escape a hanging this time!"

He stared at her, stunned by her vehemence. "Have I already been tried? And will someone, sometime, tell me what I must be hanged for?"

Her face had grown paler with the force of repressed anger.

"Oh! You . . . you hypocrite! Don't you dare think you can fool me by pretending you don't recall what you did! Or does murder come so easily to you that you've lost count of your killings?"

She snatched up the lamp and marched to the door, her back stiff with anger while he watched her silently, feeling frustrated and mad. Damn the woman!

The next time she came in her face was cold and purposely expressionless. She wouldn't even look at him as she proceeded efficiently to change dressings and bandages. Equally silent, he watched her, knowing that his fixed, steady gaze was getting to her as the color seeped into her face.

She wasn't really beautiful, of course, but she had a slim, supple figure and an upright carriage. High cheekbones, a generous mouth when it wasn't set tightly in a disapproving line and a rather determined chin. Her eyes were her best feature—a particularly translucent green-gold, wide apart and fringed with thick black lashes. Her hair grew thick too, springing back from her temples in curly tendrils all her scraping back couldn't control.

Suddenly, compulsively, he broke the rather taut silence between them, forcing himself not to wince as she tightened a bandage.

"Is the Doc coming back?"

She gave him a composed look. "It won't be necessary now. You're mending fast, and I'm quite capable of changing dressings and bandages."

He was pushed into remarking caustically: "Don't see why you bother to go to all the trouble. Why, feeling the way you do, didn't you just let me die? You could enjoy sitting back and watching me bleed to death just as well as a hanging, couldn't you?"

"I've already *told* you what my feelings are, mister. And anyhow, hanging you might just act as a warning to others of your kind."

"Do you usually hang people without the benefit of a trial?"

"And why would there be a need for one? You gunned down three people in cold blood, one of them my husband—and you wounded another who might not live. There were enough witnesses too, so you can save your breath if you were lying here thinking up some lie with the idea of saving your skin!" Her face was flushed with anger. "No, mister. You came here to kill for the blood money Prendergast offered—"

"Seems like whoever I killed in cold blood did some pretty good shooting of their own," he said ironically, meaning to say more, but she ignored him again, slamming the door as she left the room and leaving him to stare at the ceiling and the walls again—to guess at what was outside the window. It was hot; he could almost smell the dust outside. How long had he been here? How long before she decided it was time for him to die?

When she came in with lunch he tried a different tactic.

"It might be easier if you unhitched me long enough to let me feed myself," he suggested.

"I don't trust you," she pronounced coldly, and continued to feed him as if he had been a recalcitrant child, sitting on the edge of the bed.

"May I have a smoke?" he asked her afterward, and she frowned.

"I don't keep any tobacco around this house. And besides, one of those bullets you took grazed a lung and it wouldn't help your recovery to indulge."

He burst out laughing—his whole chest beginning to ache—

caught by the incongruity of her statement with its macabre humor, and she flushed angrily.

"You're insufferable!"

"And you must admit there's a certain grim humor in this whole situation! You nurse me back to life from what I presume was death's door, and you sit on the edge of this bed and feed me as if I was a baby—even fuss disapprovingly when I ask for a smoke. . . ."

She was in a rage, her usually pale face had become redder, making her look pretty.

"How dare you talk to me in such a familiar way? A man of your kind—an *animal* . . . !"

"Is that why you have to keep me chained up like I was a pet wolf? Or did you have some other reasons too, lady?"

"Ohh!" Gasping her fury, she hit him. Her hands, as he'd noticed before, were rough and calloused, as if she'd had to work hard all her life. She had been bending over him, and the sheer force of her openhanded slap made her lose her balance now, so that she fell over on top of him.

He put his free arm about her waist, almost a reflex action. And maybe that was the reason why he was suddenly kissing her— because her face had ended up so close to his. For an instant he sensed some kind of response, almost a surrender in her; and then, with a muffled exclamation she tore herself away, wiping the back of her hand across her mouth ostentatiously as she glared down at him speechlessly before she whirled away.

# Chapter Twenty-Seven

An old Mexican man brought Steve his next meal; muttering and grumbling under his breath. This gringo pig should have been left to die like a wounded coyote—even hanging was too good for him. The señora should not have had to soil her hands taking care of such carrion. . . .

"Where is she? Gone to make arrangements for the hanging?"

The old man shot him a startled look, his lower lip sticking out as he squinted at the man on the bed.

"So you speak Spanish, eh? You have the look of a bandido, except that your eyes are blue. But," he added hurriedly as if regretting having spoken, "that is no concern of mine. Eat—and be quick about it, for I tell you that I have much to do outside, and I do not care very much whether you starve or not!"

Ill-humoredly, Steve lifted his shoulders, wincing immediately with pain. "And I can tell you, *viejo*, that I don't care either way myself—except I'd like to know why everyone seems so hell-bent on hanging me. First I ever heard that a man who defends himself when he's ambushed deserves lynching—or perhaps the laws in this part of the country are different?"

He was still weak as a kitten and in a great deal of pain, and he realized immediately from the old man's frown and averted eyes the futility of his speech. Obviously—and memory was coming back to him—he'd been mistaken for someone else and set up. And when they hadn't quite succeeded in killing him they'd made up a story that would make sure of it.

Obdurately, the old man refused to say anything further, and after he had left Steve had to force himself to lie still, resisting the urge to throw himself off the bed just to find out how strong that manacle really was. Trouble was, *he* didn't have much strength. He hated the weakness that held him trapped; the sickening waves of agony that accompanied his every attempt at movement. Damn it—even trying to *think* was too much effort. It made his head pound, sending him sliding off into the blackness of sleep or unconsciousness to escape from it. There was no time to measure out a day by—hardly any difference between day and night. He was being turned into a goddamned vegetable, and he would almost rather welcome the sounds of the booted feet of men who would come to take him away and hang him.

Twice more the old Mexican man came to attend to his needs, still refusing to speak except to himself, and under his breath at that. And then at last *she* came again, and he realized that he had missed her—even the feeling of tension she brought with her.

She was still silent, her high-boned face still coldly set, and he looked at her without speaking, closing his eyes as she began with her usual efficient motions to change dressings, tighten bandages. Damn her for a cold bitch anyhow! Her or the Mexican, what difference did it make?

He fought against pain, feeling the sweat popping out all over his body, stinging the cuts and wounds that seemed to cover it, and heard her voice say "Here . . ." as she held a cup of water to his mouth.

If his left arm hadn't been strapped against his chest he would have enjoyed knocking the cup away, no matter how futile the gesture, but as it was he drank obediently, his eyes now as hard and scornful as hers.

She set the tin vessel down on the washstand with an unnecessary thump and paused there with her back stiffly turned. Angrily, almost compulsively she said: "You feel any better?"

"Does it matter?"

She had turned around in time to catch the sardonic lift of one eyebrow, and the color rose in her face. "I see you're well enough to be rude!"

"Then I'm well enough to be hanged—right? What are you waiting for?"

"If *ever* I met a man who deserves to hang it's you!" she burst at him vengefully, hating the mocking smile he gave her in acknowledgment. "Don't you have any conscience at all? Any regrets for all the men you've killed in cold blood?"

"Hard to feel regretful over trying to fight off a pack of drygulchers," he drawled at her infuriatingly. "Although of course I might end up regretting they didn't finish the job—or else *they* will." There was a cold-steel threat in the way he said those last words, and her temper flared higher.

"Don't think to save your skin with that feeble lie you thought up! Domingo told me what you said to him too, and let me tell you that you're not going to save your neck by—"

"Lady, I think you've just made up your mind to watch me hang, and nothing's going to change it, so why the sermonizing and why the delay? Or do you purely enjoy just thinking about it, picturing it in your mind? Maybe you're one of those folks who enjoy hangings as much as holidays."

"*You!* Only a mind that's unbelievably corrupt could think up such an evil thing to say!"

He grinned at the loathing and venom in her voice.

"What's the matter, lady? The way you enjoy talking about it the thought of a pleasant little necktie party in the name of revenge shouldn't worry you."

Speechless, she sent him a look of pure hatred before she turned her back to march herself out of the room with the sound of his soft, mocking laughter following her until she closed the door with all the force she could muster.

With a frown, Steve regarded the closed door. Another no-win skirmish, and now she probably wouldn't come back again until they came to get him. He wished he didn't have to remember the way it felt to be hanged, the slow choking . . . but the memory came back to him with too-sharp clarity. A cellar in Dallas and a rope flung over a hook in the wall.

"You bastard—you're going to hang!" And the high-pitched, excited giggle of a blond-haired woman called Toni Lassiter ringing in his ears before the roaring of his own blood drowned it out as they hauled him up slowly, slowly. . . . Shit, he was beginning to get morbid and there was no point in it. Better hope, though, that they planned on using a horse or the gallows *this* time.

He welcomed the unexpected distraction that took him away from his backward-turning thoughts.

"Señor? *Psst*—señor!"

A pair of button-dark eyes peered at him from under a badly

cut thatch of black hair as a small boy carefully eased open a wooden shutter to look in curiously.

Steve looked back at the urchin whose round brown face was screwed up with a mixture of caution and inquisitiveness. "Holá, muchacho," he said at last, and the head came up higher, unblinking black eyes regarding him.

"Is it true, señor, that you are a real bandido?"

"Well, I've been called that, but it kinda depended on which side the people who did the calling were on. Right now I could use some company, and as you can see I'm not very dangerous hitched to the bed this way. Why don't you come on in?"

"Well . . ." There was a slight hesitation, and then with a gusty sigh and a furtive backward look the boy eased himself onto the windowsill. "As you can see, señor, I am not afraid—of anything, even bandidos. I have learned how to fire a gun too. Can I see your bullet wounds? There must be very many. . . ."

"You'd have to come closer for that. Or are you afraid?"

"Afraid? Me? I am ten years old, and a man already."

With another swift backward glance the boy was in the room, approaching the bed hesitantly until the blue-eyed stranger's smile disarmed him and he smiled back.

"You don't look very bad, señor." He peered at all the bandages and at the livid scar that creased the man's temple and his eyes widened. "Ay! My abuelo says it is a miracle you are alive."

"Well, it probably won't be that way for too much longer, it seems like."

"They are going to hang you, sí? Are you not afraid?"

"Not much point to that when you know it's coming. I only wish I knew what made them decide I needed hanging."

"Oh—you shot many men! Bam-bam-bam—like that! You pull a gun very fast, señor. I think I like to learn how, one day."

"I wouldn't if I were you—you might end up the same way." And then he casually eased the question in: "I wonder how I got shot up so damn bad if I'm as fast as you say? My memory seems to be kind of hazy. . . ."

"Oh, but you did not know they were waiting for you outside the saloon, señor. Me, I am only a small muchacho and they do not pay attention to me. I heard them talk of it, how they will get this bad hombre that has been sent to kill everyone here. When you came outside the cantina they all start shooting, and then you start shooting too. There was so much big noise and everyone was shouting. . . ."

"You sure tell a good story, *niño*. Sounds almost like you were right there!"

"But I *was* there—I stayed hidden very small, flat on my belly under the sidewalk. Twice I could feel the bullets go by my head, but I was not afraid. The *patrón*, the Señor Cady, told me to go on home to tell the señora he would be late, but I stayed to see what would happen. You fought well, señor. I am sorry they shot you so many times."

"But you enjoyed watching a real gunfight, huh? You tell anyone what you saw?"

His eyes round with alarm the boy shook his head. "Oh no, señor! And you wouldn't tell, would you? My *abuelo* would beat me, and the señora would be very angry. I am not allowed to go to the town by myself, but sometimes the Señor Cady would let me come in the back of his wagon so I could drive him back when he had had too much tequila to drink and wanted to sleep. But if my *abuelo* knew . . . why, he might even send me back to Mexico to live with my aunt in Sonora who has too many children already and would beat me every day. . . . I have to go now señor, for he would also beat me if he knew I was here and he is calling me."

"Wait a minute—"

"I have not been here—you have not seen me!" the boy said rapidly as he scampered off, easing himself out through the window with the agility of a monkey and leaving Steve swearing under his breath with frustration.

Damn! A few more minutes and maybe he'd have been able to persuade the boy to repeat his story. But would she listen? Would she *want* to listen? It would be his word and the boy's against all the others'—probably men who were considered solid, upstanding citizens of Prayers End. And maybe after all, it was fate that he should have decided to get off there. Prayers End. Rope's end.

He became aware, suddenly, of sounds outside. The pounding of hooves and men's voices shouting. Even a little boy's voice, shriller than the others. Company, then—for her or for him?

The woman came in, saving him further wondering, her face paler than usual. She was biting her lip. Following her closely were four men, and he recognized at least one of them as the swaggering blusterer in the saloon. Milt, the others had called him. Looking at their eyes and at hers Steve knew suddenly that it was time. So she'd gone right out and got them! Bitterness rankled, tasting sour in his throat, but he stared back at them coldly with nothing at all showing in his face.

It was Milt Kehoe who spoke first, pent-up excitement seeping through his voice. "Surprised you gave him a bed, Lizzie. You ought to have kept him chained up in the cellar—that's all a murderin' coyote like him deserves!"

"We all been waiting for this time, stranger—bet you have too, huh?"

"That's enough!" the woman said sharply, and almost abstractedly he noticed how her hands clutched at the corners of the apron she still wore over her faded cotton gown. The knuckles were red and raw as if she'd just finished doing her washing. She said more strongly: "There's no need for . . . for all that. He's going to hang and that's punishment enough."

For a while after that things became blurred as they dragged him outside, wrists manacled before him. He could feel the sweat pouring off his body and cursed himself for his own weakness as he stumbled, too dizzy to walk on his own. Someone boosted him onto the back of a horse, and roped him to the pommel, and from then on it took every effort of will to keep his jaws clenched against the groans that threatened his pride as every movement of the horse sent arrows of pain that seemed to pierce him everywhere, much worse than the bullets had been.

Some miles further on another, larger party of men caught up with them. Elizabeth Cady was with this group, driving a light wagon with the old Mexican sitting up beside her, his seamed face sour.

*Now?* But he was almost past caring, except to hope grimly that he'd be lucky enough to have his neck broken right off.

"Get down off that horse! Lige, why don't you undo that rope and get him off? We're gonna do this in style."

The rope they put around his neck was Milt Kehoe's. And now, in the suddenly taut silence, an older man cleared his throat awkwardly.

"Now wait a minute here. Mebbe we ought to get his name or somethin'. . . ."

"Yeah," someone else said. "We could pin a note on his carcass afterwards, so Prendergast finds out what's gonna happen to any other hired killers he sends out."

Steve felt a wave of fury jolt through him, pushing back some of the weakness and nausea. He lifted his head, and strangely, it was the young woman's eyes that he met before she averted them hastily.

"One thing I'd like to know," he said suddenly and evenly, silencing them all for a moment. "Why am I going to be hanged?"

They were all staring at him now, faces portraying various degrees of anger and incredulity. It was Kehoe, acting as spokesman as usual, who burst out furiously with:

"What the hell you trying to pull? You know damn well what you done, gunning down innocent men!"

"Since I was jumped first, how does that add up to murder? Or is it for revenge that this lynching party has been arranged?"

"What do you mean by that?" Kehoe yelled, his face going almost purple. "By God—Lige and I were there, and you drew on Jared without warning—you never gave him or Red a chance—"

"That's a lie. I walked away from the fight you tried to provoke me into in the saloon—and right into a nice little ambush outside. And as for the rest of you men—don't you believe in giving a man a trial or at least checking up with *all* the witnesses before you take it on yourselves to pass sentence? I've been accused of being a hired gun and a murderer, and all without my getting a chance to defend myself. You folks do that to every stranger that passes through?"

"Goddamn it—don't you all see what he's tryin' to do? He's playin' for time, that's what! As for you, you bastard, I'll teach you to start spoutin' your lies. . . ."

It was the change in the timbre of Milt Kehoe's voice that warned Steve as the rope tightened about his neck, jerking him forward. He brought his manacled hands up to clutch at the rope, trying to ease the terrible, choking pressure against the corded muscles of his throat, and felt his body hit the ground.

From very far away he seemed to hear a woman scream. "No—

oh, no! Not like that. . . ." And suddenly he was lying on the ground feeling the blood seep out of him while he choked slowly to death. Cool hands like ice touched his throat, easing the rope loose while he breathed again at last, sucking in great lungfuls of air. From everywhere behind the red mist that blinded him he could hear voices that seemed to rise and fall like wind-sounds. Nothing they said made sense and nothing mattered. There was only one way to escape from the pain that engulfed him in wave after wave, and that was to pass out.

This time it was Martin Burneson, the biggest of the small-holders, who took charge, ignoring Milt Kehoe's vituperations.

"I'm sorry I had to shoot your horse, Milt, and I'll replace it with one of my own. But you had no right to do what you did. And what he said—this man we were all so ready to hang—it made me stop and think some. For instance, how *can* we be so sure he was one of Prendergast's men? And he said something about witnesses. . . ."

"You doubtin' my word and Lige's to take *his* now? By God, I hope I did manage to kill him, that . . . that . . ."

It was at that precise moment that the old Mexican who worked on the Cady place came up, dragging his reluctant grandson with him by the wrist.

"Fidelito was hiding under the sacks in the back of the wagon," he said heavily in explanation. "This was not a good thing for a boy to see. But he also heard what this man, this stranger, had to say, and he tells me—he tells me it was true. It had been planned that many men would wait outside the saloon to kill him if those who were inside could not do so."

"He's lyin'! You want to believe a Mexican brat? This old man's as crazy as his grandson!"

"Milt Kehoe if you don't quiet down I'm going to shoot you myself!" Her face as white as paper, her skirts covered in blood that was caked with dust where she'd been kneeling, Elizabeth Cady looked up, silencing the sputtering man. "You almost made us all murderers along with yourself. And I tell you now that I believe Fidelito. I . . . dear God, I can't believe what I nearly did—what we all nearly did!"

"I think," Martin Burneson said firmly, "that what we ought to do is call in the Sheriff. No need to tell him what we almost did, but he can surely find out if this man is wanted or not."

"If he lives!" Milt Kehoe jerked out viciously, and Burneson nodded.

"Yes. If he lives. But at least we are sure that the Sheriff is our friend, and that's lucky for all of us, particularly for you, Kehoe."

# Chapter Twenty-Eight

❦

The Sheriff was leaning back in his chair, fingering his reddish-brown mustache thoughtfully when he saw Elizabeth.

"Well, Miz Cady . . ."

"Doc Wilson said . . . he told me he was in *here*."

"Sit down, Lizzie. Chair ain't too uncomfortable."

She sat, wincing at his sudden, familiar use of the hated name of her childhood. Liz . . . Lizzie. Why christen her with a pretty name like Elizabeth if no one used it? Not even Jared. . . . She closed her eyes quickly to the thought of Jared, her widely spaced hazel eyes meeting Sheriff Blaine's squarely.

He was regarding her with a kind of tolerant amusement, to-bacco-stained finger still rubbing at his mustache as if it itched.

"You want to see him, that right?" His look was quizzical, making her feel humiliated for coming here at all. "I guess that'll be all right," he allowed, still giving her that faintly tolerant look she detested. "Can't keep him here much longer, anyhow. As far's I can find out he ain't wanted—not in this territory anyways. 'Course, that don't mean too much. He could be one of them renegades from across the border who keep crossin' back and forth and changin' names. . . ."

She had almost forgotten her mission in her fascinated interest in the Sheriff's discourse.

"But is he really a professional gunman? Isn't there a way you can find out that much at least?"

"Without a name to hang on him?" His choice of words made her flush, but he went on thoughtfully, pretending not to notice. "I don't know, Lizzie. Heck—I can't tell you how many John Smith's I've encountered in my time! But if this hombre is really a professional gunslinger, stands to reason that someone around here'd have heard of him, just from the description I've passed around. An' I've sent a wire to Texas Ranger headquarters in Austin, just to make sure he don't come from *their* neck of the woods. Best I could do—but he coulda come from almost anyplace, and he ain't tellin' where. Claims his getting all shot up wiped his memory clean away." He gave her a sly look. "He could be a drifter, just passin' through, or escaped from a jail somewhere, like the Doc seems to think. Just passin' through would be *my* guess, now."

"No one just passes through this town, and you know it!" she said quickly and rather bitterly. Without her willing it her eyes went beyond the Sheriff to the shadowy passage leading to the cellblock. He caught her wandering glance and gave her a benign smile.

"Look here, Lizzie," he said kindly, if a trifle heavily, "I ain't got no right to stop you, if it's what you want. He's alive and well enough to travel, and if he ain't wanted, that's where my responsibility stops. But if I was you . . ." He saw the tight, closed look on her high-boned face and sighed. "He's trouble. At my age, and as long as I bin doin' the job, a man gets to sense these things. Don't know where he comes from or what he is, but I can tell when a man's dangerous—an' this one is. I'd prefer it if he just keeps riding and gets clean outa my territory. We got enough problems as it is, and I'm an old man, Lizzie."

"I'm only asking to talk to him, Sheriff Blaine." Her voice was coldly taut, giving nothing away.

He sighed again, reaching for his key ring. "Well . . ."

He rose from his chair and she followed him, standing beside him with her head slightly bowed as he began to unlock the door that led back into the cellblock. Then he said unexpectedly, voice lowered, "Prendergast sent one of his boys in here yesterday, askin' questions about him—his description an' everything. Why don't you do us all a favor and persuade him to move on? Soon's I get a reply to that last telegram I sent to Austin I kin turn him loose. . . ."

She said in a low, bitter voice: "Don't you think *he* might have other ideas? He was ambushed and nearly killed—and then they . . . we . . . almost hanged him. If he's the kind of man you think he is . . ."

"Mebbe he'll just decide to feel grateful he's alive. After all, you did save his hide, didn't you?"

She cried out, "Ohh!" It was a sharp sound of mixed despair and frustration.

The Sheriff said with a sudden bunching of his thick shoulders: "Talk to him then, if you're bound an' determined!" He went on in a grumbling voice, "Lord knows I don't want him mixing up in this war on the side of Prendergast, but—hell—I don't want him mixing up in it at all, not on *any* side!"

She wouldn't give him the satisfaction of hearing her comment and he shrugged in resignation, standing back to let her precede him into the shadowy coolness of the small corridor that fronted on three cells.

Elizabeth hadn't been afraid at all when she'd walked into the Sheriff's office, buoyed by her confidence in herself and her new black taffeta gown that was hardly suitable for just-a-visit-to-town in the buckboard. She had even done her hair differently, in a big, smooth coil at the back of her head, showing her neck and small ears with her mother's jet earbobs. She had felt the *rightness* of her errand. For, after all, *somebody* had to be the one to tell him how sorry they all were at the mistake that had been made; and it should rightly be her—to show him she didn't blame him any longer for Jared's death. And then there was also the other mission they had entrusted her with—just because she was a woman it didn't mean that she couldn't take her equal share of the responsibility now, as a ranch owner in her own right.

The thoughts had stopped there, until she had been unfairly forced to sit down in the hard wooden chair in the Sheriff's office, and to listen to the old man's dire warnings and unasked-for advice.

But now that she was locked into a small cell alone with *him*, Elizabeth felt all her confidence ooze away; and for a moment, when she met his expressionless, darkly blue eyes, she couldn't find a single word to say. She was barely aware of Sheriff Blaine's departure with the hearty admonition over his shoulder that she was to holler when she wanted out.

He wasn't making it easy for her. He had been lying on the narrow cot with his back propped up against the wall; one long leg dangling to the floor as he idly flipped over cards from a greasy deck that was spread out over the blanket-covered mattress. When the Sheriff had let her in he'd come slowly to his feet, face betraying no surprise—eyes turning first wary and then carefully blank.

Neither of them said a word until the Sheriff had gone and they heard the closing of the outer door. Elizabeth stood there in her stiff taffeta dress, suddenly miserably conscious of its newness, her fingers going up to fiddle nervously with the cameo brooch she'd pinned to its high collar. She was taken with a sudden sense of panic that made her want to turn and run, following the Sheriff to safety; shamefully, Elizabeth felt that *he* had sensed her fear.

Lifting her head high, she met the mocking tilt of his mouth with her lips pressed tightly together, but she suddenly began to wonder if he thought—dear God, could he possibly be thinking that she . . . the unbidden, unwanted memory of that night in the lamplit bedroom, when he had kissed her, came rushing back, making her face grow hot. She felt beads of sweat trickle down her neck and thought wildly, "Why doesn't he say something? Why can't I?"

"Ever play solitaire?" He broke the silence abruptly, stooping to gather up the dirty cards off the blanket where they lay scattered carelessly.

"No, I . . . I never have played cards."

The unconscious primness of her voice made him smile. He turned back to her, flipping the deck of cards at the corner of the cell where they fell with a soft, pattering sound that made her jump.

"Had you figured for a nice, God-fearing lady," he said, a tinge of mockery underlying the statement. It made her angry, and she was able to look back at him fearlessly, meeting his eyes and refusing to let hers drop.

He wore a faded blue linsey-woolsey shirt, open at the collar, and darker blue denim trousers. In the weak light that filtered through the one barred window, his face showed a shadowy beard stubble; and when he smiled, as he did now as if her sudden bravado amused him, deep creases appeared in his lean cheeks—a thin scar on one emphasizing the piratical ruthlessness of his face.

"Dangerous," the Sheriff had called him, and she felt she had always sensed it, even when he was so weak and ill and mumbling God-knew-what words in his delirium.

She had been staring at him for too long and now she said quickly, "I . . . I'm glad you're better. . . ." The words sounded stiff and stilted, even to her.

"Oh, I'm all healed up," he said carelessly, and with a return of the irony, "can't you tell? Sheriff's even been talking of letting me go."

"That . . . that's what I came to talk to you about." She let the words tumble out, ashamed of the awkward nervousness he made her feel. "Have you thought where you'll go? Or . . . what you plan to do?"

"I guess you're still thinking of Prendergast." He answered her suddenly shocked look with a lift of one black eyebrow. "Sheriff Blaine told me someone had been asking about me."

"I . . . I don't know *what* to think any longer. I . . . we are all sorry about what happened. . . ."

"We? Are you speaking for Milt Kehoe too?" A note of barely suppressed violence had suddenly appeared in his voice, frightening her.

To cover her fear she said sharply, "Milt was sure you were one of the professional gunmen he'd heard Prendergast had sent for—and I'm sure Jared thought so too. I'm not saying their methods were good, or right, but you don't understand how fear—panic if you will—can affect people! And all of us here have been living under the shadow of that fear—and of violence—for too long. Is it wrong to try to meet force with force?"

"For a God-fearing lady you sure talk a lot of violence." His eyes had narrowed, and the flat, unequivocal statement dropped like a stone between them.

She wasn't going to let anything he said deter her now that she was fired up. "Well—but you *could* have come here to work for them. The word was out all over the territory. Why shouldn't you have been one of the wolves who came looking for high pay for killing?"

"So without bothering to make sure, that gave the wolvers the right to exterminate me. Is that what you're saying?"

"No!" She said it violently, wondering how he continued to put her in the wrong. She fought for control of the mixture of emotions he managed to arouse in her, wishing she could see his face more closely to judge his expression. Why did the very blueness of

his eyes act as a barrier against her reading his thoughts? She had
to explain. . . .

"Elizabeth." His unexpected use of her full name choked her
into stillness. "You didn't come here to fence with me, did you?
Why *did* you come?" His voice had gentled almost imperceptibly,
suddenly leaving her with nothing to say. How *could* she put it to
him? As a blunt proposition? What did *he* think she had come
here for? And—how dare he call her "Elizabeth"!

She resisted his attempt to disarm her. "I came here to talk to
you." She wondered right after she'd said it why she had placed
such emphasis on the word "talk," and saw from the crinkling of
his eyes that he had noticed. She went on quickly, before her resolve faltered, "We . . . I . . . wanted to explain to you just how
things stand here—and to . . . to make you a proposition."

There, it was out! And now that she had said the words her eyes
dropped before the suddenly cold and merciless scrutiny of his.

"Well—I guess you've already explained, so that leaves the
proposition, doesn't it?" His voice took on a sarcastic drawl as he
added with deliberate suggestiveness, "I must say that any proposition put to me by a pretty woman would be very hard to resist."

He took a step toward her and Elizabeth shrank back instinctively, feeling herself menaced by his closeness. She had an almost
overwhelming impulse to turn and run from him, to call for the
Sheriff. But instead she forced herself to stand still, to throw her
head back and meet his mocking, impenetrable eyes.

"Mr.—" She had meant to sound cold and cutting, but the sudden lack of a formal name by which she could call him defeated
her and she said instead, fury making her voice tremble, "You
. . . you pretended to misunderstand me on *purpose!* You are not
a gentleman!"

"Obviously not, from the look in your eyes," he drawled hatefully, a taunting grin pulling at the corners of his mouth. Then
the grin disappeared and his eyes became narrow and cold and she
knew he was closing in for the attack. He was so close to her now
that she could feel the heat that emanated from his body, smell
the sweaty man-smell of him. And she could not have spoken,
could not have moved to resist him if he . . . if he . . .

"Well? What will you do now? Finish telling me all about that
interesting proposition you had for me? Or will you scream rape

and provide your fat Sheriff with an excuse to keep me locked up in here? Is that why you came to visit, Elizabeth? All dressed up in your pretty new gown with the rustly petticoats underneath it, and that cameo—" He reached out then and actually touched her brooch, startling her into a gasp of terror as she stood there like a mesmerized rabbit.

"Is that pinned to your collar to tempt a man to tear it away and pull off all these little buttons, one by one, to see what your breasts look like? By God—even in that high-necked, long-sleeved black widow's gown you're damned desirable. Tell me"—his voice became softer, and to her, infinitely more menacing—"are you a part of that proposition they told you to offer me? Because in that case you might just persuade me to consider it."

His fingers moved very gently down from the pulse in her throat to her waist, tracing the outline of her breasts on the way; and it was then, when she felt he was about to pull her against him, that she recovered her sanity.

Elizabeth recoiled against the bars of the cell door, feeling them digging into her back through the tightly laced corset. "Oh, no!" Her shaking whisper flung an accusation at him. "What do you take me for?"

He stood staring at her for a moment, making no further attempt to touch her, and then turned away with a shrug that infuriated her even more than his earlier advances had.

"Took you for a woman, I guess. But I should have remembered. You're obviously a churchgoing, God-fearing lady. All right, then . . ." Unbelievably, he had thrown his full length onto the cot and was looking up at her with his arms crossed behind his head. "I can't ask you to sit down because there's no other place to sit except for this miserable cot. And that might not look very . . . respectable, if the Sheriff should come back. And I guess you have to act respectable above all things, you being a recent widow and all. So why don't you go on and finish what you came to say— that is, if you haven't changed your mind?"

She was still standing braced against the cell door, staring at him with glazed, unbelieving eyes.

"Oh! But you . . . you . . ."

"It's already been established that I'm not a gentleman. And that I'm probably a professional gunfighter and a murderer into a bargain. But maybe that's what you came looking for. Isn't it?"

If it would not have seemed, under his mocking gaze, to be total and abject surrender, she would have called for the Sheriff and stalked out with her head held high. But she had come here for a purpose, and she would *not* have the others think that she had failed, simply because she was a female and this man had made use of that fact to humiliate her. So Elizabeth gathered what shreds she had left of her self-possession and looked back at him coldly.

"Are you sure you still want to listen? After all, Prendergast can offer you much more than we can."

"Prendergast again? Well—I can't really tell what I might say to their offer until you make yours, can I?" He had the insufferable gall to raise one eyebrow at her, underlining his sarcastic drawl, and her anger snapped inside her, making her stamp furiously across the room to stand looking down at him with her eyes shooting sparks.

"And *you*—what kind of man are you, do you enjoy the feeling of . . . of power it gives you to play us against each other? Or is it your idea of a good joke to play on us? All you've done is . . . is make a fool of me ever since I came in here.

"I was going to make you an offer on behalf of the smaller ranchers and homesteaders here—hard-working, decent folk who settle here legally and ask only to be let alone to try and earn an honest living. We have water, and we share it and we put up fences to protect our property—but Prendergast thinks he needs all of this range, all of this county, to run his cattle on! And he's trying to squeeze us off with his barbed wire and his hired killers. Jack Prendergast boasts that *he* brought the railroad in here to ship his herds to market. He calls this town his too, and . . . and —but I guess none of this matters to you, does it? I came to make you an honest, decent offer, but I guess Prendergast got to you first—or is that why you came here in the first place? Why couldn't you have said so in the beginning? Did it give you pleasure to humiliate me and insult me?"

Sudden tears blinding her, gasping for breath now, she whirled around to run from him, but with surprising speed he came up off the bunk like a cat, catching her wrist to swing her around again.

"Whoa now! What a hot temper you've got hidden under that prissy look you put on. Were you going to leave without telling me exactly what kind of offer your friends had in mind?"

She glared at him through moist eyes, and he laughed shortly. "That's better. At least you haven't screamed yet. And you've got gumption, I'll say that much for you." Surprising her again, his voice turned coaxing, shocking her into silence. "Look—would you like to start over? You sit down and I'll stand over here. And I promise you I'll listen to whatever you have to say. Won't utter a single word to interrupt you until you're all through. Is it a deal?"

He caught her doubtful look and grinned crookedly. "I really mean it. I keep forgetting it was you who kept me alive when I should have been dead by rights. I guess I owe you more than cheap insults for that."

How quickly he had disarmed her—even made her feel slightly guilty because after all she had only kept him alive in order to have him hanged. But now he'd restored her pride and recalled her mission, just as quickly as he'd driven her into a hysterical rage a few moments before.

Not knowing how to answer this new approach, Elizabeth walked stiffly to the bed with its dingy grey blanket and sat gingerly on the very edge, still eyeing him suspiciously even though he'd taken up his stance a few feet away. He leaned his shoulder against the mortared wall now, his eyes inscrutable.

Elizabeth found it difficult to collect the scattered threads of her carefully planned words. She regretted bitterly now that she had come here at all, but it was too late for regrets, she was *here*; and because she felt cornered and ill at ease she forgot all her carefully planned strategies and let her words come out as bluntly and as plainly as possible—keeping what she had to say to him short, as a man might have done. When that was done she folded her hands on her lap primly, waiting for his reply.

"Kehoe. Is *he* one of your bunch?" His question took her off guard, making her eyes widen almost guiltily.

"Milt Kehoe *is* a member of our Association. But . . . but I was asked to assure you that there will be no more trouble. He's a fool and a hothead, but he realizes that he needs the Association. No— I'm sure he'll stay out of your way."

"And supposing I don't want to stay out of *his?*" His words challenged her, but this time she was ready to meet it.

"If Milt Kehoe starts any trouble he . . . he'll be on his own. He already understands that."

"You haven't answered my question." She flushed as the dark blue eyes narrowed on her face, and was saved a reply when he shrugged. "But I suppose your answer will do."

"Then you . . . you agree?"

"Now look—hold on!" Almost angrily he pushed himself away from the wall and started to pace the length of the cell; the quick, soft-footed way he walked reminding her of a caged beast. "How can you be sure you need a hired gun? For that matter, how do you know that I'm a gunman at all? Damn it, everyone carries a gun now. Even drummers!"

"The Sheriff thinks you are. And then there's Fidelito—he says that even though they took you by surprise he's never seen anyone pull a gun as fast as you did."

"And how many gunfighters has that kid watched? Hell, blind panic could make a man clear leather faster than he ever thought he could before."

She was regarding him thoughtfully now, her head tilted to one side. "But I think it wasn't that way with you. You're . . . you're a—"

"A murderer? A killer?" He stopped his pacing to sneer at her and then waved an impatient hand when she started to retort. "All right—it's your purely female instinct. Maybe you're right. But do you and your friends of the Association know what you're getting into? My horning into this war that's been building up here might just touch off the powder keg—and once it blows up there'll be no stopping more explosions. There'll be death and destruction and bitterness and sorrow on both sides. Have you ever been mixed up in a range war before? Do you have any idea what it could mean?"

"Have *you* been mixed up in one? Was that what you were running from when you came here?"

She had the feeling that a mask had suddenly dropped over his face, turning it to wood, before he made an angry, strangely foreign gesture with one hand as if he was brushing away some unpleasant memory from his past.

"All right. Touché."

She had a vaguely puzzled look on her face that made him frown. "I guess you don't understand French. It means—hell, it doesn't matter—it means, your point, Mrs. Cady."

She felt herself stiffen primly. "There's *no* need to swear. Or to try and frighten me with dire warnings. Do you think we haven't discussed all this? Or thought about it? Or agonized over it? We *know* what a range war could mean. But on the other hand there's something called pride—and wanting to defend what's ours. If we don't show them we're ready to fight back if we have to they'd . . . why, they'd just run all over us and run us out—it's being done in other places! That's why we formed the Association."

His eyes were as blue-bright as polished steel. "Oh sure—your Association. Did they tell you to warn me what might happen if I *don't* agree to their proposition? I'd sure hate to be a main attraction at another hanging—or another ambush."

She flushed, coming quickly to her feet with her long skirts impeding her. "That was uncalled for! I've told you—you're perfectly free to make up your own mind—and there'll be no trouble made for you if you decide to move on instead of staying around to get involved."

"So that's the choice, huh? Stay on *your* side or leave town."

"It's fair enough, don't you think?" she flashed back at him, and the mocking, piratical lines in his face deepened.

"I guess so. Especially from your point of view. All right, Mrs. Cady. I'll think about it."

"You'll *think* about it?" She was immeasurably disappointed and let it show for just an instant before she caught herself, forcing a note of coolly unconcerned civility into her next words. "Oh —very well. I suppose that is only fair. I . . . . I'll speak to Sheriff Blaine about—"

"About when he's going to let me out? I wish you'd do that. It gets real boring, playing solitaire all day."

He shouted down the passageway for the Sheriff, and suddenly, taking her completely by surprise, tilted her chin up with one finger. "Oh—one more condition."

"Please!" she murmured hastily, hearing the outer door squeak as it was opened. He laughed.

"*You* come for me. And wear this gown. It becomes you."

Sheriff Blaine was in a jovial mood when he lumbered down the passageway to unlock the cell door. A folded piece of yellowish paper stuck out of the top of his vest pocket.

"Well, well! You all had a nice visit Miz Cady?"

So he was back to being formal again. She lifted her chin into his oversolicitous smile. "Thank you, Sheriff Blaine."

She expected him to lock the door again after she had passed through it, but for some reason he stood there, grinning at his prisoner, forcing her to wait for him.

"Got good news for you, whatever your name is—Smith, you said?" Getting no reaction to that he shrugged. "Well, had that telegram I was waitin' on from Austin, Texas, and it seems like you're clean—or at least, they ain't got no record on you." His stubby fingers touched the yellow paper in his pocket and he shook his head. "Sure is strange, that. Wired them a full description on you—an' they never heard of you. Dunno—maybe you came up here from the south side of the border, would I be guessing right. Anyhow, the Rangers don't want you, and you ain't any known gunman far's I can find out, so—"

"Are you telling me I'm free to walk out of here right now, Sheriff?" The lazy voice sounded calm and expressionless, but Elizabeth could not help giving him a slanted, slightly alarmed glance. If he was free, why could he not change his mind about helping them out? Perhaps this was a private matter between this hard-faced man and the Sheriff, but she was determined to stand right here and listen. And why not?

"Well, I guess that's about the size of it," the Sheriff was saying reluctantly. "If you want to come back into the office here with me an' sign the paper for your release . . ."

The Sheriff had begun to walk back to his office but *he* waited politely for her to precede him. She thought he did little things like this automatically, from habit. Strange that his very politeness was in such sharp contrast to the leashed violence she sensed was in him! Elizabeth was very conscious of his tall, striding presence behind her, and while the Sheriff was pushing open the outer door, he caught her elbow and bent his head to whisper, "Aren't you going to wait for me?"

Elizabeth didn't know what she should do now. If she went back to the ranch alone it was certain that the Prendergast faction would get to him—or that he might just decide to go to them. What did she, or any of her friends and neighbors know about him after all?

Feeling stupid and self-conscious she pretended she wasn't there, studying the far corner of the Sheriff's desk with concentration.

"You sure didn't have much with you when you was brought in here, but Miz Cady was good enough to hand over the guns you were wearing. You kin have 'em back." The Sheriff unlocked a glass-fronted cabinet and produced the twin-looped cartridge belts and holstered guns, their dull black handles looking vaguely ominous.

"Should have a name of some kind to put on this here paper . . ." the Sheriff hinted, and the man looked up from his thoughtful examination of the guns.

"Oh, had you forgotten? John Smith." And then, with an amused glint in his blue eyes, "What else?"

Elizabeth watched, with the first faint creeping of fear mixed with resentment, the methodical, dangerously efficient way he handled those guns. He had already buckled the twin cartridge belts around his waist, letting them sag to hip level so that the holsters rested along his thighs. Almost too well she remembered removing these same belts from his unconscious body, with a feeling of revulsion that made her toss them away from her. She had only insisted on keeping them to give to the Sheriff to prevent Milt Kehoe from taking them.

Now, that man who had worn those guns twirled the cylinder competently; replacing spent cartridges, frowning all the while.

"Kinda newfangled guns, ain't they?" the Sheriff said conversationally. "Saw they was Colts, but I never seen that particular model before."

"Colt .44's—'73 model. Center-fire metal cartridges." He'd said the words almost mechanically.

"Well now, ain't that something!" the Sheriff said, adding casually: "Hope you don't aim to use them guns around here, Mr. er . . . Smith. You'll be ridin' out now, won't you? Still got your horse over at the livery stable—you'll remember which one? I mean—there probably ain't nothin' to keep you here any longer. . . ."

Mocking laughter lines deepened in "John Smith's" face. "That anxious to get rid of me Sheriff? Thought for a while you were planning to keep me here. But you see, I promised Mrs. Cady here that I'd have supper with her, first night I got out of jail. You *did* mean that kind invitation, ma'am?"

Outside, he took the reins of the dilapidated-looking buckboard she had brought to town, lifting her up first. She was still unaccountably flushed and breathless from the pressure of his hard hands around her waist when he climbed up on the seat beside her.

Elizabeth saw his blue, long-lashed eyes flicker over the horses and the badly sprung vehicle itself and said defensively: "I *know* I should have had it painted and new springs put in, but there's so much to be done around the ranch, and with all the trouble . . ."

He deliberately avoided her stumbling excuses and said instead, "Should you be driving yourself to town alone?"

"I'm a woman! Even *they* wouldn't dare molest me," she said sharply.

He raised an eyebrow and gave her a rather doubtful look, but didn't make any further comment on the subject, and they rode down the town's dusty main street with Elizabeth sitting stiffly erect beside him—looking straight ahead, as if by doing so she would make herself invisible to the curious, staring eyes that must surely follow their rather slow progress out of town.

# Chapter Twenty-Nine

❧

The members of the newly formed Smallholders Association hadn't expected him to attend their meeting that night—that much was certain. But Elizabeth, without having too much choice in the matter, had taken him directly to Frank Dean's house, where they were holding the meeting. It had made for a more lively gathering than usual, she thought unhappily now, trying to avoid the reproachful look that Frank's wife, Millie, sent her.

"You'll have to do things my way," John Smith had warned them, adding, "And I don't want to hear any complaints about my methods either." His voice had softened then, almost as contemptuous as the way his eyes flicked over them, taking their measure. "You don't like me—I can tell that. To you I'm worse than a wolf. But you need me—or one of my kind, right? That way you can all keep your hands clean."

"Now look here, Mr.—"

His voice had cut through Brad Newbury's uneasy bluster as if the small man hadn't spoken. "And now there's the question of wages. . . ."

"Well . . ."—Frank Dean cleared his throat hastily—"we've already discussed that, and we're each willing to pay our share. Come fall and roundup time we should have enough head to . . ."

His voice trailed off uncomfortably when he saw that Smith was looking straight at Elizabeth Cady.

"And you, ma'am?"

She flushed, ashamed of herself for that self-betrayal.

"I . . . I don't know yet what I'll be able to raise, but I . . ."

As if he'd suddenly lost interest he swung around, letting his eyes flick over the rest of them.

"Now that I've heard your side of the proposition I'll give you mine. Take it or leave it." He took the time to light a cigar, flicking the dead match with careless ease to land between Milt Kehoe's booted feet. Kehoe reddened, his eyes shifting uneasily, but he didn't say anything.

They watched while the tall man drew on the cigar, making them wait until he finally looked up.

"I'll fix you up with a plan of defense after I've had a few days in which to look around. And I'll need whatever maps you have around. But remember that every man does his share. And remember what I've already told you: I don't want to hear any complaints—not *any*, understand—about the way I make war. I'll count on you fine upstanding citizens to square things with the Sheriff."

His caustic tone raked at their pride, but they were nodding agreement in spite of it, and Frank said hesitantly: "But your . . . your wage? You haven't . . ."

Smith shrugged. "Food and ammunition to start off with. And I'll need a new Winchester rifle. Also, I'll take five dollars a month from each of you, and one percent of the money you get from selling your stock; but that only if I'm the one to lead the drive safely through to the stock pens."

Those standing to the rear of the small room were muttering in low voices, and he raised an eyebrow. It was Milt Kehoe, unable to keep silent any longer, who said belligerently: "But my God! Most of us could pay that much money if we had to but some—like Felix here and Lizzie—damn it, man, they just ain't got it to give! You mean to say—"

"I was coming to that. Felix can provide me with horses. I'll need a couple of good ones in addition to my own . . ."—he paused pointedly before adding—"and as for Mrs. Cady here . . ." For the first time Elizabeth felt the frontal attack of his eyes, holding hers against her will. He said softly: "I guess I kinda enjoyed those woman-cooked meals and the fussing over I got when I was mending. And she's the one who talked me into attending this meeting anyhow. So her part of the bargain can be . . ."—he hesitated, a half-smile on his face as he surveyed the shocked, embarrassed faces that stared back at him, *hers* becoming red all over again as she bravely tried to meet his stare—"I get my board and lodging right at her place. There's room, isn't there? Besides, Mrs. Cady needs a man around the place to look after things for her."

On a long breath, she fought the reality of the thing he'd suggested, saying nothing herself. It was Milt Kehoe who again pushed himself to the front of the group, clearly disgusted and angry.

"By God—you all going to take *this*? Even for the kind of hombre we all know he is, it's going too far! We gonna listen to him talk about a woman that way without doin' nothin' about it?"

"Milt!" It was Elizabeth's voice that stopped him dead, sounding cold and clear. "Milton Kehoe, you'll permit me to speak for myself, if you please. I'm a free woman, able to do as I please, and I . . . I accept the . . ."—she almost choked on the words, angrily wishing her telltale blushes gone—"the proposition Mr. Smith has suggested. If we're all in this together I want to give my share too —I insist on it."

"Guess it's settled then?"

Elizabeth felt both anger and shame overriding her scattered emotions for her friends who stood there shifting on their feet with low-voiced mutters that didn't quite become objections and eyes that wouldn't quite meet hers.

She heard *his* voice, sounding as coolly dispassionate as it had been while he'd been telling them what he would and wouldn't have—and she was almost relieved.

"Maybe it's time I drove you home—there's quite a ways to ride yet if I remember right, and I'm hungry." He took her arm, just above the elbow, and led her out then—right under the surprised, shocked eyes of all the others, none of whom made a move to stop him.

Elizabeth was unutterably thankful now that she had asked Domingo to ride over with Fidelito to the Dean place because she didn't want to drive herself home alone. Now she insisted that the chattering boy should ride in the buckboard with them. He had been upset to the point of sickness at the thought of what he had almost caused by his silence—a few words might help. . . .

She found that she was talking for the sake of the sound her voice made and she knew from the way his mouth twitched slightly at the corners, lines deepening in his face, that he knew very well what she was up to. Still, he made no objections and actually talked to the boy in surprisingly idiomatic Spanish; being rewarded by a flood of speech that ceased unwillingly only when they had reached the house and Domingo went grumblingly to unhitch the horses—shouting to his grandson to follow him, for he was no longer a young man and needed help.

She didn't want them to go and . . . leave her! The way his hands had gripped her around the waist as he lifted her down from the buckboard had left her breathless and shaken inside, and now, almost running away from him and up the steps to the house she caught her heel in a cracked board, falling against him.

"Be careful. Why don't you let me go ahead?" His voice sounded dispassionately quiet, but he had taken her hand, disregarding her attempts to tug it away from him.

"I can find my way, thank you. It's just this darned skirt. . . ."

"I'm glad you don't wear a bustle." His voice turned impatient. "Come on!"

She tried to hang back, her nerves jangling. "But . . . but there's no light. I . . . I have to light a lamp. . . ."

"What for?" He'd already shouldered the door open and his blunt, almost brutally direct question terrified her.

"I can't *see!* I have to . . ."

Behind the cover of her stumbling words her mind raced as fast as her heart. Dear God—what did he mean to do with her? She felt herself bump against furniture, drawn through an open doorway, hearing the door kicked shut behind them in the shuttered gloom of her bedroom. Her *bedroom?* . . .

"No!" But she'd said it too late, and the word was a choked sound trapped in her throat as he took her in his arms, kissing her hard and almost harshly, without mercy, until her head fell back weakly and her body felt as if it were made of rubber, like a doll without feeling.

Gasping for breath now, Elizabeth was suddenly aware that his hands were moving down her back, fumbling with hooks and buttons. And "no" her mind shouted fiercely, while from somewhere she discovered the strength to push him away with both hands, falling back hard against a wall.

"No!" she uttered the word at last, panting. "What do you think you're doing?"

Faint light filtered in now from outside—the old man had lighted the lamps in the kitchen and stoked the fire, and *he,* silhouetted against the window, was taking his gunbelts off, unbuttoning his shirt.

"You want me to undress you? It might be quicker if you did that yourself, and I wouldn't want to rip your dress. But hurry. Christ, I feel like I've waited forever to have you!"

The feelings rolled over her like waves, battering at her. Shock, terror, raging disbelief.

"*What?* What did you say?"

"Why waste time playing coy games? You've known I've wanted you from the beginning, haven't you? Get those clothes off and get to bed, Elizabeth. Unless you prefer to be taken standing up."

He had flung aside his shirt and was coming toward her when her voice, rising hysterically, stopped him.

"Why *you*—what kind of man *are* you? How dare you presume that you . . . you've *bought* me just as if I was a . . . a . . . get out, do you hear? Get out of my bedroom right *now* or I'll . . . I'll . . ."

He stood very still, staring at her. His voice was hard and cold when it came at her out of the darkness.

"I thought you understood what I was talking about back there. Goddamn it, you're a woman, aren't you? And you knew damned well—I thought I'd made my intentions pretty damned clear! I want you, Elizabeth. What were you looking for from me? A long courtship maybe? Or a proposal of marriage before I broached the subject of sharing your bed? Is that how a decent, God-fearing *lady* quiets her conscience?"

Tears stung her eyes at his brutal words, but they had made her angry enough to fight back. "And does it not matter to you that *I* do not want *you?* No—I guess nothing really matters to you besides grabbing whatever it is *you* happen to want and you don't really care about stepping on anyone else or their feelings or . . . or anything, do you? And I haven't given you any reason to presume I'd let you drag me in here and treat me like I was the kind of woman you're obviously used to dealing with! I'm not a part of your wage, mister. I'll feed you and I'll house you and I'll wash your clothes and sew for you, but me—I still belong to myself!"

She faced him with clenched fists and angry eyes, waiting fearfully for his reaction, wishing she could read what must be in his face right now. But when he spoke at last he surprised her. All the passion and the anger had gone out of his voice, leaving it soft, and without feeling. She could sense the shrug he gave before he said: "All right."

And then, to her utter surprise he picked up his shirt and slung his gunbelts over one arm while she watched, hardly daring to believe her victory.

"I'm sorry I presumed too much, ma'am."

As he turned to leave her Elizabeth remembered, belatedly, why he was here, and before she could prevent herself she started to say, "You . . . where—" Stopping short to bite her lip.

"You going to let me use the same room as before or would you rather I bunk outside?" Still the same indifference in his voice; how quickly his moods could change!

"The . . . the other room will be all right. I . . . changed the bed linens. . . ." As he opened the door she pressed the backs of her shaking hands against her mouth, stifling a shaken cry when he turned.

"I'd appreciate some supper, if it's not too much trouble. The food the Sheriff serves over at the jail isn't fit for dogs."

And then he walked out, leaving her to stare unseeingly at the door he had closed carefully behind him.

Elizabeth began the usual evening chores moving like a sleepwalker. Lighting lamps, putting more wood in the big stove; rubbing bare arms that had become goose-pimpled in the chilled air. The black taffeta dress had been carefully folded away again in her precious cedar chest, and as if to chastise herself she'd worn her oldest, shabbiest gown.

As she went through the motions of fixing supper her mind kept questioning, taunting, scolding: "So why'd you have to wear *that* dress? Could it be that you're vain, Elizabeth Merrill Cady? You went there to tempt him—no! No, I didn't. Just wanted to look nice, that was all. It was nothing to do with *him*. I don't like him. Don't trust him. He's a loner, like a killer wolf. I shouldn't have said 'yes' to his coming here. Wonder what all the others are thinking now?"

She broke one of her favorite dishes—one of the few left from a set Mama had given her—and she burned her fingers on the edge of the big skillet, making the tears start to her eyes.

"What am I doing? Must be crazy! Letting him get that forward and not even slapping his face . . . and now fixing supper for him! . . ."

All the same, she took her apron off and hung it on a hook behind the door before she opened it to call across the yard, "Supper's ready!" making her voice sound curt and rather sharp.

Maybe he hadn't heard. Maybe he wouldn't come. But she heard faint sounds of splashing at the pump outside the door to warn her, and when he walked in he acted as if nothing had happened—real polite, like any stranger asked to share supper.

"Sure smells good. I've been looking around some, and you have a nice little spread here. House has good thick walls too, in case you ever had to hold off—Indians. Got a few things that need doing, though."

He lowered himself into a chair and she began to heap food on his plate with hands that shook only very slightly, not quite hiding her amazement at his casual air.

"I . . . I know there's a lot that needs doing. The corral's about to fall to bits. But there's only Domingo and Fidelito, and with a million things to be seen to . . ." She sat opposite him, wiping her damp hands down the side of her dress, forgetting about the apron. She went on quickly to forestall his question, "We used to have three men working for us, but after Jared started to get real friendly with Milt Kehoe and that Talley Burton he . . . he wasn't used to saloons, you see, or gambling. He was raised even stricter than I was! But everything is so different here from back home! I'm pretty strong for a woman, though, and we didn't really need the help except at roundup time. I—"

She had been talking nervously to avoid having to look directly at him, but now she suddenly cut herself short, remembering that this man sitting right across from her had killed her husband. How strange life was! So many things happening, seemingly all at once.

Fortunately for her state of mind he didn't comment on her sudden lack of words, but continued to eat hungrily after giving her one long, unreadable look.

"You're a good cook," he said after a while, and she was able to respond dryly, "Thanks!" Wishing for silence which he seemed willing to grant her until, when she got up thankfully to clear the table, he asked her if she had anything stronger than coffee to drink.

Frowning her disapproval, her lips set tight, Elizabeth poked in back of a cabinet that was cluttered with bits and pieces—souvenirs of St. Louis, visits to Kansas City, funny-shaped little vases that had seemed pretty at the time. "I'd rather you didn't drink the loathsome stuff in my house, if you please," she said stiffly, holding out a bottle that was three-quarters full of whisky as if she was afraid it would contaminate her. "I don't hold with drinking hard liquor!" she burst out fiercely, seeing his mouth twitch, "but Jared always insisted we should keep some for his friends."

"Thoughtful man in some ways, your Jared," he commented sardonically, pouring from the bottle into his half-empty coffee mug and looking up to meet her wary, ready-to-pounce eyes. "I won't drink it in here—but do you mind if I keep the bottle? Seeing that you don't hold with the stuff, that is," he added hastily. Then he lit up a cigar that Domingo must have given him from his own carefully hoarded supply.

She wanted to protest once more, but he had risen and started pacing about the room impatiently, making her nervous.

"You got a map?" he asked abruptly.

"I . . . I really don't know," she said helplessly, trying to occupy herself with finding a dry dishcloth. "There were a whole bunch of papers Jared had—they're still there in that box over in the corner. I haven't had time to go through them yet, though, I—"

"Well, maybe you'd better make the time to do that," he said, adding offhandedly, "reckon I'll just step out for a while. Finish this good cigar and have me a drink and an all-over wash at the pump before I turn in."

"Oh!" She blushed in spite of herself and turned away, angry for having let him notice. "Well," she flung over her shoulder, "I'll be sure and not put my head out back until you . . . you're all through, then. Although I could heat up some water for you if you'd like that better. . . ." She offered it reluctantly, doing her duty. "There's an old tub I use sometimes, back in the store-room."

He gave her a rather wicked smile as if he enjoyed causing her discomfort.

"Thanks all the same, ma'am, but cold water and outdoors is good enough for me. Don't let me stop you from taking *your* bath, though, if that's what you had in mind. I'll get back to my room through the window so I won't bother you."

The inclination of his head as he left her was impudent, making her clench her fists at her sides. She wanted to throw the sopping wet old dish towel at his back—tell him to go wash himself with that. But the thought was hardly Christian or ladylike, and she mustn't let him have the satisfaction of angering or embarrassing her. Thank the good Lord she wouldn't have to face him again tonight!

She had the rest of the night to herself—Elizabeth found herself relishing the thought, and she walked aimlessly through the small parlor she had insisted Jared must add to their house, wondering rather sadly why she never sat there any more. There was that book she had promised herself that she would finish, with a blue ribbon marking the place where she'd stopped reading. And the pictures of Mama and Papa taken on their wedding day . . . *her* room. Familiar room. But it was shut tight, and smelled slightly musty from not being used and she just didn't have the heart to sit there tonight, alone in her rocking chair and trying to lose herself in another world of people she couldn't recognize and would never know. Jared hadn't liked the idea of his wife reading novels. He'd often lectured her about it, even had the preacher talk to her, advising her that reading that kind of book might give her ideas—tempt the devil inside her. . . .

No, Elizabeth thought, closing the door firmly behind her, she didn't want to sit in the parlor tonight. She should go to bed, of course, but all his talk about taking a bath had suddenly made her conscious of feeling hot and sticky and uncomfortable in her scratchy old gown. It had been over a week since she'd had a *real* bath—and it was something she liked to do often, the only real luxury she allowed herself apart from the reading.

Why not? It would be nice to go to bed feeling fresh and clean for a change; nice to wash the dust and sand out of her hair.

It didn't take too much effort to drag the tub out and into her bedroom, and because the stove was still hot and she had almost a full kettle of boiling water still on the simmer it seemed like no time at all before her bath was ready for her. She kept her door and the window closed, only the coals in the small fireplace across from the bed giving off light. It was enough, and she didn't spend long sitting in her tub, hearing the splashing sounds outside and ignoring them by humming to herself while she scrubbed vigorously at her scalp.

Baths were necessities, not meant to linger over. Disciplining herself, Elizabeth was finished before the water had a chance to get chilly. She dried herself quickly, standing in front of the fire, and pulled on a wrapper that belted loosely around her waist. Putting more wood on the fire she brushed out her hair vigorously, then tied it back from her face with a ribbon. "There!" she thought, satisfied. The bath and a steaming cup of camomile tea would put her to sleep soon enough—as soon as she got the tub emptied. She was sorry that she had dragged it all the way into her bedroom, to be sure of privacy. Now she had the chore of emptying it or facing dirty, soapy water in the morning.

"I'll do it now and have it over with," she thought determinedly, struggling with the tub which really wasn't all *that* heavy, she told herself bracingly as she dragged it into the kitchen, stopping to catch her breath back and to listen. Only the soup kettle bubbled softly on its perch at the back of the stove. Outside, the sounds of splashing had stopped. Except for a coyote's howl in the far distance, everything was quiet.

Just a few short feet further, and she had the kitchen door open and the tub tipped, emptying it out. Maybe it was because she'd been concentrating so hard that she didn't hear him come up behind her until he was right *there*, arms reaching out to help her, his voice impatient as he said, "Why didn't you call out and tell me you needed help with that?"

She had almost died of fright, but she couldn't tell him that; her heart was still thumping so loudly she didn't care to speak yet, could only shake her head, pushing the tub under the sink and straightening up to face him, only to have her heart start racing again like she'd been running for a long time.

He wasn't wearing a shirt—white scars stood out against the brown of his skin. And suddenly, frighteningly, Elizabeth was only too conscious of herself—her warm nakedness under her

robe, the blood rising warmly to stain her face, her damp hair be
ginning to curl as it dried.

She looked at him. He was standing between her and the open
door to her bedroom, his eyes shadowed so she couldn't see what
was in them. Nervously, Elizabeth brushed back a stray strand of
hair. She wetted her lips: "Well I . . . I guess I'll turn in now.
You want more coffee? There's always some in the pot there,
although it gets rather strong. . . ."

"You know what I want." He was close enough to reach out,
pulling the ribbon to let her hair cascade around her shoulders
like a darkly shining cloud. His fingers touched it, touched her
face gently, sliding down to her shoulders and from there—suddenly the robe seemed to come loose by itself, slipping away from
her body as he took the one step that was all he needed to take
her against himself.

Had this been something she had secretly been waiting for?
Why wasn't she fighting against him this time? Her breasts were
bare, nipples tingling against the slight roughness of hair on his
chest, and his kisses, gentle and searching this time, lulled her into
a false sense of being comforted.

Whatever was happening had started to happen inside herself
too, like water that trickled at first and then came bursting
through a dam. His hands caressed the length of her bare back,
and somehow the robe was about her ankles now, hobbling her.
She murmured incoherently against his mouth and he swung her
off her feet, still holding her closely against him as with long, urgent strides he carried her to the doorway and into her bedroom,
lowering her down onto the waiting bed. She turned her face
aside, not wanting to see his eyes watching her, and closed her
own against the light of the lamp she had lit a few minutes before. "Please . . ." she whispered. "The lamp . . ."

Without a word—humoring her shaken whisper—he blew it
out, and now she was conscious of his movements in the sudden
red-coaled darkness; she had barely time enough to wonder desperately what she was doing here with him, what he might do with
her, before he came to her again, naked himself this time—holding her closely while her body shook with chills and her teeth
chattered.

"P—please! I'm not—I haven't . . ."

His mouth hushed her and his hands warmed and explored her; very slowly, very gently, as if he'd meant only to memorize every inch of her flesh. She began to twist under him with her breath coming in gasps as she tried to escape. It wasn't *right*, what he was doing! Not even Jared had dared to touch her so intimately. This man was kissing her face, her ears, her neck and even her breasts in a way that made her feel she would faint—or go mad if he didn't stop. Or perhaps she was mad already—she must be, to be lying here, letting a stranger use her so familiarly.

"Please don't!" she whimpered, but he was already between her thighs, and now suddenly her body was burning hot, her skin so sensitive that she could feel even the warmth of his breath against it. Her own breathing came in shaken, ragged gasps and she moaned softly, wondering at the new feelings that were beginning to flow through her, taking away her will to resist any longer.

It had never been this way with Jared! The thought should make her feel guilty, she thought detachedly as she lay here with the man who had killed her husband—but she was already beyond guilt.

She and Jared—both so young, both hardly knowing what was expected. She remembered that first night—Jared had been so drunk he'd fallen asleep snoring, while she lay beside him in her new, scratchy nightgown, stiff and afraid. And the next morning there had been the excruciating pain when Jared, waking up, had discovered her there. She'd bitten her lip to stop from screaming, and afterward there had been the shame—the bitter humiliation of the bloodstains on the sheets to be scrubbed and scrubbed away.

After that Jared would climb on her maybe once or twice a week, pushing up her nightgown and muttering unintelligible words while he took her clumsily and quickly. Elizabeth remembered the sound of his breathing, heavy and gasping, while she'd had to will herself to lie there and submit until it was over at last and he'd roll away, starting to snore almost at once. And then she would creep out of bed to go clean herself and come back to lie there—as far away from him as she could get. That was the ugly, unspoken side of marriage. Her mother's embarrassed hints about "wifely duties" and "submitting to certain things a man wants" hadn't prepared her for the disgust and the dirtiness she'd felt every time *it* happened. The act without words, always reminding her of barnyard animals.

But now—now *he*, this stranger in her bed who hadn't yet used words either, was showing her how different the same act could be as he made love to her in wondrous ways, with his hands and his lips and his hard male body, bringing feelings to her she hadn't thought possible and couldn't describe, even to herself. A wild, pulsing churning in her belly that spread and spread until it reached everywhere and she began to arch and shudder and clutch at him wildly with her head thrown back.

"You're so beautiful, Beth. . . ." he whispered to her, and she moved, gasping, to accommodate her body to his. No more shame, no more holding back, only a *wanting*—a needing of him deeper inside her—beyond herself now, beyond thought, only *feeling* as she cried out fiercely and wantonly and her body began to move almost of its own accord to keep pace with his. There was a rising and a falling and a tight-gathering and then a flood of release in her like the sun's warmth after a rainstorm and like rain after a drought. It was as if he sensed it—everything inside her that had been trapped there and pushed down for all this time and longed to be free, sensed when to be gentle with her and when to be hard and almost brutal. And there was no longer time —only motion and feeling.

Sometime during the long night the fire died but she didn't mind the lack of its warmth, lying cradled in his arms, held close, with her face pressed against his shoulder. She didn't want to move, and her thoughts were cloudy and unfocused. She, Elizabeth Cady, had just fornicated with a man she hardly knew—and she felt neither shame nor regret. No. She felt spent and at peace with herself at last. Set free!

# Chapter Thirty

❧

The valley and the plains beyond brooded under the scorching sun, and there was an uneasy sort of peace that held everyone in a kind of suspension, waiting. The Apaches, renegade bands of them, were on the warpath again, and from the north the Comanches ranged further than usual. Not only the small ranchers and the homesteaders but even the Prendergasts prepared to defend themselves against this different but ever-present enemy, and so for a while there was a respite of a sort, even while they all prepared for war.

Elizabeth Cady had learned not to ask too many questions, among other things, but she was happy, hugging fiercely to herself the knowledge and feeling of that happiness. It was as if she had only existed before, not knowing what it was to *live* and to savor each day fully, whatever happened.

Whatever happened . . . sometimes she felt choked with fear and a sense of presentiment, as if she *knew* inside of herself that she was a guilty sinner and would some day be punished—not only for sinning but for glorying in it and deriving happiness from it. But most of the time she would push such thoughts away; keeping herself busy while *he* wasn't around.

There was a lot to do. There always had been of course, but now things got done. Domingo strutted around as if he was a man twenty years younger, filled with a sense of responsibility—the corral fence looked better than it had when it was spanking new, and there was livestock behind it now. The buckboard had been fixed up and given a new coat of paint, like almost everything else around. And the cellar that she'd hardly ever used was all cleaned out and stacked at one end with guns and ammunition. She didn't like to think about *those*, or the times Smith would leave and stay away for days at a time. Sometimes, she was almost certain, he went across the border. And at other times . . . she told herself that she didn't want to know. Some of the members of the Association, led by Milt Kehoe, grumbled; but others, like Martin Burneson and Frank Dean who were older men and more experienced, seemed to go along with what was happening. They all had maps now, and had studied the terrain around them, finding what were their weakest sections and which were the best places for a massed defense if it came to that. And each of them had turned their houses into miniature forts, with an eye to a supply of water and enough food to last for a while.

"What we needed, I guess, was someone to organize us. . . ." Martin Burneson said in a gusty sigh. He had taken to coming over sometimes, and when Smith wasn't there he would stay and talk to Elizabeth. She knew he liked her, and that he always had. He was a widower with a grown son of sixteen and another who was only ten, and everyone said he'd been a good husband and should get married again, but he seemed content enough as he was. Elizabeth liked Martin because he was a kind man who didn't judge, and now that the women—the righteous wives—had gradually stopped coming over to visit she enjoyed the company, especially when she was on her own.

For the most part, Elizabeth preferred to live each day for itself. It was strange how different she felt, even to herself! Sometimes she could feel her mind spinning, as she tried to absorb too many new things, new ideas. Things she had been brought up to believe were wrong or bad weren't that way at all, like reading; or even silk underwear, or not wearing anything at all and letting a man look at your body and kiss it all over. . . .

"John Smith—huh!" Her hair tickled his face as she stirred against him, tilting her face to watch his. There were times when he detested her early-morning wakefulness, forcing him into a show of energy he could not quite feel yet; and he only grunted, turning his unshaven cheek against the pillow, hoping she'd let him burrow back into sleep.

No use. Teasingly, her fingers traced patterns against his back.

"Smith. It reminds me of that story Mama told me once, about the English Captain who married an Indian Princess."

"Yeah—" he said shortly. "Pocahontas. Wonder if she was as restless as you are this early in the morning."

She giggled, pressing her body against his and rousing him against his will.

"Damn you, Beth!"

He had told her in exasperation once that he could not remember who he was—thinking of the time when that had been true. It had been the same story he'd told the Sheriff, not caring if the fat man believed it or not, but with Elizabeth he felt almost ashamed for having used that particularly flimsy subterfuge, especially now, when she asked him guilelessly:

"Don't you ever wonder? About who you really are, I mean?"

He kept his face stubbornly turned away, but he answered her, still only half awake.

"Sure. Doesn't everyone?"

"There! That's what I mean." Beth sat bolt upright, startling him into rolling onto his back, squinting at her through lazy eyes. "You—I only meant, did you wonder about your real *name*, but you took what I said differently, didn't you?" She sighed. "There are so many times when I don't really understand what you're saying—or the *meaning* of what you're saying under the words on the surface. I wish . . . Smith, who are you really?"

Ignoring her question he countered, "Well, how about you, Pocahontas? What kind of woman are *you* under that cool, prissy exterior? Haven't you found yourself wondering? For instance, what you're doing here in bed with a bastard like me."

"Don't!" She bent her head in defeat, nuzzling it against his shoulder. "I was only trying to say . . ."—her voice sounded muffled as she hugged herself to him closely—"that you're *different*. Mama taught school before she married my father, and I guess that was why I had more schooling than most girls my age, but I still don't know even half as much as you do. I don't . . . talk as good, for one thing. I don't understand the meaning of some of the words you use."

"For Christ's sake, what is this? Soul-searching day? What are you trying to tell me, Beth?"

"Smith—don't be angry with me! It's just that sometimes I need to *talk*—you know? A little more than . . . than just falling into bed when we're together. *You* taught me that. And there's something else—I . . . I love you, Smith. At least, I think I do."

"Beth . . ."

"No—please don't try to stop me now, I have to say it all. It'll be better for both of us afterward."

He said nothing, merely tightening his arms around her, and after a moment she continued: "Jared—yes, I've got to talk about *him* too! Jared and I—well, he was the first young man who came courting, and I didn't want to be left on the shelf. My family wasn't rich, you know, and there were a lot of us to feed. And Jared, he was full of dreams in those days. Dreams of going West —homesteading, building us up a nice place of our own. And that's what I wanted too. To have dreams, to travel—to end up *being* someone. To have space around me. And . . . and I didn't care too much that he drank liquor sometimes, even if I didn't dare let Pa find out. And I didn't even care when . . . that when we were . . . you know . . . it wasn't very pleasant. I thought that was the way it was supposed to be. Mama told me that men wanted to do . . . certain intimate things with their wives, and a wife had to submit, that was her duty. And I did—even if I didn't like it at all and I felt . . . don't laugh . . . I felt defiled!

"But that was the way it was until . . . well, after we came out here and Jared made friends he began to take to drink much more. And he'd go into town all the time and leave me to run the ranch and do *everything* and I . . . I was actually glad that he didn't come into bed with me as often as he used to! I used to . . . sometimes I'd deliberately pick an argument with him so he'd get mad and go into town. He hit me sometimes, and it was my fault, because I'd provoked him. And when he . . . when it happened, I felt guilty—sick with guilt inside because . . . because I felt God was angry with me for being such a bad wife and because I didn't feel any sorrier than I did! And now with you . . ."

"Beth, honey, that's enough, huh? Come here." He moved over her, kissing her tear-stained face, trying to kiss her into silence.

"Smith—oh . . . oh, Smith!" She put her arms around him, pushing her warm, fiercely responding body up against his. "This *isn't* wrong, it isn't!"

"Shut up, Beth!"

"I love you," she whispered, her lips pressed against him. "I know it isn't the same with you, but it doesn't have to be. I even know that someday you'll leave—but it doesn't matter. You hear? It doesn't matter, if all I have is now and today!"

He stopped her wild, incoherent speech with his mouth, telling himself it was only a mood—wishing she wouldn't talk so damn much sometimes. She was warm and sweet and giving, and he didn't want to think of her being hurt.

His assault on her body was almost angry, but she met it with a fierceness of her own—for once not protesting that it was daylight and the covers had fallen off the bed onto the floor; not even afterward when he pulled back and looked down at her naked quivering body, running his hand very gently down the length of it.

"You're lovely, Beth."

But he had never told her that he loved her.

He left again soon after that on one of those mysterious errands that neither she nor any of the others dared ask him about. Beth always pretended that she knew where he went and had promised not to tell—it made her feel better, having them all think she was so close to him. By herself, she wondered like the rest, although he'd never offered to tell her where he went or when he'd be back—and she had too much stiff-necked pride to question him.

She thought about him a lot though, missing him with an ache inside her that was like an emptiness wanting to be filled. And she wondered how she could ever bear it if he didn't come back. Because, deep inside, she knew that one day that was what would happen. He was that kind of man. He'd finish what he'd begun here—or settle it one way or the other—and then he'd get bored and someday she'd wake up to find him gone.

Martin Burneson, now a frequent visitor, was Elizabeth's only real friend—the one person she could confide in, even though she knew, guiltily, that this was only because she had already sensed he loved her.

"Elizabeth," he'd say in his slow, slightly pedantic way, "you must be practical. Even if he stayed, what kind of a future would you have with him? You will always be afraid—always wonder if *this* time he will not come home. . . ."

"Martin, *don't* . . ." she cried out but he went on inexorably.

"Yes. It must be said and you must hear me. And I think that *you* think the same thing too—too often, if I can judge from those dark rings under your eyes. You keep wondering about him, and worrying, don't you? You say he still says that he does not remember who he is or where he came from, but this I do not believe. However, to me it does not matter. Have you thought that he might be married? That there is another woman somewhere who waits for him to come back?"

"No! No—he's not the type, not the kind of man for ties. . . ."

"And are you not looking for ties? And if he is not that kind of man, what kind is he? Will he give you what you are looking for? It is you I worry about, Elizabeth. Me, I do not like your man, but neither do I dislike him. He is . . . a certain breed of man. I have seen his kind before. They stir up things and sometimes they settle things, but always—they move on. But you—yes, *you*—what will you do when he goes? You tell me you are living for now, for one day at a time, but when that particular day comes will you be content to stay here or will you try to run after him, hold him, no matter what kind of life he offers you—if he offers you anything at all?"

He had not offered her anything. For the moment he was her man. He shared her bed and he was kind to her and even tender with her. He talked to her—but of *things*, not of himself. And he wanted her—and in taking her had given her something precious. He'd given her herself and the knowledge of her own femininity. He'd also taught her how wonderful it was to love—and at the same time how frighteningly vulnerable it made her, loving him as she did.

Beth told herself over and over again that what he gave her was enough. She had no doubt that he could be cruel and completely ruthless, as Martin kept warning her, but all that mattered was that he was gentle with *her*.

She tried to tell Martin that, stumbling over the words because she cared enough about Martin to want him to understand, but he only shook his head forebodingly.

"Elizabeth, you say one thing and you *look* another! Where has he gone this time? And for how long?"

"I don't know! Very well—you're the only one I can say even *that* much to. But I do know he'll be back. He's given his word—and you know he hasn't taken any pay yet. . . ."

"Yes. He's a man who asks a high price for his services, and yet he does not seem to need money, does he? He has it—as much as he needs."

"Or *we* need!" She leaped to his defense. "We have guns now, and ammunition—had you forgotten that? And a *plan* in case of any trouble. We're *doing* something instead of sitting about *talking*. . . ."

"And who is he talking to? Don't look at me that way, Elizabeth. I say these things only because you must think them yourself—and must know what your friends are thinking. We *know* that he knows Jack Prendergast—he said as much to Lefty the day he arrived in town. How do we know—"

"That's disgusting! If you think that way, what a bunch of hypocrites you all are! Why don't you come out and tell *him* what you think? He's not setting us up for the Prendergasts—why, that's impossible, and you have to admit it yourself! We're in a better position to fight back now than we ever have been."

"Elizabeth! That is not what I am saying. I am saying that . . . ah, now I have made you angry and brought tears to your eyes and that makes me angry with myself. I do not want to see you hurt."

She dashed the back of her hand over her eyes, blinking away the tears he'd accused her of. "Then . . . then don't say such things to me, Martin Burneson. Or I couldn't think of you as my friend any longer. Smith isn't a traitor and he wouldn't hurt me—and please, can we stop talking about it now?"

Martin asked her again to marry him, and she shook her head miserably.

"But Martin, I *cannot!* Don't you understand? I couldn't, feeling the way I do about him. Please don't ask me again."

"I will wait. I am a patient man, and I have come to care for you very deeply. Later, perhaps."

"But I—how could you want to marry me when I . . . we . . . Everyone *knows!* Everyone knows we live here together—that I—"

"To me, nothing matters but *you*, little Elizabeth. I'm not as young as you are and I know more of human nature. But that's enough. For now we will talk of other things, yes?"

The days dragged on into a week. Where *was* he? Suppose something had happened, suppose he was lying dead somewhere. . . . Elizabeth tried not to worry, but it showed in her face and she was aware of Martin's pitying looks—clumsy attempts to comfort her by Domingo and even Fidelito. Dear God! —what if *this* was the time—and he wouldn't return?

Beth told herself that it was only because she wasn't feeling well that she worried so. He'd told her he might be away for longer than usual this time—yes, he'd told her that much at least. He could take care of himself. . . . But all the time she felt listless and uneasy and didn't sleep well at night; and there were times when she wanted to burst into tears without any reason at all, which wasn't at all like her.

It was only when she started feeling nauseated in the mornings, sometime during the second week of Smith's absence, that the truth hit her like a blow and a revelation at the same time:

"I'm . . . I'm going to have a child! Oh, God—it's happened. It wasn't *my* fault all these years, then—it was Jared's. And now I'm going to have a baby—*his*." And on the heels of that thought, sneaking up on her unbidden, "When he knows—when I tell him —it's going to make everything different. He'll want to settle down and stay with me, I *know* he will!"

# Chapter Thirty-One

∞

Beth. Warm and soft and sweet. The smell of fresh bread baking. Beth waiting—just being *there*. Her body refuge and comfort and pure pleasure. The kind of woman a man wanted to come home to.

He laughed caustically inside himself. Shit—he had been riding too long; he was thinking like Martin Burneson now. Coming home to the same woman night after night would probably get damned boring after a while, as he ought to know. And yet—what *was* it that he was looking for? The answer came unbidden to his mind, even though he tried to erase it. Fire and passion. A laughing, teasing, sensuous green-eyed woman he'd once taken and loved—and let go. Bright flame of a woman, leaving the scar of her loss like a brand on him; etched all the deeper because he had been responsible for killing her. But how long was he going to keep running because of it? The scar, like the others he bore, he'd carry with him always—he might as well learn to live with that thought.

Steve Morgan was suddenly angry with himself, suddenly impatient. There were things he had to do, and so far he'd merely been playing war games. Playing for time too, in one sense, because he'd needed time in which to heal and mend—not just his body, which seemed to cling to survival, but his mind as well. And then there had been—there still was—Beth.

The sky had begun to turn dark and menacing with lightning flashes lacing through the clouds when Steve turned his horse to head north. Once before, on a day like this in the mountains of Mexico, he'd had the same kind of thoughts. Thoughts about having spent most of his life running—or chasing. Always moving, taking what amusement he needed along the way. Ginny had made him stop for a while, but Ginny was gone out of his life forever, her defiant fire extinguished. Damn her! He was going to get her out of his mind no matter what it took!

Riding cautiously because of the ever-present danger of coming across a band of marauding bandidos, Steve kept moving. Prayers End, where he'd been heading in the beginning, lay a long way behind him now.

If he had known that he was the subject of a long and heated argument between Renaldo Ortega and his wife Melissa, Steve would have smiled, knowing the impossibility of staying angry at Missie—but not for very long.

Renaldo was not precisely angry himself, because he happened to worship his young bride, but perdition!—sometimes Missie did not understand, and in the face of her simplistic way of looking at things, he found it hard to explain.

In spite of being seven months pregnant, Missie managed to look impossibly slender—a fact that worried everyone but the Doctor that Don Francisco had called in. She wasn't above taking advantage of her pregnancy either, Renaldo decided wrathfully, as she tilted her pointed chin at him with unusual defiance.

"I *still* do not understand, and I will *not* quit asking questions until I do, so . . . so there! Renaldo, why do *you* think she did it? And I can't understand why your uncle who is so stern and so . . . so *straitlaced*, should have allowed it! I thought she *loved* Manolo —I mean Esteban, of course, only I can't quite get used to—"

"*Tesoro*, my treasure," Renaldo interrupted gently, "don't you see that it is no use making yourself upset about something neither of us can do anything about? Ginny's gone off to Europe with this Lord Tynedale and her children—and surely my love, you can't deny that she has the right to take them with her? Esteban hasn't been back to see them and nor has he sent as much as a message to ask after them. My cousin can be quite . . . dispassionate."

"He's not! Well, not really—you saw how nice he was to *me*, and even to Pa and the boys afterward. He saw to it that they have all the land that should have been my mother's, didn't he? He's *not* really bad or wicked, and I don't think it's fair—I think someone should have told him. I think Ginny should have told him, and I don't care if you were a little bit in love with her before you met me or not!"

Distracted, Renaldo clasped her in his arms. "I never loved anyone but you, my treasure, and I never will—how could I, when you've made me the happiest man in the world? But—"

"Then you will write a letter to Steve and *tell* him. Or let me. And *I* will write a letter to Ginny, and send it to—you have the address of her aunt and uncle in France? Those poor little babies —all that *traveling!* And in the end she's going to leave them there while she goes traipsing off to . . . to Turkey of all places, with this Richard. I *know* I haven't met him and I shouldn't judge—and I *do* like his sister, but that doesn't signify, does it? If you want to know what *I* think, I think Ginny's just run away to make sure Steve follows her—to *prove* he loves her. And I think Richard took advantage of her when she was so ill, and if Steve knew . . ."

The thought was enough to make Renaldo blanch, although he consoled himself with the knowledge that his uncle would surely handle matters in his usual autocratic fashion. Esteban would be made to understand, and he would, of course. He had too much pride to go running after a woman who had shown so openly that she didn't want him. And with Steve, there were always other women. . . .

Wanting to end their disagreement, Renaldo said quickly, "I think we should keep only to facts, don't you, my love? But I promise you that I will write to Esteban—will that bring back a smile to your face? His partner, Sam Murdock, is bound to have some idea of his whereabouts."

Sam Murdock had only a gut feeling that Steve would turn up in answer to his message, but Sam was a patient man, and he hadn't taken a vacation in years, so he was prepared to wait. If Steve wasn't coming he'd have sent a message back.

The Prendergast ranch, with its Double P emblazoned everywhere, stretched from the hills to the valley that the ranch house overlooked, and Jack Prendergast, a big bear of a man, ruled his domain like a king. He had three sons by his first wife, a long-suffering woman who had simply faded away as her husband seemed to grow stronger and more bullheaded. And a few years after Amelia had died, Jack Prendergast had met and married an attractive Frenchwoman in her thirties—a distant cousin of the Marquis de Mora, who had decided to try his hand at ranching in New Mexico. By Francoise, who was still attractive and quite as energetic as her husband, Jack Prendergast had sired a daughter whom he named Lorna—and Lorna was the only member of his family that Jack Prendergast did *not* rule. The Crown Princess, she twisted her father and her brothers about her little finger; all with a wide-eyed, innocent air. The only thing that Lorna wanted and hadn't got yet was a vacation in Europe—her mother wouldn't leave her father and her father wanted her to be at home. He didn't trust those decadent European men, he'd confided to his friend Sam Murdock. What did his baby girl want to go to Europe for anyway? Anything she wanted from there he'd have shipped out to her—like the grand piano she'd asked for a few years back. And a dance teacher. And her own dressmaker—a woman who had worked for Worth in Paris. He'd sent Lorna to an Eastern school, and having her away from home that long had been bad enough. Better that she stayed around for a while, and this was no time for traveling anyhow, with the Indians on the rampage and those miserable homesteaders making trouble. . . .

Sam Murdock was a good listener, and when he did talk, he made good sense. He was one of the few men Big Jack called "friend" and would listen to. On this particular evening they were rocking on the porch while supper was being fixed; they'd had a rainstorm and the air smelled fresh and clean with the lemony scent of sagebrush and pine.

"So what do you think?" Jack Prendergast said abruptly. "Dawson talked to Sheriff Blaine himself and he says this hombre the Sheriff was holding sure matched up with the description you gave me of your partner. He'd been shot up bad and almost got himself hanged after that—by those smallholders I was tellin' you about. Thought he was one of my boys, I guess. But all of a sudden he drops out of sight. Doesn't sound right. I want to know what's going on, and I'd have sent my boys down to find out 'cept for the damned 'paches making trouble."

"It doesn't sound like Steve—letting himself get shot up," Sam Murdock said dryly. But he added in a grimmer tone, "I must say

I'm surprised that he hasn't showed up here before now, though. Maybe we should make some inquiries."

Lorna came out onto the porch at that moment—she had auburn hair and tawny eyes to match and dimples when she smiled. She wore a fashionable evening gown, for since Francoise's coming it had become the custom at the ranch house to dress for dinner.

"Are you men still talking about that *fascinating* sounding Steven Morgan? I wish he *would* turn up—he'd be someone new to practice my French on. And perhaps he could tell me more about Europe. . . ." She rolled big, reproachful eyes at her father, who pretended to scowl and succeeded only in smiling fatuously.

"Lorna's got a one-track mind."

"And Lorna's also bound and determined to get to Europe before she's too much older! You promised to think about it, Papa! Wouldn't you like me to come back with a titled catch?"

"I'd—" Jack Prendergast was spared finishing his comment when there was a hail in the distance.

"Sounds like Clint, and he's late for supper. Wonder why he's hollering?"

"Oh, Clinton's always late and he always has an excuse!" Lorna shaded her eyes from the light of the big hanging lamps and squinted into the darkness before she whirled around with a trace of excitement tinging her voice.

"Papa! I do believe we have company for dinner. That's a strange horse and rider with Clinton."

Curiously, she stayed out on the porch, pretending not to hear her mother's voice calling her from inside. Company was always exciting—at least in the beginning. Until, as it usually happened, they turned out to be dull, dull people with the same limited horizons her father and her brothers had. Still, she kept hoping that someday—why couldn't things in real life happen as conveniently as they did in books?

And then something did—and Lorna caught her breath, forgetting all her sophistication as she stared like all the others at the tall man who walked up the steps with her half-brother Clint.

He was as tall as her father—that was what she noticed first. Tall, but not half as wide-bodied, except for his shoulders. IIis hair was black and his eyes were dark blue and his face was as brown as an Indian's, except for a thin scar on one cheek and another that ran across his temple. In spite of the scars and the dark beard stubble, Lorna thought he was surely the handsomest man she had ever seen—and the most exciting. Even before she heard Sam Murdock greet him, she'd already guessed who he was. And never mind how he was dressed now, she knew this man moved in sophisticated drawing rooms as easily as he did right now in his shabby range clothes. She was glad she'd worn her best jewels tonight. He'd be bound to notice—and notice *her!*

For Lorna Prendergast, at least, the evening passed far too quickly. She had noticed Steve Morgan's eyes on her at dinner, and had engaged him in conversation, but she had also realized that the blueness of his eyes, shadowed by those ridiculously long lashes, gave away nothing at all. He had been polite to her, and yet had turned most of his attention to her father and her brothers. Their conversation had not interested her all that much. Did men have nothing to talk about but cattle and guns and the Indian Problem? *This* man was different—she could sense it. And the idea that he could treat her with casual politeness even when she sparkled and set herself out to be enchanting both piqued and intrigued her.

After dinner, he had gone off with the rest of the men to smoke cigars and drink cognac on the porch and Lorna, left with her mother, looked directly at the older woman.

"What is he doing without his wife—if he has a wife? I think I would like to tame him, Maman."

Francoise shook her head, wishing her daughter were not so headstrong and willful. "My treasure—be careful! I do not think he is an *easy* man. And I recall that he has a wife—or had one. In any case he is here on only a very brief visit, to see Sam and to talk to your father—and from the sound of it, I do not think the business he comes to discuss is pleasant."

Sure enough, Lorna could hear raised voices from outside—she recognized her brother Joseph's bellow and she grimaced.

"Joseph always *blusters* so! And Pete is sneaky. Clint doesn't really care, as wrapped up as he is in that woman he's been seeing. None of them is half the man Papa is, or as smart as he is either.

But I think this Steve Morgan is a smart man too. I wonder what they are arguing about?"

They were arguing about squatters rights and the rights of the homesteaders and small ranchers—Jack Prendergast and his sons being noisily forthright about *their* viewpoint, while Sam Murdock continued to rock and hide his quiet smile behind the cigar he fussed with. Steve had turned up at long last—with not many explanations to offer for his delay. But he certainly wasn't wasting much time, now he was here! He wondered if Jack Prendergast would choke on his words when he was told politely that he was outdated in his ideas.

"If you'll pardon my saying so, sir, a range war would only cost you blood and money—and not gain you much. You'd be too busy attacking or defending to tend to business. And you're into ranching for the money, like the rest of us, aren't you? It wouldn't do you any good in the long run to force a few miserable settlers off land that's legally theirs—those days are gone, I'm afraid. You should have filed on that open range before, when the land cost no more than a few cents an acre. Now someone else owns it, and they've banded together, determined to fight if they have to, in order to hold what's rightfully and legally theirs. Wouldn't you do the same in their place?"

"It ain't the same thing!" Joe Prendergast shouted. He leaned forward in his chair, his face red. "We were here before—it was Pa and his friends who came here first and fought off the Indians and fought in the goddamn war, and fought to keep this land free. And then the damned nesters get here with their little pieces of paper that say they own this or that. And their fences—forcing *us* to put up fences too. It's getting so we don't have no place to run our cattle—and that means they better get the hell off the land. Or get put off!"

"They've learned from other range wars, and they're determined not to be pushed. They've formed an Association and they're ready to fight if necessary to keep what they consider to be theirs."

"They're a bunch of sniveling cowards—dirt farmers and ex-cowpunchers with a few rustled head of cattle, hoping to start their own herds. They don't know the first thing about fighting!"

Steve Morgan said quietly, "They're learning—from me." And

then he sat back and waited for the explosion that would surely follow, and did.

Lorna waited, pouting, for what seemed like ages—but the men still didn't come inside, although she continued to hear their raised, angry voices. She wanted to go outside on the pretext of serving them coffee, but her mother, putting her foot down for once, forbade her. At last she went to bed, still sulking, but determined to get her turn next morning. She liked to lie abed late and let one of their Mexican maids bring her café au lait in her room, but *this* morning would be different. She'd be up for breakfast with the rest—or even before. . . .

Their house was built U-shaped around a courtyard for coolness. A Spaniard had designed it long ago, but he'd been killed off by raiding Comanches before he could complete it, and for the safety of his family Big Jack Prendergast had only had to add outbuildings and a stockade fence. It was a comfortable house, and Lorna called it home for now, but since she had been to school back East and visited the homes of some of her friends she'd been discontent with the remoteness and loneliness of her life here. More than anything she wanted to travel—and especially to Europe! Her maman still had relatives there—why shouldn't she go?

Lorna had dreams that night that kept waking her up, and it had to be only about six o'clock when she forced herself out of bed; taking a long time with her toilette before she was finally ready. She admired herself in the long mirror her papa had had shipped here for her. Her newest riding habit of black cloth made her look older than her eighteen years. It was trimmed with gold-colored satin and she wore a scarf of the same fabric tied loosely about her throat, pinned with a diamond and topaz brooch. She was an excellent horsewoman too, as Steve Morgan would find out if he took her hints and offered to go riding with her.

To her chagrin, Lorna found that almost *everyone* in the household was up already by the time she emerged into the courtyard, where an impromptu breakfast was usually laid out on long tables.

Her brother Pete brushed by her with a slyly whispered: "Who're you out to catch *this* time, sis?" That made her want to kick him with her high-heeled boot.

"What are *you* doing up this early, baby doll?" her father questioned tactlessly, and her brother Joe whistled loudly, but Lorna was determined not to let them spoil anything for her.

"Good-morning, everybody!" she said sweetly, holding her skirts up with one gloved hand while she signaled to the maid to bring her a cup of coffee.

Sam Murdock was already there, but *he* wasn't. Lorna hid her disappointment well enough as she joined the older man after kissing her father.

"I couldn't sleep at all this morning, it looked so pretty outside! And Gypsy needs exercise, so I thought I'd go for an early ride. Will you ride with me, Mr. Murdock?"

From the way his eyes twinkled she guessed he had a very good idea whom she *really* wanted to go riding with her, but he was nice enough not to let on.

"Well, Miss Lorna, if I was a few years younger I'd jump at the chance. But I guess I'm going to have to start packing, now that my partner's decided to show up."

"You're not *leaving*? Why, we'll all miss you so, I was hoping you'd persuade Papa to let me travel with you—at least as far as San Francisco. My aunt and uncle there have been begging and begging me to come visit, and I have two friends living there I went to school with, too—oh, Mr. Murdock, *do* talk to Papa!"

Sam noticed with amusement that all the time she was talking to him her eyes kept going beyond him, searching. Lorna was used to getting her own way, and he had seen the way she looked at Steve across the dinner table last night. It was just as well they'd be leaving today.

Just then Steve Morgan came outside, dressed for riding—with a gunbelt around his waist. He was wearing black pants and a faded blue shirt with a leather vest over it—a darker blue bandanna knotted about his neck. Now that he'd said what he'd come to say he was anxious to be gone, to be *doing*. He and Sam had had a long talk after the others had gone stamping off to bed, and now he was impatient to get back to the challenge of business and the things he'd left undone. Work was what he needed to get his head straight again—and there was Beth. Goddamn it, he needed to do something about Beth.

What Steve didn't know was that Francoise Prendergast, knowing her daughter, had already talked to Sam, drawing him out with her studiedly casual, shrewd questions that told her several things about Sam's partner—including the fact that he'd recently been widowed. And she'd spoken after that to her husband, who had still been smoldering after the talk they'd had last night. Now Jack Prendergast was thoughtful, trying to make up his mind; keeping whatever he felt inside to himself. He watched his daughter's face, and he watched Steve Morgan.

Lorna helped him make the decision—he never could resist her pleading for too long. "Papa, *please!* Please may I go riding? I'd go by myself, only I promised you—"

"You know it's dangerous out here, daughter. Not just from Indians but damn sheepherders and homesteaders as well. . . ." From under lowered brows he flashed a belligerent look at Morgan, who looked back at him with his face as impassive as an Indian's. "Hell . . ." Jack thought to himself, Lorna could take care of herself and she could reduce almost any man she came in contact with to malleable putty in no time at all. Why should Morgan be any exception?

"But, Papa—"

"Tell you what, I'd promised to show Mr. Morgan here those old diggings on our north range—you know what place I mean. Maybe you can ride out there with him. I still think there's silver there—just didn't want any folk from outside nosing around. Sam here says he thinks the rocks look right—I'd appreciate a second opinion."

Lorna Prendergast, with her rich auburn hair and her tawny eyes, was quite a woman—and a challenge she kept throwing in his face. Manned by experience and indifference, Steve parried easily. No more eager, panting little virgins—and he thought she was one, for all her boldness. In Lorna he kept seeing Ginny, as Ginny had been when they'd first run into each other. Only, instead of being forward, Ginny had begun by hating him . . . and had ended hating him. . . . What he should keep in mind was that she had gone off with Andre Delery of her own free will. That she had died was an accident of fate—if she hadn't, he might have felt impelled to kill her himself.

"Are you going back to Prayers End or directly to San Francisco? You have a house there, don't you?"

He had houses everywhere—and not one he lived in and called home. Lorna's question brought her back into focus for a while and Steve looked her over as he would any woman who kept throwing herself at him. She colored slightly, but kept her eyes fixed on him.

"I'm going back to Prayers End first. I've unfinished business there. And after that maybe I will go back to San Francisco. Or to Mexico."

"You must travel a great deal. I wish that *I* could too. Most of all I want to go to Europe." Lorna sighed. "Papa's so stubborn, but I'm working on him. I know I'm going to have to settle down sooner or later, but I—there are so many things I'd like to do and to see first!"

She had stopped playing flirtatious games for a change, letting some of her real feelings show through, and Steve gave her a thoughtful look.

"Moving around can get mighty tiresome and boring after a while—but I guess you *would* enjoy Europe. You'll make quite a hit there, I'm sure."

"Do you think I'm pretty?"

"You're a beauty, and you know it too."

"Then—why haven't you tried to kiss me yet?"

This time he laughed outright, and the laughter made him look younger and less dangerous. "I'd thought about it—but I was waiting to be asked."

"Ohh!" He thought she was going to forget all about being a lady and swear at him, but she decided to give him a cat-smile instead, and half closed her eyes provocatively. "I'm asking now. I think I'd like you to kiss me. And I haven't been kissed by too many men, not really."

He brought his horse in close and kissed her without another word, and the way he kissed her was like no other time before, making her weak and breathless, making her want . . . she didn't know what! And then he ended it with a harshly muttered: "That's enough. You'd better start to understand that if you go kissing men back that way you might end up with more than you asked for, Miss Prendergast." Lorna was silent for once, trying to collect her scattered feelings. She wanted him to kiss her again, but she was afraid too. Not just of him but of herself as well. Maybe *this* was what Maman had meant by her warnings about emotions getting out of hand; she hadn't wanted him to stop kissing her, and yet—what would have happened if he hadn't stopped? Girls got in trouble—oh, not just from kissing, she wasn't as ignorant as some of her classmates had been, but women always had to pay a price while men walked off scot-free. Glancing sideways at Steve Morgan as they resumed their ride just as if nothing had happened, Lorna wondered resentfully how many other women *he* had kissed, and if he had a woman right now to whom he did more than just kiss.

# Chapter Thirty-Two

❦

The dark fell very suddenly here on the plains, marching down from the mountains in the wake of the shadows of the mountain peaks that lay black against the orange-red glow of sunset. Time to light the lamps and stoke up the fire. Time to try even harder not to think, not to look toward the bedroom and long for his presence there, waiting for her. But then he wasn't the kind of man who enjoyed waiting—that was for her; the waiting and the enduring.

Beth moved slowly in the kitchen, dragging out each task for as long as she could. Martin had been over again today, and again he had asked her if she would marry him. This time, her worry and her distress had made her burst out with the bald, unvarnished truth.

"Martin, I . . . you don't understand. I have good reason to believe that I'm . . . expecting."

She had half expected him to turn from her in disgust. She waited dumbly for his face to change, and instead, he reached out for her hands, gripping them very tightly.

"Ah, Elizabeth! I was married once, you know. I had already begun to suspect. There is a look a woman gets. . . . And so—what will you do? Does he know?"

"No. I haven't told him yet. I didn't know—I was only sure after he had left. When he comes back—"

"*If* he comes back. It has been three weeks, Elizabeth. That is a long time."

"He *will* come back!"

"No matter. Do you think he will marry you? Would you be happy married to him? Is this place big enough for him?" He made a wide gesture, and Beth knew what he meant. Martin was a wise man in lots of ways. He went on before she could answer: "To me—it does not matter. Knowing what you have told me, I still want you as my wife. I would try to make you happy, Elizabeth, and I would bring the child up as my own." He smiled crookedly. "I hope it is a girl who looks like you. I would like a girl child to spoil and carve dolls for. Did you know that I am very clever at carving dolls? I had a niece once—she died of the typhoid when she was only five years old. But she always asked for Uncle Martin's dolls—always a new one, and my sister would make clothes . . . you are crying. What have I said?"

"I am crying because you are a good man, Martin Burneson. And because . . . I am grateful to you for asking me to share your name in spite of what you know about me. But, Martin, I—"

"I know." He had risen then, looking down at her with sadness in his face. "You don't wish me to talk of this until he comes back and *you* are sure. Isn't that so? Well, you have to make up your mind. If you say yes to me I shall know it is because you have thought very carefully and it is what you want to do. So—I will come again tomorrow?"

The thought came to her all over again that Martin was sureness—Martin would come tomorrow because he had said he would. But Smith . . . dear God, she didn't even know his real name—or where he'd come from or where he went when he left her. All she knew about him was the way he made her feel when they were in bed together. Was that enough to build hopes on, build a life on? And what name would her baby bear, what kind of existence would the poor mite have? Ostracism she couldn't stand—for herself maybe, but not for her child. *His* child too.

"Beth?" He had come up behind her so quietly that she hadn't heard—not even the opening and closing of the door. And she jumped so hard that she fell against the stove and he had to grab her, brushing sparks off her sleeve while he swore.

"Oh, Smith!" she said. "Oh—darn you, Smith! Where have you been? I've been worried sick!"

"Fine defense you have here against an Indian attack! I rode right up to the corral and unsaddled my horse, and all without a peep out of either of your two brave cowpunchers!"

"Domingo was going to give Fidelito a bath—you know what a chore *that* is! He was probably hollering so loud neither of them . . . where've you *been*? Three weeks without a word. . . ."

All the time she was scolding, her eyes couldn't take in enough of him. He looked sun-browned and fit, and he was wearing a new shirt made out of some blue cloth that felt soft enough to be real linen, open down the front with an unfamiliar dark jacket over it. She'd never seen him wear a jacket before, and it made him seem . . . almost removed from her.

Beth let her words trail off as she kept staring at him, wishing he wouldn't stare at *her* so hard. She had a smudge on her face and her hair was knotted up any old how—and she hadn't bothered to change her gown all day. What was he seeing when he looked at her? Why hadn't he kissed her yet?

"Smith? . . ." she questioned on a rising whisper—and that was when he took her in his arms at last, holding her in a hard embrace that locked her body against his.

"Beth—I've missed you. Jesus—how I've wanted you!"

He could still make her blush when he said those things out loud, and he laughed at her blushes, scooping her up off her feet to carry her—protesting feebly—into the bedroom.

"Not now—put me down! The stew will burn . . . ohhh . . . Smith, you're tearing my dress, stop it!" There was a note of something barely held back in his voice that she hadn't heard before.

"The hell with the stew and the hell with your dress. I've brought you a new one, and you'll model it for me—afterwards. Right now I want you *without, querida.* Without clothes—and without reservations."

When he started kissing her all over every argument she could muster seemed to dissolve away; even shame, even the ever-present guilt that still enveloped her when she was alone. There was something she had to tell him . . . but even that didn't seem to matter now—not right now when he was doing what he was with her body and making her want it, making her cry out with a need as fierce as his wanting.

Later, lying lazily satiated beside him, Beth asked her questions again, the need to know pushing at her.

"Where did you go this time? What did you do? I was afraid . . ."

He had rolled over to lie with his head pillowed on his arms, but she could feel him turn to her. His voice was quiet and without inflection.

"I crossed over into Mexico first. Had some business there. And then I headed north, to visit the Prendergasts."

"You did—*what?*" She sat upright as if he had pushed a spring inside her. "*What?*" she repeated, feeling stupid for having done so; wishing she could see his face in the gloom.

"Lie down, Beth. I have a lot to talk to you about. Stop glaring down at me that way."

"I want to know why—"

"I didn't go up there to sell you out, if that's what you're wondering about. I figured that maybe by talking to Jack Prendergast I could stop this damned war that's building. In any case my partner has been staying there, and Sam was the reason I came up here in the first place."

"Your *partner?* Partner in *what,* Smith? What would he be staying at the Double P for?"

"Quiet down, Beth. . . ." He said on a sigh. "I'm trying to tell you. And to begin with, my name isn't Smith, it's Morgan. You could start calling me Steve, if you aren't too mad to talk to me after I've finished explaining."

She couldn't know, of course, that he wasn't a man much given to explaining. She lay there beside him as stiff as a poker and almost as hot with the rage she was holding bottled up inside her. He had lied. From the beginning he had lied! She was glad it was dark enough in the room so he couldn't see the tears in her eyes. She didn't really want to listen to anything he had to say, but the tears would have betrayed her if she had tried to say so, and that alone kept her silent until she could no longer hold still.

"How could you—why did you as much as listen to us talk? Why'd you say you'd take the job? Was it just for spite, or was it a game you enjoyed playing? You—"

"I took the job because I wanted *you,* damn you, Beth! And because—hell, you might say it was a challenge, and I needed something to do. But mostly because of you. Christ—what did you want, a bloody range war? I talked to Jack Prendergast, and I told him which side I'd be on if there was trouble; and he has agreed to sit down and talk things over with your spokesmen. In fact, he'll be at the Denver House tomorrow night, and if you'd climb down off your high horse you could meet him yourself—and his wife and daughter."

Her mind urged the practical *sense* of what he was saying and her feelings ached with hurt and anger.

"What kind of a man are you?" she said at last in a repressed voice.

"By now you ought to have been able to make up your mind about that!"

"And that's not what I meant either. Are you a gunfighter, is that it? Is that why you have even Jack Prendergast talking *reason* now? What are you, Mr. Steve Morgan? What do you do for a living besides . . . besides amuse yourself with people like us? Where'd you get all the money from for the guns and the ammunition and—"

"I didn't rob any banks, if that's what you're thinking. Not recently, anyhow."

The next day she was to remember his saying that—when Sheriff Blaine came by the house. By then Beth didn't feel worth anything. Last night had been like a bad dream, except for the part when he'd made love to her. And after that—she guessed part of it had been her fault, with anger making her question and nag like a shrew until he'd rolled off the bed and begun to dress. It had scared her when he did that, and still a devil inside her made her scream at him in a voice that was clogged with tears: "Where do you think you're going? You promised me some explanations, and you—"

"I'm going into town, and you'll find me at the Denver House when you're ready to listen instead of screeching like a goddamned washerwoman!" And then he'd turned at the door and said in an ugly voice: "Or maybe you'd prefer to send Milt Kehoe after me?"

She had too much pride left in her to follow him, and she spent what was left of the night in utter misery, weeping until she could hardly see out of her eyes, or breathe except through her mouth. Why hadn't she listened. What should she do now?

Martin Burncson came over early, and his coming helped Beth's state of mine only a little. He told her that Steve Morgan (she must stop thinking of him as "Smith") had dropped by his house last night and they'd sat up a long time talking. Tactfully, Martin didn't comment on the way she looked, nor did he stay for too long.

"I promised to talk to the others, Elizabeth. What he says makes sense. Why get caught up in a range war where there will be no winners, and maybe a lot of losers? He suggested that some of us might lease some grazing land to Prendergast in exchange for water—yes, it makes sense, if we are all able to sit across from one another at one table and talk over our grievances, instead of resorting to violence."

"You sound like *him!*" she snapped unfairly. "*He's* a violent man, don't we all know that? And then he dares to talk peace. . . ." She thought then of Jared and why he had died and how she'd lain night after night with his killer, and her face grew first red and then pale.

Martin didn't pretend to misunderstand her vehemence. He had not been in the house long enough to sit and have a cup of coffee, and now he sighed as he jammed his battered old hat back on his head. "I do not like to see you like this, Elizabeth, and you know it. But you must think carefully about . . . everything. I will stop by again on my way back, if I may?"

She couldn't ask Martin her questions—the answers she sought could only come from *him*, from Steve Morgan—blue-eyed, hard-faced stranger who had shared her bed and told her he wanted her and had lied to her. How many more lies? Or should she have let him tell her the truth at last before leaping in with her accusations? If only he'd told her just once that he loved her!

When the Sheriff came that afternoon Elizabeth had been bathing her reddened eyes, and still fighting a battle with herself. Was she going to town, running after him as she'd done before, or wait for him to come back to *her*? Would he come?

At the sound of hoofbeats she had been unable to stop herself from running out onto the porch, her cheeks flushed with a mixture of fear and excitement. What would she say, how should she act—but it was only Sheriff Blaine, of all people, clambering off his horse to throw the reins at Fidelito, who looked as downcast and disappointed as *she* did.

"Afternoon, Miz Cady. You home alone?" The question was unnecessary—she felt he *knew* already, for all that his eyes glanced around casually.

She couldn't leave him standing out there. Sometimes polite

lies were necessary. "It's good to see you, Sheriff. Would you care for some coffee and a slice of pie I baked yesterday? . . ."

Thanking her, rubbing at his mustache in his usual way he followed her indoors, seating himself comfortably at the kitchen table.

"Big doin's in town—I guess you've been told already?" Her closed, high-boned face gave nothing away as she busied herself at the stove, and he continued, after an inward sigh: "Been a long time since any of the Prendergasts have come to town, and I'll be durned if it isn't the old man himself this time, along with his missus and their little gal—only she ain't so little any longer. Purtiest gal you ever did see, and dressed all fancy. Heard one of the ladies say her daddy gets her clothes clear from the East and from Paree too. Must be going on eighteen and not yet married—looks like she could be a spitfire, with that hair an' all."

"Oh?" Elizabeth said with what she hoped sounded like disinterest. Inwardly she had begun to seethe with resentment again.

"Yup!" The Sheriff leaned back, carefully wiping crumbs from his bushy mustache. "But that ain't really why I came by, Lizzie."

She looked at him crossly and he grinned as if he knew very well how mad it made her when he used her given name. Putting on a solemn look right after that he said portentously: "Got some information I reckoned you might appreciate hearing. Real interesting information. You know Milt Kehoe's been after me to keep digging on that hombre who calls himself Smith?"

"I didn't—" Elizabeth began, when he cut her short with a wave of his beefy hand.

"Oh, I know why, and what Milt's beef is. But I'm a curious man myself, you see, and it just didn't strike me as bein' *likely*, if you know what I mean. A man gets off the train wearing two of the newest-model guns—and I happened to find out they're real hard to come by—and shows he knows how to use them real accurately and fast. Well, it stands to reason that someone's got to have heard of such a man, you get my meaning?"

Elizabeth poured herself another cup of coffee she didn't really want and leaned over to refill the Sheriff's cup, wanting to keep her hands busy.

She said coldly: "I know his real name isn't John Smith—and I know what it is."

He caught her right up on that. "The name's Steve Morgan—sometimes known as Sam Whittaker, although that was long ago. Sam Whittaker was supposed to have been hanged by vigilantes in Dallas last year, but stories do get around sometimes. Getting back to Steve Morgan—reason it came up was accidental. Isn't it the durndest coincidence, after all the checkin' I'd bin doing?"

"Sheriff, I can't really see—"

"Gimme a minute, Lizzie, an' you will. You see, I had this visiting U.S. marshal in my office, goin' through wanted posters and the like, and we'd just stepped out when down the street come the Prendergasts—had an older man with them by the name of Murdock—a millionaire. Self-made, so I've heard. And your friend Smith was riding right alongside him.

"Now, that Marshal Seymour recognized him at once. Said he'd heard of him in Texas, and even saw him in a shoot-out once. Wasn't wanted, though, until . . ."

Elizabeth knew Sheriff Blaine was pausing for effect and she knew she should try to hide what was in her face, but by this time she couldn't. She kept her hands clenched in the folds of her skirt, pinning her eyes on his face until at last he cleared his throat awkwardly and let his look slide away from hers.

"Story goes that he stole a wagonload of gold belonging to a U.S. Senator—a Senator Brandon. Took it over into Mexico—and not just the gold, but the Senator's daughter as well. Took her hostage, they said, and her pa had marshals and posses and bounty hunters chasin' both sides of the border for them, with blood money on this Morgan's head. That is, until he turned up a couple years later, married to the Senator's pretty daughter—and the charges were dropped. Wonder what in Hades he's doin' here?"

# Chapter Thirty-Three

❦

The Denver House boasted that it could hold its own with any fine hotel in the whole territory, even as far north as Santa Fe. Tonight, the management had attempted to outdo themselves in providing the very best. Wines had been hauled up from the cellars. Whole sides of beef, smoked salmon and fresh river-caught fish, and chickens that had been scrounged from farmers' wives at outrageous prices—all were prepared for the guests. The chandeliers had been taken apart and polished before being hung again; floors and tables had been scrubbed until everything shone. Rumor had it that there might even be dancing—the real fancy kind that the ladies loved.

The men had been talking all afternoon and most of the previous night, Elizabeth had heard from Martin. Tonight was to be a night for celebration, for festivity. But she didn't feel festive; she had spent most of last night crying too, after she'd composed the cold little note she'd sent off by Domingo in reply to the one Martin had brought *her*.

There was no need for Mr. Morgan to come all the way out to pick her up. If he did, she would refuse to come. She certainly planned on joining everyone else for dinner tomorrow—why shouldn't she?

*Beth—I'm sorry I lost my temper,* he had scrawled. *I hope you'll wear the gown I brought you when I come to pick you up. I think it will become you.* And further down: *I think there are still things we must talk about, and there is something I would like to ask you.*

He would never ask her to marry him because he was a married man. And no doubt he was used to keeping mistresses wherever he went—when he had the time to spare for a woman! He had only wanted her because there was no one else available and she had let him see that she hated him. Oh, but she should have kept it that way!

Elizabeth arrived at the hotel with Martin Burneson, holding her head high. She knew that the other women, all her "friends" who had whispered behind her back, would be whispering even more loudly and watching to see how she acted and how he acted in front of his fine friends. Well, let them!

She was prepared for all that—but she wasn't prepared for how beautiful Lorna Prendergast was, as she stood in her elegant ball gown with diamonds sparkling at her throat and ears, her fingers resting possessively on Steve Morgan's arm. And she wasn't prepared for the look that leaped immediately into *his* eyes when he saw her—disappointment turning into black fury that he hardly bothered to mask.

She should have been flattered that he left Lorna at once, with a casual word and crossed the room toward her with angry, purposeful strides that made her want to shrink back. Elizabeth said in a shaking voice: "Martin! . . ."

Martin Burneson gently disengaged her suddenly clinging fingers, giving them a gentle squeeze. "I think, my dear," Martin said firmly, "that this is a matter you must deal with yourself."

Did he never pay attention to what other people might think? Without a word he had seized Elizabeth's wrist with fingers that felt like steel, propelling her across the room with him with no regard for the looks they got from everyone, even *his* friends. Now he had her pinned in a far corner of the room, between a large table that was laden with pastries and a monstrosity of an urn that held a large palm.

"Why in hell didn't you wear the dress I brought you?"

A sense of desperation upheld her now and made her face him bravely.

"Because it . . . it wasn't right for me. It showed too much of me, and women don't dress that way here, you know that. Besides you always said you liked this gown."

After much deliberation, she had worn her black taffeta, and had carefully wrapped and put away the beautiful, beautiful dress he had brought her that was made of embroidered silk and must have cost a fortune. The silk had become spotted with her tears, but he would never know that.

"Dear God, Beth! Do you see what Lorna and her mother are wearing. Respectable women *do* wear gowns that show their arms and a little more than their necks! What do you care what anyone else thinks, anyhow?"

She didn't know how she managed to keep her voice steady. "I care because they're my neighbors and my friends; because I plan to spend the rest of my life here among them."

"I see." His voice had become dangerously quiet, and his eyes narrowed on her, making her feel pinioned in her corner. "Is that meant to tell me something, Beth? I'd planned to ask you to come to San Francisco with me. Lorna and her mother are going there too, and Jack's arranged for an escort of soldiers—at least through Apache country. I'd like you to come, if you can manage to stop worrying about what your gossipy neighbors might say. Wouldn't Mrs. Prendergast do as a chaperone?"

"Oh, God!" she was praying silently, "make him stop talking, make him stop tempting me, make me strong!"

She surprised herself with the coolness of her voice. "Chaperone or not, you're still a married man, Mr. Morgan. Or don't you care what your wife might think? How would you pass me off—as Miss Prendergast's maid, perhaps?"

She heard him suck in his breath and she quailed a little, seeing the taut white lines around his mouth.

"I should take you by the shoulders and shake you until your stupid little brain rattles!" he said between his teeth. Then with a harsh travesty of a laugh: "Oh, you don't have to worry that I'd do anything to shock your *friends!* But while we're on the subject I might tell you that whoever gave you your information failed to add that—my wife is dead. She died some months ago, so I've had time to become used to being a widower." Something about the *way* he said it, the cold intensity of his voice and the impenetrable hardness of his eyes made Beth want to run away and hide, without hearing any more. But it seemed now as if they were both trapped, standing here, by the words that had been said between them, and she blurted out almost without thinking:

"I'm sorry! I should not have said—"

"For Christ's sake! Never be sorry for anything you've said! And you haven't given me an answer yet, now that we've done away with your excuses. Well?"

"Do you have children?" She didn't know why she asked that except that it had suddenly become important for her to know. He looked taken aback—and then angry.

"What in hell has that got to do with—yes, there are children. Twins, as a matter of fact—a girl and a boy, I believe. I have never seen them."

"You haven't—"

"Beth, I'm just not cut out for parenthood, I guess. And I like to keep moving. I'm just a restless man, I guess."

Now it was her turn. She said in a dead voice, "I see." And then, when he waited deliberately, she drew in her breath to say steadily: "I really shouldn't have . . . asked all the questions. I had no right. But it *was* right that we should speak, and . . . and be honest with each other for a change." She was watching his face almost hungrily as she spoke, memorizing it, longing to be able to reach out and run her fingers down that scar, the way she'd done before when they were happy together and he was just plain "Smith." But that time was past and now, at last, she said what she had come here to tell him. "Thank you for asking me, but I can't come with you. You see, I've promised to marry Martin Burneson."

Silence. She watched his mouth harden and half expected him to stride away and leave her without another word. But he stood there studying her thoughtfully, his face a mask again.

"Beth—you sure you're doing what you really want?"

Now it was easier for her to talk. She swallowed the lump in her throat and said defensively: "I'm sure. And Martin's a good man—a kind man. A man with roots. It's what I need. I wouldn't belong in San Francisco or most of the other places you'd be going to. I like staying put, and I love this land here. I think . . . I'm sure that in time I'll come to love Martin as much as he loves me. I respect him and I trust him."

They looked at each other, and at last he put out his hand and touched her face very gently.

"You're a beautiful woman, Beth," he said softly before he took her by the hand and led her back to Martin Burneson.

He missed Beth. But, wryly, Steve Morgan admitted to himself that it would only be for a while. She had been right—what he had been offering her was nothing, while Martin Burneson was offering her not only the kind of life she wanted but marriage as well.

In an introspective mood, he spent most of the journey to California acting as scout for their party, and his spare time talking either to Sam Murdock or the taciturn man who called himself Burrows and had attached himself to them in Arizona. Burrows had known Steve a long time ago, when they had both ridden shotgun for a stage line, and he was also acquainted with Sam Murdock. He was a good man to have along.

Francoise Prendergast bore the journey very well, but her daughter was frankly bored—and piqued as well because the elusive Mr. Morgan didn't pay her more attention. She was used to talking quite frankly with her mother, an understanding and worldly wise woman, and she said one day:

"I want him, Maman. And I'm going to have him!"

Francoise, knowing her daughter only too well, merely raised her eyebrows. "Oh? And what will you do with him when you have him, petite? He is not an easy man to manage. Also the things I have heard tell me he would not be easy to live with. His wife was a very lovely, accomplished and well-born young woman, and it was said they were madly in love—before he sent her off to Europe and took up with an opera singer. He is a . . . singularly dangerous man, I would think, the kind I have heard called a 'loner.' The expression is correct?"

"Oh yes, it's correct, Maman, but . . . you know what it is? He's the kind of man that every woman would like to tame and have for her own?"

"Very clever of you, *cherie*, and you're right—but I don't think he'd be too easily trapped. No, I do not think he would make a good husband."

"I think he would make a wonderful lover!" Lorna said boldly, and her mother gave her a reproving look.

"Best not to let your papa hear you talk that way, hear? You know how he feels."

"He wouldn't object to my marrying Steve Morgan! In fact, I think he'd rather like it. Why do you think he changed his mind about letting me travel?"

In spite of her mother's forebodings, Lorna made the best of things by never complaining and making sure Steve Morgan noticed what an excellent horsewoman and good shot she was. The more she studied him the more fascinated she was. He was so different from any of the other men she'd met, and so . . . so changeable! She had seen him wearing impeccable evening clothes with the same animal grace that he wore shabby range clothes. And when he took the time to sit and converse with them he was *interesting*—he had been all over the world and spoke several foreign languages. Lorna meant to learn as much as she could about him!

She gained more of his attention, and certainly found more excitement, after they had reached the Port of San Diego in California. Here Steve suggested, as casually as if he'd asked them to go canoeing, that they might sail to San Francisco by ship, if they pleased. It might be quicker, and there was a ship in the harbor that belonged to the Lady Line, in which he had an interest.

"We'll stop in at Monterey for a day—I have a ranch there, and it's a beautiful and unspoiled part of the country. We should have a clear run to San Francisco after that."

Ever since he had kissed her that day he was always so ridiculously *formal* with her, Lorna thought rebelliously, even while she vowed it would soon be different. Wait until they got to San Francisco and she acquired some beaux. *That* should bring his attention back to her!

"Do you think he could be mooning over that dowdy farm woman he started off paying so much attention to that night at the Denver House, Maman? It was obvious they knew each other very well. . . ."

"I believe she nursed him back to health after he'd been shot," Mrs. Prendergast said mildly, although she *had* heard some gossip.

"Well—even if they did have an affair it couldn't have meant anything!" Lorna said scornfully, dismissing Elizabeth Cady from her mind. "I suppose men must have their . . . amusement!" And her nose wrinkled disdainfully.

Elizabeth had dropped from Steve's mind too, by the time the clipper *Green-eyed Lady* had left San Diego, although Lorna would have been angry if she knew that his courteous attentiveness to her was no more than politeness. It was the same green-eyed lady he'd named the ship after who stayed in his mind

—and his decision to travel to San Francisco by sea had been made deliberately as a form of exorcism. He would return to Monterey, where he'd been forced to keep Ginny a virtual prisoner while that doctor worked to rid her of the opium habit. He had the feeling that she had never forgiven him for that. Ginny—damn her memory that wouldn't let him alone!

"How long will you stay in San Francisco?" Sam Murdock asked casually, guessing from his partner's black frown where his thoughts were.

Steve came back to attention with a shrug. "I'm just not certain, Sam. Long enough to look into that mining deal, though. And to show Mrs. Prendergast and Lorna around so that it won't appear rude when I get ready to leave." He saw the watchful look that Sam gave him and began pacing from one end of the stateroom to the other. "I guess I'll go back to Mexico—" Steve said abruptly. He stood with his back to Sam, staring morosely at the flying water as it whipped past the porthole. "I don't fancy tangling with my irascible grandfather again, but something someone said reminded me I have some obligations to take care of. *Two* in fact—" he added grimly, and wondered as he said so if they both looked like Ginny.

The two letters, one written by Renaldo and the other by Renaldo's wife—whose style of writing was much more colorfully dramatic than her husband's—did not arrive until they had been in San Francisco two weeks.

Renaldo Ortega had, after much thought, also written to Sam Murdock, who was a friend of Don Francisco's. If anyone could pour oil on troubled waters, he thought grimly, Sam could. Privately, Renaldo hoped that Steve's sense of pride, if nothing else, would prevent him from going after his errant wife. Perhaps Don Francisco was right, and theirs had been a marriage that only a divorce could cure. If Ginny was happy with her new love, then God knew the poor girl deserved that happiness, and Steve should bow out gracefully. After all, Steve had never lacked for women, or consolation in their embraces!

What neither Renaldo or Missie nor even Don Francisco himself could have known was that Steve believed that his wife was dead. And when Sam Murdock, who also believed the same thing, opened Renaldo's letter and perused it, his first feeling was of fervent relief that Steve was away—spending a week in the Portola Valley with the Prendergasts and some other friends. Sam's next impulse was to purposefully "mislay" both the letters addressed to his partner—but then, he thought dourly, sooner or later Steve would find out. Good God, what a damned mess! He thought about Ginny, whom he remembered with some affection as a lovely woman, but unhappy—at least, at the time he'd known her. What had driven her into running away? They had seemed meant for each other, she and Steve—and he'd never seen his partner so obsessed by a woman before. What would happen when he found out that the wife he grieved for was not dead at all but had gone off to Europe with their children, determined to get a divorce and marry an English Lord she'd met God knew where?

Sam Murdock was a brave man, and a hard man when he had to be, but at that point in his thoughts he shuddered inwardly. God help both Virginia and her husband to be if Steve ever caught up with them! And what had his friend Don Francisco been thinking of to allow such a thing—even to encourage it?

## Part Four

# "THE GAME OF LOVE"

## Chapter Thirty-Four

❧

The green lawns of the chateau stretched smoothly all the way down to the lake, with its small artificial island and summerhouse in the center. And a little further on was the river, hidden by great willows whose trailing branches brushed the dancing waters. Two small children playing on the lawn under the watchful eye of their nurse and the group of well-dressed people partaking of tea on the covered terrace overlooking the rose garden made an idyllic picture of leisure on this lazy summer afternoon. One would have thought, looking at them, that they had not a care in the world! The faint perfume of roses drifted up to the terrace as the dignified butler retired within the house, leaving his mistress—an older lady with silvering hair—to pour tea for her son and his friend. Celine Dumont looked with worried eyes, eyes a softer brown than those of her son, from one young man to the other.

With a muttered exclamation Pierre jumped to his feet as if he could not bear to sit still any longer. "Well, now that Broussard has stopped hovering about us I can ask my question. Michel, what do *you* think of the change in my cousin? I hope you will be frank, for I know you have always been fond of Virginie."

Michel Remy, Comte D'Arlingen, cleared his throat a trifle awkwardly before he answered. He had at one time been Virginia

Brandon's lover and protector and had, in fact, wanted to marry her. And in spite of the fact that she had carried on under his nose with a Mexican Colonel forcing him to break their engagement, he was *still* inordinately fond of her. Why, just a few years ago on Virginie's last visit to France he had been on the verge of leaving his wife for her. *Sacre!* It was not quite fair of his old friend Pierre to ask *him* for an opinion, and especially in front of Madame Dumont.

"Yes, please do be frank," Celine Dumont said in a strained voice, adding, "we have all been so worried, you see, but it is so difficult to talk to her without . . . without letting her feel that we *pity* her. She would never want that!"

"She has lost her sparkle, her spirit!" Pierre exploded in a suppressed voice. "Surely you cannot fail to have noticed for yourself? She was always so full of life—yes, and full of mischief as well! And you'll remember how much she enjoyed riding—she was forever wanting to *do* something in case she should become bored. And now—well you can see for yourself! She spends most of her time cooped up in her room or with him. . . ."

"Isn't he good to her?" Michel could not help asking, and got a preoccupied frown from his friend.

"Oh, he's devoted to her, and hardly leaves her side," Pierre said with a shrug. "But that is not the problem. No—the problem is Ginnie herself, and it is for that reason that I am asking your opinion. After all, you knew her quite well in Mexico, did you not? And you have met this man she is married to?"

"She gave me to understand that she has applied for a divorce," Michel said a trifle stiffly. "Naturally I could not pry!"

"But does she seem happy to you?" Pierre went on persistently. He ran his fingers through his thick blond hair. "This Lord Tynedale she plans to marry certainly seems to be a decent enough fellow, even if he's a trifle old for her. And he has money, so that's no problem, but still . . . no, it's in Ginnie herself that I sense something lacking!"

"She is . . . quieter than before," Michel said cautiously while he tried to order his thoughts. "But have you considered, my old one, that she must feel . . . well . . . how can she possibly enjoy any of the things she used to enjoy so much when she is . . ."—he found he had to swallow before he pronounced it—"when she is blind?" He had said it at last, feeling his heart sink.

Ginnie! Ginnie of the laughing, flashing green eyes and temptress mouth, who had led him such a dance—how could such a tragedy have come about? If it had anything to do with that bandit, that ne'er-do-well outlaw she'd married—he'd a good mind to call the bastard out himself! But with total composure she had told him that her blindness was only a temporary thing and that Richard, her fiancé, was taking her to visit a famous doctor in Vienna who would soon put her right. Undoubtedly she had complete trust in this man Richard, who was a doctor himself. Michel could not help feeling, even now, a pang of jealousy as he thought of the man who must surely share Ginnie's bed and her wildly passionate embraces. *Dieu*—what a lover she had been! And sometimes, in spite of all the pain she'd put him through, he'd have given anything to put back the clock and go back to those months when she'd been solely and exclusively his.

For Ginny herself, Michel's unexpected arrival at the chateau had brought back a flood of unwanted memories. Poor Michel! She hoped she had not appeared rude or too abrupt when after a few minutes of stilted conversation she had begged to be excused —an appointment with her dressmaker, she had told him, adding that she would surely see him at dinner. She wondered now if it had been as uncomfortable for him as it had been for her. Dear Michel—no doubt Pierre had warned him, and she could sense how very tactful he was being, but the truth was . . . what was the truth? Undoubtedly that she was a coward who preferred to live within the confines of the safe, happy world that Richard had created for her. She needed nothing else—and especially not memories.

Sitting in her comfortable chair by the window, Ginny could feel the late afternoon sun warm her face and her shoulders. She could smell the roses as a slight breeze wafted up to her—and the rich smell of Havana cigars. Richard and his visitors, no doubt. Tante Celine, ever-thoughtful, had given them a whole wing of the rambling old chateau—"so that you may be quite private and feel as if you are in your own home, my dearest love," tante had said, and Ginny could imagine the tears standing in those softly kind brown eyes. Poor tante, whatever must she think? Pierre had been more outspoken.

"As long as you're happy, that is all that counts," he had said gruffly. Hard to imagine the young man who had always been her "cousin Pierre" was now an eminent lawyer and a diplomat and, some said, a future cabinet member for certain. To her, at least, he hadn't changed at all!

Below her window was a private, stone-flagged terrace where the sunlight was filtered by the leaves of old, gnarled trees. When she had come here to the chateau, which had been in her mother's family for generations, to have her children, she had loved this particular terrace and this particular room that was now hers. *That* had not been a very happy time, but this time she had Richard, and the children as well. "We are a family!" Richard had told her happily, and it was true! It was perhaps what she had always secretly wanted and would not admit to herself because she had been so stubborn and headstrong; rushing at life and an experience without thought. But now . . .

In the distance Ginny heard the laughter of the twins, and a smile curved her lips. Pierre had promised to paint them. How well she remembered the day he had begun on *her* portrait!

Almost unconsciously, Ginny had been listening for Richard's voice. The bell cord that would bring her personal maid running was within reach of her fingers, but Richard enjoyed having tea with her, an English custom he laughingly urged on her. Perhaps his visitors were getting ready to leave at last, for she thought the murmur of voices below became louder as the men emerged from the study below her room onto the terrace.

"Is there no chance," the voice said, "that she might see again?"

Catching her breath, Ginny froze, hearing Richard's voice reply with controlled anger:

"There is every chance that she will see again . . . when she is ready. There is nothing physically wrong with her, and when I have taken her to my friend in Vienna she will see as well as she did before—as well as you and I!"

"I beg your pardon if I have caused you to become angry, but you must surely understand why I ask questions? For a woman, and a blind woman at that, to travel all the way to Stamboul with you—"

"She is not a blind woman, she is my wife. And this conversation is ended. If you wish me to come to Stamboul with you I will do so, but only because of the promise I made to your uncle the Sultan some years ago."

"Under the law of Islam a true believer is allowed more than one wife."

Had she actually heard or only imagined that last comment that had floated to her ears? There had been a pause after Richard's icy dismissal of the man's objections—perhaps the speaker had addressed his words to a companion as he descended the steps to where a carriage was no doubt waiting, not realizing that as she sat at her window in the sun she could hear everything that went on below.

Ginny clenched her hands over the book that from habit lay in her lap. She was surrounded by voices without faces, by sounds without images to match. Why couldn't she see? What was the real reason, the reason that this friend of Richard's was supposed to try to ferret out? And suppose . . . suppose she remained blind, what then?

Richard had an answer to everything, even to her question: "How can you stand to be tied to an invalid?"

"But you are by no means an invalid, dearest. You are a healthy and very beautiful young woman with whom I happen to be deeply in love. I am lucky to have found you, and you fill my days and my nights with happiness."

As he filled hers. And her happiness was contentment, for wasn't that where lasting happiness lay? She was so lucky that Richard had found *her*. He told her that she was his fate, the woman of his destiny, and that was why he had not taken a wife before. Richard was a man of his word, a man she could trust.

The voices had faded away, and any moment now Richard would be coming to find her. She must greet him with a smile. Love wasn't to be taken lightly, nor was mutual trust. That word again!

Suddenly, and quite against her will, Ginny's mind went back two weeks before, when they had spent some days in Paris, leaving the children here at the chateau with their nurse. At Pierre's urging they had gone to the theater together for a performance by a troupe of Spanish musicians and dancers. Pierre was right and Richard was right, Ginny had thought then. She couldn't hide herself away as if she was suffering from some frightful disease!

Several of Tante Celine's gossiping friends had visited their box, and in the middle of a general conversation one of them had said:

"Oh look, my dear, at the box opposite to us! Isn't that the Princess Di Paoli? The opera singer, you know. It's said she's to do poor Bizet's *Carmen* in London next month—she made a tremendous success of it in America, I'm told. Such a handsome woman—and those jewels!"

"She's with my friend the Duc De Courcey," Pierre said with a laugh in his voice, "and *he's* accountable for that magnificent diamond bracelet, at least. He tells me she believes in *acting* her roles as well as singing them—she's probably here to learn something about Spanish dancing."

Ginny had been aware of a buzzing in her ears and the strangest tight feeling in her chest that she could not control. Di Paoli! Thankfully, the music started up at that moment, accompanied by the lusty foot stamping of an arrogant, cocksure male and the seductive click of castanets. Unexpectedly, Ginny felt tears sting her eyes and then, without warning, begin to stream down her face without her being able to check them.

"My dear! . . ." Richard said in a whisper, but she shook her head fiercely at him, not wanting anyone else to notice, and picturing the stage—seeing herself as she must have looked when she danced one night for the Emperor Maximilian at Chapultepec and the handsome Miguel Lopez had leaped up onto the stage to join her. Oh, God, how she had loved to dance, to forget everything in the frenzy of the dance itself! And now Steve's mistress, that woman he had almost married, was watching, learning. . . .

"And I cannot even see what she looks like, that predatory bitch!" Ginny thought rebelliously. "But *she* can stare all she pleases at me—and no doubt the gossips have already pointed me out to her—'See that poor blind creature over there? That's Steve Morgan's wife, his ex-wife-to-be, that is!'—oh, it's not fair!" And she cried all the harder—silently and desperately until her little lace-embroidered handkerchief was quite soaked through and Richard had to pass her his. And then a singer had taken up the plaintive, sobbing flamenco in the background, and Ginny would have liked to shut out sound—would have liked to and could not. It was all she could do to manage to regain some control over herself before the intermission, when she would make some excuse and ask Richard to take her home. *He* at least wanted no other woman but her!

Now Ginny could hear him opening the door, and she lifted her face for his ardent kiss as he crossed the room to her, hugging her as if he had not seen her for weeks.

His voice was cheerful. "Well, my darling, it's all decided! We're to leave in a week's time, if that will give you enough time to pack?"

Kneeling beside her chair, holding her hand, he began to describe to her the journey they would take and what might lie ahead, drawing word pictures for her, and holding her fascinated.

As a child she remembered reading highly romanticized tales in books filled with colored illustrations of the barbaric splendors of the Ottoman Court. She remembered the story of Suleiman the Magnificent and the Spanish slave girl Roxelana whom he had made his Empress; and the story, more recent, of the Empress Josephine's cousin Aimee Dubuque de Rivery who had been carried off by pirates to end up a Sultana and the mother of the great Sultan Mahmud. She had read accounts of the fabulous palace of Topkapi—the Grand Seraglio with its Cage of Princes and its fountains and marble courtyards and twisted corridors where intrigues were whispered. Like her friends, Ginny too had wondered how it must have felt to be an innocent young girl, strictly brought up, who was captured by pirates and auctioned in the slave market—bought as a gift for a Sultan and trained in the arts of pleasing him; praying, if she caught his eye and traveled the Golden Road to his bed, that she might bear him a son and become a Sultana.

To the young girl who would later attend the intellectual salons of Paris, the stories had been romantic to read about, but even then she had been sure that *she* would not have enjoyed such an empty life. Imagine being cloistered forever behind harem walls to be the plaything of a man who had as many other women as he could want as well—she wouldn't have borne it!

"I would have planned and schemed to run away," Ginny had exclaimed. "Even if I had to *pretend* to be happy and contented with my lot at first."

"Oh, yes!" one of her friends had giggled. "And when they found you out you would have been sewn up alive in a sack and thrown into the Bosphorus to drown!"

"I would have killed myself first!" Ginny had returned passionately and had gone back to her Geography, eyeing her maps with distaste.

But now those old remembered maps came to life again as, following Richard's patient descriptions, Ginny tried to trace in her mind the route they would be following.

From France to Austria—that was familiar enough, for she had been to Vienna. They would spend at least a week in that city—

"And we'll dance together, you and I to the music of Johann Strauss the Younger. I will be the envy of every man there!" Richard said extravagantly, making her smile and forget for a moment why they were *really* going there.

From Vienna they would travel overland again to Italy—to Venice.

"You have never been to Venice? Then we must certainly make it a point to go there. There is no other city quite like Venezia!"

Trying to catch his mood, Ginny smiled. "I've heard it's very romantic—will you take me on a ride in a gondola by moonlight?"

"I'll do more than that, my dearest love," he whispered, leaning over her, and for a time her geography lesson was forgotten.

Later that night, as Ginny lay drowsily in bed listening to Richard's deep and even breathing beside her, she found herself picturing the rest of the journey that would take them from sea to sea. They would sail down the Adriatic, perhaps visiting Italian ports, and then to Greece—oh, she loved the sound of Greece, remembering pictures of all its ancient splendor, and wondered what it would be like now. And to the island of Mykonos to see the white-painted villa overlooking the Aegean that Richard was thinking of buying from the Turkish friend who owned it.

"You see, my dear, the Turks aren't too popular in Greece just now, and my friend says he wouldn't feel comfortable going back there. I thought that we could take the children there for summers, they would love it, and you would too!"

"I'm sure I will! Describe the rest of it for me Richard, please!"

"You'll see it all for yourself!" he assured her stoutly, and then he had gone on to tell her how they would sail through the Dardanelles to the Sea of Marmara past Seraglio Point with the Golden Horn and Pera to their left, to Constantinople, the city that the Turks called Stamboul. And so to the Dolmabahce Palace that had been built by the Sultan Abdul Mejid, facing the Bosphorus in all its neoclassical splendor of marble and gold leaf.

"I'm glad I'm not one of the Sultan's poor concubines—what a terrible way to die, sewn up in a sack and thrown into the Bosphorus!" Ginny murmured and heard Richard chuckle.

"Hmm! Does that mean that you would have been unfaithful? Now if *I* were the Sultan I'd keep only you and dismiss all the others. How could any man need more?"

Soon, Ginny had found herself sighing, letting Richard take her with exquisite tenderness and expertise to heights of pleasure from which she usually slid, contented, into sleep. He was always so considerate of her feelings, her pleasure! And she really should ask him where he had learned to please a woman so! On how many women had he practiced? The strange thing was that she wasn't in the least bit jealous of Richard—did that mean that she was maturing?

With a slight feeling of resentment, Ginny remembered something that Michel had said to her when he had held her hands to wish her good-bye before he returned to Paris.

"I ask you if you are happy and you answer that you are content. Think, Ginette, is that really enough after you have known the depths and the heights?"

Ginny stirred uneasily, wondering why she was not yet asleep. How strange of Michel to say that to her! What had he really meant? But it didn't matter. . . .

# Chapter Thirty-Five

❦

Why did it always seem as if the preparations, the anticipation of any long journey actually seemed much longer than the journey itself? Everything was behind her now—the coaches and the hotels and the rented villas; even the gondolas of Venice, and the long, boring instructions in Turkish etiquette, including a few words of the language itself. The latter she had received in Crete, which was still a Turkish province although the Greeks were eyeing it. To her in Crete also had come a wizened, disapproving old man whom Richard had explained was an Imam—or holy man—to instruct her in the teachings of the Prophet.

"You want me to—"

"I am asking that you take his instruction and repeat certain words after him. It will be painless, my love, and will not commit you in any way. It is just that it is best that we should be married officially according to Islamic law, before we go to Stamboul. It will make things very much easier for us both—and I will be able to call you my wife in all honesty then!"

He had been right of course—after all, what did the repeating of some words she did not even understand mean to her? If it pleased Richard, it was little enough for her to do for him, especially in view of all he had done for her!

"I am surprised that you still want to *marry* me!" Ginny had said shakily. "You could keep me as your concubine with much less fuss, you know!"

The disappointment of her visits to Dr. Wundt in Vienna still stayed with her, spoiling even Venice. He had talked and *she* had talked—they had talked for hours and Ginny had told him all her life history. And after all of that the only thing he had said was:

"And can you think what it is that you do not *want* to see, madame? When you have discovered that for yourself you have found the key. I cannot put it into your hand, I am afraid."

She had cried, despising herself for such an exhibition of weakness, and Richard had comforted her with his assurances that she *would* recover her sight. It might take time, but eventually . . .

"Eventually you'll find that key my friend Dr. Wundt was talking about, my love. And in the meantime I love you to distraction!"

In the meantime, she had learned to do things for herself, to memorize the placement of furniture in a room, and even to arrange her own hair or pick out which gown she would wear by the feel of it.

"When we get to Pera," Richard promised, "you won't have to lift a finger to do anything for yourself if you don't wish to. Since I will be the Sultan's personal physician we will have a magnificent house, with servants."

Now, looking back, Ginny could not *quite* believe that she was actually in Turkey at last, living in splendor and luxury that far exceeded the magnificent house with servants that Richard had promised her. In her wildest dreams she had not imagined that within a few weeks of her arrival in Constantinople she would sail up the Bosphorus in a heavily curtained caique that was taking her to the Sultan's Palace of Dolmabahce.

How could either of them have known how it would turn out? The Sultan Abdul Aziz was not only an absolute despot but an eccentric whose idiosyncrasies grew daily, and he had a phobia that everyone about him was trying to poison him. For days on end he would eat nothing but eggs that had been boiled by the Queen Mother Pertevale herself—and these eggs had to be delivered to him carefully wrapped in black crepe and sealed with his mother's own seal. How could one deal very well with a man like that?

"All I did was nurse him through an attack of acute dyspepsia!" Richard announced distractedly. "He eats far too much, of course, even when he's only eating hard-boiled eggs! And all the wrong kinds of food and far too much to drink, even though he *is* a Moslem. But he believes I saved his life, and so . . ."

"And so? . . ." Ginny had echoed, sensing his hesitation even before he said slowly:

"My darling—do you know that I almost wish I had not brought you here with me? We are ordered to the palace so that I may be near the Sultan in case he should need me. I daren't refuse. I can only hope that he will soon forget we are there at all and will find a new favorite."

But for the moment, here they were, and she—as well as Richard—must make the best of it. In the face of Richard's distress, Ginny had at first actually found humor in *her* situation. It had not entered the minds of either of them that while they resided in their quarters within the Sultan's palace, Richard, as a "true believer," would be expected to conform to Islamic law—and so was she!

Yes, at first Ginny had thought it amusing that she should find herself in a harem, of all things, with slaves to attend her. It was the custom, Richard had explained in an embarrassed fashion. And not only must she occupy the women's quarters, unseen by any male except himself, but if she went out in public she must be veiled!

"It's only for a short time. Do you think you could bear being so constrained for a while?"

Poor Richard, Ginny thought now, with a half-smile curving her lips. *He* was much more upset than she. He had actually been angry with her when she had teased him about the lack of concubines to occupy the extremely spacious quarters which had been allotted for the use of his women. Why, there was even a walled garden where she could walk every day and even ride. Richard had found her a horse and a groom—a silent man whom Ginny imagined, uncomfortably, must be a eunuch. She didn't really care for the idea of owning *slaves*, but since they were all presents from the Sultan, what could one do? Her personal maid, as Ginny preferred to think of the soft-voiced woman, was a wonderful masseuse as well as a companion who acted as her eyes when Richard was not around, and Ginny could feel herself becoming quite spoiled.

In spite of a certain lack of freedom that she *sensed* rather than experienced, Ginny found that she enjoyed the luxury of a warm, perfumed bathing pool and deft hands that helped her with everything, even drying her and massaging scented oils into her body. And the clothes! Although she could not *see* them, Ginny could imagine from remembered pictures what they must look like. She was sensual enough to enjoy the feel of silk against her skin and the heaviness of barbaric gold jewelry around her neck, wrists and even her ankles. Certainly the costume that Turkish women wore within the seclusion of their own quarters was much more comfortable and practical than the layers and layers of petticoats and whalebone corsets and bustles that European ladies of fashion were forced to wear. She thought of a letter she might compose to her Tante Celine and could not help giggling out loud—her laughter echoed by the young woman who was massaging her back with hands that were strong and yet gentle at the same time. Poor tante—how shocked she would be if she could only see her niece now!

"But I really must write to her," Ginny thought lazily. "I must ask how the children are—and I do hope her letters in reply get delivered!" She must speak to Richard about that when he came back from dancing attendance on Abdul Aziz or one of his nephews. And there was another matter also, that she must speak to Richard about. . . .

She thought she was to bear a child again, Richard's child; and it seemed as if the poor infant would be born in the palace of the Sultan of Turkey! Mihri Hanoum, the golden-haired Circassian who was the Sultan's favorite concubine was also pregnant, and the only humor that Ginny could find in the situation was that they both might be delivered together—with, no doubt, Richard's first priority being the Sultan's offspring.

As it happened, Richard sent word that he would be late in coming to her that night, for the Sultan had summoned him and would keep him at his side. The two men would dine together, and in a postscript written in English that was to be handed to her and not read aloud in formal Turkish style, he had written:

*My darling, forgive me, for you know where my heart is. I will come to you as soon as I may.*

Frowning over it, and then shrugging, Ginny decided to dine lightly before she went to bed. The meal was served as usual with ceremonious splendor, each course carried in on covered silver platters so as to remain either hot or cold depending on the dish. She was trying to accustom her palate to Turkish food and while she enjoyed the inevitable pilaff, there were certain other dishes that were too sweet, like the quail browned in butter with garlic and onions and then steamed with a combination of rice, currants, raisins and nuts. Anything too sweet and heavy made her feel slightly nauseated, although the sherbet served at the end of every meal, along with mint-flavored tea, was always a delight.

It was difficult to sleep tonight. Her maid, Fatmeh, had told her there was a full moon, and perhaps that was why. Ginny wondered, "Will I ever see the moon again or will I only feel it in the tides of my body?" She felt alone and lonely in her corner of that enormous marble palace, longing for someone to talk to, something to do. She wondered what the Sultan's bevy of concubines did to occupy themselves, guarded by over a thousand eunuchs. Some of the women and girls, she heard, slept five or ten to a room on sleeping mats while they waited, hoping and praying to catch the Sultan's eye. Some of them would never know what it was to sleep with a man. And all of them, except for the new Queen Mother, would be banished to the Palace of Tears at Adrianople when the Sultan died. Those of his women who became pregnant, on the other hand, would meet with the usual fate —sewn up in sacks to be cast into the Bosphorus. What a truly barbarous country, Ginny thought with a shudder. It seemed as if the spread of civilization had stopped short at the borders of the vast and sprawling Ottoman Empire. "I will be glad when we can leave," she thought, and suddenly there was no humor at all in the position in which she now found herself.

It must have been very late or very early when Richard finally came to join her. Ginny woke from a light, uneasy sleep to find him lying next to her. Was he asleep? She moved, and was enfolded by his arms.

"I am sorry, dearest. I couldn't help it," he whispered against her shoulder. She thought he sounded tired.

"Was it very bad?"

He sighed. "He was . . . very high-strung tonight. Dinner was interminable, although *he* hardly ate. And then he had his soldiers stage mock battles that we were all forced to watch. Ginny, I swear I had no idea how far his mind had deteriorated when I agreed to come here. When I met him in London he seemed . . . a trifle overpowering, but *sane* all the same. Now—but who dares to say so aloud? I'm as big a coward as the next man. He had one of his servants beheaded today for some trifling offense. And he rules a vast empire!"

"Don't think about it now," she soothed. Now was not the

time to tell him anything, but perhaps tomorrow? On a whim, Abdul Aziz might spend several days in complete isolation except for his mother and his Circassian, and it was this Ginny hoped for. *Then* they would have time to talk and make plans, Richard and she. Cut off, she felt, from everything except smell and touch, she was doubly lonely in this enclosed world of the harem, with no companions except slaves whom she could not trust and could barely converse with. If she had the company of other Europeans it might have been bearable at least.

Richard held her closely, but did not attempt to make love to her, and after his first outburst and her reply neither of them spoke. Ginny fell asleep again and slept heavily this time. When she awoke to the singing of birds, Richard was gone once more, and there was the interminable routine of a day to be gone through, from her "breakfast" of fruit and goat cheese to the constantly proffered sweetmeats she just as constantly brushed away; the walking in the walled garden with its various perfumes of herbs and flowers and her short ride; and then the long and leisurely ceremony of her bath which was followed by a massage and then the combing and dressing of her hair, the choosing of garments to wear. . . .

"If I could see! . . ." she thought fiercely, "if I could see, then perhaps this would all be fun—an *Arabian Night's* entertainment!"

When Richard came she was gowned and perfumed and her flesh felt silken and polished like her hair, which had jewels threaded in it on little chains.

She bowed with her hands held together and said in her newly acquired Turkish:

"Behold thy slave who awaits thy pleasure!" and promptly burst into tears—an embarrassing habit she could not seem, recently, to control.

# Chapter Thirty-Six

❧

She had been comforted in Richard's arms and soothed by his voice and his words. And still, with her senses more finely tuned since she had lost her sight, Ginny could feel an air of tension that Richard seemed to carry with him more and more.

She told herself that it was because they were both living here with their very existence dependent on the whims of a madman who happened to be Sultan. And because Richard felt guilty for having brought her here. There were other things, she was sure, that Richard did not tell her for fear of upsetting her more—and Ginny was fiercely ashamed of her tears. She let another occasion go by when she might have told Richard that she was almost certain she was carrying his child—part of her mind was even rather resentful because he, as a doctor, had not yet discovered it for himself.

At least, he still thought she was beautiful.

"You are so lovely. I am glad that the Sultan has not seen you or he would desire you for his own. I am becoming quite Turkish— do you know that I am jealous that his nephews have seen you unveiled? I know I must take you away from here, and soon, but we will take all these new clothes of yours with us, and you must promise to wear them for me. . . ."

And then, when dinner was over and they had retired to their chambers he said quite abruptly and without preamble:

"I saw General Ignatiev today—he is the Russian Ambassador to the Porte, you know."

Ginny had been feeling languid and ready to be undressed and taken to bed, but now she stiffened.

"Oh? And was your meeting significant?"

"I suppose so. . . ." Richard said on a sigh. "I told him that you were here. It might be helpful at some time if—" He broke off to say carefully, "He is also a friend of the Sultan, who trusts him more than he trusts the British or the French, much to *their* annoyance. I think the Tsar of Russia is the one ruler that the Sultan respects."

"Did I tell you *that* too?" Ginny said questioningly as she tried to search back in her mind. She felt Richard come up behind her, his fingers beginning to slip off the fastenings of her thin night robe.

"You've told me everything about you!" he said teasingly, but she thought, in spite of all his attentions, that she detected a forced note underneath the teasing. The feeling went with her to the low, cushioned bed that they shared and it was hard for her, this time, to let herself relax. Suddenly it was as if there was another part of her that was detached and observant, even questioning.

Why had Richard suddenly told the Russian Ambassador of her existence here? Of course he would have mentioned it with exquisite tact—the Tsar's illegitimate daughter, cloistered in a Turkish harem—and just in case . . .

What was Richard afraid of? What did he think might happen? Gently, he lowered her back on the bed, his hands sliding over her body, and for the first time Ginny wondered if the lamps were still lit or not.

"Your skin is like silk," he whispered, and she felt his lips at her breasts. "You are my beloved, and it is my pleasure to pleasure thee. . . ."

It was true, he was always patient, always considerate, always seeking to give *her* pleasure. But of himself? It came to her with a small, ashamed feeling of shock that *she* had never reciprocated his caresses. She had let him take her gently, oh so carefully and gently, to mountaintops—finding his own pleasure somewhere along the way, but in such an unobtrusive manner that she was scarcely aware of it, so wrapped up was she in her own body's sensations.

"How selfish I've been!" Ginny thought contritely. "I should have . . . should have . . ." She stretched out her hand to touch him as he was touching her and felt his withdrawal.

"Richard—"

"No! You are no odalisque, no slave bought for pleasure who

has been instructed in such arts. You are my beloved whom I worship—whom it is my privilege to worship. Just let me love you, my darling, as you deserve."

The next day, late in the afternoon, Ginny had a visitor. A very important visitor obviously, for Fatmeh, who was dressing her hair, smashed a bottle of expensive perfume on the tiles at their feet when the eunuch who guarded the women's quarters made his announcement in a trembling voice.

"You must make your obeisance, my lady!" Fatmeh whispered urgently, her voice sounding muffled, so that Ginny guessed that she was on her knees with her forehead pressed to the ground. Well, no matter who it was, *she* wasn't about to do any such thing!

She curtsied, though, the way she had been taught to before she'd been presented to the Empress Eugenie so long ago. After all, Pertevale the Queen Mother was a powerful figure who demanded respect, and there was Richard to think of.

"You speak French?" The Sultana Valide's French was heavily accented and difficult to understand, but Ginny inclined her head, not wanting to offend.

"Good, then we will speak." There was a sound of rustling, with whispers in the background that prompted Ginny to think that the woman had brought a small entourage with her. And after a few moments: "You may sit now."

She felt hands—Fatmeh's—guide her until she was sitting on a cushion, cross-legged, as she'd been practicing.

And what was she to do now? Offer refreshments? She had no idea of what protocol was involved—oh dear! Richard should have prepared her. Now she would be thought a barbarian, no doubt. Perhaps the best way would be to confess her ignorance.

In carefully enunciated French, Ginny apologized for her lack of preparation for such a distinguished visitor, and her lack of knowledge of what was proper on such an occasion as this. The perfume of attar of roses almost overwhelmed her, making her feel slightly sick, while she thought with a sense of panic that *that* would never do! What would they do with her then, throw her out of a window into the Bosphorus?

"So you are the blind woman. Are you the wife of Tynedale

*effendi* whose true name is Fuad? Were you married according to the laws of Islam?"

How dared she be so personal? Ginny's first impulse was to retort in kind, and she had to bite her lip in order to hold back the caustic words that rose to her lips. Forcing her voice to remain cool she said:

"Yes, I was married to my husband according to Moslem law, in Crete. And I . . . cannot see now, although my husband says it will not be so for always. May I offer you some refreshment?"

"Later. We have brought our own sweetmeats, my daughter and I. Everything that passes our lips has to be especially prepared —but of course you could not be expected to know that." This last sop that was thrown to her like a bone to a dog made Ginny grit her teeth. She felt frustration pour through her, and the old familiar refrain in her mind: "Oh, if only I could *see*—why then I'd be able to cope with anything. . . ."

Another voice, belonging to a much younger woman and also speaking in stilted French said:

"My mother and I are here because I desired to meet you. And also because I desired to look about this place. For when *I* come to live here there must be room enough to house all of my slaves. Room also for you, of course."

"*What?*" After she had said it, Ginny felt the one word imprinted in the air between them like a frozen banner.

"Well, of course he could not have told you yet. My son, the Sultan, has only just made up his mind." It was the older woman's voice again, interposing smoothly. "My daughter Gulbehar is his favorite sister, and that is why she has not been married yet. But you realize of course that a follower of Islam is permitted more than one wife? So it should not come as a shock to you."

"I am sure we will be as sisters to each other," the younger woman said in a falsely sweet voice. "And I shall make sure that you also will have more slaves to do your bidding, for a man's wealth is measured by the size of his household—and my brother is a generous Lord."

Ginny said carefully, picking her words, "I am sorry if I seem stupid, but I don't quite understand. You are saying . . ."

"My son," the Sultana Valide announced shortly, "has decided to marry my daughter to your husband. It is the greatest honor he could bestow. My son is not given to trusting easily."

"My brother," the younger voice chimed in, "has been kind enough to ask me what *my* feelings are. I have watched . . . our husband through the latticework and he is truly a handsome man as well as being blessed with the gift of healing. Or have you not been fortunate enough to see his face? Perhaps I will describe him to you after I have come here."

She felt smothered by the raining down of their words and by the effort of holding back her emotions. She would have liked to cry as well, but not in front of these women who faced her and watched her without her being able to see their faces.

"When is the ceremony to take place?" Ginny said in a voice that was as cold as a blade—and ordered refreshments.

They had gone by the time Richard came to her. She was sitting in the garden taking in all its different scents and hearing the restive whinnying of her horse—all without being able to move from the marble bench where she was seated as if she had been turned to marble too.

"Ginny . . ." There was agony in his voice, but there was agony inside her as well and she did not—could not—turn her head toward him.

"Had you guessed? Or did it come as a surprise to you—as it did me?"

"Oh, my God—I had no idea, and I swear it! And then, after he had made the announcement, I heard that . . . that you had had visitors."

He had seated himself beside her now, but she could sense that he was almost afraid to touch her.

"Ginny . . . believe me, I . . . I am in torment! I don't know what to do!"

"There is nothing much that you can do, is there?" Long ago, after *they* had gone, she had been emptied of tears. "I . . . understand how helpless you are—just as I am. But you must tell me exactly what it means. . . ."

At that point he caught her in his arms, holding her against him.

"I wish I had never brought you here! I wish I had never come here! It was bad enough before, but now—do you understand that I had no hand in this, no idea what he was thinking of? If I could —but my will is not my own any longer. My master the Sultan has given me his favorite sister and there is no possible way in which I can refuse her. Tell me you understand. You *must* understand!"

With a part of her mind she *did* understand. Even to the extent that Richard, loving her as he did, was thinking of *her* safety beyond his own.

But what would this new "marriage" mean? Dared she ask him for fear he'd answer her? Stories that Ginny remembered hearing came to her mind now. Wives or concubines who bore children to the same man within weeks or even days of each other. Would it be the same way with her and the Sultan's sister? For surely, along with another marriage went another set of responsibilities. Richard would have to bed his new wife, there was no question of it. And then? . . .

He swore to her that he loved her, and no one else but her. That it would make no difference to their relationship, and would, in any case have to be endured only for a short while. Sooner or later the Sultan Abdul Aziz would find another doctor, and his sister another husband. Divorce was easy for a man in the Moslem world.

Ginny found herself comforting him—her mind still not *quite* able to grasp the enormity of the thing that was facing them both. One more night went by without her being able to tell Richard of her suspicions, and yet another. In the end she told him at the worst time possible, blurting it out on the night before he was to be married for a second time—to another woman.

"I . . . I think I'm with child. I'm sorry to have to break it to you *now*, but for days I . . . just haven't been able to find the right time! Not that this is the right time, but . . ."

His explosion was all that she might have hoped for under different circumstances. Joy mixed with excitement, concern—and then a passion of self-reproach.

How could he possibly go through with such a mockery of a marriage ceremony *now*? Perhaps the Princess would change her mind, for she wouldn't want to be relegated to position of secondary wife. And as for Ginny, she must rest, she must not ride, she must . . .

She could not help laughing weakly, almost as a reaction to the tension that had built up between them of late.

"But you're a *doctor*, Richard! And I might be wrong. Please . . ."

He insisted on examining her himself, finally confirming what she had already known in her heart. But even so, it was too late to back out of marriage with the Sultan's sister, and they both knew it.

Ginny shut herself away in her wing of the women's quarters, trying to pretend that nothing was amiss, even when she could hear the bustle and hubbub that was taking place on the other side of the marbled courtyard as the Princess Gulbehar's retainers began to arrive with her dowry and all her possessions. The formal marriage ceremony might take days, and in any case it was unlikely that Richard could come to *her* soon afterward. The more she thought about it the more impossible and dreamlike the whole situation seemed to be. Even her thoughts had begun to feel confined, just as she herself was. She could not think of anything further than passing one day at a time, and even that was an effort. It was then that she really realized the extent of her dependence upon Richard.

# Chapter Thirty-Seven

❧

Hardest of all to bear, Ginny thought, was the fact that Gulbehar seemed deliberately to cultivate her company; especially now that she was swelling with Richard's child.

Richard himself told her, with an air of embarrassment, that the poor girl was probably lonely. He seemed to think that Gulbehar was as much of a pawn as *they* were, and therefore deserving of pity, and Ginny had to bite back her comments. No matter what she said, she would only be thought a jealous shrew—or else pitied because of her so-called "delicate" condition. All the same, it *was* a strange and uncomfortable position that they all found themselves in, Ginny supposed, forcing herself to think *charitably*. Richard still spent most of his time with her; and if, as her pregnancy advanced, he no longer lay with her, it was only because of his love and consideration for her health. As it was, he usually sat with her until she was on the point of falling asleep, helped by his gentle, soothing voice as he read to her.

Ginny tried not to wonder how often he went to his *other* wife, and when; although she knew he must. It was better not to know, and then she wouldn't be inclined to dwell upon it. She must think only of the child—Richard was sure it would be a son—and of her own health. He told her so, over and over.

Days passed—and she had to suppose that weeks passed; but time had become meaningless to her, and as the child within her womb became heavier and she more clumsy in her movements she could only pray and hope that it would be over with quickly, leaving her free again.

"There will be no pain this time," Richard had assured her. "I promise you, my darling—no pain. When your time comes I will be with you, and you must only listen to my voice. I will bring you through it without your feeling any of the agony you had to go through the last time. Do you still trust me?"

"Yes," she whispered, and felt him lean over her to kiss her—tenderness turning into passion until at last with a smothered exclamation he pulled away.

"How I want you! And the waiting is almost unbearable. Ah, my love, never doubt that I love you!"

A letter from her Tante Celine arrived during this time, and it helped to cheer her up—if only to be reassured that her existence here was recognized by the outer world.

The children were well and happy—Laura Louise had had a cold and a slight fever but she had soon mended. Francis—or Franco, as they all called him—was a handful. They all missed her and waited for her return.

Tides of homesickness washed over her, and Ginny tried not to let herself sniffle like a baby. It was almost better, she thought, to join Gulbehar in the garden where it was pleasant at this time of the evening, rather than sit in her room moping. Richard, having read her letter to her, was gone again; and she, who had never minded being alone before, could now hardly bear her own company. She could not read and she could not sew. The music she heard was unfamiliar and full of strange, sensuously twisting rhythms. There was nothing familiar in her surroundings, that was it—and nothing she could do about it since she had become so helpless.

"But I am *not* helpless," she thought, "I have only lost one of my senses, and that only temporarily. I must not let myself forget that. I can think, and I can plan and hope. . . ."

Through the arched, open doorways and through her windows a soft breeze came to play with loose strands of her hair, bearing on it the heavy perfumes of musk and ambergris and attar of roses, and very faintly the smell of crushed herbs as well. There was a world outside, even if it was only, at this point, a walled garden. And she was *not* a prisoner unless she thought herself so. Perhaps *that* was the key that the learned Doctor Wundt had referred to.

Like the Lady of Shalott in the poem by Tennyson she had recently read, Ginny rose purposefully to her feet. She knew her way out to the garden; through the marble courtyard onto which her room opened, and past the bathing pool and so through a wide, vine-bowered archway into a place of tinkling fountains and flower scents.

There was no need to call for Fatmeh—she was not an invalid and did not need a keeper. Pausing in the doorway to regain her bearings, Ginny could feel herself flinch inside. She had suddenly been reminded of the time when, without her realizing it, she had become a slave to the opium habit, walking in a daze, existing only for that short-lived feeling of uplift she obtained soon after she had taken one of her powders. And how she had suffered, without wanting to, in order to break her dependency on a drug! *Steve* had made her suffer, and she had hated him for it—never quite forgiven him. Steve, who was now free to marry whomever else he chose. Would it be Di Paoli?

"It doesn't matter to me any longer. *He* doesn't matter to me, I have set my life in a different direction!" Ginny warned herself. She brushed through the doorway of her room and heard her footsteps echo in the marbled bath chamber.

In the garden, as she had half-expected, Gulbehar was eating her favorite sweet pastries, kadin gobegi and lokma and baklava, and sipping khoshab, a special fruit drink made from peaches and other fruit and flavored with musk.

There was a ripple of voices and movement as Ginny emerged, and out of the ripple Gulbehar's high voice, filled with a concern she could not really feel.

"Are you here without your servant? You might have fallen in the bathing pool, and made our lord very sad. Navsad, help my husband's other wife to sit down—yes, there, among the cushions." Almost without a pause the high, light voice with no depth to it ran on: "Do have some sweetmeats, they are freshly baked and delicious. My servants found a new pastry shop in Pera run by an Alexandrian. And have some ayran to drink, it is good for you in your condition. *I* have begun taking it too, since . . ."

There was a giggle from Gulbehar's numerous attendants, and Ginny chewed on an overly sweet, nutty pastry without really tasting it while she tasted those last coy words instead.

"Are you *enceinte* too?" she said clearly in French, and her drink tasted sour while she waited for the answer that came in the same language, just as clearly phrased.

"I too am blessed, and pray to Allah that I may bear a son to my lord—and many others after that." After a pause the other woman said with a false question in her voice, "And is it true that you have been married before and have other children?"

Knowing what store the Turks set on the virginity of their women Ginny received the full effects of *that* barbed dart, although she merely shrugged casually and said: "Yes—twins. Richard plans to adopt them. . . ." And wished she could see Gulbehar's face.

After that, her pride, if nothing else, forbade her to retreat to her room again too soon. Setting her chin, Ginny stayed, forcing herself to finish her yogurt drink, the ayran that was supposed to be so good for her. She listened to music that she didn't really understand, and heard a singer wail in a high-pitched voice—a love song, Gulbehar told her condescendingly.

From somewhere in the distance there was a sound of shots and then shouting that made her jump—and she felt tense until she understood from the chattering that was going on around her that it was merely the Sultan playing his war games. And finally, to Ginny's relief, it had been time enough and she could politely leave.

"Richard will come to *me!*" she thought, and was ashamed of the thought, finding in it a form of defeat and the subjugation of her spirit. Was it possible that she was making Gulbehar a *rival?* That because she was locked in by circumstances, she was beginning to *adjust* (horrible word!)? Of course Richard would come to her, and of course they both realized that she was not a prisoner here but stayed of her own accord because *he* had to stay. Or was that strictly true? Was she, perhaps, a prisoner of herself?

Ginny had gained her room by now, and she was about to call for Fatmeh, who was always about, when the first cramp took her by surprise, doubling her up. She caught at the edge of the bed, and the covers slipped off in her clutching fingers, falling with her to the floor. She felt as if a knife was slicing at her stomach, cutting her in two with thrust upon thrust of agony.

Afterward she supposed that she must have screamed. There were shadowy figures all about her, holding her; voices talking to her—when all she could do was scream until her voice gave way; feeling pain piling upon pain, thinking "it's not yet *time*, it can't be!" until everything was blacked out.

* * *

Even in her unconsciousness there was pain—pain remembered and pain present when she woke up sobbing, feeling each breath trapped in her throat. And she saw Steve's face bending over her. It took some time for her to realize—and then only after she had heard him speak to her—that it was not Steve she saw but Richard. And it took more time before she became aware that she was *seeing* again, just as if nothing had happened.

Before she could say so, Richard's voice was soothing her, carrying her away from the knife-edge pain inside her that kept on and on, trying to kill her.

"No!—no, no!" The voice she heard was hers but sounded separate from her.

"Hold on to me. Here's my hand. Hold on, my darling. And now—the pain is going away. You are going to sleep—not to die, but to *sleep*, do you understand? You will listen to me—you will hear nothing but my voice. . . ."

His voice—and nothing after that until much later, when she opened her eyes to sunlight and bright silk hangings that covered stone walls—azure-tiled ceilings and floors that were also tiled in what looked like mother-of-pearl.

Everything she saw—oh, God, she was *seeing* again!—seemed extraordinarily sharply in focus, and bright, while at the same time she seemed to be viewing it all from a dispassionate distance. Even Richard.

He was a handsome man, in spite of the faint imprint that the smallpox had left on his face. Ivory complexioned, it was his blue eyes and black hair and perhaps something about the shape of his mouth that had reminded her so forcibly of Steve at first. But Steve would never have looked so haggard and so concerned.

"Ginny. Oh, my beloved, don't close your eyes again." His hands, strong hands, held hers tightly. "You are back with me, and you are going to become stronger with each day that passes. You are going to be all *right*, do you hear?"

Like everything else about her, her voice sounded detached too.

"And why should I not be? Richard, why do I feel so weak? What happened to me? All I can remember is the pain. . . ."

His face changed, growing tighter, and his eyes fell away from hers.

"You . . . I wish you had not asked me that yet, but I cannot lie to you. You lost the child. I don't know what caused it—something you ate or drank, perhaps. But the important thing is that you are alive, and you are here with me." He gripped her hands harder, until she murmured softly, and then he loosened his grip almost unwillingly. "I will be with you more often from now on, I promise you. I'll look after you."

Why did she need looking after? As soon as she felt stronger . . . sleep attacked her again, laying her low in spite of herself; but this time it had some good effects. She felt stronger, and she remembered.

Everything she had read about the Ottomans and their history came back to her. Everything she had experienced since she had been here should have taught her. She had regained her sight and lost a child—"an eye for an eye"? When they brought her food or drink now she said politely:

"Please taste it first. You know how fussy I am." And when Richard came to her again she said to him directly, "I was poisoned, wasn't I? Someone wanted to kill me—or make me lose the baby."

"You're overwrought, my love, because you lost the child." His voice lacked conviction and his eyes could not meet hers. He looked drawn and tired, with dark crescents under his eyes. She saw strands of grey in his hair and wanted to reach out and touch them—and wanted to comfort him because he had comforted her and been kind to her.

"Richard—"

Again he evaded her. "General Ignatiev is coming tomorrow. He wishes to . . . talk to you."

"Will he be allowed to see me?" He ignored the mockery in her voice.

"You will have to be veiled, of course. I'm sorry, my darling, but by now you must surely understand . . ."

"I don't understand what I cannot accept. Not the veil, not this enforced seclusion. She does, perhaps, because she was born to it. She tried to kill me because she wanted her child to be born first. The history of the harem is full of such stories, isn't it? What are you going to do about it, Richard?"

She saw him wince at the cruelty of the cold, evenly expressed facts she had laid before him, and winced inside herself; still wanting to reach out to him. If he would take her in his arms; if he would promise to take her away; if he would *do* something, anything, instead of staring at her as if she mortally wounded him!

Finally, he bowed his head—and she saw him press his fingers against his temples, realizing suddenly that he would not have shown her such despair if he knew that she could see him. For some reason, perhaps because she had not thought to do so, she hadn't mentioned anything to him.

It was on the tip of her tongue to tell him when he raised his head, his eyes looking at her with such an expression in them that she almost wished herself blind again. His voice sounded dead—devoid of all feeling.

"What am I going to do? I had hoped to see you stronger before I told you, but since you have forced the issue upon us both: I am going to divorce you, Ginny. The laws of Islam make it easy for a man, for all he has to say is 'I divorce Thee' three times—and it is done. Tomorrow, in the presence of an Imam I shall say the words, and you will leave here. Ignatiev knows your story and he has promised to make sure you reach St. Petersburg safely."

# Chapter Thirty-Eight

❦

General Ignatiev, a tall, spare man with ferocious mustaches, questioned her only cursorily, and it was one of the most humiliating experiences of Ginny's life. She knew the Tsar? She had been to his court? Who had been her sponsor? Ah, she had been married to a Russian, and knew the Tsar's personal physician . . . yes. She had the feeling that he believed nothing, or very little, of what she said—and she said very little, except to tell him that she had no desire to go to St. Petersburg.

The General merely *looked* at her—as if she had been a fly or some other annoying insect.

"I have been given to understand that you are a . . . ah . . . protégée of my master the Tsar. That is why I have made certain arrangements to have you escorted from here. If St. Petersburg proves too dull for you I am sure there are other places you could travel to from there—and no doubt you will not lack for escorts." His icy gaze put her in her place; just as his next words quieted her protests.

"You could, of course, stay here—if you prefer such a life as I am sure you have already sampled. I understand that the Prince Abdul Hamid has expressed an interest . . ."

She had not seen Richard since his pronouncement of their divorce. She had seen hardly anybody; except for the condescending General. And by this time, all she could wish for was freedom—something sane and civilized beyond the walls that hemmed her in.

Now that she had no pipeline to the outside world, Ginny only heard vague rumors of what was going on. There were societies, such as the Young Ottomans, formed by the free-thinking Turks, which were making more of an impression in other countries than in Turkey itself. Midhat Pasha, one of the leaders of the Young

Ottomans, had been banished to some distant province. But now, since the present Grand Vizier was pro-Russian, there were rumblings that sought the recall of Midhat Pasha as Vizier—as well as unrest in Bulgaria, where two bad harvests had brought the people to the verge of revolt.

General Ignatiev had too many other things on his mind and so, when the time came, he sent Ginny on her way under the escort and personal protection of one of *his* protégés—a Colonel Taras Barsovich Shevchenko.

She left the Dolmabahce Palace heavily veiled, through an unobtrusive garden gate that led down to a small stone pier; and stepping into the gaily painted caique with its silk canopy, Ginny saw for the first time the blue waters of the fabled Bosphorus and, facing her, the distant green shores of Asia.

All the time she had not said a word, ignoring the big, burly Russian officer who sat opposite her with his arms crossed over his chest. He glittered with decorations, this Colonel in his resplendent uniform, and from the glum expression on his face she was certain he was no more looking forward to the journey that they would share than she was.

Through the thin piece of net that covered her eyes, Ginny continued to study her surroundings—mostly to keep herself from depressing introspection. She had done enough weeping and enough thinking to last her forever! A part of her life was behind her. . . . She thought again of Richard, who was surely sending her away because he was afraid for her life. The suffering on his face when he had told her he was divorcing her had been evident, and he had not given her an opportunity to argue with him or to question him. There was a feeling of cold emptiness inside her— but with a deep breath of the fresh sea-smelling air, Ginny firmed her stubborn chin under the ugly black veil. From now on she would be completely independent! Never again would she let herself get too attached or dependent on a man. Even Richard's constant concern for her had tended to become overpowering, almost smothering. He had been as protective of her as if she had been a child, and she too in her turn had played the role. No more!

The Russian broke the silence. "The Golden Horn there—and on this side Pera. On the other, Constantinople, that the Turks call Stamboul."

He obviously spoke very little English and his accent was heavy, but at least the man was trying to be polite. Ginny inclined her head, perversely determined to remain silent, but she had followed the direction of his pointing hand, and could not help a swift intake of breath at a sight that must have remained the same for centuries.

They were moving in the direction of Constantinople, past Seraglio Point where the old palace of Topkapi stood, veiled by its dark green cypresses and plane and willow trees. Through the water gate there had come the hundreds of captive girls chosen as slaves for the Sultan, never to leave the harem again. Ginny gave an involuntary shiver, and looked instead toward Pera, with its collection of white, red-tiled buildings that sloped upward to vine-covered peaks. It was here that many of the Europeans lived, and church spires penciled the sky along with domed minarets.

One glance backward—the marble and gold-leaf Dolmabahce Palace with its tall Grecian columns and sprawl of buildings gleamed in the sunlight with the ever-present cypress trees brooding dark green against the hillside behind. She would never see it again. Ahead of them now lay Constantinople, built, like Rome, on seven hills.

The Colonel cleared his throat—Ginny could tell that he was having a hard time coping with her veiled silence. Good! she thought. The more constrained he felt in her presence the easier it would be, in the end, to persuade him that there was really no need to take her all the way to St. Petersburg. In fact, Ginny had made up her mind that she was no longer going to allow herself to be moved this way and that like a pawn. St. Petersburg indeed! Her children, and indeed all her ties, were in France.

"We are here," Colonel Shevchenko announced unnecessarily. He sounded relieved. For the first time, Ginny really regarded him thoughtfully, wondering what he had been told about her. He *looked* like the kind of man who had hearty peasant appetites and enjoyed hearty peasant women. While he was only slightly taller than she, he had the build of a wrestler, with a massive chest and shoulders. He had dark brown hair that curled tightly against his head and was sprinkled with grey at the temples, and he sported luxuriant mustaches over a wide, full-lipped mouth. He was perhaps forty or forty-five years old? It was hard to tell—and it didn't

really matter. She didn't intend to be a burden on the Colonel for
longer than she could help!

Still veiled, and to any idle onlooker, every inch a respectable
Turkish woman, Ginny allowed herself to be escorted to the Colonel's own quarters. He informed her stiffly that *he* would of course
reside in the Embassy until they were ready to set out. And in the
meantime her baggage would be brought in and unpacked for her,
if she wished, by a maid he had hired. If she lacked for anything,
she had only to mention it. She inclined her head again; he
clicked his heels and then left. She was on her own!

"She did not say a single word to me!" Colonel Shevchenko
complained to his superior officer, standing at attention before the
General's desk. "I watched my manners, I pointed out the sights
to her, and I left her to the full use of my house and my servants.
And still not one single word. Is she a deaf mute, perhaps?"

"Nonsense!" General Ignatiev said impatiently. His eyes were
busy with documents that were piled on his desk, and a thoughtful frown creased his forehead. The trouble in Bulgaria was building up to some kind of explosion—he wondered what form it
would take. He also happened to know that Turkish troops had
been dispatched to the unruly province, as well as a detachment
of Circassians who fought not for pay but for whatever plunder
they could take. It did not look good—or was it perhaps the best
thing that could have happened? Fine threads—all of them when
carefully woven together forming a pattern. . . . And at a time
like this he had to be bothered with a woman!

The General looked up at last into the red, expectant face of
his friend, Colonel Shevchenko. What on earth had Taras just
said? Well, no matter—he was a good man and he would follow
orders.

"The lady is, very possibly, the natural daughter of the Tsar
himself. She was at his court, and made much of by him a few
years ago. She was also formerly married to the Prince Sahrkanov
—he was one of my predecessors here. So you'll understand the extreme delicacy of your mission?" A few more well-chosen words,
and Colonel Shevchenko was fully aware of the delicacy and the
difficulty of his task. He was to escort a lady who was American
born, but a Russian Princess with estates of her own in Russia,

to St. Petersburg. In doing so he would, of course, greatly further the chances of his own advancement. And, the General added in a voice devoid of expression, the woman was extremely attractive— or so he had been told. *If* this was the same woman, and it had damned well better be!

"He picked *me* of course—this Englishman-turned-Turk who was her husband—because I am the only foreign ambassador the Sultan trusts well enough to visit him. He seemed extremely anxious that she should be sent safely home." He did not add that the lady in question had not seemed very willing. Let the Colonel find that out for himself and deal with it. As for himself, General Ignatiev thought, the matter was taken care of, and *his* responsibility was ended.

A few hours later, with his uniform changed and his mustaches carefully trimmed, Colonel Taras Barsovich Shevchenko presented himself at his own house on the pretext of making sure that his guest had everything she wanted. He was fortified by the vast quantities of vodka he had consumed with a few of his cronies, and General Ignatiev's carefully dropped tidbits of information had made him curious. Quite curious.

He was already standing at the door to the living room when the servants announced him in a low, rather frightened voice. And now, in spite of himself, the Colonel found himself at a loss for words. Instead of the veiled Turkish woman he remembered, he saw a young woman dressed in the latest European fashion, her hair caught up in braided loops that showed off to perfection her small ears with their dangling diamond eardrops. Her eyes, studying him coolly and quite openly, were a peculiarly luminescent shade of green, and she had a mouth . . . caught staring at it, the Colonel reddened and bowed belatedly.

"I came to see . . . if there was anything—"

"How kind of you. And as a matter of fact . . ."

As a matter of fact it turned out that there were a number of things she desired. Writing paper, pen and ink—there were letters she had to write. And champagne. . . .

"Champagne?"

"Is it obtainable here? They don't believe in alcoholic drinks in a harem, you see. I've been positively thirsting for some champagne. And oh yes, I would like to visit the American Embassy, if I may. I happen to be a citizen of that country."

"Most of the foreign embassies are located in Pera." She wished he wouldn't keep staring at her with those red-rimmed pop eyes of his. "And we will be leaving for St. Petersburg tomorrow, so that there will hardly be time—"

"Colonel . . ."—now she faced him squarely with her chin tilted defiantly—"I will not be leaving for St. Petersburg. I will write a letter to my . . . to the Tsar which you may deliver if you wish, and it will absolve both you and General Ignatiev of all blame. But you must understand that I have two young children in France, and I am longing to see them again."

"Madame, my orders are that you are to be escorted to St. Petersburg!"

"And the only way you'll take me there will be as a prisoner—a *very* recalcitrant prisoner, I might add! What will you do," she added scornfully, watching his face, "keep me in irons? I am the Princess Romanov and I've committed no crime against the State!"

"Of course not. But all the same, you are going to St. Petersburg. My orders—"

"Colonel Shevchenko, I am not a member of the Russian Army! I refuse to follow these . . . these *orders*. And you tell General Ignatiev that. Or *I* will tell him so if you are afraid to do so."

He stared at her, hardly able to believe his ears. She was defying him! What was more, she was even defying the General! But *he* was the one who was being made to look like a fool, unable to control a willful woman.

He took a step toward her and then controlled himself, finally repeating stiffly: "General Ignatiev has told me that I am to take you to the Tsar at St. Petersburg, and that is what I intend to do —whether you come willingly or not. But I think you will come!"

Now she was studying his face measuringly, noting the vein throbbing in his temple and those big hands that were clenched at his sides. He looked like a burly bear—a man given to violently ungovernable rages. Perhaps she should try other tactics?

Ginny sighed, and bent her head, looking down at her clasped hands.

In a small voice she said: "Would you separate a mother from her children? At least let me take *them* with me to Russia. Please. Is there anything in your orders to say that you cannot take a roundabout route to St. Petersburg?"

She had taken him by surprise and there was hesitation in his voice when he answered. "I will . . . have to speak to the General about that. But plans have already been made for us to travel by sea to Sevastopol—leaving tomorrow."

# Chapter Thirty-Nine

❧

The Colonel had left—no doubt to see the General again. Alone once more, Ginny prowled about the small house like a young cat—and just as restless. It was late, but there was no question of sleep—her mind was too full, too occupied for her to contemplate lying down. She felt as if she had been *resting* for months now, caught in a web of protection and kindness and—yes, there had been love! Richard had loved her and she had loved him. She had been content to be looked after and pampered and cosseted, and now—oh, but it was difficult to decide just *what* she felt at this point in time.

"I must have a very shallow nature," she thought. "How could I put Richard out of my mind so quickly otherwise? I'm selfish. . . ." Perhaps the word was unfeeling. But it seemed as if, when she suffered such agonies only to lose the child she had been carrying, not only her blood had run out of her but her capability for deep feeling as well. Once before, she had learned to control her feelings and to skim the surface of life as lightly and as carelessly as a butterfly. Feelings only got hurt.

Thoughtfully—and yet deliberately—Ginny unearthed the bottle of vodka that she had noticed earlier and poured some into a glass, toasting herself before the mirror. The face that looked back at her as she swallowed all its contents at once, grimacing, was overly pale—with eyes that looked large and haggard. Eyes that could *see* again—she really ought to keep that in mind.

Once before, opium had brought her forgetfulness. She had none now, but the vodka might do. Locking the door, Ginny sat down on the divan, making sure that the bottle was close by her on an ivory-inlaid table. Her body had begun to feel warm—a few moments before she had had to fight to keep from chattering with the coldness that was inside her like an icicle.

"Sempre Libera!" she said, toasting herself with the name of an aria from *La Traviata*. Ever free. No more ties. Aloud she said experimentally: "Richard?" And missed him. Richard had always comforted her when she felt unhappy, when she was afraid of the darkness pressing in on her. Richard had made tender love to her —*not* the way Steve had ravished her! Richard would never ravish a woman. *How had he taken Gulbehar?* Had it been with the same gentleness, the same attention that he used to make love to *her?*

"Richard . . . Richard!" Say his name so she wouldn't say another. Richard had looked almost frighteningly like Steve—but not close-up. How was it possible that two people could love each other and hate each other at the same time? She had never hated Richard, and she didn't now. It was the vodka and not her thoughts that made her head ache, and she should have insisted upon champagne. Why couldn't that silly Russian Colonel . . .

The throbbing in her temples sounded like drumbeats.

"My goodness!" Ginny said and put both hands up against her ears as the knocking ceased and the door burst open with a horrific crash. Seeing him there, a great big bear of a man with a case of champagne under one arm, she began to giggle. "I conjured you up! I was just thinking about you, and there you are— with my champagne too; how very thoughtful. Only . . . I am already more than a little drunk on *your* vodka!"

"Oh, is *that* what you've been doing? The servants thought you might have killed yourself! And so you found my vodka, did you? It's much better than your silly French wines! Perhaps you're more of a Russian than you know!" He strode up to her, depositing the champagne carelessly on a table as he came.

Ginny frowned up at him. "I don't like Russians!" she said coldly. "I was married to one, once, and I didn't like *him!*" And then, belatedly, "What are you doing here?"

"I thought you'd like to hear the good news—at least it's partly good and partly bad." He sat on the divan beside her, grinning, and began, quite unconcernedly, to undo his tight uniform jacket. "Do you want to hear it now? Or shall we have more vodka first? Or shall it be champagne for you?"

"Champagne," she said automatically, and then, becoming angry, "and what do you think you're doing?"

"What do you think? Getting comfortable. Ah—now I feel I can breathe!"

She blinked her eyes to clear them, and he had risen, walking over to the case of champagne, which he ripped open easily with one great hamlike hand, while she stared in awe.

"Champagne!" he said, and gave a great, hearty guffaw of a laugh. "I have an easy way of opening one of these—quick too." And with that he proceeded to knock off the neck of the bottle against the table edge. He did it very quickly and neatly, and brought the bottle, still fizzing and overflowing, to her, filling her glass while it splashed all over her.

"You are a maniac!" Ginny said wildly, feeling herself one too. She had to be!

"Take a swallow of that champagne and you'll feel better!" he said comfortably, and pushed the glass up against her lips so that she had hardly any choice but to do so.

"Finish it, finish it! There's more where it came from, you know! Yes—I'm glad I came back here. And I didn't forget what you wanted either."

"You're drunk!" she said in what was meant to be a quelling voice, but he only laughed so hard that she was forced to start laughing with him.

"Drunk? Of course I'm drunk! But so are you—so are you! And you're a lovely woman, wasted behind that ugly veil you were wearing when I first saw you. I'm sure you were wasted on that husband of yours too. A woman like you—"

"You don't know anything about me!" She swallowed more champagne, enjoying its familiar tickling taste.

"No—perhaps not yet, but I do know women. Why d'you think I came back here tonight? Give me a kiss!"

Before she knew what he was about he had seized her about the waist, pulling her against him as he pressed his lips over hers.

"Stop it!" Ginny tried to say, but his mouth stopped her words, and helplessly, she felt his hands fumbling at her breasts. This was forgetfulness of another kind . . . pure sensation, nothing else— thank God, nothing else! And he was right, this great big hairy brute of a man—it was exactly what she needed.

"What pretty little breasts you have—perfectly shaped! See how each one fits in my hand? Just the kind of breasts I like!" He made a kind of running commentary of the different parts of her body as he uncovered them, his fingers making short work of the fastenings that held her gown together. And she did nothing to stop him, realizing that it was already too late, and by then not wanting to stop him—no, not even when he poured cold champagne over her body and lapped it up greedily, making smacking noises.

He was nothing but a crude animal of a man, a typical Cossack! And yet his very roughness and directness drew a response from her body and she succumbed in spite of herself, letting him do whatever he wanted with her until at last she reached that place of self-forgetfulness where she wanted to be.

Sometime during the night it became cold on the divan and he carried her to bed in his arms—*his* bed, she thought drowsily and supposed it was only fair. She slept after that and was warm because his body was warm. And the next morning, when she was only half awake, her head aching, he made love to her again, forcing her into awareness with his bearlike playfulness—biting her breasts, forcing his big hands everywhere until again she gave in, and in giving in found for herself a perverse kind of release.

"I'm a born whore!" she thought before she stopped herself from thinking and concentrated only on sensation.

At least he had said nothing else about leaving. Ginny had no idea what time it was, or whether it was afternoon or evening when she opened her eyes next. The heavy shutters remained closed and the room they were in smelled of sour liquor and lovemaking. She tried to move, but her body was trapped under the weight of one big leg as massive as a tree trunk.

He must have felt her struggles, for he reared up to look down at her.

"Ah, so you're awake again? Are you ready for more? I haven't had anyone quite as good as you before, do you know that? And I've had quite a few women in my day, believe me! I haven't upset you by saying that, have I? You strike me as being a practical, sensible sort of female, and this was good for both of us, wasn't it?"

"I would like to take a bath," she said faintly, and he chuckled.

"I already guessed that! I ordered the woman to get everything ready for you—and you won't mind if I join you, will you? I'm not much for baths back home, but in this climate . . . come along then! We'll rub each other's backs, shall we?"

Ginny could hardly believe that she had allowed herself to get on such familiar terms with "The Cossack" as she had nicknamed him in her mind. She must have been crazed last night! But still, here she was, and here he was, and perhaps she could talk him out of dragging her off to Russia after all.

As it was, she need not have worried. Sipping iced pomegranate juice mixed with tangerine, Ginny let her Cossack massage her back while he told her his "news" of last night.

"You distracted me, my dear, and that's the truth! But I brought the champagne—and had the devil's own time getting it, too!—because I thought you might want to celebrate. Or you might not—it depends on how fond you are of the Turks!"

"What do you mean?"

"There's been an uprising in Bulgaria—started in the mountains around a small town called Batak. I'd never heard of it myself, but the General thinks the whole world will, before too long. They—the Turks that is—put down the revolt with their usual brutality, only this time there was a newspaper correspondent there to witness everything, including the burning of a church with women and children inside! There's likely to be a bloody war over this, you know! In England and America they've got softer sensibilities than we Russians have."

Ginny twisted around so that she could see his face better, and found him beaming down at her like a genial giant.

"So I don't have to go to Russia?"

"Quick-thinking, aren't you?" Leaning down, he gave her buttocks a pat before he said, "No—not with a threat of war. The General only heard last night, and after what I told him he relented. I'm only to see that you leave safely for France on the first possible ship—there, doesn't that make you feel better?"

It took three days to find a ship going to France with suitable accommodations available, and during that time Ginny felt herself nothing but a plaything. The Cossack Colonel was both insatiable and indefatigable, and she felt, dazedly, that all she did during that time was eat—he loved to eat—drink, make love and sleep. They went through three cases of champagne as well as innumerable bottles of vodka, and he used her unmercifully, but with laughter and a rough heartiness at the same time so that she could not object too much. Whenever she started to protest he would find ways to silence her, so that in the end she stopped protesting and let herself be carried along on the wave of his boundless enthusiasm for whatever it was he was doing at the moment.

By the time he escorted her to the ship, an English vessel, Ginny was exhausted—and sore. She told him so, in the carriage that was taking them to the docks, and he merely burst into uproarious laughter, pinching her breasts surreptitiously.

"Ah! So you'll remember me for a while, eh? I'm really sorry to lose you, you know! If I could afford you—or the consequences—I'd have liked to have kept you for a while. But in my profession I have to keep moving. So maybe now you won't have such a bad opinion of all Russians?"

He kissed her soundly just before the carriage stopped, pushing aside the heavy veil she had worn draped round her fashionable bonnet. But when he escorted her on board, he was perfectly correct in his behavior and extremely formal, as he had been when they had first met.

"In a way," Ginny surprised herself by thinking after she'd gone below to her cabin, "I'll actually miss him!" For after all he *had* been what she needed. A pure sensualist who didn't pretend to be anything else!

She undressed and lay down, feeling the ship creak and sway beneath her. How tired she felt! And how many more journeys lay ahead of her? But *that* was something she would think about later.

# Part Five

# "LAST LOVE"

## Chapter Forty

&~@

France was shrouded in the faint mists of late spring when Ginny arrived, having cabled ahead. Coolness and pastel colors after the blaze of heat and color and light and shade of the Mediterranean countries.

France was familiar voices and intonations and a feeling of excitement welling up in her as she joined the others at the rail. Once she had called Mexico home, but she had put that behind her. Was *this* to be home now? "I can decide everything after I've seen the children and I'm back at the chateau," Ginny told herself. And there was Pierre! And Tante Celine as well—had they brought the twins? Her longing to see them was suddenly like an emptiness she hadn't realized existed, waiting to be filled. They wouldn't recognize her of course, they were still so young. But this time she would spend all her time with them, and then . . .

"Here you are!" Pierre said briskly as he bent to kiss her. And then, "I'll see to your baggage. . . ."

She was enfolded in Tante Celine's welcoming embrace, feeling tante's cheek damp against hers. Tante Celine always cried!

"Where is Richard? We were all so puzzled. . . ."

"I'll tell you the whole story later—there is nothing to be concerned about. Can't you see how well I look? I have been enjoying the sunshine and being out in it!"

"Come, let's go!" Pierre said, coming up behind them. He cast a warning look at his mother, who continued to dab at her eyes. "We'll talk in the carriage," he said unnecessarily, shepherding them ahead of him before Ginny could protest. But why was Pierre in such a hurry?

"How are the—"

"Ah—there it is! Ginnie, you remember Joseph? You get in with Maman and I'll see to everything else, shall I? There is plenty of room for your trunks."

She settled in against comfortable velour cushions with a sigh.

"Oh, it's so good to be home again! Shall we be staying in Paris or going straight to the chateau? I can hardly wait to see the children, they must have grown so much!"

"Yes . . . yes, a few inches at least!" Tante Celine answered distractedly, her eyes searching for Pierre.

"Have they been keeping well? The last time you wrote—but that, of course, was several months ago, the mails are not the swiftest in Turkey! That was why I did not mail the letter I wrote to *you*."

"My dear—what happened?" Tante's eyes were still filled with tears as she leaned forward to hold Ginny's hands.

The young woman shrugged insouciantly. "What usually happens? Richard was devoted—at first. But living in a harem was like living in prison for *me*, and after a while he . . . he decided it would be better for me to be free of the walls. *He* could not leave himself, for the Sultan had taken a fancy to him, and that meant—" She realized she was speaking far too fast, trying to keep her tone light, and that her aunt had seen through it all. It was with relief that Ginny saw Pierre come to join them at last, slamming the door shut as the carriage bounded forward.

"Well, here we are!" The note of forced gaiety in his voice was obvious enough to make Ginny frown inquiringly at him.

"Pierre—whatever is the matter? You ought to know that you can't hide anything from *me*! Tante—what *is* it?" Her eyes went from one to the other of them, and she could feel the blood draining from her face as she whispered: "It's not . . . the children? Nothing's happened? Oh, for God's sake, *tell* me!"

"The children are fine—just fine! For heaven's sake, how like a woman to jump to the worst possible conclusion!" Pierre said roughly, and that for him was unusual enough to make Ginny stare.

"Well then—but I know there is something wrong! Why won't you tell me what it is? If it's not the children, where are they?"

Tante Celine was twisting her small lace handkerchief round and round her plump fingers, her eyes not quite meeting her niece's. It was left to Pierre to answer her with a sigh as he stretched his legs out before him.

"Now, Ginnie, you must remember that—well, as a matter of fact the children are in England, I believe. And you must not worry, for I am sure they are being very well taken care of."

"In England?" Her voice had gone high as she gazed at him with her eyes bright with disbelief. "In England?" she repeated stupidly, wondering if she had heard right. "But . . . but what are they doing in England? How? . . ."

Tante Celine had started to sob. "There was nothing we could do to stop him, Ginnie! After all, he *is* their father and . . . and he had a court order—"

Pierre cut her short, making Ginny's head turn slowly—feeling as if her neck was so brittle it might break—from her aunt to him.

"Ginnie—what Maman and I are trying to tell you in our clumsy, bumbling way is that your husband has the children. Steve Morgan . . ."—he said it carefully, watching her eyes dilate, his voice turning slightly caustic—"is a very . . . forceful man. Although believe me, I would have stopped him if he had not taken every legal precaution beforehand. We had not expected him, you know!"

"We couldn't very well keep him from his own children, my love, although I did try very hard to talk him out of taking them away with him! But with you away, and . . . and . . ."

The *enormity* of what they were saying to her suddenly hit Ginny like a blow and she started upright, her hands fisted.

"Ohh! Oohh! That *would* be exactly the kind of lowdown, despicable trick he'd pull! He's . . . he's—*my* children! They're *my* children. I bore them, and he never even bothered to . . . to take the time to see them! And now—ohh! How well he plays the hypocrite! But he shan't get away with it!" She paused for breath, looking at her aunt's aghast face and Pierre's unreadable one. "I am going to get my children back, do you hear? He shan't—did he ask where I was?"

It was Pierre who said carefully: "He . . . er . . . seemed to know. All he said about you was he hoped you were quite happy. And he's not an easy man to read, Ginnie. He—"

"Oh, yes!" she said between gritted teeth, "oh, yes, how *well* I know that!"

She felt as if she'd been hit by a bolt of lightning. Steve—and that he'd dared to use the children to perpetrate his revenge on her! She'd like to kill him, stab him through his black heart with a dagger. Perhaps she would when she caught up with him!

It was sheer rage that made her cry this time. Pierre put his arm around her and Tante Celine offered her a clean handkerchief.

"I want . . . to know everything—" she said through her heaving sobs. "Everything! Where he was taking my children, what . . . what he intends to do with them—everything!"

Gradually, the whole story came out—and mostly from Pierre who, being a man, was more open with her.

Steve had arrived unexpectedly, with friends. One of them, Pierre was forced to admit, was a very attractive young woman— an American.

"But there is nothing between them—I am sure of that, for she was chaperoned by a formidable mother. She is so beautiful—she has hair the color of leaves in autumn."

By this time Ginny had recovered some of her self-control and she only said tightly: "How very *like* Steve! And you sound quite smitten with this American beauty! Tell me, how many other women did he have in tow? What about that . . . that opera singer?"

Pierre had the grace to flush. "Well, I—naturally I did not ask! But it's true that I heard they had been seen together in Paris. I believe she also left for England a few days ago."

"And darling little Concepción is there too. I'm sure he'll have his hands full!" Ginny said furiously. Unable to sit still, she began pacing; stopping to glare accusingly at her cousin.

"And *you*, Pierre—you are a lawyer, are you not? You let him steal my children without lifting a finger to stop him!"

"Ginnie, I tell you that *everything* was legal! And they *are* his children too, after all—" Catching her look he flung his hands up in mock defense. "Oh, very well! You have my promise that I will help you in every way possible. And so will Michel, if you ask him. I swear, he still has an inordinate *tendresse* for you! But what do you plan to do, Ginette? I hope you will not act too recklessly. . . ."

Breathing deeply, Ginny put her hands behind her, gripping the edge of the table she leaned against. And Pierre, watching her, thought suddenly that she looked very Russian at that moment, with her upward-slanted eyes that flamed emerald fires and her soft mouth tightened with resolution.

"Why," she said in a disarmingly sweet voice that did not deceive him in the least, "I intend to go to England to see my children! *That* much at least you will agree I am entitled to? And as for Steve Morgan, who is no longer my husband . . ."

"Ginnie, beware! Your divorce is not yet completed—"

"Did *he* try to prevent that too?"

Pierre shook his head ruefully, as he eyed her warily. "No . . . ah . . . no, not at all. In fact he . . . told us that he would do everything he could to make sure you obtained a divorce as speedily as possible since he too was contemplating matrimony sometime in the future. He said . . . he said that the children needed a mother."

A precious vase smashed against the wall just beyond his shoulders and Pierre flinched. *Dieu!* What temper—and what temperament! How his docile little cousine Ginnie had changed!

She had become a schemer, a planner. And she had learned—most of the time—to keep her temper in check.

When Ginny left France again it was in style, with a whole wardrobe of new gowns and jewels. With her cousin Pierre and another man—a new admirer—also in tow. On her engagement finger sparkled an enormous emerald ring that she was sure outshone the one Steve had presented to Di Paoli. Herr Frederick Metz, her friend, was a Swiss banker, and enormously wealthy. He was also happy enough to be seen in her company, and did not make any demands of a physical nature on her, for his taste in sexual partners veered towards his own sex. Still, he was a comparatively young and good-looking man, in a Teutonic, blond fashion, and he'd do. . . . He'd do to impress Steve with, and this—she al-

ready knew inside her heart—was going to be a battle to the
death.

"So—we go to London first?" Frederick said. He was enjoying
this, his first venture into international society. Since his father
had died, leaving him everything, his life had developed new horizons. France had been but the first stop on his grand tour. And
now London—in the company of such a lovely woman that all
men envied him. Yes, he was enjoying himself!

"We go to London first," Ginny said, and her smile was brilliant, deceiving Herr Metz, but not her cousin Pierre, who eyed
her with some uneasiness. What did she have up her sleeve this
time?

It had been arranged for them to have the use of one of the
town houses belonging to Lord Dalbey, a close friend of the
Prince of Wales and a fellow member of the Eccentrics Club.
Dalbey himself was going to shoot tigers in India because, he
swore dramatically, the fair Ginette would not yield to him. "I'll
think about it when you come back," she promised him, smiling,
and he had taken himself and his broken heart off, leaving her his
house for as long as she needed it.

"I always knew you'd turn out to be a heartless flirt!" Pierre observed, shaking his head as he observed his cousin, whose surface
sparkle and brilliance only made him wonder what he was doing
trailing behind her to London—except that she needed a man to
keep an eye on her; not one of her many admirers that she could
twist around her finger but someone who knew her and the mischief she was capable of getting into.

Ginny was patting her carefully curled and artfully arranged
hair in front of a mirror and she lifted one shoulder in response.

"But my dearest cousin—and dearest friend—I've always been a
flirt! What fun it is, to be sure—and it is perfectly permissible, you
know. What *isn't* is to give in, and then if you're a woman you
become *bad* and no one wants to flirt with you any longer. Isn't
that so?" She spun around to face him, inviting his comments on
her elegant new walking dress, adding coaxingly when he merely
eyed her severely, "Oh, Pierre, *please* try to understand me! I
know I must seem shockingly willful and independent to you, but
that is the way I am. And you know very well why I have come to

London and why I charmed poor Dalbey into leasing us his house. But now that we are here—"

"Now that we are here I do hope you will do nothing to injure your reputation!" Pierre said sternly. "I do not mean to lecture you, dear cousine, but the English are not half as liberal as we are in France—that is why they all escape to France to have fun! But if you intend to get your children back, you must be very careful not to turn public opinion against you—no matter how little you care for it!"

Ginny's face turned serious, and she bit her lip. "I know. And I . . . I really do promise that I'll try to be as discreet as I can." With a feeling of relief she saw her maid come in and she leaned forward to press her cheek lightly against Pierre's. "I'm going to do a lot of shopping so I might be a little late coming back—but we *are* going to the theater tonight?"

She was aware, as she left, that Pierre remained frowning after her, and a slightly guilty feeling tugged at the edges of her mind for a while. Well—but there were things it was much better for Pierre *not* to know! He had become so . . . so staid and so proper!

# Chapter Forty-One

❦

Ginny's arrival in London had been without fanfare, and her first week there spent quietly, without any public appearances. If she went out frequently during the day it was always, she assured Pierre, to go shopping. He in his turn had promised to find out, if he could, where Steve Morgan was residing with the children.

But now Pierre was frankly worried. Ginette was up to something—he knew her well enough to be certain of it. For instance, when she found out that her twin infants and their father were presently sojourning at the country home of the Viscount Marwood and his beautiful Spanish wife, she had taken the news almost too calmly.

"Oh, so he's staying with Concepción? He *would*—and so would she! I wonder what they do with poor Marwood?"

She had even dismissed the fact that the opera *Carmen* with Francesca Di Paoli playing the leading role was due to open on the stage at Covent Garden this week with no more than a casual: "Oh really? We *must* obtain tickets!"

No—after the exhibition of fireworks he had witnessed before they left France, Ginette's new quietness and docility was almost ominous! He could only hope it wasn't a case of the calm before the storm!

When Herr Metz, who was staying at the Claridge's Hotel, came calling and professed himself disappointed at not finding Ginny in, Pierre said casually: "She's never at home in the afternoons! And as a matter of fact, I had a message for her. Do you have any idea? . . ."

Frederick shrugged, brushing off an imaginary piece of thread from his immaculate black broadcloth suit. "Indeed no, unless she is still sitting for that portrait—you know, the one that that fellow

Alma-Tadema wanted her to pose for. He's quite famous, I understand. Fellow of the Royal Academy and all that—"

Sir Lawrence Alma-Tadema's house at Grove End Road had indeed become a favorite refuge for Ginny, and the artist's red-headed wife and daughters her friends. And as for the portrait itself . . . well, it was not exactly a *formal* kind of portrait, and Ginny continued to shy away from having to explain to Pierre that she was posing in the semi-nude for a portrait to be entitled "A Gift for the Sultan." Of course, in her pose she was looking down as if in acute embarrassment, and her face was shadowed, but to those who knew her the likeness would be unmistakable. And only today, as he was putting the finishing touches to his latest masterpiece, the painter had announced rather slyly that the Prince of Wales himself had expressed an interest in purchasing it.

"*After* it has been hung, I told him of course. And I must tell you again that it has been a pleasure to have you as a model—also your descriptions of the inside of a . . . hmm! . . . harem, were most helpful, most helpful! You might have noticed from my other works what painstaking attention I pay to the smallest detail. . . ."

It was easy to stand there and let her mind wander, Ginny thought. She had grown used by now to the extremely flimsy gauze (so very different from what was actually worn!) chemise that revealed even the rouged nipples of her breasts and the even more flimsy harem pants held in place around her hips by a belt made from gold coins. The "Moorish eunuchs" who were supposed to be holding her captive and helpless would be painted in later.

"I hope it makes him furious!" Ginny thought, and immediately forced her thoughts away. She wasn't going to spoil today by thinking about Steve, and there were other things on her mind. There was the news from Bulgaria—its details much more horrible as published in the newspapers than the casual way in which her Russian Colonel had mentioned it. And the *Times,* just today—belatedly, since news took so long to reach London from Stamboul—had carried the news that the Sultan Abdul Aziz had been deposed and his nephew Murad put on the Ottoman throne instead. Oh, her well-meaning friends were eager to read aloud to her every tidbit of news about Turkey, since they knew she had lived there for a time.

"Richard," Ginny thought, and was asked solicitously if she was cold, should another log be put on the fire perhaps? She shook her head, smiling a vaguely polite smile, while her mind continued to worry at the thought. Richard—what would he do now? Leave Gulbehar and follow her? Or would his sense of responsibility toward the woman who carried his child prove too strong? The truth was—Ginny drew in a deep breath and closed her eyes slightly as she tried to be completely honest with herself—the truth was that all the months she had spent with Richard now seemed like a nebulous dream! He had been a voice that coaxed her out of unconsciousness and despair. He had been kindness and comfort and clever, knowing hands that had brought her to physical fulfillment when she needed it. He had tried to shield her from all unpleasantness and unhappiness, right up until the very last, and she would always be grateful to him, always! But—like an arrow from out of the past—she heard Michel Remy's words that he'd flung at her in the room of the little house they had shared in Mexico:

"Gratitude! I don't want your *gratitude!* . . ." No, Michel had wanted her love, and she had been unable to give it to him because she had been in love with—"a ghost," as he had put it.

"I didn't even know what love was," Ginny thought somberly. "Perhaps I never did and never will. It's just an illusion, that's all —a weapon that people use to hurt each other."

"Ginny—you are looking so sad!" Sir Lawrence's oldest daughter, who was the closest to her age, was looking at her with concern. "Aren't you excited about going to the theater tonight? They say the Prince of Wales will be there—and of course Papa designed the sets. I wish *we* could go tonight, but Papa says he has too much work to finish and we have to wait until next week."

Thank God for light dialogue, Ginny thought, as she forced a smile and brought her thoughts back to the present and her reason for being here. For the rest of the hour she spent there she discussed with her friends the much-talked-about Oscar Wilde and his clever comedy *The Importance of Being Earnest,* which had taken London by storm.

\* \* \*

"I have a surprise for you," Pierre said when Ginny arrived back at the house later that afternoon. "I hope you don't mind," he continued in a casual voice, "but I have asked two more guests to accompany us to the theater tonight—and I have reserved a table for us in one of the private rooms at Romano's for our supper afterward. Frederick was here earlier and he said he would be here promptly at seven." Pierre pulled out his gold fob watch and looked at it before saying, "Which gives you, my dear cousine, exactly an hour and a half in which to complete your toilette. Do you think you can manage it?"

Ginny was already making for the stairs, relieved at not being questioned.

"Of course I can be ready! But who have you asked? Are they people I know?"

She was already halfway up the stairs and could not quite catch his reply—shrugging, she continued on her way up. Trust Pierre to pick friends who were invariably dull as well as being quite unexceptionable socially! Well, she'd find out who they were soon enough.

For some reason, Pierre seemed in a great hurry. Ginny had barely swept down the stairs, acknowledging Herr Metz's extravagant compliments on her gown of pearl-grey faille, richly trimmed with bands of dark crimson and pearl-grey velvet, when her cousin, looking at his watch again, announced that their carriage was waiting and they must leave at once or be late.

Looping her train over her wrist Ginny allowed herself to be hurried, although once they were settled in the carriage, she said: "Pierre, whatever is the matter with you? And who *are* these people that you are so anxious not to be late for?"

"They are friends of mine." She thought he sounded slightly uncomfortable. "They are—actually they are Americans. A mother and her daughter—actually the mother is French, a relative of the Marquis de Mora."

They were, as Ginny was to discover for herself, none other than the Prendergasts—Francoise and Lorna—whom *Steve* had personally escorted to Europe. And Lorna Prendergast, in a gown that was every bit as fashionable as Ginny's, was a beauty.

How *could* Pierre do this to her? And without any warning—

although at least he had not thought to ask Steve himself to be one of their party! Ginny was in a temper, and trying not to show it. She had been charmingly polite to the two women who eyed her curiously—what had Pierre told them?—but gave most of her attention to Frederick Metz, who basked in it proudly. There were, naturally, many eyes turned on them, for they were comparative newcomers to London society.

"I wonder who they are? Seldom see two such striking women together, by jove! Lucky fellers with them. . . ."

"Isn't that the young American heiress? I hear Marlowe's quite captivated by her, although her mama stays close."

"Someone was saying she was already engaged—to an American. They were at Ascot. . . ."

During the first intermission the men left to bring the ladies refreshments, and the gaslights reflected brightly off the opulent brass and crystal of the Haymarket Theater. Lorna Prendergast, with a defiant glance at her mama, leaned across an empty seat to say to Ginny:

"Do you mind very much if I'm frank and ask you if you are still married to Mr. Morgan? I've heard that divorces in France take a much shorter time than anywhere else, but . . ."

"Of course I don't mind that you are frank!" Ginny answered in kind, her voice as lightly brittle as glass. "And to tell you the truth it is something that I too would like to find out for myself. If our divorce is final or not, that is. But why—if I might be frank in my turn—does it matter to you?"

Lorna Prendergast smiled, leaning back again in her chair, and her mother only shook her head as if to say, "What a naughty child!"

"Mr. Morgan—Steve—is an attractive man, don't you think? I could think of a lot of women who would like to marry him if he was free."

Ginny smiled back at the russet-haired girl. "Oh, yes," she said clearly, "I'm sure there are a lot of women who find Steve attractive. And he does not turn down many of them—but I'm *not* talking of marriage of course. Personally, I had begun to find his series of mistresses rather tiresome, especially when I could not help running into them everywhere. Have you met Concepción yet?"

She had the satisfaction of seeing hot, angry color rise in Lorna

Prendergast's face before the arrival of Pierre and Frederick put an end to their barbed dialogue; but for the rest of the second act Ginny missed most of the witty dialogue she had so appreciated when the play began. Damn Steve! He had a lot to answer for!

Steve Morgan had just returned to London from the docks at Southampton—and before then he had been on a long and arduous journey that he hadn't wanted to embark on in the first place. He was tired and hungry and irritable, and the prospect of sitting down to write a long and detailed letter to his grandfather did not entertain him in his present frame of mind, although he knew it had to be done. Abdul Aziz, the deposed Sultan of Turkey had killed himself by slitting his wrists with a pair of scissors, and his concubine, Mihri Hanoum, was dead also—in childbirth they said. Murad, the new Sultan, had been declared insane and his brother Abdul Hamid had just been appointed Sultan in his place. These were things that most people in Europe did not know yet, but when the news broke, Don Francisco and his wife would naturally be concerned for the safety of their son—Richard Avery, Lord Tynedale.

The impassive-faced English butler who let Steve into the house he had rented for his use and the use of his friends in London informed him that the ladies had gone out to the theater and would be back late, after supper.

"If the cook's still up I'd appreciate some supper myself," Steve said. "Something cold will do. And I'd like something warming to drink. You may bring a tray in to me in the study."

He hadn't been expected, of course. He had told the Prendergasts that he intended to spend some time in the country with the children. All the same, the butler showed no signs of being flustered or even surprised.

"I shall have the fire in the study lit immediately, sir. You will find everything else in order."

The pretty parlor maid who came in to light it reminded Steve of Juana, who had been popular in the bachelor wing of his grandfather's house. She had the same pert, somehow knowing look. And for some strange reason—because he was so damned tired, perhaps—that in turn reminded him of Ginny. Ginny of the false green eyes, who ought to be safely ensconced in the Russian court at St. Petersburg by now. Steve found himself scowling—and the pert maid scuttled away with a backward look over her shoulder.

"Ooh—wasn't *he* in a bad mood!" she said belowstairs later.

Steve tore up the first sheet of paper he had begun to write on, and threw it into the fireplace. Damn Ginny anyhow—he hoped he would never have to run into her again. What she had done was unforgivable, and he intended to put her completely out of his mind as soon as possible. To think that he had actually thought her dead, and had mourned her! . . . And had even blamed himself—that thought alone was enough to throw him into a black rage. She was nothing but a teasing, tantalizing slut who gave in far too easily to every new man she met and he was well rid of her.

A second sheet of paper went the same way as the first, and the butler, carrying in a tray that was temptingly arranged with a variety of cold meats, pasties, pies and an assortment of fresh vegetables vinaigrette—just the way Mr. Morgan liked them—was met at the door of the study by Mr. Morgan himself, his greatcoat slung over his wide shoulders like a cloak.

"I'm sorry, Ross, but I shall be going out again. I shall probably not be home until some time tomorrow morning. Perhaps you will inform the ladies? . . ."

Perversely, Steve looked for some sign of discomposure on the man's severe, pallid face, but found none.

"Certainly, sir. Have a very good evening, sir."

Damn—the man had obviously missed his calling. He would have made an excellent poker player—perhaps good enough to best Jim Bishop!

He wondered what *his* luck would be like tonight, at rouge et noir. Well, Francesca always brought him good fortune at gambling, and he knew where he would find her tonight, in spite of the late hour. Once he had talked her out of shooting him or stabbing him or throwing some heavy crystal object at his head they would probably end up having a very entertaining evening together. It would certainly prove less frustrating than staring into a fire in which his imagination burned a series of green-eyed, copper-haired witches!

# Chapter Forty-Two

❧

"Wait till he hears that *she* is here!" Lorna Prendergast said to her mother, her topaz eyes brilliant. "Wait until he knows! What do *you* think he will do, Maman?"

Francoise, who had had quite as much of a difficult and puzzling evening as her daughter, only sighed. "*Ma cherie*, how is one to know? I must admit, however, that she is not quite what I had expected. She is beautiful and she has wit. It is a pity you two could not get along. Perhaps . . ."—she looked at Lorna, who had begun to pout slightly—"perhaps it's time we went home? I must admit, my dear, that I have begun to miss your father and the boys. And the cleanness of the air and the size of the sky. I had forgotten how small and cramped Europe can be, and I do not care very much for the London fogs."

"But Maman! I have only just started to have *fun!* Monsieur Dumont has asked me if I wish to visit the Crystal Palace. And the opera next week. Please, Maman!"

"Sometimes, Lorna, you become a child again! Pierre Dumont is Madame—is Ginny's cousin. Heavens, was it ever decided whether she and Mr. Morgan are still married or not?"

"Well," Lorna confessed sulkily as she began to brush her hair, "I don't really care! He has paid me hardly any attention at all since that . . . that Italian opera singer arrived on the scene. I only said what I said to . . . to see what *she* would say in return! And anyway, I do like her cousin. He's nice, and he's a real gentleman, *and*—I really don't think he's after my fortune, Maman! I mean, he's not the type to boast, but did you notice . . ."

While Lorna and her mother were talking, Ginny too was lying awake—tossing uncomfortably in her bed that seemed suddenly too big and too soft. What a strained evening! It had only been for Pierre's sake that she had borne it until the very end, and had tried hard to be civil to that sly-tongued little bitch. She frowned into the darkness. She had found out nothing at all about Steve except—and this by accident from Lorna's mother—that he had kept up his acquaintance with Francesca Di Paoli. And with Concepción. How dare he leave her children in the care of Concepción, of all people? Her heart ached when she thought of them. It had been over a year since she had seen them, and children's memories were so short. No doubt, without her Tante Celine or Pierre to remind them, they had forgotten all about her. And Steve—why had he suddenly taken an interest in their existence when at first he had not even acknowledged the poor little mites? But that, she supposed, was typical of Steve. Obviously he was as unpredictable and as changeable as ever, and she hoped it would not be necessary for her to see him again. If only the persons that Frederick had hired on her behalf were half as clever in their profession as they were supposed to be, then she should have her children back and be on her way to . . . to . . . perhaps it might be just as well if she did go to St. Petersburg, at least for a while. Her father the Tsar would be delighted to see her, and there at least she would be safe from Steve!

"Do not worry," Frederick had told her. "I am able to hire the best—men that some of our leading clients use for their business. They are quite professional, I assure you, and no one will be harmed." He had said on a questioning note, "unless you wish it? . . ." which made Ginny flush. Did he think her vengeful? She had, in the end, avoided answering directly by telling Frederick to warn his men that Steve Morgan must not be discounted as an adversary.

"He used to make his living as a mercenary, and for all that he can give the impression of . . . of almost foppish elegance, he can be as merciless as any savage when it comes to fighting. And above all, I do not want the children alarmed."

Frederick Metz had smiled, patting her on the shoulder. "You do not have to worry, I assure you! It will all be taken care of— including this brutish ex-husband of yours."

There was something she had not quite liked about the way he had said those last words, but she had been prevented from saying anything further when Pierre had walked into the room. And

above all, as she had impressed upon Frederick, Pierre must not
know anything. He would *not* approve!

When Ginny had finally fallen into an uneasy sleep that was
run through with dreams of unpleasant events in the past that she
always tried to thrust out of her conscious mind, the blanket of
fog outside her windows had begun to thin and look lighter with
the advent of dawn.

Not too many streets away, a lone hansom cab clop-clopped to
a halt before the elegant apartments occupied by the Princess
Francesca Di Paoli. A drowsy footman let the Princess and her
companion in, and once in her room she quickly dismissed her sullen, scolding maid Costanza, who gave the man Francesca called
Stefano her most baleful glare.

"So—again! And always, nothing but trouble to follow from it.
Much better this Duke, for all that he is an Englishman. At least
he is not some *banditto* from that uncivilized country where everyone carries guns. . . ."

Steve burst out laughing, at which Costanza glared all the
more, surreptitiously making the sign to ward off the evil eye.

"Oh, do go away, Costanza! The nagging, always the nagging—
it makes me so tired! I will undress myself—or better, my *banditto*
here will help me, *sí*? And tomorrow—remember that tomorrow I
do not wish to be disturbed too early!"

When the door had banged shut behind the woman, they
looked at each other, Francesca's great dark eyes reflecting the
candlelight.

"Well? And so here I am with you, when I should have been
with poor Alberto instead! You are bad for me, Stefano!" With a
supple movement she turned her back on him, wriggling her
shoulders. "Here! *You* will have to do it since I have sent my poor
Costanza away. Oh, how I hate these corsets!" She felt his warm
fingers brushing her skin and could not help a slight shiver of
desire. He was an animal—like herself. When she was with him
she could be herself, not an actress playing a part. They knew
each other almost too well! With a sigh, Francesca leaned back
languidly against him, feeling the frou-frou of her expensive gown
as it slipped unheeded to the floor. Without it, she was just as
beautiful—her mirror, and the eyes of the men who languished
after her, told her so!

He unlaced her corset, and she sighed as it came loose. "Ah! How good that feels! You see—I don't really need it! My waist is just as small—"

She spun around, pressing her breasts against him as her hands began to undress him in their turn. "And you—you have not changed either. I love your body, Stefano, it is so hard and so . . . so fierce—yes . . . yes now, now!"

The candles guttered out after a while, drowned in their own wax, and after a long while the two who had played at make believe war with their bodies fell asleep. Through the heavy ruby-velvet draperies of Francesca's bedroom the morning light tried to penetrate and could not.

It was afternoon when they woke, and as usual, did their talking then.

"So—and will I see you again soon, or not at all? You are a papa, with two children—I find that so strange! You are not the type, Stefano! And will you marry again? Or have you chased *her* out of your mind yet, that red-haired wife of yours? I think you like red-haired women—the other one I saw you with, what was her name?"

She did not realize until afterward that *she* had, as usual, done most of the talking. All he had told her was that he would be leaving London again the same night—probably for a few days, and that when he returned he would be bringing his children and their nurses with him.

"You are planning to leave soon? Back to America or to Mexico? Will you marry again, Stefano?"

He surprised her by answering *that* question, his fingers lightly tracing the outline of her breasts—going down her belly and back up again until her breath came shortly.

"I have to leave soon, 'Cesca. I've spent enough time here and I want my children to know a different place as home. There is more room—much wider spaces where I'm taking them. But I'll miss you." He grinned at her. "You wouldn't make a good wife— or a mother, *cara*."

"Ha! I have not failed to notice that you have not been brave enough to ask me either! But never mind—" Her eyes began to dance. "There is always Albert! What do you think, shall I let him make love to me or wait for . . . a certain gentleman whose

name is Edward? He sent me a ruby in a bouquet of red carna-
tions—how clever! But I almost threw it away!"

One black eyebrow lifted. "The Prince of Wales? By all means!
Although his grand passions never last. Perhaps Albert might be
useful to keep in reserve." He added as an afterthought, "Remind
me to send you white roses next, 'Cesca. Each with a pearl in
their center, and one extra large one for *here*."

"Oh, *yes!* I would love that—don't tease me, Stefano!"

It was early evening when he left, with some regret, because
Francesca always managed to keep his mind on her—while he was
with her.

Back at his own lodgings, Steve found that he had missed the
ladies again. They were out for the evening, but looked forward to
seeing him on their return. On the point of asking where they had
gone, Steve hesitated and then shrugged. If he missed them, he
would leave a note. It was more important to set out for Devon
this evening, as he had planned. His senses always attuned to danger, Steve had had a strange feeling of late, and the letter that he
found waiting for him only intensified it.

Now that he had made up his mind, the letter to his grandfather was written swiftly, and without many pauses for thought.
He had only to seal it, write another short note for the ladies telling them of his plans, and he was ready to leave. He missed the
Prendergasts by only two hours, and had no idea of the news that
they were longing to give him.

"He'll be back within the week," Francoise said, tapping the
folded sheet of paper against the table as she spoke. "That isn't
very long, and there is so much to be done here if he is bringing
the children with him, *and* their nannies. My dear, I know I had
promised to visit the Tower with you, but we have been in such a
rush of late, and I *do* feel an obligation to see that everything is
made ready. After all, Mr. Morgan was kind enough to escort us
here!"

"Well, it's the least he could do after Papa agreed to tolerate
those nester friends of his!" Lorna flashed, and then, soon after,
touched her mother's hand in apology. "Oh, I'm sorry, Maman!
It's just that I cannot help being disappointed! I want to see as
much as I can before we have to go back, and I do so love it here

—although not as much as I loved France!" Her eyes became dreamy. "Maman, can't I go all the same? You know very well I'd be safe with Pierre—Monsieur Dumont. I promise to behave myself—and you know that *he* will. Please?"

"I'll think about it!" her mother said distractedly, drawing a glance of surprise from her daughter. Francoise added thoughtfully, "Do you think . . . that he has found out she is here? I cannot help worrying about what may happen when they meet! Those poor children . . ."

In the end, Mrs. Prendergast allowed her daughter to coax her into just one more expedition. Quite exhausted after their talk, the older woman insisted that she *must* lie down and rest, although her daughter might—if accompanied by her maid—allow M. Dumont to take her to view the paintings at the Royal Academy.

It was then that Pierre realized, with horrified embarrassment, exactly what kind of portrait his cousin had been posing for during the past few days. There was a cluster of people around the latest Alma-Tadema picture to be hung, and he overheard a whispered comment that the paint was not quite dry on it yet! Recognizing the subject at once, Pierre would have hurried Lorna past, pointing out another portrait a little further down, but his face had gone quite red, and she had noticed it. He watched, with a sinking feeling, how wide her eyes had become as she in turn realized who the odalisque in the painting was. This time, he thought furiously, Ginny had really gone too far, and he must certainly tell her so! Yes, and he would take no further part in her schemes, either.

"Ohh!" Lorna breathed, her fingers tightening on his arm, "how *could* she have dared! And how thoughtless of *your* feelings! Why, I'm sure all London will soon be talking of nothing else!"

If Pierre was touched by Lorna's obvious concern for him, his anger at Ginny had by no means abated. He had no idea where she was—his preoccupation with Lorna had made him forget his duty toward his cousin. He should have insisted that she not go jaunting around London on her own, just as he would have to insist, now, that she must accompany him back to France immediately.

It was Lorna who put another, worse thought into Pierre's already troubled mind.

"Oh, Monsieur Dumont—Pierre!" she breathed, making his pulses race by her use of his first name, "wouldn't it be just terrible if *Steve* found out? Perhaps they are *almost* divorced, if there's such a thing, but he does have such a . . . a very bad temper! And naturally he will think of what it might mean to those two poor innocent children. . . ."

*Dieu!* He had not thought of *that*. Of course Lorna was right!

"There is nothing to be done," Pierre announced firmly and with more courage than he felt, "but for me to meet with this Mr. Morgan and . . . and explain everything to him. I would rather he heard from me than from some stranger."

He was praying, even while he spoke, that Ginny herself was not up to more thoughtless mischief at this very moment.

# Chapter Forty-Three

❦

With no idea in the world that that nemesis was about to overtake her, Ginny was enjoying herself. It had been a long time since she had gone riding, and she was glad that Frederick had suggested it. Riding in the park! What could be more exhilarating? Ginny's stylish riding habit in striped golden-brown shades, trimmed with bands of silk in green and gold, was topped by a cravat of green grosgrain. A gauzy veil of the same shade was wrapped around her black beaver hat. She was well aware of the admiring masculine stares she received, although she pretended not to notice and turned all her attention upon Frederick, who looked extremely good himself.

"We make a well-matched couple," he told her when they had stopped to rest their horses in the shade of some trees. "Ginny," he added diffidently when she turned to him with a surprised look, "I . . . realize how I am—or thought I was. But you are the first woman in whose company I have been for so long—and the first woman whose company and conversation I enjoy! I . . . I even think that I would like to . . ."—his face reddened and he went on with a rush—"to make love to you. There, I have said it!"

"Why, Frederick . . ." She didn't know how to answer him, and worried her lip with her small white teeth while he, seeing he had surprised her, put out his hand to touch hers.

"I am asking you to be my wife, of course," he said. "And I do not expect you to give me your answer at once. But I must tell you that I desire children—and beyond that you may be sure I will not interfere with you too much. You will have a more than generous allowance to do with as you will, and always more if you need it. And if we do not, in time, frequent each other's beds but prefer others—well, there is that too, as long as there is discretion, yes?"

Discretion, she thought, and remembered with anger that Steve had said the same thing to her. Discretion—but he had applied it to her only, and not to himself! And she didn't want to spoil the day by thinking again of Steve or of what might happen when the children were taken from him.

As if he had been able to read a part, at least, of what she was thinking, Frederick Metz leaned over and said gently: "Sometime today you can expect to hear . . . about your children. There's no need to worry, I tell you! And perhaps after that, when your mind is at rest, you will give me an answer?"

"Yes," she said. "After that I will give you an answer. And thank you, Frederick."

He had moved out of his hotel suite into lodgings of his own by now, and Ginny had fallen into the habit of going there quite freely. She did so this afternoon, to change out of her riding habit while Frederick waited patiently in the other room, reading the newspapers that he had sent to him from Switzerland. Frederick was really very sweet, and perhaps he was the sort of man she *should* marry. Quite uncomplicated and undemanding—and very rich into the bargain.

Sighing, and wondering why she had sighed, Ginny began to arrange her hair in front of the mirror, forcing her mind to dwell on her appointments for the rest of the day. From here she would go to Bond Street for the fitting of a new evening gown she had ordered especially for the opera. And if her new dinner toilette was ready she could change into *that* and be ready for the supper Frederick had promised her before they went to the Palace Theater to watch a variety show which featured such popular entertainers as Lottie Collins, the Levy Sisters and Marie Lloyd.

Ginny could not help but smile when she imagined how Pierre would raise a supercilious eyebrow if he knew! He did not approve of variety theaters—or music halls as they were more commonly called—although the Prince of Wales and his friends of the Eccentrics Club were among the "stage-door Johnnies" who seldom missed a popular act. Poor Pierre—she really should send him a note, but then he should be getting used to having her go off on her own by now, and he in his turn had been keeping busy squiring Lorna Prendergast and her mother around. . . .

"I will take you to this place you have to go and come back for you later," Frederick announced as he handed her into a smart-looking hansom.

True to his word he was waiting for her when she emerged, looking ravishing, as he told her later, in her new dinner gown. But at the moment he was too full of news to keep it from her for one more moment.

"See?" Frederick produced a square of yellow paper from behind his back and handed it to her. "I told you it would all go well, did I not?" He caught her puzzled look as she read the message imprinted on the telegram and laughed. "Oh that—it is a code we had agreed on, you see. 'Johnnie and Sarah both recovered and able to go back to school. . . .' That means it all went off exactly according to plan, and that very soon, you will be reunited with your children."

Ginny swallowed hard. "*When?*" she whispered, and then, with a hundred different emotions scurrying around in her mind, "and was there—do you think that it was necessary for them to use . . . violence?"

An expression crossed Frederick's face—so quickly gone that she might only have imagined it. An expression of—perhaps—satisfaction?

He said bluffly, "Not unless, as I told you, it was necessary. And I am sure it was not. The important thing is surely that your *children* are safe and will soon be in their mother's arms." He smiled at her. "Soon, my dear. Very soon. Tonight, it is important that you act just as usual, as if you know nothing. Tomorrow morning you must tell your cousin that you are going riding again, and we will meet at my lodgings and travel together to where your children will be waiting."

Ginny was silent, almost too shocked by the suddenness of it to speak. She had not expected it to be so *easy*, after all! And now for some strange reason she could feel all her nerves jangling.

"I know how relieved you must be!" Frederick said kindly as he handed her into the waiting carriage. Once they had started off he said judiciously, "I think . . . perhaps that it might be good to go to Ireland, yes? For a few days, until you have had the time to think of where you will wish to go. *I* shall dare to hope that you will choose Switzerland. It is a very beautiful country, you will see. Very healthy for children!"

"Yes," Ginny found herself answering mechanically, "I am sure that it is. Perhaps it *would* be a good idea in case we are—in case I am followed."

As he leaned back comfortably against the plush upholstery of the carriage, Ginny thought she saw the same strange expression cross Frederick's fair, handsome features.

"Oh—I do not think you need to fret yourself about *that*," he said, adding smoothly when he saw the unguarded look on her face, "Don't worry, I am quite able to look after you. I always carry a pistol and a sword cane with me, and I am accounted an expert with both weapons!"

The rest of the evening went by in a whirl of, for Ginny, forced gaiety. She drank champagne and nibbled on caviar and drank more champagne during the intermissions, laughing as merrily, as did everyone else, at the risqué jokes and songs. And during one of the intermissions they joined up with a group of people that Ginny had had only a nodding acquaintance with before—all of them going to supper together afterward. It had been, Ginny decided a trifle tipsily later, a deliciously *vulgar* evening, and just what she had needed!

"Yes, my dear!" Frederick said smoothly, and when she leaned her head against his shoulder as the carriage wheels jounced over cracks in the pavement, he put his arm around her and felt tentatively for her breasts, half-exposed by the fashionably low-cut square neckline of her new gown.

"Why do I always allow men to take liberties with me after I have had too much champagne?" Ginny thought. But she was beginning to feel drowsy, and it would have been too much effort to pull away, so she let him touch her, and after a while, as if embarrassed, he gave up and only held her.

It was a long ride home! Ginny fell asleep and woke up and drowsed off again. "I wish we had some more champagne!" she murmured after a while, and Frederick, without a word, produced a bottle, still chilled, from under the seat opposite them.

"You see—I attempt to fulfill your every wish!" he said gallantly.

Perhaps she had never really appreciated Frederick before?

She tried to tell him so, between sips of champagne and a fit of the giggles, and he smiled and patted her shoulder.

"Ah—but you see, you have brought such laughter and excitement into *my* life! When my papa was alive it was always study, study, study and work, work, work. Now, with you, I have learned to play, yes?"

"*Everybody* ought to play—and *everybody* should learn to laugh!" Ginny pronounced, wondering what it was she was trying not to think about. Perhaps it was better not to remember. She much preferred being happy to being sad.

Finishing another glass of champagne, she started to tell Frederick so—dear, kind Frederick!—when he said:

"Ah, here we are! I hope there will be someone up to let you in? I will wait, of course."

"Oh, Pierre will be *very* angry! Perhaps you should come in and . . . and explain? You *will* be gallant and take all the blame?"

"Yes, yes! I will take all the blame."

He supported her to the door, still trying to suppress her laughter in case Pierre heard and came downstairs to scold. "I have to knock," she explained, "so that someone will hear—but not loud enough to wake Pierre!" The brass door-knocker banged loudly, causing Frederick to wince.

"And *now* I have a case of the hiccups—oh dear! Perhaps if I drank more champagne—out of the *wrong* side of the glass? My old nurse always said—"

"I do not think more champagne would be good for you!" Frederick said gravely, and Ginny wrinkled her nose at him.

"I *hope* you are not going to be *dull!*" She knocked again and almost immediately heard the bolts being slid open from the inside. "See, there *is* someone awake, and *they* will get me more champagne if you won't!" She almost fell into the dark hallway and was rescued from falling by a hard hand closing over her arm to steady her. "Frederick, you promised to come in, do you remember? We are going to drink more champagne—"

And then, from out of all her darkest nightmares, she heard the one voice she had not expected to hear, saying politely:

"By all means, do come in, Herr Metz. I take it you *are* Herr Metz? And please do close the door behind you."

When she felt him release her to turn up the lamp, Ginny

found herself suddenly and coldly sober, as if someone had
thrown a bucket of ice water over her.

"*Steve?*" It was a disbelieving whisper. Ginny backed up against
the papered wall with her palms flat at her sides to hold her upright.

"You didn't expect to see me alive again?" His voice had turned
coldly caustic, like a knifeblade that cut through her nerve ends,
paralyzing her.

It was Frederick who said: "You are her . . . her . . ." As he
hesitated, Steve broke in flatly with all his attention on Frederick
now.

"Her husband. Yes, I am afraid so. For the moment at least. It
was kind of you to bring Ginny home, Herr Metz. I presume you
are just as kind to her in other ways?"

"How is it you are here? I will not let you hurt her!"

She was still quite incapable of movement, and only barely capable of thought. Through dilated eyes Ginny saw Frederick
reach into his pocket for the small pistol he carried; and saw
Steve, with no apparent effort at all, but with all the speed of a
striking snake, reach out and disarm him, throwing the gun behind him.

"And now," the hard voice edged with contempt, "will it be
the sword stick next? You are an arsenal of weapons, Herr Metz!
Is it all for my wife's protection, or perhaps to keep her faithful?"

"If necessary," Frederick said in a voice Ginny had never heard
him use before, "I will kill you." The exposed blade from the
sword cane glittered evilly in the lamplight with golden ripples
running up its length.

Steve laughed softly, and the *way* he laughed made Ginny's
blood run cold.

"You mean to do the job that your paid assassins could not ac-
complish?" There was a flicker of change in the wooden, concentrated expression on Frederick Metz's face, and Steve said jeer-
ingly, with his eyes not leaving the flickering blade, "Oh yes—I
know about that. You see, I happened to pass, quite by chance on
my way to Devon, the carriage that was carrying my children
away. One of them waved to me from the window or I might not
have noticed them at all."

"Yes?" Frederick said and took one step nearer.

Steve stood still, his hands relaxed at his sides, but his stance was like that of a mountain lion before it springs.

"Yes," he said. And casually: "I have the children now. Ginny should have told me she was so anxious to see them. And as for the other—I learned of the extra five hundred pounds they were to have been paid for *my* convenient demise from one of your hirelings. It was not hard to make him talk."

"You are talking too—perhaps to put me off guard? You will not do that. I think I must put an end to this nonsense you are talking."

The sword blade moved and Ginny screamed, "No!" She was sobbing now, trying to make her words intelligible. "No—you must not! Frederick, don't—he'd kill you! I saw him . . . kill another man once—on the deck of a ship. A man who . . . who had been my husband. *He* had the sword, and Steve—he had only his bare hands. But he . . . he killed him all the same! Oh, God!" The memory sent her fisted hands up against her mouth to stop herself from being sick, as she had been that day on the swelling deck of a ship with the bloody and broken *thing* that had been the Prince Ivan Sahrkanov lying at her feet.

Frederick Metz hesitated slightly, and at that moment, releasing the tension that bound them all, Pierre Dumont's voice came from the stairs:

"What *is* all this? Frederick, I hope you intend to put that sword away now that you have learned who this gentleman is. I should also ask you why you have brought my cousin home so late?"

"Frederick," Ginny said urgently, touching his arm, "please—it is all right. You must believe me—and . . . and I am sorry, for whatever happened was all my fault!"

Pierre came downstairs in his embroidered dressing gown. His face was stern and not at all sympathetic when he looked at Ginny.

"I certainly agree that you ought to be sorry! We will talk in private later, shall we not, cousine? But for now . . ." He looked inquiringly toward Frederick, who, nonplussed, had begun to back off with a muttered apology.

"Don't forget your pistol," Steve said pleasantly, his eyes still not touching Ginny, and it was Pierre who retrieved the little Derringer and handed it to its owner.

"I think we may all talk more sensibly tomorrow. The servants will soon be awake, if they are not already, and I *think*," his voice sounding ominous, "that it is time that Mr. Morgan and his *wife* had some privacy in which to discuss their affairs and their children."

# Chapter Forty-Four

❦

Frederick had taken his somewhat shamefaced departure, and Pierre—the traitor!—had merely gestured wearily at the door to the small library that opened off the entrance hall.

"I presume you two would like to speak in private in spite of the early hour? You may, of course, ring if you need anything. There is liquor in the sideboard, although . . ."—his eyes fixing themselves on Ginny in a particularly steely fashion she had never seen before—"I hardly think that my *cousine* needs any. So, I will see you after we have all had a chance to rest and compose ourselves."

Far from being able to compose herself or even plan what she might say, Ginny found herself alone with Steve in silence—a silence that grew as her stubbornness asserted itself.

"He cannot do anything to me, he wouldn't dare! And when I explain to Pierre, he will have to understand. What did he *mean* about assassins paid to kill him?"

And still she did not say anything, listening to the sound of the fire as the silence between them stretched and Steve poured himself a drink at the sideboard without offering *her* one.

How dared he walk back into her life in such a casual fashion, as if he'd never been out of it—into *her* house, treating her as if he still had some rights over her? As if he *owned* her? Ginny could feel her heart begin to pound with a mixture of fear and anger. She would not let him discover how unsettled and confused she felt! She would *not* give in; no matter what he said or what he tried to do with her, she would never give in to him again!

She watched him turn, with a glass in his hand now, to regard her intently and almost *strangely*, Ginny caught herself thinking as she forced herself to return his gaze. Without wanting to at all she noticed, almost as if she was seeing him for the first time ever, the intense blueness of Steve's eyes; their blue rendered even darker by the overshadowing length of his eyelashes. They were strangers to each other, evaluating each other, and with a sense of shock Ginny realized that he too was looking at *her* as if he hadn't seen her before.

God, but he was a handsome man! In spite of—or even because of—the thin scar that Ivan Sahrkanov's saber had carved across his cheekbone, and a new scar that burned against one temple. The unwanted thought that had shot into her mind made Ginny annoyed at herself, and she clenched her hands on her lap. Of course she should remember that she knew Steve almost too well! Women always looked at Steve—and it seemed as if, after all this time, she was no better than any of them! And he—his eyes, still watching her, gave nothing away.

A dart of annoyance shot through her, tightening her lips. Damn Steve, she had never been able to read his thoughts, except for a few occasions when she had managed to catch him off guard. And now—what was he seeing when he studied her so? Why didn't he *say* something?

There had still been no words between them as they looked each other over. Ginny noticed with a little shiver that Steve was wearing a white linen shirt that lay open at the throat, and was splotched with bloodstains. Over it, as if it had been an afterthought, he had shrugged on a black broadcloth jacket that looked crumpled, and was darkly stained too. He looked . . . he looked as if he had been in a war! And as if he didn't particularly care what she or anyone else might think of his appearance, either. . . .

The least he could do, after the way he'd startled and embarrassed her just now, was to make some apology or give her some explanation! He had cheated and tricked her and humiliated her while they had been married—yes, and he'd actually had an affair with her demure stepmother too. He'd practically *forced* her into leaving him! And had stolen her children. . . .

"Do I . . . do I look so very different? Why are you staring at me so?"

She hadn't meant to be the one to speak first, or to sound so defiant when the words spilled out of her without volition. Ginny saw, with irritation, Steve's mouth twitch at one corner, even though his voice was as precise and as evenly toned as if he spoke to a stranger.

"How could I help staring at you, *ma mie?* You're still a very lovely young woman, even after—how many years has it been? Two? Three? And you're alive—did you know there was a long time when I thought you dead? Andre Delery thought so too. But now *he's* dead and here you are in the flesh . . . you survived, didn't you, Ginny?"

While he was speaking he had crossed the room to her with that long and particularly catlike stride she remembered all too well; and his fingers, long and sunbrowned, touched her face lightly, eliciting a gasp from her before she flinched away, her spine stiffening and her chin tilting.

"Yes, I survived! And so did you, obviously! In spite of . . . should I dare ask what happened to Andre? Or why . . . or why there are bloodstains all over you?"

She resented bitterly having to look up at him as he stood before her with his eyes narrowing hatefully. Had she only imagined that he intended either to strike or to strangle her?

He said smoothly and almost lightly, with one eyebrow raised, "Do I actually detect concern in your voice, or . . . frustration, perhaps?" He gave a short laugh that made her jump. Why did he keep looking at her in such a . . . a gauging, measuring way? She was reminded of another time when she had questioned him just so—in Mexico, it had been; and coming across a certain knife in his baggage she had questioned him, and had been told about Matt Cooper. . . . Did she really want to know about Andre Delery?

He was so close to her that he almost straddled her pressed-together knees and she felt his fire-shadow fall across her face and her shoulder, making her shudder.

"Do you really want to know? I dueled with Andre Delery and came off the victor—that was the first of your questions, was it not? And as for the second—the bloodstains you noticed came from . . . shall we say my *argument* with the persons who had abducted my children? Ginny . . ." And then on an expelled breath of exasperation he veered to a completely different subject, his voice giving away nothing. "Do you know that your skin is just as soft and as smooth as I remembered it? To look at you, you haven't changed too much, but I seem to detect a lack of the old sparkle in your eyes—there's even a touch of sadness there. Can it be that you're not too happy at being reunited with your husband as well as your children? Should I have let you leave with your handsome Swiss banker who adores you enough to have me killed if he could? But then . . ."—stepping away from her with steel underlying the deceptive softness of his voice now—"I do not care for men who send hirelings to kill me and wave their little pistols and sword canes in my face. Why did you want to have me assassinated, Ginny? Our divorce is almost final, and I would not have stood in the way of your next marriage—if marriage was what you had in mind! In fact, I had made up my mind not to interfere with you in any way, not even to see you again if I could help it—until you forced my hand!"

"You took my children from me! And I didn't . . . I didn't know that Frederick had—"

How she hated and mistrusted the controlled softness of his voice!

"Ah, yes . . . Frederick," he said, dismissing Frederick as if he had ceased to exist. He dropped into the chair opposite her and said evenly, "But as for the children, they are mine too, are they not? Or so you told me . . . but in any case I suppose I have developed a certain . . . fondness for them. And as for you, my dear, it seemed obvious to me as well as to everyone else that you had abandoned them yourself while you sought and experienced the delights of a Turkish harem! What did you expect me to do, Ginny? Abandon them in my turn once I had . . . made their acquaintance?"

Quite suddenly, as if the combat between them had completely exhausted her, Ginny leaned back in her chair, tension-white knuckles pressing against her eyes as if she had been a child herself.

"Steve—don't! Oh, don't play your usual cat-and-mouse games with me again—not now! I'm too *tired*, do you understand? I'm . . . I'm . . ."

Before she could prevent it, he had seized both her wrists, pulling them down and away from her eyes, which had started to overflow with the tears she no longer had the strength or the will to hold back.

His voice was as inexorable as his grip.

"You're—*what*, Ginny? For God's sake, why won't you start being honest with me for a change? And with yourself too. Christ! —you're a woman desperate with unhappiness, it's written all over you. And it's not only because of the children either. I think— *look* at me, Ginny!—I think my taking the children only made you angry. And perhaps gave you a reason, also, for existing . . . if only to take them back from me in your turn, to defeat me? . . ."

She had already begun to shake her head vehemently, rejecting his calm reasonableness.

"No, you're wrong! And you have no . . . no right to pry, you have no—"

"What is it, Ginny? Is it because of Richard? Do you still love him? Do you feel mortally wounded because you imagine he rejected you?" He released her hands as suddenly as he had taken them, and she fell back in her chair to sit huddled there, crying as if her heart would break.

"Oh, *hell!*" Steve's voice came from somewhere above her, and through the rainbow-hued sheen of her tears Ginny could barely discern that he had walked away from her, as if he could not bear to be near her any longer. She heard the clink of a bottle against glass and his voice, controlled again and without emotion as he said, "I've just returned from Stamboul, Ginny. And I found out that he's safe. He, your Richard, and his wife who was the sister to the dead Sultan, and their son—they have gone to Persia to live. I had some conversation with a General Ignatiev, who was on his way back to Russia at the time. It was from him that I learned you had already left—for France, or St. Petersburg—he wasn't quite certain. And he also informed me as to the circumstances of your . . . 'divorce.'" Steve's voice had turned dry, still betraying nothing of what his feelings might have been. "As I understand it, Richard Avery did not divorce you because he wanted to, but because of his concern for your continued safety. He also felt a sense of responsibility, I was told, for the woman who had borne him a son—not to mention the child itself. He appears to be a man of some sensitivity—a contrast that I'm sure you appreciated!"

Ginny couldn't be quite certain if she had made some half-smothered noise of protest or not—she felt a glass thrust into her shaking hands.

"Here—drink this!" Steve said roughly. "It's only cognac, not poison. And you don't need to cower away like a whipped bitch. If I was going to kill you I would have done so earlier!" His voice lashed her into sitting erect again and trying to control her voice in order that she might fling some suitable caustic retort back at him; but his next words held her silent in spite of herself. "I have a letter in my possession—still sealed, by the way—which was given to General Ignatiev by Richard Avery. It is addressed to you, and I suppose it contains some explanations that might make you feel happier than you seem to be now. I had thought to leave it with your cousin, but since we have run into each other . . ."

Ginny took a gulp of the cognac, almost choking on it as it burned like liquid fire down her throat. At least it helped her find her voice again.

"No. I don't want to read it. I . . . I thank you for bringing it, but I . . . do not think there is any point in—it does not matter to me any longer." She forced herself to look up at Steve and found, through her tears, his shadowed eyes regarding her. She could see neither anger nor contempt nor condemnation in his face, only a certain amount of curiosity, perhaps. It made it easier to finish what she had begun to say. "I did love him—or, at least he made me feel that I did, for a time. He was kind to me and he was gentle. He made me feel as if I was the only woman in the world, protected and cosseted. I was blind then, and I—God knows I needed comfort and understanding! But when it was over, by the time it was over, I felt empty—and I felt free! Even if I despised myself for feeling so! You won't understand. . . ."

"Won't I?" He sat down beside her again, and she heard his breath expelled in a sharp sigh. "I met someone too. Her name was—it doesn't matter. I thought you were dead, and I blamed myself for killing you. It was my goddamned hotheaded pride that made me challenge Andre Delery to a duel. And after that I left Cuba and I traveled a lot—and I met her."

"And?" Ginny's voice was a whisper, not wanting, suddenly, to break the tenuously spun thread of communication between them. She felt, rather than saw him turn his face away from the fire to look at her.

"And? I'm here, as you see. I asked her to come away with me and she turned me down—for security and for *kindness*, she said.

*She* was comfort and sweetness and woman-waiting and all the things a man is supposed to need, but I couldn't offer her what she was looking for, I guess—like forever."

Ginny sighed. "Oh—what *is* forever?" And then, suddenly realizing it, "Do you know that . . . that I cannot remember that we ever really *talked* before? We merely said words to each other. It feels so . . . strange!"

He started to laugh, surprising her all over again. "Yes, it certainly does feel . . . unusual! And I'm afraid that your cousin Pierre will be disappointed. He felt I ought to be extremely annoyed because you had posed for a certain well-known artist in—I take it there were *very* few strategically placed veils?—not much beyond your skin and your hair. 'The Sultan's Captive'—is that what it was called? Should I buy it?"

Suddenly, and she did not quite know how it had happened, Ginny felt as if a heavy stone had been rolled off her chest, leaving her free to breathe . . . and to laugh—even if her laughter sounded shaky, as if she still had the hiccups.

"I . . . I didn't know it was going to be hung quite this soon! Oh, poor Pierre, no wonder he was *glaring* at me so! And as for your buying it, I believe that the Prince of Wales has already—oh dear! . . ."

She had choked on her drink, and Steve slapped the flat of his hand between her shoulder blades, assuring her as he did that it was a tried and true cure for the hiccups and no, he was *not* trying to assault her!

"The Prince of Wales?" he asked her finally with one black eyebrow cocked. "Is he another of your admirers?"

"Oh, he admires any attractive woman he sees! Music hall performers and opera singers . . ."

Her words trailed off as she found herself *looking* at him, this man she had known for years and yet *didn't* know. And wanted to know—she had suddenly discovered that too.

"Ginny—" He had not taken his hands away from her, and she felt them on her shoulders, turning her to face him. And now, for the first time his eyes were as unguarded, looking into hers, as hers must have seemed to him.

Almost blindly, she put one hand out, touching his face, tracing the new scar she knew nothing about yet.

"Yes," she said, committing herself all over again. Knowing intuitively that there would be the lessons of the past to learn from and the future to explore together.

Forever was a long, long time, Ginny thought, as she felt herself drawn to her feet, going willingly against him with her face turned up to meet the question and the answer that his lips gave to hers.

Forever was the future and the hard-won knowledge of needing and being needed. *Now* was the fresh understanding they had gained of each other—and the tolerance, and the love. Her arms went up around his neck while he locked her close with his, and somewhere behind them the fire sputtered into oblivion and the sun forced itself between carelessly drawn draperies.

It was a new day. It was the beginning of forever.